HOPEFUL
Hearts

HOPEFUL
Hearts

Two Historical Romances of Following Dreams to Love

Diann Hunt

BARBOUR
PUBLISHING

Print ISBN 978-1-61626-954-8

eBook Editions:
Adobe Digital Edition (.epub) 978-1-62029-418-5
Kindle and MobiPocket Edition (.prc) 978-1-62029-417-8

Cover image: Curlyson Photography

Published by Barbour Publishing, Inc., P.O. Box 719, Uhrichsville, Ohio 44683, www.barbourbooks.com

Our mission is to publish and distribute inspirational products offering exceptional value and biblical encouragement to the masses.

 Member of the
Evangelical Christian
Publishers Association

Printed in the United States of America.

A WHALE OF
A MARRIAGE

Chapter 1

M rs. Markle, times have changed. This is 1856, and women are allowed aboard whaling ships these days." Adelaide Sanborn stuffed another bolt of material into the slot on the shelf. The playful banter amused Adelaide, though she knew all the while she wasted her breath on her dear friend.

"Adelaide, I know all about the changing times. Some women are sailing, true; but mind you, those few are married women. A whaling ship is no place for a single woman, and that's the truth of it." The boards beneath Ida Markle creaked in protest as she pushed her broom in short, determined strokes.

Just then a bell jangled atop the door of the only general store in Yorksville, Massachusetts. A customer stepped inside.

A salty gust of October wind swished through the room, causing the invoices on the counter to flutter. Ida's husband, Caleb, quickly gathered the restless papers and placed them under a large scoop normally used to dish out candy from the nearby jar.

Paying no heed to the interruption, Ida continued. "Things are what they are; you can't change them. And further, if you want my advice, Adelaide, you'd better settle down and have yourself a family. Forget that fool notion of going to sea." A growing mound of sand lifted from cracks in the floor with every strong sweep of the older woman's broom.

Adelaide let out a sigh. "I don't want to have a family. Not yet. I have dreams." She stopped stocking the shelf. Lost in thought, she stared at the bolt of cloth beneath her fingers.

Ida walked over, reached up, and rested her hand on Adelaide's shoulder. "Of course it doesn't hurt to dream, dear." She paused a moment. Her voice softened. "You've worked so hard since your pa died."

Adelaide placed another bolt of cloth on the shelf and faced Ida. The older woman patted Adelaide's shoulder. "With no children to call our own, you are like a daughter to us, Adelaide. I pray you find your happiness someday." Her gaze drifted toward the window with the ocean in plain view. "Mind you, I know the dangers of the sea, and well"—she pulled a handkerchief from the pocket of her apron and wiped her nose—"I just want what's best for you, that's all."

Adelaide reached her arms around Ida's ample frame and gave her a tender squeeze. "I thank you for caring, Mrs. Markle. I'm sorry for carrying on so. You know I've always been too independent for my own good."

Mrs. Markle let out a chuckle. "That you have, dear. That you have." She patted her nose once more then stuffed the handkerchief back into her pocket. With a swish of her broom, she continued on her way across the floor.

Once Adelaide finished stacking the various bolts of material, she gathered a pile of oil pants into her arms then walked toward the bare shelving in the front of the store. Taking great care, she stacked the pants in organized rows.

No matter how hard she tried, Adelaide's passion for the sea overcame her good sense most times. She knew that. She also knew she could not bear the thought of living a dreary life on land.

She supposed she should give up on the notion of sea life altogether, yet something deep inside compelled her forward. A stirring. A longing she couldn't describe to anyone. After all, what woman would understand how Adelaide's heart quickened with the arrival of a long-awaited whaling ship, or how stories of the crew's adventures would fill her dreams and waking moments? Such ideas made most womenfolk squeamish.

With much regret, she resigned herself to the fact that there was little she could do about it. So each afternoon she stood outside the general store and watched the distant docks where families clustered to wave good-bye to the brave sailors. The big ships rolled out of the bay into the expanse of ocean that would be their home for months to come. Adelaide dreamed of being carried out to sea with them.

"Morning, Josiah," Caleb Markle called to the customer.

Until that precise moment, Adelaide hadn't noticed who had entered. She glanced up to see Josiah Buchanan, known around the village as the best of all whaling captains. She'd heard of his adventures at sea. Folks said year after year he brought in the biggest catches of the deep. Many times his ship carried sperm whale, the richest cargo a whaling ship could haul into port.

Adelaide went over to sort through the woolen shirts and catch a better look at him. His muscular frame towered, she guessed, slightly over six feet. She stole glances and noted his confident walk. She studied his profile. A strong, sturdy jaw suggested that most likely once he made up his mind, it would not be easily changed. She decided he had the appearance of a grand sea captain. Absently rubbing her hands along the thick wool and pushing aside all remembrances of proper etiquette, she continued to watch him.

The warmth from the potbellied stove caused her to slip into her usual daydream, the one that always carried her out to sea.

Josiah turned her way. He took off his cap. "Morning, ma'am."

Adelaide snapped to attention and muttered a short greeting. She spun around to hide the color she felt rise up her cheeks. What would he think of her, gazing at him like a silly schoolgirl! The very idea! Not that it mattered. He didn't know who she was and certainly would not care to find out.

"So you want to sail the seas, do you?" The strong voice was beside her now.

Adelaide glanced up with a start. Her breath stuck in her throat as she found herself looking into the most intense blue eyes she had ever seen. Powerful yet inviting, like the sea. She could scarcely pull herself away.

"I. . ." She got no further, for the word lodged itself midway in her throat. Adelaide swallowed hard. Suddenly it seemed of the utmost importance for her to straighten imaginary wrinkles from her dark skirt. With some effort, she pulled in a long breath. "Very much," she finally managed. She tried to speak the words lightly, but passion weighed them down.

"I told her the sea is no place for a woman. I'm sure you quite agree, isn't that right, Captain Buchanan?"

From the reflection in the storefront window, Adelaide could see Ida had joined them, hands placed firmly on her hips, clearly waiting on Captain Buchanan to echo her beliefs.

Turning to them, Adelaide looked first to Josiah for his response. Her heart paused as she waited for him to speak. It should not concern her to know his position on the matter, yet somehow it did. Before she could think further, Josiah broke the silence.

His mouth split into a wide grin. He looked at Ida. "Seems to me if I'm going to engage in so lively a debate, I ought to at least be introduced to this lovely young lady." He turned his smile toward Adelaide.

Ida pulled her hand to her mouth and covered a slight giggle. "Oh, my, of course." She cleared her throat and seemed to pause for effect. With a sweep of her hands, she began, "Josiah Buchanan, I would like to introduce you to Adelaide Sanborn. Adelaide, Josiah."

"It's my pleasure to meet you. . .Mrs. Sanborn?"

"Oh my, no, she's not married," Ida said as she absently straightened a pile of mittens. "She's about as easy a catch as a sperm whale." Ida laughed heartily at her own comment until she spotted Adelaide's expression. The old storekeeper feigned a cough and busied herself further with the mittens.

Adelaide thought she heard Caleb chuckle across the room. She stood speechless, wishing with all her might that the sea would break through the store and carry her away at that very moment. Before she could find her voice, Josiah came to her rescue.

His eyes held a smile. "Ah, a very worthy catch, indeed." He winked at Adelaide as if they had a private joke between them then turned back to Ida. "Sperm whales, as you know, Mrs. Markle, are the hardest to catch, but the most worthwhile."

"Yes, well—" A slight crimson crept up Ida's neck, a sure sign she was flustered. Seemingly at a loss for words, she turned to join her husband.

Feeling a bit uncomfortable with the discussion, Adelaide couldn't change the subject fast enough. "My pa served on a whaling ship."

He raised a brow. "Not Elijah Sanborn?"

"You knew him?" Excitement filled her. Five years after his death, she still found herself longing to hear of her pa's adventures.

"I knew him well. I served with him in my younger days."

Adelaide couldn't imagine how young Josiah must have been when he knew her pa. She studied him in an attempt to guess his age. *Twenty-nine, thirty, perhaps.*

"He kept the crew going with his laughter and music." Josiah's eyes took on the look of one remembering the past. He shook his head. "What a voice!"

Adelaide laughed and nodded. A comfortable pause followed. "I miss him still."

"That must be why you love the sea, because you miss him?"

"That's true, but it's more than that." A seabird swooped toward the storefront window, catching Adelaide's attention, mocking her with its freedom. "Certainly his adventurous tales livened my childhood, but I've always been different than most girls. I've wanted to go to sea for as long as I can remember. To feel the adventure of a whale hunt, to see the sunset spill upon distant waters, to watch the glimmer of moonlight as it prances across midnight waves; that's what I want." She pulled her hand to her mouth. "Oh, I'm sorry to prattle on so."

A tender smile lit his face. "Not at all. I understand completely."

She looked away but felt his gaze linger on her. Though in her mind she had imagined sea captains as stern and unbendable, she sensed this man got along well with his crew.

They both turned back to peer through the window. The sun hung in noonday position. A brisk breeze churned the ocean, causing the sun's rays to sparkle like scattered shards of glass across a base of blue. Gulls flew low over the docks. Though the store's door was closed, the afternoon air squeezed through tiny cracks, releasing a fresh, salty scent into the room.

"It is beautiful, isn't it," he commented more than asked.

"Yes. There isn't anything more beautiful." A thought struck her. Perhaps he could find a way for her to travel the seas! If he stayed around long enough, she could prove to him her longing for the sea was more than a silly notion. She might convince him to help her, maybe even convince him to take her along. . . .

"I'll be setting sail around the end of November," he said, breaking through her thoughts.

Her building dreams stretched out of reach. Not much time to convince him of her seaworthiness. "You'll be gone awhile?" she asked, trying not to show her disappointment.

"Eight to twelve months, perhaps. Maybe longer. Sometimes we don't know until we get out there just where the whales will take us."

Adelaide nodded. "I didn't mean to pry—"

He shook his head. "It's a logical question, really."

"We'll be praying for the *Courage*'s safe return," she said.

Josiah cleared his throat. "Yes, well, I thank you for that. It's nice to be remembered." He stared at her for a moment. "Maybe I'll see you at church on Sunday?"

Her heart quickened. Perhaps there was still time to gain his help. She nodded as enthusiastically as befit a proper young woman.

"Good. It was a pleasure, *Miss* Sanborn," he said, emphasizing the "Miss." With that, he turned and walked out the door, leaving Adelaide to stare after him.

The bell on the door jarred her back to reality. Looking out the window, Adelaide took a minute to calm herself. When she turned around, she found Ida Markle watching her.

"Are you all right, dear? You look a little flushed. You're not coming down with a fever, are you?"

"I'm fine. Just a little. . .tired, I suppose." Tired? How could she be tired when her heart pounded like that of a chased whale?

"No wonder, child. You've been working too hard. You didn't need to help us today. You have enough work of your own with the mending you do for people."

Adelaide nodded. "You know how I love to come here, Mrs. Markle."

Ida sighed. "To be near the sea, no doubt," she said with a tease in her voice.

"I'm fine, really."

"You let me be the judge of that. You come sit over here." Before Adelaide could protest further, Ida Markle appointed herself head nurse, promptly placing tea and crackers before the ailing patient.

The store was quiet as Ida pulled up a chair beside Adelaide. "He is quite a man, isn't he?" Ida asked with indifference as she stirred her own tea.

"Hmm?"

"Mr. Buchanan. He's quite the captain, they say."

"Oh yes. So I've heard." Adelaide sipped her tea, her thoughts tossing about like a battered ship on a restless sea.

"He was married once."

Adelaide's ears perked up.

"Catherine was her name. She kept to herself. Came into the store once in a while. Not a very friendly sort." Ida shrugged. "Before he left for the sea, she moved away. They hadn't been married long. He later got word that she died. No one ever said how she died. Must have been the plague or some such thing. Now he stays on the seas, hardly ever coming home. Folks say he loved her something fierce." Ida tapped her spoon on the rim of her cup then took a slight swallow.

Adelaide wondered what kind of woman could capture the heart of a sea captain. Before she could come to a conclusion, her thoughts drifted back to how she might convince Josiah Buchanan to help make her dreams come true. . . .

Chapter 2

Josiah dropped his other boot to the floor. What had gotten into him to tell Adelaide he would see her on Sunday? He had given up on church and friendships long ago.

There was a time when he believed the best in people, that churchgoing folks really cared, but Catherine changed all that. She used him. Took his love and threw it aside once she realized it didn't have lots of money attached to it. He had made a good living but obviously not enough according to Catherine.

If only he hadn't taken her to Yorksville, maybe things would have been different. She had grown up in Bayview, Massachusetts. Her ma still lived there, but Catherine had wanted to move to Yorksville to be near a friend. No sooner had Josiah and Catherine arrived than the friend and her husband moved out west.

Josiah paced restlessly across his bedroom, the memories battering him like a nor'easter. Catherine had delighted in the cruel words she'd flung at him when she told him she was leaving. Even as he'd chased the elusive whale, the sea's siren song failed to silence her hurtful words. She had never loved him. His eyes burned. He rubbed them as if to wipe away the memories.

The next thing he knew, he received a letter saying she had died. Before he could blink, it was over, as if it had never happened. Like the fact that she stole his heart was just a dream—or a nightmare. His fingers massaged his temples as he sat on the edge of the bed.

Josiah put on his nightclothes, climbed into bed, and stared into the darkness. In all his pain, it seemed no one had cared. At church, instead of showing compassion, folks had whispered. Some walked by without a word. Passed judgment on him, no doubt. He decided then and there that since the church folks didn't care, God must not care either. He figured he'd just have to make it through life on his own.

Still, he couldn't deny the lonely ache in his heart. Was it for the love he lost with Catherine or something else?

❧

An unseasonably balmy sun warmed Josiah's back as he climbed from the carriage. Each step felt like he had an anchor chained to his ankle as he made his way to the church. He didn't want to be there, but being a man of his word, he had to go.

Someone called out, "Morning, Josiah."

Josiah turned to see Harrison Neal and his wife, Rebecca. "Harrison, good to see you, old man."

Harrison reached out to grab Josiah by the hand. The two men shook hands heartily.

Josiah took off his hat and turned to Rebecca. "Ma'am."

"Morning, Josiah."

"How long you here?" Harrison asked.

"Till the end of November."

"Well, it's good to have you for as long as we can." Harrison slapped Josiah good-naturedly on the back.

Josiah smiled. No matter what he thought of church and the "Christians," he always thought Harrison a good man.

"Hey, a few of the families are meeting for a picnic after church. Why don't you join us? We've plenty of food. Bring a guest if you'd like." With his elbow, Harrison ribbed Josiah in the side.

"Harrison!" Rebecca scolded.

"Aw, Becca, Josiah knows I like to tease."

Rebecca smiled and held up her head with an air of reprimand. "Just the same…"

"Thanks for the offer, Harrison, but I—" Josiah spotted Adelaide. Their eyes met for an instant. Josiah turned to Harrison and saw him glance at Adelaide.

"Like I said, if you want to join us and bring a guest, you're more than welcome." Harrison laughed and pulled on Rebecca's arm. "Come on, love, it's time we get to church." He threw a wink over his shoulder at Josiah.

Though Josiah wanted to keep his distance, he didn't want to appear rude. He made his way over to Adelaide. "Good day, Miss Sanborn." His voice cracked. On his ship he spoke with authority. His mind was sharp and decisive. In front of this woman, before he could form a single word, his mind clogged with confusion and his voice crackled like a broken foghorn. Being on a ship had made him forget how to behave in front of womenfolk.

She turned to him. "Hello, Captain Buchanan."

"Beautiful day for a picnic," Josiah said as he opened the church doors for her. He couldn't imagine what made him mention the picnic. Though not interested in settling down with any woman, he had to admit the idea of a friend comforted him. Life as a sea captain could get lonely. Still, he wanted to keep his distance.

She smiled. "Yes it is. One of the few left before winter, I'm afraid." She looked at him. "Were you about to say something?"

The words crowded just inside his mouth. Her smile shook them loose. "I don't suppose you—"

"Why, Captain Buchanan, how nice to see you," Mrs. Sanborn said with a warm smile.

"Ma'am."

"Will you be with us long, or will the sea take you away soon?"

"I'll only be around till the end of November, I'm afraid."

"Ah, I see." Mrs. Sanborn's glance went from Adelaide to Josiah and back to Adelaide. "Are you ready to sit down, Adelaide?" Before her daughter could respond, Mrs. Sanborn turned back to Josiah. "Good day, Captain." Adelaide's expression held an apology before she turned and walked away with her mother.

Josiah sat down on the bench. He appreciated Mrs. Sanborn's kindness. Still, he clearly got the feeling she didn't want him around her daughter. He wondered what people said about him. Did they blame him for Catherine's death?

☙❧

Pastor Malachi Daugherty's voice boomed through the air: "Husbands, love your wives. The Bible tells us in Ephesians five, verses twenty-eight through thirty, 'So ought men to love their wives as their own bodies. He that loveth his wife loveth himself. For no man ever yet hated his own flesh; but nourisheth and cherisheth it, even as the Lord the church: for we are members of his body, of his flesh, and of his bones.'"

Josiah shifted uncomfortably on the bench as painful memories shadowed his thoughts. *Didn't I love her enough? I tried to provide for her. That's why I had to go to sea, to provide for us, for our future. The sea was the only life I knew. She didn't care; she never loved me. She wanted wealth.* Emotion crept up his throat. Someone next to him stirred, pulling Josiah to the present in time to hear the pastor's final prayer.

People slowly ambled out the church doors, talking in a friendly manner along the way.

Josiah wanted to get out of there before he ran into Adelaide again. He didn't want to give her the wrong impression.

Making his way through the tiny gathering, he offered greetings here and there until an elderly woman stopped him. She held him in conversation for a few minutes. When he turned around, he bumped into Adelaide.

"Oh, excuse me," Josiah said, turning his cap nervously in his hands.

Adelaide tossed him an understanding smile.

"Good sermon." Why did he say that? He'd hardly heard a word of it.

"Yes it was," Adelaide agreed.

They stood in a moment of awkward silence. Josiah cleared his throat.

"So is she coming?" Josiah and Adelaide looked over and saw Harrison Neal grinning widely.

Josiah cringed. He didn't want to get himself into an uncomfortable situation before he set sail. He shot a warning glance at Harrison.

"Oh, sorry." Harrison backed away slowly and melted into the tiny crowd.

Adelaide chuckled. "What was that all about?" Her eyes teased as she waited for an answer.

Josiah sighed and stared at his cap.

"Well, are you going to tell me?"

Josiah looked up to see Adelaide smiling. Oh, what did it hurt to have a friend? He would be leaving soon, anyway. "They're having a picnic—a few of the families today. We're invited."

"We?"

"Well, Harrison asked me to come and said I could bring a guest, and, um, well. . ."

"I'd love to."

Josiah felt like he'd swallowed a fish bone. He coughed. "You would?"

"Do they have enough food?"

Could she hear his heart thumping like a hammer nailing a loose plank? "Yes, they said they have plenty."

Her eyes twinkled with amusement. "I'll let Ma know." Adelaide turned away from him, and Josiah shrugged. It wouldn't hurt to have some friendly company.

"I don't think it's proper that you should prance around the beach with Captain Buchanan, Adelaide." Ma aired her cross feelings as quietly as she could so the church people wouldn't hear.

"Ma, you know other families will be there. There's truly nothing improper about it. We will be in the open for all to see."

"That's what I'm concerned about." Ma bit her lip.

Adelaide put an arm around her ma. "I'll be fine. I will behave as a lady the entire time." Adelaide kissed Ma lightly on the forehead and felt her ma's resolve melt away.

"It's just that, well, you know how people like to talk, and I want you to be careful with your heart."

"I understand." A laugh escaped her. "It's not as though I'm getting married today, Ma."

At this, Ma couldn't help but chuckle herself. She paused for a moment. "Well, you certainly can't go without contributing something. You'll need to come home. You baked two apple pies yesterday. Take one of those."

Adelaide squeezed her mother tight. "Thank you!"

"Adelaide, watch yourself. Don't let him see you carry on so. We must keep the menfolk guessing."

"Yes Ma."

Ma laughed behind her handkerchief.

❧

The sun sailed high in the sky, spreading its rays across the waters with flecks of gold. Josiah helped Adelaide from the carriage, grabbed the apple pie, and together they walked across the sandy beach to join the others.

The sun slipped toward the distant horizon while they passed the afternoon visiting with friends. Josiah shared stories of his whaling expeditions, and Adelaide found herself in an emotional whirlwind, caught between laughter and tears with every story. Josiah made the sea come alive to her the way her pa had done.

By the end of the picnic, Adelaide wanted to escape to the sea more than ever before. A melancholy mood shadowed her heart. She sat quietly, lost in thought.

"Have I bored you with my fish tales?"

"Oh my, no!"

His expression relaxed. "I'm glad." They sat in silence, staring out to sea.

"Adelaide, I must say your ma's apple pie is the best I have ever eaten. You tell her I said so."

"Well, I'll be happy to tell her; however, she didn't make it."

His eyebrows lifted.

"I did." She pretended a slight curtsy.

His eyes smiled in surprise. "Not only pleasing to the eye but a good cook as well!"

Not used to such compliments from gentlemen friends, Adelaide felt her face flush.

Josiah studied her for a long moment, looking as though an idea had just struck him. Before Adelaide could question him, he blurted out, "Allow me to take you to dinner tomorrow night."

Adelaide looked at him wide-eyed and hesitated.

"I'm sorry, Adelaide, I'm forgetting myself." He slapped his cap on the side of his pants like a little boy who had just been chastised.

Adelaide willed her heart to stop pounding in her ears. "Tomorrow?" She could already hear her ma's disapproval, but the idea of having more time to convince him to help her. . . "I—I—"

His eyes looked hopeful, yet something in his expression told her there was more to his request. After a moment's pause, a smile stretched across his face.

Did she dare hope? A quick flutter made her lose her breath. "Tomorrow would be just fine."

His face brightened. He pulled his cap snug on his head and gave it a jerk. "All right, then, tomorrow night at seven o'clock?"

"Why don't you come to my house? I'll cook dinner; then Ma and my sister, Esther, could get to know you better."

"If it means I get to eat more of your apple pie, I'll be there."

She smiled. "Seven o'clock, then?"

Josiah nodded. They looked around and noticed the others gathering their things and loading them onto wagons. Everyone said good-bye and headed for home. Josiah aided Adelaide into his carriage as dusk settled upon the small village. Josiah drove the carriage along the seashore; Adelaide lifted her gaze to the heavens and reveled in the stars that hung bright in the dusky sky.

With the thought of her dreams becoming a reality, Adelaide felt she would burst. "Josiah, I had a wonderful afternoon."

He coughed. "I, uh, did, too."

Could he guess her true motives? Would he mind? She suspected he had been pressured into taking her to the picnic by Harrison, but what about the dinner invitation? No doubt he spent time with her because of their common bond with her pa. She mentally shrugged. Whatever the reason, it gave her time to prove to him her love for the sea.

Once they arrived at her house, Josiah helped her from the carriage. He walked her to the door. "I'll see you tomorrow." He tipped his head then turned and walked back to the carriage.

"Tomorrow," Adelaide whispered, her mind already wondering how she could prove herself seaworthy to this mighty captain.

Chapter 3

Adelaide Sanborn, you need to hear me out," Ma said in exasperation. She stuffed the log into the fireplace, sending the scent of pine throughout their cottage. Tiny sparks shot about then quickly melted into the flames.

"Ma, I respect you, and I love you. But I know what I'm doing. Josiah is a gentleman. There's no harm in seeing him."

"He is a fine man, Adelaide, but you have been with him every evening this entire week. Have you lost your good sense? What will people think?"

"Ma, please, I don't care what people think! I have never fit into their mold. You know that." Adelaide felt the sting of another reminder of how different she was from other women her age. "I'm merely enjoying a friendship."

Adelaide shot a glance at Esther, who pretended not to listen as she swept the kitchen floor. "Ma, you told me I should have a gentleman caller—"

"But Captain Buchanan? He lives on a whaling ship!"

"So that's what this is about?"

"I've lived that life, Adelaide. I don't want my daughters to go through it as well!"

"He's only a friend." Adelaide hesitated a moment. She felt a lump in her throat. "Was it so terrible, Ma? Pa provided for our needs. He left us with happy memories."

The lines on Ma's face softened. "Your pa was a good man," she said quietly. Her voice grew more intense. "But that doesn't take away from the fact that I lived a very lonely life without him and practically had to raise you girls by myself. It's a hard life, Adelaide."

Silence, like a brick wall, separated them.

"Are you forbidding me to see him?"

Ma waited a moment. "No, I'm not. You are twenty-four years old, Adelaide. I had two children by the time I was your age. I'm only asking that you consider your steps wisely before taking them."

Adelaide went over to her ma and embraced her. "I will, Ma. I will."

∽

Sunlight peered through the windows of the church, washing the rough benches with the light of a new day.

A family with children sat beside Adelaide. The children wiggled and scooted in their seats. Their constant movement distracted her. It took great effort for her to concentrate on the sermon.

"As you know, many of our men will be leaving within the next few weeks as the whaling ships set sail," Pastor Daugherty explained. "We hope you will join us for a farewell social this Friday, weather permitting. We've been real fortunate that the cold hasn't overtaken us just yet. Isaiah and Ethel Clemmons have graciously offered to hold the social in their barn."

After the announcement, Pastor Daugherty dismissed the congregation. People talked excitedly about the social as they left the church. Adelaide wondered if Josiah would ask her.

For all her talk of the sea, she didn't feel Josiah understood in the least what she wanted. Frustration filled her. Meeting Josiah had stirred hope to life within her. No one else she knew had the connections with ship captains that Josiah had. But he would be leaving soon, and her dreams would sail with him. Because she was a single woman, she would never experience life on the sea.

Determined to enjoy the day, she pushed aside her moodiness.

Stepping into a blaze of sunshine, Adelaide drank deeply of the damp, salty air. Nearly the end of November, it seemed a magical autumn day as the season's warmth, still refusing to give way to winter's icy breezes, surrounded them.

"Good morning, Adelaide."

Josiah's voice startled her. She felt her breath catch in her throat. "Good morning, Josiah."

People mingled all about them. The children happily ran to and fro, enjoying the moments at play while their parents talked with one another.

"If you're not tired of my company yet, I was hoping you would accompany me to the social on Friday."

Adelaide felt almost giddy with excitement. One more chance. "I would be happy to accompany you, Josiah."

Josiah nudged her elbow away from the crowd of people. "You know I'll be leaving in twelve days?"

Adelaide nodded and tried to swallow but couldn't.

He cleared his throat and kicked the ground with his boot.

"What is it, Josiah?"

He looked up at her and shook his head. "Well—"

"Adelaide, are you ready?" her ma called from behind them.

"Yes, I'll be right there," Adelaide responded over her shoulder. She looked at Josiah once more, waiting for his response.

He brushed the matter aside with a wave of his hand. "I'll talk to you about it on Friday."

Seeing he was not going to talk further, she nodded. "Friday." Secretly she was hoping she would see him before then. Every moment counted now.

"I wish it could be sooner, but I have to make preparations for sailing. Gathering my crew, loading the ship, that type of thing."

"I understand."

"Six-thirty, Friday?"

She nodded and waved good-bye. As Adelaide made her way to their buckboard, her thoughts were filled with making preparations for the social and wondering what Josiah would tell her come Friday.

Josiah walked through the *Courage*, making note of inventory and wrestling with his decision. Was he taking advantage of Adelaide? Wouldn't this help them both? Over and over, he argued within himself. He stopped in front of the goose pen and checked to see what vegetables were needed. Jotting a quick note, he moved on.

Hadn't people called him "the Wise Sea Captain"? Of course, he didn't let the name go to his head. Still, he figured he had some sense of business. With heavy, dark clouds looming overhead, the skylight allowed little visibility for descending to the lower deck. Josiah stepped carefully down the steps to check on the livestock.

It seemed to him no matter how he worked the matter through, this decision seemed the best option for everyone involved. For Adelaide, for him, and for the ship. She'd certainly made it clear to him she wanted to sail. What was the harm in asking? She could always say no.

After throwing scraps to the pigs and sheep and chicken feed to the hens, Josiah trudged his way back to the upper deck. Adelaide's comments had made it obvious to him she had no idea of the harshness of sea life. That's what bothered him. He pushed aside the nagging thought that he was taking advantage of her love for the sea to meet his needs. Instead, he convinced himself he was helping her live out her dream. If that helped him in the process as well, what did it hurt?

Adelaide let out a contented sigh as she rode with Josiah along the seaside toward the Clemmonses' house. Although the night was a bit chilly, Adelaide thought it a perfect evening. She looked toward the glow of pink that covered the horizon with the setting of the sun. Shredded clouds floated aimlessly about. She closed her eyes and listened as the echo of the sea whispered through the evening air like a steady breeze.

"You happy?" Josiah's words broke through her contentment.

"Very." She was, too. Her hopes told her the night held endless possibilities.

"Me, too."

The distant lighthouse flashed its searching beam across the waters, threatening to shadow Adelaide's joy with thoughts of Josiah at sea and her left behind. She refused to linger there.

When they arrived at the social, Adelaide took in the scene before her. Though held in a rough barn, the place was clean and warm. Enormous trays of food lined up on a large table provided plenty to eat. Local fiddlers played for the adults while children huddled in circles for stories and games.

Adelaide and Josiah passed the evening with friends and laughter. All too soon the social drew to an end.

"Adelaide, could we go outside for a moment?" Josiah asked as he handed her some hot tea.

"Certainly." Suddenly her hopes fled and concern filled her. Was he going to say good-bye now? So soon?

They stepped into the brisk night air. Adelaide pulled her cloak closer to her neck and took a sip of tea.

Moonlight now bathed the sea in a romantic glow. The scent of homemade pies and cakes followed them from the barn, filling the air with fresh sweetness. Josiah edged her away from the barn, stepping around the front of the house facing the sea. The moon provided enough light to make their steps secure.

He turned to her. "I have something on my mind. I'm not sure how to say it."

She felt her heart turn to liquid. The next few minutes could seal her fate forever. Would her dreams come true, or would a part of her die?

"I received word my cook has decided not to sail with the *Courage.*"

Confusion filled her.

"I know you love the sea, and I thought, I mean, I was wondering, uh. . ."

Her mind tangled with his words. What was he trying to say?

He must have seen the concern on her face. He lifted his free hand. "Just hear me out before you say anything."

She nodded, trying desperately to keep her wild thoughts in check.

He looked down and nervously marked the sand with his boot. After what seemed an eternity to Adelaide, he looked out to sea as if the words he needed could be found there. "Having a good cook on my ship is one of the most important aspects of my job, the very reason I'm successful as a captain. Most ships employ a crewman, whoever they can get. I refuse to do that. The men need good food. They need their strength and health. It's a hard life out there."

He finally lifted his face to her. "What I'm trying to say is you want a life on the sea. I need a good cook for the crew. There's no time to search for one. You are a great cook."

Her heart soared! She wanted to run the beach, to shout from the rooftops, but his next words stopped her cold.

"I thought perhaps if you married me, you could have what you want, and I could as well."

Her thoughts swirled in a flurry of confusion. He wanted her to marry him? She gulped. Before she could utter a word, he continued.

"Please understand. I acknowledge it's a marriage of convenience. We would marry in name only. I would respect and honor you. You would cook for the crew. In return, you would experience life on the sea." He searched her eyes, as if trying to read her answer. "It's the only proper way for you to sail."

Mixed emotions closed in, making it difficult for her to breathe. How long had she dreamed for this day? Yet marriage? She hadn't thought of that. Marriage was saved for love, wasn't it? Still, why hadn't she seen this coming? He and Mrs. Markle were right. Adelaide couldn't possibly sail the seas as a single woman. What foolishness that she had allowed her dreams to carry her onto a ship without thought of propriety.

Well, Josiah was her friend, after all, not a total stranger. His love had died with his first wife, so there would be no romantic illusions on Adelaide's part. A business deal. How odd that she should feel a tug of sadness.

"I know this is all so sudden, but—"

"I'll go." Her dreams would come true—or did she seal a fate of loneliness and endless days without knowing love? "It is the only way I can get to the sea," she explained.

If he noticed indecision in her eyes, he said nothing. "You will? Adelaide, that's wonderful!" The thrill of the moment seemed to get the better of him. He pulled her into an enormous embrace, causing her to spill the remainder of her tea.

Oh, how she wanted to free herself from the fear of the unknown, to embrace her rescuer fully in return, to let her heart soar. Instead, she bristled a little. This was not about them. This was a business arrangement. True, she would get to sail, but was this the way she wanted it?

He must have sensed her awkwardness. "Forgive me. It is such a relief to know you will go." Upon seeing her face, he cleared his throat. "Of course, we must behave as though we are happy about the whole affair in front of others, or surely they would try to stop us." His eyes searched her face.

Understanding dawned on her. That was the reason for the endless evenings together. Josiah had been working up to this point. He wanted the town to think they were courting. It all made sense to her now. "I understand, Josiah." She dropped her voice to a whisper. *What is wrong with me? This is exactly what I've wanted all my life.* Yet she couldn't stop the disappointment swelling inside. She would never have a family, never know love.

"Shall we go tell the others?"

"I'd rather you let me tell Ma alone before we make it public."

"I understand." He escorted her back toward the barn. "I was thinking we could get married at your house in, say, five or six days?"

She turned a surprised look toward him.

"I'm sorry, Adelaide, but there isn't much time."

She nodded. The magical feel of the evening disappeared with the ebbing tide. Her life would be forever changed from this night forward. The worst fear of all grabbed her. She had not even thought to pray about the matter. . . .

⌒

"Oh Adelaide, that is so romantic!" Esther said dramatically when Adelaide revealed her wedding plans.

Adelaide shifted on her bed. "Shh, I haven't told Ma yet." She could hear Ma in the kitchen. The smell of simmering vegetable soup filled their cottage.

"Oh dear. She will not be happy about this," Esther whispered then nervously rubbed her hands together.

"I know." Adelaide fell back against the bed. *If Ma knew the truth, she would positively forbid it.*

Esther's face brightened. "She will change her mind when she sees how happy you two are, Adelaide. She worries about us."

The room fell quiet. The only sounds came from the kitchen, where Ma clanged pots and dishes. Adelaide needed to go help. She straightened herself back up and threw a weak smile toward her sister.

"You're sure about this, Adelaide?" Esther's expression showed uncertainty.

Suddenly Adelaide knew she would have to do a better job of pretending than this. She mustered the courage and put on a happy face. "Positive."

Esther's anxious expression broke into the most pleasurable of smiles. "Don't worry, then. Everything will be fine. Now, let's go tell Ma."

Esther extended her hand to help Adelaide from the bed, and together they walked into the kitchen.

"Well, I'd wondered what you were up to. Adelaide, would you place these bowls on the table, please? Esther, get the water."

The sisters shared a glance then commenced to set the table. Once seated, Ma prayed over the meal then spooned the thick soup into heavy bowls.

Esther nodded encouragement.

Adelaide took a deep breath. "Ma, I have something to tell you."

With reluctance, Ma placed the soup ladle back in the bowl and wiped her hands. As if waiting for this moment and knowing the dreaded time had arrived, Ma looked at Adelaide. "Go on."

"Josiah has asked me to marry him, and I have agreed."

"I see." Ma lifted the ladle once again and continued serving the soup. Adelaide and Esther exchanged a glance of disbelief.

"Did you hear me, Ma?"

"I heard you, Adelaide." Ma concerned herself with the meal before them. Without looking at Adelaide, she asked, "When are you leaving?" Her face remained expressionless.

"We set sail November 25. We would like to get married here, if you don't mind. Just our family with Pastor and Mrs. Daugherty and the Markles, of course."

"So your mind is made up, Adelaide?"

"Yes."

"Then there's nothing I can do to stop you." Tears glistened in her eyes as Ma turned toward Adelaide and reached for her hand. "I love you, Adelaide. I want what's best for you. I trust your judgment. If this makes you happy and you feel this is God's will for your life, I will not stop you."

Adelaide was caught off guard by her ma's response. If only Ma had scolded her, it would have made things easier. But her blessing? Her trust?

"Thank you" was all Adelaide could manage.

Plans for the wedding, which they decided would take place in two days, consumed the rest of the mealtime.

Once alone with her thoughts that evening in bed, Adelaide felt relief that the task of telling her ma was over. The days ahead would fly by, and she mentally made a list of things she wanted to accomplish.

She knew this should be the happiest time in her life, but deceit weighed on her heart. What kind of life would she have at sea? With Josiah?

"Father, what have I done?" Silent tears washed her face.

Adelaide listened as a ruffle of wind tapped against the windowpane, lightly at first, and then growing stronger. Misty rain blurred the glass. Soft thunder pealed from the heavens.

Adelaide pulled the thick blankets closer to her neck, suddenly feeling an icy chill. She closed her eyes to sleep, but the storm pulled her thoughts into a torturous theatrical play. A play in which she portrayed the lonely wife of a sea captain. . .

Chapter 4

Though the wind brought fragmented conversations from nearby warehouses and other various establishments bordering the waterfront, Adelaide felt glad she had insisted the wedding take place near the *Courage*.

Just beyond their gathering, four wharves reached out more than a hundred yards into the harbor. Tethered to the wharves, eighteen to twenty whaleboats, along with dozens of smaller vessels, creaked and groaned with the churning waters that sloshed against their hulls.

The wind whipped through Adelaide's dress, causing it to snap at her feet. The noontime sun did little to warm her from the nippy breeze, but she assured herself the ceremony would be over soon and she would spend the afternoon packing before setting sail.

Josiah and his crew had spent several days loading the ship with casks of water, firewood, food, equipment, clothing, charts, medicine, nautical instruments, and the like. Adelaide could hardly believe they were almost ready to sail.

Adelaide Sanborn—rather, Buchanan—would sail on a whaling ship.

The pastor's words mingled with the murmur of the sea, and Adelaide's thoughts drifted to the evening ahead of her. Josiah had told her she would need to spend the night at his land home or people would wonder. He had assured her she could sleep in a guest room. Not that she minded. She certainly didn't want it any other way. Still, she couldn't deny it was hardly the wedding night of which a young woman dreamed.

Where were all these silly romantic notions coming from? She sounded as bad as Esther. Adelaide glanced at her sister. Esther's face beamed with pure pleasure. Adelaide couldn't help but let out a slight smile.

She straightened her shoulders and turned her attention back to the pastor's words. The soft cadence of the seashore echoed against the solemn vows Adelaide and Josiah repeated in front of the few witnesses.

When they came to the ceremony's end, horror filled Adelaide as she realized Josiah would have to kiss her. Her breath felt as shallow as the shoreline. Her mind raced with the tide. She had to remain calm. Act natural. After all, this was their wedding day.

"You may kiss the bride," the pastor said with a smile.

Josiah looked uncomfortable as he reached for her, unnerving her all the more. She tried to swallow, but her mouth was too dry. *Keep up the act or the people will suspect,* she told herself. She closed her eyes, not daring to look as his face drew closer, closer. She felt his breath upon her cheeks. Still, she waited. Her heart pounded hard against her chest. It seemed an eternity. His breath grew stronger upon her skin. What was taking so long? Reluctantly, she peeked through one eye. Amusement stared back at her.

Why, he mocked her! Both of her eyes popped open. Before she could give herself over to a full fit of temper, he kissed her. Pure and simple. Just like that, taking both her temper and breath away at the same time.

It suddenly dawned on Adelaide that she had never been kissed before—unless she counted Johnny Black under the apple tree in first grade.

The tiny crowd chuckled and clapped as the couple turned to face them. Hearty congratulations filled the air, and Adelaide felt the tension fall away.

It was done.

She was now the wife of Josiah Buchanan, the grand sea captain, and Adelaide would soon sail the seas. . . .

After the wedding and celebration meal, Josiah and Adelaide decided to check on the progress of the *Courage*'s preparation for sea.

Stepping carefully along the wharves, they dodged barrels, boxes, cordwood, heaps of heavy chains, and various other whalecraft. Harpoons, lances, cutting spades, and oil ladles littered their path.

Adelaide watched as ship carpenters and caulkers worked to make the *Courage* sound below the waterline. She and Josiah stepped past shipwrights who busied themselves with repairing damage to the hull from previous voyages.

Once they arrived on the top deck, Josiah stopped to talk to a couple of crewmen. Adelaide looked around. She stared in disbelief at the magnitude of the square-rigged ship. Closing her eyes for a moment, she took in the sounds of the busy crew around her: the swish of the paintbrushes, the thump of hammers, men calling out to one another.

The ship stirred as heavy waves slapped against the hull. Seagulls cried overhead. Adelaide looked up to watch them swarm against the backdrop of a pure blue sky. Her eyes glanced toward the massive web of giant rope overhead. She turned portside and noticed three whaleboats slung from wooden davits and two more hung on the starboard side. Josiah had told her they would use three boats; the other two would serve as spares.

"Good afternoon, Captain," a seaman called out as he worked with others to hoist the topmast into place.

Josiah smiled and gave a quick nod.

"Is that what they call the tryworks?" Adelaide asked, nodding toward the men who worked on a brick structure forward of the fore hatch.

Josiah turned a surprised look her way. "Yes, it is. The whale blubber is cooked into oil in those large iron try-pots," he said, pointing toward the big kettles. "And the copper tank is for cooling the hot oil."

Adelaide thought it all very fascinating.

"Here's where you will spend much of your time." Josiah took her into the cookhouse.

The cookhouse. Her new job. The reason Josiah had married her. Reality seared through her romantic ideas of the sea. Adelaide glanced at the stove and goose pen where vegetables were stored. She scolded herself. After all, she couldn't sail in such a fine vessel without working like the rest of the crew. Her chin lifted. Yes, indeed, she'd pull her weight just like everyone else and be glad for the opportunity to do so. They stepped back onto the deck.

Workers nodded their greetings as she and Josiah continued on their way toward the stern of the ship. Josiah pointed out the skylight that would provide some lighting to the lower deck.

They came upon two small deckhouses connected just over the ship's helm. Adelaide caught Josiah's questioning look.

"Hurricane house, right?"

"Right again."

She noticed he seemed pleased with her knowledge of the ship. They slipped into the hurricane house, and Josiah helped Adelaide down the steps that led to the lower deck.

Painters worked hard washing the cabin and officers' quarters with a fresh coat of white paint.

Josiah stepped through the cabin and turned to grab her hand. He escorted her inside.

A couple of painters offered their greetings then went back to work.

"This will be our room." His voice cracked.

Adelaide looked at him with a start. For a moment, his expression held a little-boy-like quality. He seemed as uncomfortable as she felt. Suddenly, the very idea made her want to giggle, but she dared not. Josiah was a proud man; she'd best not make him think she was poking fun at him.

Josiah cleared his throat.

Adelaide quickly turned and glanced around the room. The cabin held a sofa, desk, chair, and table. The adjoining room held a small washbasin and privy and a small bed hanging from gimbals. Josiah must have seen the concern on her face.

"We'll talk about that later," he whispered into her ear. His breath brushed against her face with the softness of a goose feather.

Josiah once again took her hand and led her through the lower deck, showing her the officers' cabins; the steerage rooms for the skilled workers, such as harpooners and boatsteerers; the livestock pens; and finally, in the bow of the ship, the forecastle where the foremast hands, or ordinary crewmen, slept. She looked on the room with disappointment. Thin mattresses filled sparingly with corn husks lined the bunks that would be their beds for the duration of their journey.

Josiah, seeing the concern on her face, shrugged with apology. "It's the best I can do with what the owners give me."

"I understand," she answered lightly, though concerned by the injustice of poverty and wealth.

"I guess we'd better head back so you can pack your things and move."

A smile lit her face before she could stop herself. She had to admit she could hardly wait for the new adventure awaiting her. But what did the future hold for her and Josiah? She cast a sideways glance at him and found him staring at her. He swallowed hard and turned away at once. His pace quickened, and Adelaide struggled to keep up.

She told herself to get used to it. No doubt her life would hold many challenges in the days ahead.

❧

Shoving the last bit of clothing into her trunk, Adelaide gently closed the lid and turned to find Ma and Esther standing behind her. A downcast expression covered her ma's face. Esther's eyes shone bright with dreams.

Adelaide smiled at them both. She walked over to her ma and placed an arm around her. "I'll send letters as often as possible."

Ma nodded. She wiped the tears that stained her face. "Be happy, Addie."

Ma used Adelaide's nickname sparingly. To hear her say it nearly melted Adelaide's heart. "I am happy," Adelaide assured her. "I've always dreamed of going to sea—you know that." Seeing a flicker of surprise cross her ma's face, Adelaide quickly added, "Josiah is a good man. We'll have a wonderful life."

Ma eyed her with suspicion. Adelaide shifted from one leg to the other. Her ma knew her all too well. If Adelaide and Josiah stayed around much longer, Ma would see right through their pretense. "Well, I guess I'd better go. Don't want to keep my husband waiting." Her voice sounded much lighter than she felt.

"You're sure about this, Adelaide?" Ma's eyes studied her.

Never one to back down once she had made her choice, Adelaide answered with finality, "I'm sure." She pulled one end of the trunk; Esther quickly lifted the other. Together they carried it to the front door. Dropping it into place, Adelaide brushed her hands and looked at them once more.

"I'll miss you, Addie." Esther gave her an enormous hug.

Adelaide felt her throat constrict. "You take care of Ma," she whispered. When she pulled away, Adelaide added, "And go easy on the fellows."

Esther's eyes twinkled as her cheeks turned a rosy hue. Then a sad look crossed her face.

Adelaide knew Esther was thinking of Adam Bowman, a man who had courted her but from whom she had not heard in a while. "I'm sure you'll hear from Adam again. Don't worry," Adelaide encouraged.

Esther nodded reluctantly. "I hope you're right."

Adelaide turned to Ma. "I will miss you. You'll be all right?" Adelaide needed to hear it one more time. She had taken responsibility for the family since her pa had died, and it worried her to leave them behind. Why she worried, she didn't know. Ma and Esther were in good health, and they would do just fine without her. The enormity of her decision made her waver for a slight moment. She had allowed her passion for the sea to bring her to this point. Would it hold all the wonders of which she'd often dreamed? As much as she wanted to go, the little girl in her wanted to change her mind, run to Ma, and hide behind her skirts.

Ma took a deep breath and straightened herself. "Of course we'll be all right," she said matter-of-factly. Her tone softened. "But we will miss you."

Ma's embrace felt like a year's worth of hugs all rolled into one. Adelaide wasn't sure if it was the tight embrace or the heavy weight on her chest that made breathing difficult.

Outside, a gentle *clip-clop* sounded the arrival of Josiah's carriage. Ma pulled away in a manner that said she didn't want to, tears still glistening in her eyes. Adelaide looked at her family. "Well, I guess I'd better go. . .to my husband."

Esther chuckled and Ma nodded.

Adelaide opened the door and looked up to see Josiah coming toward the house. "Are you ready?"

"Yes."

"Good," he said, grabbing one end of her trunk as she lifted the other. "I was hoping we could stop by the *Courage* once more to check on a matter."

Adelaide nodded.

Ma and Esther followed them to the carriage. Josiah heaved the trunk into the back.

"You'll take care of her," Ma said more as an instruction than a question.

Josiah stopped scooting the trunk and looked at Ma. "You have my word, ma'am."

Ma's shoulders relaxed. A slight smile touched her lips. "All right, then." Her practical side kicked in. "You have everything, Adelaide?"

"Yes."

Another round of hugs and tears followed, and then Josiah lifted

Adelaide to the carriage. She waved good-bye to Ma and Esther as they stood watching.

A knot formed in her throat. Carriage wheels bumped against ruts in the path as they rode along in silence. The horses snorted and bobbed their heads, but Adelaide paid little heed.

"You all right?" Josiah asked.

"I'm fine."

"Look, Adelaide, I—"

She turned to him, and he stopped. "What is it, Josiah?" She wondered if he had changed his mind. "Would you rather I not go?"

Surprise lit his face. "What? No, of course not!"

The intensity of his words convinced her that at least he wanted her on the ship.

To cook.

He reached for her hand. "Thank you for saying yes."

"Why, it was my pleasure," she said. Then realizing she sounded a bit too bold, she quickly added, "I told you, I'd do just about anything to get to the sea."

"Of course." His lips drew into a thin line, and he jerked on the horses' reins. If Adelaide didn't know better, she would have thought she had disappointed him in some way, though she couldn't imagine why.

❦

"It's not supposed to be like this!" Josiah paced the floor of his bedroom while Adelaide freshened up in her room. He wrenched his fists into tight balls then flexed them. His frustration grew with every step. What had he been thinking to ask Adelaide to be his wife only to serve as a cook for his ship? What kind of life was that for a woman? He'd taken advantage of her love for the sea just to fill a position on his ship. True, he had been a desperate man. After all, he couldn't sail without a cook. Still, he had been utterly unfair to her.

The vision of their wedding scene played upon his mind. Adelaide's hair sneaking free of the pins and blowing in the breeze, dancing across her forehead and brushing lightly against her cheeks, her skin tinged pink by the chill, her eyes bright with hope. How could he look at her, knowing he had ruined her future?

"A business arrangement." Those had been his words.

His words.

Now he wished he could take them back. For her sake. *Stop it!* he told himself as he stood to pace once again. *She's making me go soft. I've got to stay away from her. Far away. She's here to cook. I'm helping her sail the seas; she's helping me keep my crew happy. It's as simple as that. Arranged marriages happen all the time. She wanted this as much as I did. We will live together. I will provide for her. We'll do just fine.* A dull ache knotted his stomach like a rusty chain. She'd agreed to a future with him, a life on the sea. So why did he feel guilty?

❧

Adelaide slipped into the front room of their home and waited for Josiah to enter. After what seemed an eternity, the bedroom door squeaked open.

"I'm loading the *Courage* with our things. I need to finalize everything for the voyage. The crew will be boarding soon. I'll stay on the ship tonight and get it in order." He glanced out the window. "Although it's our wedding night, the crew will think nothing of my being there since our departure is set for day after tomorrow." His words were gruff and curt.

Adelaide stared at him, speechless.

Grabbing the first box within reach, he lifted it into his arms and headed out the door.

Well, the least he could have done was let her spend another night with Ma and Esther. Now she would spend her wedding night alone. Humiliation washed over her. *You're an idiot, Adelaide! What did you think—you would pass the hours laughing and talking with your new friend? You're his wife in name only. A hired cook. Your pay is the sea. You've finally gotten what you've always wanted.* Tears stung her eyes. In a moment, her stubborn side kicked in. No! She would not wallow in self-pity. She had made this choice, and she would make the best of it. Isn't that what she had always done?

Although Adelaide stitched other people's clothes to help with the family income, when her pa died, she also had gone to work at the general store. Between the chores on the homestead, mending for others, and working at the store, Adelaide dropped into bed each night and quickly slipped into dreams of a different world. A world filled with adventure, foreign lands, and different cultures. Though the dreams gave her hope, despair threatened many a day. She feared she would live out her days in Yorksville. The idea had almost suffocated her.

So now she should be happy. Adelaide threw a pillow across the couch. She was feeling sorry for herself, and that was not like her.

For a moment, she sat in utter silence. Her heartfelt prayer started with tears. Finally, she began to speak. "Father, Thou art able to do all things. I ask not of Thee to change the life I have made for myself. I ask only for strength to carry on and make the best of the choices I have made. And above all, may I give all glory and honor to Thee alone for all Thy mercies extended to me. Amen."

Adelaide brushed away tears from her cheeks with the backs of her hands then dabbed at her face with the material from her dress. Lifting her chin, she decided she would get through this. There would be no loneliness;

the sea would be her constant companion.

   She looked up to see Josiah coming toward the house. Just as he entered the door, she rose from the couch. Adelaide took a deep breath. "Let me help you, Josiah," she said in her kindest voice.

   And what surprised her most was that she meant it.

Chapter 5

Once he arrived at the *Courage*, Josiah checked through the shipping papers again. He decided he had the needed legal documents for all signed-up crewmen. He placed the stack of papers inside his desk.

Glancing once more through the inventory in the logbook, Josiah decided they had what they needed for the trip until they reached the next port. The food was loaded and ready to go. Potatoes and vegetables filled the goose pen. Heavy casks of beef, pork, hard bread, flour, and water spotted the deck and cookhouse.

Josiah walked through the lower deck and did a final check on the livestock. Squealing pigs, hogs, chickens, and bleating sheep restlessly shuffled about in the animal pens. Checking the livestock's food supply, Josiah scribbled some notes on the log that his first mate would be taking over. Everything seemed in order.

Finally, Josiah arrived in his cabin, tired and spent. He glanced around the quarters. His cabin and adjoining room together didn't match the size of the most modest of New England parlors. In a corner of the room sat a tiny privy. One of the few comforts of being a captain.

The skylight and a small stern window provided some lighting. Not much but better than nothing. He shrugged. The size of the room, with slivers of glimpses into the sea world, had not bothered him. Until now. Could Adelaide live in such confined spaces? She hadn't seemed to mind when she'd seen it earlier in the day. He shouldn't worry, he told himself. After all, she wanted to sail the seas. A whaling ship was no place for coddling.

He wondered how he could be tough as nails in his role as a sea captain, for lately when he thought of Adelaide, his strength turned to limp seaweed. He couldn't help feeling he had taken advantage of her. Still, she said this was what she wanted.

Once more, he looked around the cramped room. It didn't help that they had to have the stove in the room due to the cold. When they headed into warmer climates, they could remove it.

Adelaide could keep one trunk in the room if she chose to do so. It could serve as a table or bench and also be used for storage. Some things could be stuffed in the three drawers beneath the bed, but the rest of her trunks would be stowed in the ship's hold.

Although the room had little space to spare, Josiah would have to hang another bed before Adelaide arrived. For her privacy, he'd also hang a sheet of some kind between them.

Bothersome thoughts poked tiny holes into his peace of mind like determined mosquitoes. Josiah prepared for bed. Once settled under the covers, he willed himself to get needed sleep. Quieting the restless voices inside his head, he managed to shove away all thoughts but one. Could Adelaide build a happy life for herself here?

∞

The next morning, Josiah collected Adelaide and her things and brought them to the ship. After he'd seen to having her things put away, he busied himself with the tasks of a sea captain, but Adelaide stood on the wharf and drank in her surroundings. The men buzzed around the ship in a whir of activity. She marveled that this time she would not only watch the ship leave, but she would be on it! Even if she and Josiah only pretended to have a marriage in front of others, Adelaide decided to make the most of this time and enjoy her seafaring life.

She knew the morning of November 28, 1856, would go down in her memory for years to come. Her first day to set sail. No doubt her grandchildren would one day discuss it. The thought warmed her before she realized there would be no grandchildren. She would not allow her thoughts to go there, not now. Nothing would spoil this day.

"Adelaide!"

Hearing a familiar voice but not quite placing it, Adelaide turned around. "Adam Bowman," she said with surprise. "What are you doing here?"

"I've signed on as first mate." Pride filled his voice.

Adelaide thought how proud Esther would be of him. Though Adam was three years older, he and Esther had hit it off from the day his family moved to town. In the past five years, they had written to one another while he was at sea, though communication was minimal. He stopped to see her whenever he was in port. Ma tried to discourage the friendship. She didn't like having anyone who had to do with whaling associate with her daughters.

"Congratulations! We didn't know you were in town. I'm surprised you didn't stop by the house. Esther will be disappointed!" Adelaide threw him a teasing grin.

He frowned. "I had only returned from a whaling trip when I learned my grandma had died. We went to Bayview and have just returned."

"Oh, I'm sorry."

He shrugged. "She was ready, though we didn't want to let her go." He shoved his hands into his trousers pockets. "Then I'd signed up for the *Courage* and had to hurry back." He looked at her. "I wish I'd had more time. I wanted to see Esther. Wasn't sure if she had anyone special in her life, what with me gone all the time. I would have said good-bye to her if I'd known I still had a chance." He said the last phrase more as a question.

Adelaide picked up on it. "I believe you do," she encouraged. She noticed his ears turned lobster red.

"What are you doing here, anyway?"

She swallowed. "Well, uh, I got married yesterday to the captain of this ship." She tried to make the words sound as happy as a new bride.

"What?"

Adelaide thought Adam looked as though he'd choked on a fish bone. She laughed. "See what happens when you're away?"

"You've got a lot of explaining to do, young lady," he teased in a brotherly fashion.

"Mate," Josiah's deep voice interrupted, "I think you'd better get your things in order."

Adam looked at Josiah then back to Adelaide. "Yes Captain," Adam replied before quickly complying with orders.

Josiah's behavior left Adelaide mute.

"Adelaide, if you will please follow me." His voice was short and curt, leaving no room for comment.

Adelaide felt like a little girl being reprimanded by the schoolmaster. She couldn't imagine what she must have done wrong.

Once they reached the cabin, Josiah closed the door behind them. Adelaide opened her mouth to speak, but he cut her short.

"You must conduct yourself as a woman of propriety, Adelaide. These are rough characters you will be traveling alongside, and you'd do well to steer clear of the lot of them."

For a moment, disbelief caused her tongue to stick to the roof of her mouth. Though his remarks hurt and angered her, the concern in his voice pushed the sting of the insult at a distance. Oh how she wished Esther's starry-eyed ways hadn't affected her. On the other hand, Adelaide did want Josiah to know, under no uncertain terms, that she was a decent woman.

Without conscious effort, she lifted her chin. "Captain Buchanan, as you get to know me, you will find I am a woman of propriety and conduct myself in such a manner. Further, I wish you to understand that I know that young man. Your first mate, Adam Bowman, happens to be a dear friend of our family." The words were measured and meted out evenly. She hoped Josiah would see he had jumped to a wrong conclusion.

His eyes narrowed. "All the more reason to steer clear, *Mrs.* Buchanan. Wouldn't want the crew to get the wrong idea." With that, he turned, walked through the door, and closed it hard, leaving Adelaide to stare behind him.

What had gotten into him? What had happened to the kind, gentle man she had been seeing for the past several weeks? Adelaide unlatched her trunk and began to rip things from inside and throw them onto the bed. "How dare he consider I would be less than a woman of propriety!"

Dresses, petticoats, books, paper, and underthings flew from her arms onto the cluttered bed. "Just because we're married doesn't mean he can tell me when and to whom I may speak." She didn't care that her underthings lay bare for anyone to see. "It would serve him right if he walked in right now. I'd love to embarrass him the way he embarrassed me!"

She pulled out her shoes and tossed one across the floor. Of course she was behaving as a child, but somehow she couldn't stop herself. It seemed since Josiah Buchanan had walked into her life and turned her world upside down, her emotions shifted with the eastern winds.

She threw herself into her clothes and started to whimper. Before she could work herself up into a good crying spell, she heard the door open. She shot up on the bed.

Josiah walked in and stared at her. For a moment, neither said a word. "I—" He stopped talking and glanced at the floor. Bending over, he picked up her petticoat and threw it on the bed. "You dropped something." He turned and walked right back out the door.

"Awgh!" she wailed before falling back into the pile of clothes on her bed.

∽

Later that evening, family and friends gathered aboard the *Courage* in a final good-bye celebration. Together they enjoyed a fine feast, and then Adelaide and Josiah stood at the ship's rail, waving as whaleboats rowed their guests back to shore.

Once the excitement died down, the reality of her recent choices swept over Adelaide, filling her with a sense of melancholy. A quiet settled upon her as she pulled wide the curtain separating her bed from Josiah's.

Dressed for bed, she situated herself beneath the folds of blankets and quilts. Josiah's boots thumped against the floor, and she could hear him shrugging out of work clothes. She wished things could be different somehow. Their friendship had changed from the moment Josiah mentioned marriage. Things were now a bit, well, awkward between them. Adelaide took a deep breath and blew out a quick puff of air, snuffing the light from her lantern.

Josiah's bed shifted as she heard him climb in. He scooted about then blew out his lantern.

Adelaide stared into the darkness. A sense of loneliness filled the tiny room. Heavy waves rocked the hull, but sleep escaped her. She heard Josiah turn restlessly on his bed and wondered if he stared blankly through the darkness, too.

By the next morning, Adelaide's mood had improved considerably. She dressed quickly and pulled on her cape. When she opened the door, Josiah stood waiting on the other side.

"I thought I'd walk with you to the cookhouse."

Adelaide smiled and felt pleasure at the protective hand at her elbow, guiding her to her new workstation. The wooden deck sparkled from the cleaning it had received in port. Adelaide secured the top button on her cape against the eastward wind.

Once in the cookhouse, she quickly prepared a breakfast of eggs, coffee, and ham for herself, Josiah, and his mates. Although somewhat out of the ordinary, Josiah allowed the skilled members of his crew, such as the blacksmith and cooper or cask maker, as the position was sometimes called, to also join them in their cabin for meals. Adelaide knew that on most ships, the skilled workers ate after the captain and his mates. Josiah's kindness softened her heart toward him.

The rest of the crew sat on their sea chests on the main deck and ate the hardtack and ham that Adelaide made for them. They ate below deck only during foul weather.

Breakfast was soon over, and Adelaide watched as the men went to their various posts with the fire of adventure in their eyes.

After she scrubbed the cookhouse clean, she went out on the deck. The *Courage* set sail down the bay. The old ship groaned as the wind pushed it toward the high seas. Adelaide wanted to take one last look at her homeland before it disappeared with the shoreline.

The moment was bittersweet. She knew she would miss her family and her town, but as the wind filled the sails, excitement shot through her. She was living her dream.

As she made her way to the rail, sailors nodded cordial greetings, granting her the appropriate respect as befit a captain's wife. Adelaide edged closer to the rail to get a better view. Just then a sailor stepped in front of her. Deep lines rutted his forehead. Spiked whiskers poked through his jaw, reminding Adelaide of pins on a cushion.

"You want to be careful not to get too close to the ship's rail, ma'am," he said with a smile, revealing rotted teeth. He tipped his cap in a mock gesture that made Adelaide's skin crawl. No doubt the man had made his way through life bullying others. It was probably the only life he had ever known. She knew she couldn't show her fear, or she'd be miserable the rest of the journey. They had to serve on the ship together, and he needed to know up front where she stood. God's love softened her fear, and compassion filled her.

Without a blink, her gaze fixed on his threatening one. "Why, I thank you kindly for your concern, Mister—"

His eyes narrowed. Adelaide felt quite delighted that she seemed to have caught him off guard. "Ebenezer. The name's Ebenezer," he growled before stepping aside from her path and moving on his way.

Adelaide stared after him for a moment to let him know she was not frightened in the least. Which, of course, was not true. Underneath her clothing, her legs trembled. She waited until he edged away at a comfortable distance then turned her eyes toward the sea.

I thank Thee, Father, for helping me in that situation. Please help Ebenezer to know Thee as well. Amen.

She lifted her face to the sky and took a deep gulp of the fresh sea air. Sometimes the strong smell of fish overpowered the docks, but out on the sea, the air held the tangy scent of salt.

Pa, if only you could see me now. I think it would please you to find me on a whaling ship. I can't wait to experience all the excitement you shared with me as a child. Your stories built dreams in me, Pa. This is a whole new world. A world alive with color, activity. . .and loneliness.

Where had that thought come from? She hadn't a chance to feel lonely here. Too much work to do. Besides, her pa had taught her to look at the bright side of things, and she did. The sea. She was riding the seas on a whaling ship as the wife of a grand sea captain. How could she complain?

She stood in the warmth of the sunshine and drank in the awesomeness of God, the handiwork of His creation. Her spirit held her steadfast in the warmth of worship.

∞

Josiah caught a glimpse of Adelaide standing at the rail. Her eyes were closed, her face lifted skyward. The sun's rays sprayed upon her, casting her in an ethereal glow. She looked like an angel. He stood transfixed, watching her. No doubt she was praying. He had heard her whispered prayer the night before. She pored over her Bible with such enthusiasm, as if she couldn't live without it.

How did people attain such a faith? Though on land he had been a regular attender, church was more of a gathering place for him. He considered himself a good man. Never saw the need to get religion, as some folks put it. Didn't really have the time. Oh, he gave God the respect He deserved. Being a sea captain, he could do no less. Josiah believed God to be the Creator of the universe. Beyond that, he hadn't really given much thought to the matter.

Then when he felt folks let him down after Catherine—well, he didn't want to think about that. Yet watching Adelaide made him wonder. Was there more to it than what he had thought?

"You sure have arranged for a fine cook, Captain."

Josiah turned with a start to find Adam Bowman standing beside him. "A fine cook and a fine wife, Bowman." Josiah didn't smile. His own actions made him even more cross. Why did he feel he had to defend his position with this man like two roosters in a cockfight?

Adam blinked. "Yes sir. Though I don't think you 'arranged' for the wife," Adam said with lighthearted banter. He seemed oblivious to Josiah's bitterness.

Josiah cringed inwardly. He knew Adam had no clue of his marriage arrangement—or did he? Could Adelaide have told him?

"Yeah, I'll say. Mighty fine wife, Captain." Ebenezer Fallon joined the two men, his eyes filled with challenge.

This man meant trouble, no doubt about it.

"I can only wish the same for you two in the future. Now, we best get back to our posts."

Adam nodded and hurried away. Ebenezer shot one last glare at the captain then turned away. He took slow, deliberate steps, as if to let the captain know he would do what he wanted when he wanted.

Yes, Ebenezer Fallon spelled trouble.

Chapter 6

The following week, a constant gale from the west tossed the ship around like a ball of yarn between a kitten's paws. Josiah had to admit he admired Adelaide's strength. Cloaked in all its treachery, the sea caused even the sturdiest sailors to weaken at times. Yet, although Adelaide suffered with seasickness, she didn't complain. She continued to cook for the crew, ate nothing herself, then scurried to their cabin for relief. Josiah found her amazing. His own experience had told him women reveled in complaining, so he found himself puzzled by her.

When finished with his review of the logbook, Josiah snapped it shut, yawned, and stretched.

Since it was only a few weeks from Christmas, his thoughts went to the scrimshaw upon which he had been working. He hoped Adelaide would like the jagging wheels he had carved for her. Now she could crimp her piecrusts with no problem. He'd like to make her a rolling pin later. With a shrug, he told himself, after all, she was his wife; he needed to give her something.

A nagging thought agitated him. Maybe he should have purchased a gift from a store, something a little more feminine. Catherine had always complained he never understood women. Perhaps she was right. He found whales more predictable. Staring at the sea, he allowed his thoughts to continue. Even now, the *Courage* steered toward Verdade, South America, but he hadn't planned to pull into port. They had whales to catch, and so far only a few cries of "There she blows" had called from the masthead, with little hope of a catch up to now.

Josiah gazed at the rising sun. Looking at the sea, he found it hard to remember its anger of the past days. He hoped Adelaide would soon adjust to this new life.

"Good morning, Josiah." Adelaide's soft voice broke through his musings. He turned to her and nodded as she joined him at the railing.

"You're looking much better this morning," he said with more softness than he'd intended.

"Thank you. I'm quite better." A slight breeze pulled a strand of hair loose from her pins and brushed it against her cheek. Adelaide tucked it back into her bonnet.

"Good." Josiah cast Adelaide a sideways glance. Her dark brown eyes reminded him of the rich, deep soil of a freshly tilled meadow; her creamy skin, the silk of a cornstalk. A nice change from what he usually saw on his ship.

A noise shook him from his foolishness. He turned to see a chicken strutting and clucking behind them.

Adelaide laughed. "I feel right at home seeing the pigs and chickens running around the deck."

"They are a lively bunch," Josiah said with a grin. "Guess they don't know they'll be supper one day."

She laughed.

The sound made him feel lighter somehow. "You're doing a great job with the meals, Adelaide."

She turned a surprised look to him. "Thank you." Her eyelids lowered and a pink flush fanned her cheeks.

"Good morning, Adelaide. Captain." Adam Bowman greeted them with a smile.

Josiah stiffened. "Bowman," he returned, his voice hard and formal.

If Adam Bowman noticed the change in the captain, he didn't let on. "Beautiful morning, isn't it?" he continued with a pleasant smile. Before anyone could respond, he turned to Adelaide. "I haven't seen you around except at mealtime, Addie. You been feeling poorly?"

Oh, this man irritated Josiah. Still, Bowman stood there smiling as if he hadn't a clue of the captain's feelings. Not only did Josiah not like the man's cordial ways, but Josiah clearly did not like Bowman's familiar tone with Adelaide. Calling her Addie should be reserved for those closest to her. A thought struck him. Was Bowman close to her? Adelaide said he was a friend of the family. Perhaps he had called on Adelaide, but her love for the sea had won out. His stomach knotted up like a rusty chain, and he was completely puzzled as to why.

"Bowman, you would do well to remember your place," Josiah rushed in. "You will address her as Mrs. Buchanan like every other crewman."

Adam looked chagrined. "Sorry, Captain. I forget that—"

"It's all right, Adam. Josiah—I mean, Captain Buchanan just wants to keep order—"

"I understand," he managed. Embarrassment flamed his face.

The softness in her voice toward this man caused Josiah's blood to boil like blubber in a try-pot. *She is my wife, after all.* His breath turned quick and shallow as he attempted to calm his anger. An uncomfortable silence fell upon them.

Adelaide looked at each man briefly. A slight shadow crossed her face. "I'd better get started on the meal." The softness of her words, her calming ways, turned Josiah's stomach upside down more than the roughest of gales. Frustration ran through him. Despite the fact theirs was a marriage of convenience, Adelaide was still his wife, and Adam Bowman would do well to remember his place.

Josiah turned and walked away. "I can't let that woman make me soft," he muttered under his breath. Chickens clucked and piglets squealed to get out of his path as his boots stomped hard across the rough planks.

Adelaide diced through the vegetables with a little more force than necessary. She couldn't understand Josiah's harsh treatment of Adam. Something told her Adam could one day be a member of their family, judging by the way he talked about her sister. Adelaide wanted Josiah and Adam to get along. Of course, Josiah didn't think of her in that way. Would he ever feel like a part of her family? What did the future hold for them?

The knife sliced into the potato, but before Adelaide realized it, she nicked the tip of her finger. "Oh!" She grabbed her hand.

"Are you all right?" Behind her, Josiah grabbed a cloth and dashed to her side. She stood perfectly still while he held her bleeding hand and looked over the cut. He maneuvered the cloth around her finger, winding it tight to stop the bleeding. Once finished, he held her hand in his.

Adelaide wasn't sure what to do. She felt clumsy and very female for having made such a mistake. Her eyes glanced up. "I'm sorry; I should have—"

"Shh." His fingertips reached up and touched her lips. He stared into her eyes. "It's all right." Allowing his fingers to trail down her cheek, he tilted her face toward him. "I'm sorry you hurt yourself."

His eyes were so intense and kind. Like the Josiah she had met not so long ago. All sights and sounds drifted away. Her world consisted only of this moment.

Alone with Josiah.

What was happening, she didn't know. She feared the slightest movement could break the magic. She dared take a slight wisp of a breath. Josiah's gaze never left her face as he dipped his head toward her, his lips claiming her own. For one brief moment of bliss, Adelaide felt all the pleasures and wonder of a real kiss. Like a shared secret between two people who loved each other from the depths of their souls.

Yet just as quickly as the moment commenced, it stopped. Josiah broke away, his body stiff and professional once again. "I'm sorry, Adelaide. I don't know what came over me." He looked down at the floor then back to her. "It won't happen again." He turned on his heels and quickly left the cookhouse.

Adelaide stared after him, her trembling fingers tracing where his lips had been. Now that was something she hadn't seen coming. By the look on

Josiah's face, she figured he hadn't planned on it either.

She wasn't sure how she felt about what had happened. She only knew things were definitely changing between them. And where this change would take them, she could only imagine. . . .

∞

Josiah couldn't, for the life of him, figure out what had possessed him to kiss Adelaide. After he had promised himself he would stay away from her, not allow her to make him go soft, he had betrayed himself and spoiled everything. She would want nothing to do with him now, of that he felt sure.

She came along for an adventure at sea, not a romantic life with him. He shoved his fingers through his hair. He could kick himself.

Admittedly, he'd never met anyone like Adelaide. She was so complex, tougher to understand than most women. Determined, that's what she was. After all, it took a determined woman to handle life on a ship with a group of crusty whalers. But more than that, she was soft. Like a gentle breeze. Not just her skin, but her ways. She was unlike any woman he had ever seen. He couldn't put his finger on it. It was like she possessed a quiet strength from beyond herself.

Josiah raised his hands in frustration and let them drop at his side. Now he was thinking nonsense. A pig snorted at his feet, and Josiah growled at it, sending the poor creature off squealing.

Might as well admit it. You have feelings for her. The thought both surprised and angered him. Surprised him because he hadn't admitted it until now; angered him because he was accustomed to being in control of everything in his life. He felt as though his heart had committed mutiny against his better sense.

Josiah shook off the disturbing thoughts and walked through the ship, checking things, talking here and there with the crew. The men grew restless. Tension mounted daily. They were itching to kill a whale, and he knew it. They'd best find one soon.

Just as Josiah headed downstairs for the cabin to check on Adelaide, Adam's voice stopped Josiah short. Adam and the man to whom he spoke were hidden from Josiah's view.

"If I had known how she felt, I wouldn't be sailing on this ship today. I guess I've loved her since the day I met her." Adam's voice trailed to silence.

"Her father was Elijah Sanborn?" the other voice asked.

"Yeah, he's the one."

Sickness balled up in the pit of Josiah's stomach. He didn't hear the rest of the conversation. He had to get away. Never had the ship seemed so small. Going back on deck, he considered their chart. They would stop at Verdade, most likely arriving near Christmas Day. If the men grumbled, so be it. No matter the cost, he had to get away for a while, away from Adelaide. He needed to think.

∞

Adelaide situated her chair on the ship's deck. A glorious sun had risen over the waters. *Perfect for the Lord's Day,* she thought. She lifted her face to its rays. After a moment of sheer basking in the warmth, she pulled open her Bible and flipped to her reading for the day in Psalm 139. Her heart absorbed what her eyes told her. When she came to verses seven through ten, she stopped and reread the passage:

> *Whither shall I go from thy spirit? or whither shall I flee from thy presence? If I ascend up into heaven, thou art there: if I make my bed in hell, behold, thou art there. If I take the wings of the morning, and dwell in the uttermost parts of the sea; even there shall thy hand lead me, and thy right hand shall hold me.*

The passage wrapped itself around her heart like a warm embrace from God. Regardless of the circumstances, she was not alone. God would never leave her. Though her choices had brought difficulties, God would see her through. No matter how far from home, she was never out of His care. The thought brought tears to her eyes. "Oh God, Thy mercy is never-ending." She felt her heart nearly burst with praise.

Overcome with worship, her voice lifted with the melody "I Sing the Mighty Power of God."

Footsteps sounded behind her, but before the melodies stopped in her throat, a couple of male voices joined in.

Adelaide turned in pleasant surprise to see Adam and another crewman, whose name she couldn't remember, standing beside her, smiling. The three turned toward the sea and lifted their voices in further praise as they finished the rest of the song. Other sailors eyed them curiously.

When the song ended, Adam was the first to speak. "Would you share a scripture with us, Ad—Mrs. Buchanan?" he quickly corrected himself.

Adelaide smiled and threw him an I'm-sorry-you-have-to-call-me-that look. She nodded and looked at her Bible. Lifting it to her, she began to read Psalm 139. So engrossed was she in the scripture, she hadn't noticed the footsteps surrounding her. By the time she had finished, three-fourths of the crew circled her.

Not sure what to do from there, Adelaide felt she must not let the opportunity go unheeded. Whispering a quick prayer in her heart for the right words, she told the sailors that everyone had sinned and fallen short of the glory of God. She shared the message of God's love for each of them and told them how He sent His Son to die in their place. Further, she explained that because of God's provision through His Son, those who believed in Him would not perish but would have eternal life. Some of the crew shifted uneasily where they stood.

Quickly, Adelaide lifted her voice in a prayer for each of them. When the prayer was over, only a few had walked away. The others who lingered, she noticed, had removed their caps and simply stood in the warmth of the sunshine.

Greatly encouraged, she started singing "O, for a Thousand Tongues to Sing." Adam quickly joined in, and a couple of others soon followed. Though the song had been out a few years, the burly crew had probably not been exposed much to songs of faith.

At the back of the crowd, Adelaide spotted a man with cap in hand. He seemed clearly moved by their little service. His sad gaze caught hers, and he turned and walked away. She wanted to call after him but knew the time wasn't right. Oh, how she wanted to know more about this man of mystery.

Captain Josiah Buchanan.

Chapter 7

Adelaide felt lighthearted after sharing scriptures and songs with some of the crew, although she couldn't ignore the pain stabbing her heart each time she thought of the look on Josiah's face. What troubled him? Maybe the Lord had been talking to him. Perhaps a painful past plagued him. Did he regret marrying her because he still loved his first wife? Could Adelaide make him forget Catherine? Did Adelaide want to? She had to admit to herself she had growing feelings for this man. Could he ever make room in his heart for her?

Adelaide went to the cookhouse and fixed mutton stew for lunch from leftovers. One thing she had already learned in her brief stay on the *Courage*: No food was wasted on a ship. She stirred the pot of vegetables and cut up the bread she had made earlier that morning.

Sometimes Josiah and Adelaide ate in their room alone while the officers ate in the adjoining cabin. Today was such a day. Josiah joined Adelaide for lunch. She arranged the bowls nicely on her trunk, managing even a little candlelight between them. Though the sun crept through the porthole, she thought the candle might make Josiah more comfortable.

She watched as he picked up his spoon. She quickly bowed her head and said grace for them both. Afraid to look up when she was finished, she picked up her spoon and started eating, feeling his gaze upon her.

"You have a beautiful voice."

She dropped her spoon and splashed broth upon her dress. "Oh dear." She wiped at the offensive stain with her cloth napkin. "I'm so clumsy." Her face grew warm.

"I said, you have a beautiful voice."

His compliment ran clear through her like warm cream on a cold winter's night.

"Adelaide, would you look at me, please?"

She swallowed and looked at him.

"Your voice. It's beautiful." He extended his hand to her. "I had no idea you could sing like that."

She struggled to get the last bite of vegetables down her throat. Things were definitely changing between them. With another swallow, she finally managed to murmur, "Thank you."

Josiah looked down at his hand, and as if he suddenly realized he was holding hers, he quickly pulled it away.

Adelaide tried to ease the disappointment squeezing her heart.

He picked up his spoon. "My ma used to sing like that."

Adelaide's head jerked up. Josiah never talked about his family to her. All of a sudden, she realized how little she knew about him. She watched him as he stared into his soup bowl, seeming to catch a glimpse of days long ago.

"Tell me about your ma."

He shrugged and looked at her. "Not much to tell, really." Lifting his spoon to his mouth, he took another bite.

Adelaide feared she had broken their moment of sharing, but he continued. "Pa was the captain of a whaling ship; did I tell you that?"

She shook her head, praying he would tell her more.

"Ma pretty much raised me alone in Bayview. Pa was always at sea. I hardly knew him." Josiah drank some water. "For a while, she cried herself to sleep most every night. I can't say for sure when she finally stopped." He scratched his face thoughtfully. "We did all right. Pa sent money home for us. Then Ma got sick when I was fourteen. Died of the fever. I didn't know what to do. Had no other family. So I did what seemed natural. Signed up on a whaling ship. Course, I started out as a cabin boy. By the time I was eighteen, I was an experienced whaleman. Then I worked my way up to harpooner and eventually on up to captain. I guess it's all the life I've ever known." He looked at her. "Can't help but think Ma wouldn't like it, though."

"What happened to your pa?"

"Don't know. When Ma died, I just moved on to whaling. Never knew how to find him after that."

"Oh Josiah, I'm sorry."

He tipped his head. "That's the way life is out here." He suddenly looked at her as if he'd maybe said too much. "I hope I'm not scaring you about life on the sea." He seemed to almost hold his breath.

Adelaide smiled. "No. Though I've never been on a ship before, I'm aware of some of the struggles."

Josiah settled back into his seat as if he felt much relieved.

"I want to thank you for having the men slaughter the animals for our meals. That's one thing I don't enjoy. It's a chore I had to do at home, of course, but I'm thankful for the help here."

"It's called survival. You're too tender for your own good." Josiah's words were gruff, but she could feel the kindness behind them.

"I suppose you're right. But I thank you just the same."

He nodded, finished his last bite of lunch, then stood to go. He turned to her. "That little service you had this morning—good for the men. You can do it every week if you want."

Adelaide nodded. Excitement shot through her with the idea of such an opportunity. "Thank you, Josiah." Did she see a half smile touch his lips before he turned to go?

Josiah closed the door behind him. Adelaide settled back into her chair. She clapped her hands together. "Yes, Father, Thy mercy is never-ending."

⬭

The next two weeks were fairly uneventful, but for the rough, strong winds, much to Josiah's dismay. Though a few whales had been spotted, there had been nothing close enough to chase. They'd caught a porpoise or two and a few blackfish, storing away what oil they could. But he hoped they'd spot a whale soon.

Josiah had made his rounds on the ship and sat at a bench, whittling on scrimshaw for Adelaide. The gales had tossed the ship long enough, and now a pleasant breeze settled upon him, just warm enough for comfort.

All of a sudden, a flying fish plopped on the deck. A couple of men laughed then ran over to scoop it up. For Adelaide, no doubt. Flying fish were plenty. Adelaide had cooked some for breakfast. Josiah thought the way Adelaide prepared it, the fish tasted like fresh herring. A smidgen of pride overtook him for having the foresight to ask her to be their cook. Course, he knew now he wanted her for more than a cook, but that hadn't been part of their agreement. She would cook and enjoy life on the sea. He would enjoy a happy crew and good meals. Oh, how he wished he could turn back the clock. He wondered how things might have played out had there been time for courting.

What was he thinking? He had been burned once by the fickleness of a woman; did he want to go through that again? He had given his heart, only to have it smashed like a ship wrecked upon rocky shores. A part of him wanted to believe Adelaide was different. Yet another part of him warned him to stay away. He couldn't account for others, only himself. He had to make it on his own.

Besides, even if she did fall in love with him, what could he offer her? Oh, she liked the ship now, but a year from now? Three years? What then? What about children? Though he knew some captains took their families aboard the whaling ship, he didn't want that for his family. That would leave Adelaide to raise the children on land. Alone. Just like him and his ma.

If only they would spot a whale, he could keep busy and forget all the nonsense clouding his thoughts. His jackknife gouged deep into the whale-bone as Josiah worked with determination to shape it into a rolling pin. Though he knew he wouldn't have it done by Christmas, he figured he could give it to Adelaide later.

Christmas. They would be upon Verdade soon. The crew was restless, and a stop in the port would do them all good. He kept his eyes on Ebenezer. He didn't like what he saw. Seemed each time Josiah passed Ebenezer, the man was whispering to other crewmen, only to stop abruptly when Josiah walked by. What was so secret? Josiah couldn't trust the man, of that he was sure.

No, he'd better get the crew to port before Ebenezer stirred them up into a disgruntled lot.

∞

With breakfast over, Adelaide settled down to work on the unfinished shirt she was putting together for Josiah. She hadn't had much chance to sew since she'd spent so much time in the cookhouse. Her fingers ran over the material appreciatively. She hoped Josiah would like it. It hadn't been easy to keep it from him. After all, she didn't want to spoil his Christmas surprise.

With great concentration, she worked on the shirt, adding a few final touches as needed. Before she knew it, the time had come to prepare lunch. She flipped out the shirt before her and looked at the handiwork with pleasure. It turned out all right. She hoped Josiah thought so. Folding it neatly in place, Adelaide tucked the gift carefully in her drawer in a space emptied for it.

Just then their door swung open. "A whale's been spotted. "We're going out." Excitement filled Josiah's words, while a touch of fear settled upon Adelaide. With the news delivered, Josiah disappeared behind the closed door.

Adelaide could hear the crew thunder across the deck above. She put away her things and hurried up to watch the excitement.

The crew scurried across the deck in a frenzy of commotion. Tubs of harpoon line were quickly hoisted into the three whaleboats. Josiah, Adam, and the second mate, Benjamin West, took their positions at the steering oars in the stern of their respective whaleboats, and the boat steerers manned the harpooner's oar in the bows. The twelve oarsmen remained on deck and lowered the boats into the water. Once the boats floated beside the ship, the oarsmen climbed down the sides of the ship, and four men each crowded into their assigned boat.

Though Adelaide knew this was the reason they had come, she couldn't prevent the concern that shadowed her heart. Not only did she care about Josiah, but she cared about the souls of his crew.

Breathing a prayer, Adelaide continued to watch the busy crew at work. Maybe this would be the day they would catch a whale. Josiah had thought perhaps they could stop at Verdade, but if they caught a whale, most likely they would sail on. She had hoped to step foot on land and browse through some shops, but then that was selfish thinking on her part. Once again, she found herself praying for the men.

When the boats were out a distance, bobbing on the swells, Adelaide went to the cookhouse to prepare dinner. With no lunch in their stomachs, the men would be hungry when they returned.

Though the owners of the *Courage* provided little extra provisions for the sailors, Adelaide knew Josiah surrendered some of his wages to grant his crew better eating. Most sailors' meals consisted of nothing more than hardtack—biscuits so hard they could break a man's teeth—and a hunk of salt beef or pork with an occasional dumpling thrown in. Though sometimes the men had to eat such meals, and the common sailor didn't eat quite the fare of that of the officers, Josiah still saw to it that they ate a decent meal as often as possible. He insisted the success of a whaling ship depended on his crew's health.

After sticking a chicken in the oven to roast with some potatoes and carrots, Adelaide prepared some bread for baking for the officers. She then prepared salt pork with a small serving of potatoes for the rest of the crew. She would also set aside some bread for them. With the chicken cooking in the oven, she slipped back on deck. By then, the whaleboats were merely a speck on the horizon.

Adelaide decided to go to the cabin to pray and read her Bible for a while. Later, she went back to check on the chicken and to stick the bread in the oven. By the time she returned to the deck, low-flying clouds hung from the sky like a lumpy mattress. Day had surrendered to night. An eerie feel settled upon the ship and covered Adelaide with shivers. She tried to rub the chill from her arms.

"No use to fret none, Miss Adelaide."

Adelaide spun on her heels. Who would dare call her that after Josiah had given strict instructions not to do so? She turned to see Ebenezer. He looked sickly, his eyes bloodshot, his nose as red as a boil.

Knowing Ebenezer's job was oarsman on Benjamin's whaleboat, Adelaide asked, "Wha–what are you doing here?"

"Now is that any way to treat a man who's been seasick?" He pulled a bottle from his back pocket, took a drink, and swiped his mouth with the back of his hand.

Adelaide felt fear climb her spine. Her gaze swept across the deck in search of help. She didn't see the three shipkeepers who were supposed to stay behind and handle the ship.

"Oh, one of the men filled in for me. I'm sick, you know." A wicked grin heightened his evil expression. "The other two are in the cookhouse, helping themselves to your fine food."

Her head jerked around toward the cookhouse. She thought she heard distant sounds of the crew returning to the ship, but Ebenezer's hearing appeared dulled by his drink. He didn't flinch.

"I hope you don't mind," he said with insincerity. "I told them you said to eat so they would have strength when the rest of the crew returned." His lip curled into a snarl. "I'd like to help myself to a little dessert."

Adelaide gasped.

Before another moment passed, sounds of the crew climbing back up the ship came from the starboard side. Ebenezer turned with a start, searching frantically for a place to deposit his bottle. Adelaide drew a shuddering breath and watched as he ran off the deck and down the stairs. Shaken but unharmed, she turned her attention toward the returning crew.

Adelaide's heart lightened with the sight of Josiah. He came right to her. The uncomely sight before her took her breath away, but the excitement on his face lessened the trauma.

"We caught a fin. Not the biggest whale, but a whale, nonetheless."

She thought he was going to slap her on the back, but he stopped his hand midair. Her nose wrinkled with the smell.

Josiah laughed. "Sorry, but you'll get used to it. Hopefully, you'll see more than this in the days ahead."

Activity swirled around her. Wood was thrown beneath the try-pots where a fire soon commenced. Adelaide stood out of the way and watched the process with fascination. Blubber was cut into pieces and placed into the heavy iron pots. Crispy scrap pieces floated to the surface of the pot and were skimmed off then tossed into the fire for more fuel. The smell of the burning scraps created a black smoke and an unforgettable stench.

Adelaide pinched her nose to squelch the foul odor. She turned a glance toward the bloodstains, the huge masses of flesh and blubber soaking the pine-timbered deck, and decided not to announce dinner. With her hand held tight against her stomach, she slid through the greasy planks for her cabin.

"You chose this life, Adelaide Buchanan," she told herself. "You and you alone."

Her swift, uneasy footsteps carried her to the cabin, where she arrived at the privy just in time.

Chapter 8

Adelaide couldn't believe it. She had always dreamed of a whaling ship, and here she was sick at the sight of a catch! The very idea. Her pa would be shocked. She wiped her mouth with a cloth, feeling ashamed beyond belief.

She'd never seen such a sight. That thought helped justify her illness. Such a massive creature. Why, the mere sight of it took her breath away. Josiah was right. She was too tender. One look at the dying creature turned her insides soft. A nurturing instinct told her to run to the whale, defend it, nurse it to health. But, of course, the killing wasn't for sport but rather the good of mankind. A necessity. At least that's what she had always heard. Yet after seeing the whale. . .

Enough of that, she told herself, attempting to calm her stomach.

Adelaide walked over to the drawer that held her journal and slipped it out. Before writing, her thoughts went to Ebenezer. She hadn't told Josiah of the earlier episode. She felt Ebenezer didn't want a woman on the ship and hoped to stir up trouble for Josiah. Well, she decided, she wouldn't give Ebenezer the satisfaction. It seemed best to keep the matter hidden.

Adelaide settled in the chair and began to write in her journal of her experience as she had done every day since boarding the ship.

Once she finished, Adelaide pulled out some paper and began a letter to Ma and Esther. Though she'd have to wait awhile before mailing them, Adelaide decided to write and store up her letters for when they reached a port or visited a passing ship. She would send the letters all at once.

Adelaide kept her news lighthearted and happy to keep Ma from worrying. She told Ma and Esther of the beauty of the sea, the adventurous gales, as she put it, and of her work on the ship. Although Esther had been sick when the *Courage* set sail and she had missed seeing Adam, Adelaide kept her sister informed on how things were going. The mere mention of his name would no doubt set Esther's heart to flutter.

Adelaide thought for a moment. Oh, how she did miss her little family. If only she could hug them once more.

By the time Adelaide had finished writing to Ma, Esther, and the Markles, she was tired and spent. She had hoped to do laundry the following day but knew everything would be at a standstill until the final cask of oil was stowed away below deck.

She prepared for bed and slipped under the covers. She had pulled the sheet on the wall for privacy when Josiah walked in.

"Adelaide, are you still awake?"

She shot up in bed. "Yes, Josiah."

"May I come around?"

She pulled her covers up around her shoulders. "Yes," she said before gulping. Though she felt ashamed for thinking it, she'd hoped he had cleaned up a little before coming to her.

He had.

"I think things are pretty much under control. The try-pots are heavy with boiling oil, and the last of the blubber has been minced into small pieces, waiting their turn in the pots."

"Will the men have to stay up late to finish things?"

He nodded. "We have try watches, five to six hours long. They'll get little sleep." He rubbed his chin. "The oil has to be tried out then put into casks, cooled, and stowed away for market. Then the ship has to be scrubbed clean. I thought you might want to get in the flour barrels and roll out some doughnuts in the morning—you know, cook them in the scalding oil. That oil will be as sweet as new hog's lard."

"All right, I'll do that." She smiled. He was always thinking of the crew.

"We've all been snitching a bite of dinner here and there. Thank you. It sure was tasty."

She stared at Josiah. His words ran together like an excited schoolboy. Her heart constricted. She found his enthusiasm endearing. "You're welcome."

He looked at her then at his hands. He shoved them in his pockets like he didn't know what else to do with them. "Well, I just wanted to make sure you were all right. You'd never seen a catch before, had you?"

She shook her head.

"You're amazing. Most women would get sick with the sight. You're my strong one, Adelaide. Good night." With that, he turned and left.

Guilt covered her. It's not like she'd had the chance to tell him she had gotten sick, or so she told herself. She lifted her chin. Well, next time she felt quite sure she would be just fine. Each time would get easier.

She settled back into bed and snuggled into her pillow. Closing her eyes, she played back his words. *You're amazing. You're my strong one, Adelaide.* Her eyes popped open. The words played once more. *You're my strong one, Adelaide.* Into the darkness, she whispered, "He said 'my' strong one." A smile touched her lips. Somehow she liked the sound of that.

⌒

Adelaide stretched into the darkness. Though she was tired from the past few days of working around the men as they prepared the captured whale, the excitement of Christmas morning rushed through her like a child. She was delighted Josiah had decided to stop in Verdade. He said the men needed the break. On land they could celebrate the good fortune of capturing their first whale. They would arrive tomorrow, and Adelaide could hardly wait.

Quietly, she slipped from her bed in hopes of not disturbing Josiah. She wanted to get an early start in the cookhouse.

She had plans of a special Christmas lunch for the men. Not just the officers—she meant every crewman to enjoy this meal. Mentally, she went through her list. She would prepare stuffed roast chickens, potatoes, stewed cranberries, cucumbers, bread with jam, and squash. For dessert, mince pie. Coffee, tea, and water to drink. And the best of all, she'd prepared popcorn balls for each of the crewmen. The anticipation filled her. With swift motions, she dressed for the day.

While she dressed, the door of their room opened, giving her a start. "You awake, Adelaide?" Josiah's voice called to her.

She smiled. So he had already started his day. It was she who had slept too long. "Yes, Josiah, I'm awake." Smoothing out her skirt, she pulled open the curtain to see him. A smile flashed across his eyes and lit upon his mouth. The way he looked at her made her feel he approved of her appearance.

"Merry Christmas." His eyes twinkled.

She almost wanted to giggle. Christmas seemed to bring that out in people.

"I have a gift for you. Do you want it now or after breakfast?"

Adelaide couldn't hide her pleasure. She felt most happy he had thought to give her something. "After breakfast, if that's all right. We'll have more time to enjoy it then."

He nodded as if appreciating her good sense. "You ready to go?"

"Yes."

He held out his arm to escort her, and suddenly it seemed to her they were back at the church social as he prepared to escort her out to the beach where he had asked her to marry him—or more precisely, to be his cook. No matter what their original intentions had been, things were changing between them, and for that she was thankful. To top it all off, today was Christmas.

The officers ate breakfast in their cabins, while Josiah and Adelaide brought their meals back to their room, and the men ate on deck.

"Delicious meal, as always, Adelaide." Josiah wiped his mouth with the cloth napkin she had sewn before they were wed. He had eaten his meal so quickly, Adelaide wondered how he even had time to taste it.

"Time for your gift." Josiah stood.

Adelaide reached out and touched his arm. "Josiah, would you mind terribly if we read the Christmas story together first?"

Childlike disappointment flickered in his eyes. She smiled.

He tossed a halfhearted grin her way. "Oh, sure." He looked across the room for her Bible and went to fetch it. Picking up her Bible, he took it to her.

She turned to the appropriate passage in Luke and looked up at him. "Would you read, Josiah?" She held her breath, fearing what he would answer.

With a look of confusion, he reluctantly took the open Bible from her. "All right." He began to read the words. His bass voice sounded through the room as she closed her eyes and listened to the greatest story ever told. Her heart never tired of the story of the Savior's birth.

Josiah finished the passage then handed it back to her.

"Thank you." She bowed her head and led them in a prayer of thankfulness that they could celebrate such a wonderful day and that she could share it with Josiah. She hadn't meant to say those last words. In fact, she felt mortified they had escaped her. What would he think of her now? Though she felt things were changing between them, he hadn't said things were different. As far as she knew, he still didn't want another wife. He wanted a cook. At least for now, that's the way she saw it. She turned grumpy. It was all Esther's fault.

Before her mood could grow any darker, she looked up at him. His eyes were shining. She decided he must not have heard the last part. Hadn't she said them in just barely a whisper? That was it. He hadn't heard her. Relief washed over her.

Josiah rubbed his hands together. "It's time?"

Adelaide laughed and nodded. "It's time."

While he went to his drawer and pulled out something for her, she went over to her own hiding place to pull out her gift to him.

They each walked back to one another and hid their presents behind their backs. Josiah looked at her in surprise, as if he hadn't considered that she might have a gift for him.

He cleared his throat. "I, uh, know how you like to cook and all. You bake tasty pies and work so hard to make them look nice." He pulled the gift from behind his back. "Well, I made you something."

Adelaide looked at the scrimshaw in his hand. "Jagging wheels! Oh, Josiah, now I can crimp my pie shells! Thank you!" Forgetting herself, she placed his present on the trunk behind her and reached over to hug him. Overcome with excitement, she hadn't realized the boldness of her behavior until she felt his arms firm around her back, holding her tight against him. She felt herself flush. Quickly, she pulled away and hurried back to her present.

She reached for his gift and handed it to him. "Thank you for your hard work and kindness."

He ran his fingers along the material then looked at her. "You made this?"

She nodded.

"It's mighty fine," he said, looking at the shirt. He glanced back at her. "Mighty fine, indeed." A wide smile stretched across his face, causing her heart to tumble like a fish in a net.

"Merry Christmas, Addie."

After lunch, the men came up to the deck where Josiah and Adelaide sat enjoying the calm sea. It seemed to her only fitting the Lord should provide a restful sea on Christmas. Though she had to admit she had never experienced such a warm Christmas. Not the slightest hint of a breeze stirred. The canvas sails didn't have a single kink. They wouldn't make much headway today. Adelaide pulled off her bonnet and tucked stray hairs from her neck back into her hairpins. She felt sticky.

The men seemed in good spirits. Many of them thanked her for the delicious meal that reminded them of home. Adam Bowman came up behind them and pulled out a harmonica, much to Adelaide's pleasure and surprise.

He started playing some Christmas tunes. Pretty soon, others gathered round, some laughing, some singing. Before she could blink, Josiah stood and left, taking all her joy right with him. Others watched him leave but kept right on singing.

They were having such a wonderful time together; why did he have to spoil it all? Well, she wouldn't allow him to ruin her Christmas. She joined in the singing once again.

The melodies floated over the ship and surrounding waters as they each sang from their hearts. Adelaide lifted her face to the sun and sang with gusto. Suddenly a strange sound hit her ears. She stopped singing and listened. Recognizing it, she turned to find Josiah standing nearby playing a fiddle. He smiled and winked at her. Much to her dismay, she let out the most unladylike laugh. She couldn't help herself.

More pleasure than she had ever known rushed through her. Could life get more wonderful than at this very moment? Once the singing stopped, they all laughed and made comments to Josiah and Adam about their great music. Pride washed over Adelaide as she watched Josiah.

Her husband.

A whaleman named John spoke up. "You know, I can remember one Christmas our pa was away from home. He had gone to a nearby town for some seed—and I suspect a present or two. A blizzard blew in on our little community, and on Christmas morning, Pa wasn't home. We kids sat around long-faced, even though Ma tried to cheer us up, presenting us with our stockings filled with an orange and a peppermint stick. Funny how even the candy didn't matter 'cause we were worried about Pa.

"I can still remember Ma's rocking chair as it rubbed against the wooden floor, back and forth, back and forth. The wind blew hard against our homestead, causing our only window to rattle. The clock on the mantel ticked away while my brothers and I scribbled on some paper at the table.

"All of a sudden, the door blew open. In walked Pa, covered from head to toe with snow and shivering like a nervous chicken." John let out a laugh, his thoughts still seemingly far away.

"Ma gasped and ran to his side, as did we boys. We helped get Pa by the fire. Ma stripped him down to his underwear, filled him with hot coffee, and had him good as new in no time. Then Pa grabbed his bag and pulled out some dress material for Ma and little horses carved from wood for me and my brothers.

"It was the best Christmas I ever had."

Smiles lit through the crowd, and one by one the rough old whaling crew shared their Christmas stories. Adelaide scratched her head in wonder of it all. Even the roughest of characters deep down had some good in them. She had to believe that. *God doesn't give up on us, so why should we give up on others? As long as there is breath, there's always hope.*

Her gaze fell upon Ebenezer. So much had happened since their encounter on the ship's deck, she hadn't even given it much thought. Yet now the sight of him made her cold. She adjusted the shawl on her shoulders. Just then he glanced at her and caught her staring. He sneered then turned and walked away.

She watched him leave, remembering what Josiah had told her. It seemed Ebenezer had once been the captain of a ship. Something unfortunate had transpired on his journey. Josiah thought it had something to do with Ebenezer's drinking habit and some bad judgment, though Josiah wasn't sure of the details. Whatever the problem, it reduced Ebenezer from a captain to a mere worker on whaling ships. Bitterness ate away at his soul like alcohol ate away at his future.

There was always hope, she reminded herself. Even for one such as Ebenezer Fallon. Wasn't there? Still, the choice was his to make.

After the Christmas stories, the group sang a few more songs. Adam and Josiah joined in and played a couple of songs together. Adelaide thought they actually looked as though they were enjoying themselves. Maybe, just maybe, they could be friends, after all. What a wonderful day.

After dinner, Josiah walked Adelaide back to their room. "It's been a fine day, hasn't it?" Josiah asked as he helped her step through their door.

She untied the ribbon on her bonnet and straightened her hair. She turned to him. "It has been one of the best Christmases ever for me."

"Truly?" His eyes sparkled.

"Truly," she answered before staring at the bonnet in her hands.

"Tomorrow, Verdade."

She looked up with excitement. "I can hardly wait."

Josiah laughed when he looked at her. "I'm glad you're enjoying yourself, Adelaide."

She looked at him but said nothing.

"You're not sorry you've come?"

Her eyes went to her bonnet again as she shook her head.

Josiah walked over to her and lifted her chin. The very touch of his fingers against her skin made her tingle.

"I'm glad," he said. His finger traced the side of her hair; then his gaze pinned hers. "I'll bet your hair is pretty down, too."

Adelaide's heart thumped so hard in her chest, she thought sure he could hear it. Embarrassment told her to move, but her feet refused.

He stared at her, looking as though he would kiss her at any moment.

Then just as quickly as the moment had settled upon them, it left. Josiah blinked and pulled away. His voice took on a friendly yet distant manner. "Yes, I'm quite sure you'll like Verdade," he said as he turned and pulled out his nightclothes.

Adelaide said nothing. With Josiah at her side, she knew she could like anything.

Chapter 9

The next morning sparkled with promise. Adelaide quickly prepared skipjack for the crew for breakfast. Though not her favorite fish to eat, it did add variety to their daily meals.

Josiah entered the cookhouse. "We caught a porpoise."

Adelaide worked with the iron pot on her stove and turned to him. "Wonderful."

Josiah snitched a piece of skipjack. "Should get about two gallons of oil from the skin. Hopefully, that will be enough to keep us from darkness for a season until we can get some more."

Adelaide nodded. "I thought I would make sausage cakes for dinner, if that's all right."

Josiah nodded. "Good idea. They're as good as pork sausages." He paused a minute. "We'll pull into Verdade about noon today."

Adelaide felt excitement course through her. He must have seen it in her eyes.

"After lunch, I'd like to escort you through town to see some of the shops."

She eyed him closely. His clothes looked fresh, and he smelled as clean as a breeze. Without whiskers, his face looked as soft as baby skin. Her heart stirred.

"Addie?"

Oh, how she liked the way he said that. "I'm sorry, Josiah. Yes, I would like that very much."

"Good." He smiled. He was about to leave then turned an anxious look to her. "We'll only be able to stay till nightfall. The men want to keep moving."

"I understand."

He tipped his head then walked out.

Adelaide fluttered around the room with a light heart. She could hardly wait to step on land.

∞

Josiah felt quite the lucky man as he escorted Adelaide through the streets of Verdade. He noticed more than one turned head as Adelaide walked past the men on the streets. He sneaked a glance at her. She had a natural beauty about her. He couldn't quite describe it. Like she glowed from the inside out. Catherine hadn't had that. Oh, she'd been pretty to look at, but something had been missing, though he couldn't say what. His heart clenched as he thought about Catherine. Not from love for her but from the pain she had caused him.

The more he thought about it, the more he wondered if the pain he had felt those first months after her leaving him was more from a hurt ego than from a love lost. He thought he had loved her, but then he'd never been in love before, so how could he be sure? The feelings growing in his heart for Adelaide were different than what he had felt for his first wife. Catherine had used her feminine ways on him, and before he knew it, he was caught like a fish on a line.

No matter. He didn't want to think ill of the dead. She had been his wife, after all, even if only for a short time.

Adelaide broke through his thoughts as they stepped past the wharf and onto the street dotted with a couple of shops. "Were you surprised some of the men didn't want to stop here?"

"You know, I was. I thought they'd like a break. But once a man gets whaling in his blood, it's hard to let it go. There's always that gnawing need to catch another. Just the same, I think we all needed the time here. I hope to do a little trading as well." He looked at her and smiled.

"It seems odd to have such hot weather near the end of December. Back home, we'd be bundled in heavy layers of wool by now."

Josiah cast a sideways glance at Adelaide as she patted a handkerchief against her forehead, just under the brim of her bonnet. "It is, indeed, warm. Would you like to stop here?" Josiah asked, pointing toward a cozy little dress shop.

"Oh, could we?"

How could he refuse when he saw that sparkle in her eyes? "Of course."

Inside, the room smelled sharp like the sea. Colorful bolts of cloth lined overhead shelves. Laces and ribbons of assorted shapes and sizes were arranged to entice the simplest of tastes. A small gathering of stylish hats and gloves stood in a corner. Oriental silks lined a table.

Adelaide walked over to the material and began to browse, feeling her way through each fabric.

Josiah watched the scene, an unfamiliar stir running through him. He meandered through the store then turned to see Adelaide admiring a light blue gown and matching bonnet fringed with ruffles. He imagined Adelaide in such a gown and bonnet and decided she must have them.

He waited patiently as she looked around. Each time she seemed interested in an item, upon finding the price, she graciously declined. No doubt she didn't feel she could ask him for the money—probably because she knew they were only pretending at a marriage. Would she ever want it to be more?

Suddenly the bell rang on the front door, and Josiah turned to see Adam Bowman entering. Though Josiah fought against it, his muscles grew tense. He glanced at Adelaide, who hadn't yet noticed Adam.

Adam spotted Adelaide, but Josiah stayed somewhat hidden behind merchandise.

"Why, Adam, what are you doing in here?"

Josiah could hear the teasing in Adelaide's voice. He swallowed hard.

"I just thought I'd see if I could find something for my girl." He grinned. "I've been saving money for quite some time, so I have a little."

Adelaide smiled at him as if they shared a secret.

Josiah felt raw nerves. Who did that man think he was? Had he no respect for the fact Adelaide was married? Or maybe she had explained it was a marriage of convenience. Did they have plans for a future together? Josiah clenched his fists. He took a deep breath and released his fingers, noticing his white knuckles.

Suddenly his heart felt heavy. The light of the day seemed to grow dim as his thoughts took a different direction. Adelaide and Adam continued in small talk, but Josiah turned away. He could hear no more.

"Josiah." Adelaide walked up behind him and touched his arm. "I'm ready to go if you are." Her words were soft and tender, somewhat soothing his angry heart.

Josiah glanced over his shoulder to see Adam watching them. Josiah gave him a curt nod and led Adelaide out of the shop.

They walked down the street a little; then Josiah made an excuse to get away for a moment.

Once Adelaide was safely shopping in another store, he went back to the first shop. He would not be outdone by Adam Bowman! Josiah stepped into the shop, and before he could change his mind, he purchased the gown and bonnet for Adelaide. Adam was nowhere in sight.

◌

Later that evening, Josiah wondered if he had done the right thing in purchasing the dress and hat. Maybe Adelaide would think it too much. Perhaps she didn't want such a gift from him. Yes, he had gone too far. Such extravagance. But they were out to sea now. He could hardly take them back. Did he have the courage to give them to her?

He needed time to think about it. But where could he store the presents while he thought through the problem? He might have Adam keep them till the morning. Although it grated him to do it, Josiah knew he could trust Adam with the dress and bonnet. The captain wasn't so sure about anyone else aboard the ship.

Yes, he decided, that's what he'd do. Adam could hold it in his room. Josiah would explain they had little space with Adelaide's things in their rooms. They'd clear something out that night, and Josiah would fetch it in the morning after he decided what to do.

Suddenly, it became very important to Josiah that Adelaide like the gown and matching bonnet. Very important, indeed.

∞

Sticking the last pin in her hair, Adelaide turned with a start when a knock sounded at the door. She knew Josiah wouldn't knock, so she wondered if there was trouble on deck. Quickly, she pulled on her bonnet and went to answer the door. Adelaide opened it and looked up to see Adam holding a box.

"Why, Adam, is everything all right?"

A wide grin stretched across his face. "We caught some more blackfish." Then, as if just remembering the package in his hands, he added, "Oh, here. I thought I'd save you a trip and bring these to you. I hope you have room for them now." Adam stretched his arms out with the packages.

Adelaide puzzled at his comments but took them from him. She didn't know Adam would purchase such a large gift for Esther. In her heart, she was convinced the young man loved her sister. Curiosity got the better of Adelaide. She had to see the gifts. "All right if I look at them?"

Adam's face registered surprise. He shrugged. "I suppose so—"

Just then a voice called behind him. "Captain needs you on deck, sir."

Adam nodded then turned to Adelaide. He tipped his hat. "See you later, Mrs. Buchanan." With a smile, he turned on his heels and left her staring after him.

Adelaide looked at the boxes, giddy with excitement for her sister. Quickly, she closed the door behind her. She couldn't get to the sofa fast enough and pull open the packages.

She lifted the lid and peeled back the papers on the smaller box first. "Oh!" She slipped a bonnet from the box. The bonnet she had seen in the dress shop the day before. She removed her bonnet and pulled the new one ever so gently onto her head.

Then with eager fingers, she opened the next box and gasped, staring in disbelief. Adelaide had admired that dress in the shop. Oh, my, to have such a gown! She swallowed hard and lifted the garment ever so gently, allowing its folds to ripple to the ground. Draping it in front of her, she suddenly imagined herself at the most wondrous of balls with Josiah at her side. She curtsied before him, lifting her arms in a dancing gesture, and began to take a few steps in the cramped quarters. So lost was she in her imaginations, she didn't hear the door when it opened.

She turned to see Josiah standing in the entrance, a scowl on his face. "Josiah!" She stopped in her tracks. "Isn't this beautiful? Adam brought it down this morning and—"

"We don't have time for such foolishness, Adelaide. There's blackfish on deck, and you need to get to the cookhouse to prepare it."

All her dreamy notions flew away like a flock of birds, leaving embarrassment behind. What had gotten into her? She had a job to do, and she was behaving foolishly.

"Of course," she answered, humiliation knotting her throat.

Josiah opened his mouth to say something then seemed to think better of it and turned to go, closing the door behind him.

Large teardrops spilled from her cheeks as Adelaide carefully folded the dress back in place and put the lid on the box. How could she have been so silly? And for Josiah to catch her behaving in such a manner was more than she could bear. For the first time since their trip began, she truly wanted to go home. The sea in all its splendor filled her head with romantic notions. She had to get hold of herself and forget such nonsense. She was on the ship to do a job, and that's precisely what she would do. Nothing more, nothing less. Josiah would get his cook. She would get her life on the sea. That's all each of them wanted, anyway. So what was the problem?

As far as Adelaide was concerned, there was no problem. No problem at all. She brushed aside another tear, ignoring the cries of her heart. Pulling herself up, she washed her face and headed for the door.

Time to cook some blackfish.

Chapter 10

Josiah felt cross and worked with a vengeance to get the blackfish on the ship and ready for Adelaide to prepare for lunch. Why had Adam brought that dress to Adelaide? Maybe Josiah hadn't made it clear he wanted to pick it up himself. He gritted his teeth. Now Adelaide thought the gift was from Adam. The worst of it was that she appeared absolutely delighted with the idea.

The whole thing was a big mistake. Marrying Adelaide, bringing her aboard the ship. For what? So he could have a good cook for his crew? Most captains and crews frowned upon allowing a woman on the ship, let alone putting her in charge of the meals. But who could argue with his success? His voyages brought in endless casks brimming with oil and, from the sperm whale he gathered in abundance, spermaceti, the purest of all oils, and ambergris, a substance used in making expensive perfumes, so no one dared oppose his decision to have Adelaide be the cook.

Without question, he had been a fool. What could he do about it now? Approach her with the option of leaving the ship? He knew Adelaide to be a woman of faith, and most likely, she would not consider such a thing. How could he help her escape the dreadful life into which he had entangled her?

⌒

"So, what did he get you?" Adam asked Adelaide as he passed her on the way to his cabin.

"Who?"

"Who? Captain, that's who. What was in the boxes?"

She felt her mouth gape and promptly closed it shut. "I–I thought. . ."

"What?" His puzzled expression met hers.

"Well, you were getting something for Esther in the dress shop, and I assumed. . ."

Understanding lit his eyes. He whistled and shook his head. "I'm afraid I don't have that kind of money." He shrugged. "I bought her a necklace holding a stone from the island."

Adelaide could hardly contain herself. She could almost kiss Esther's friend. "Oh, how wonderful, Adam. She will love it." She barely noticed him scratching his head as she whisked past him.

Was it possible Josiah had purchased the gown and bonnet for her? Did she dare presume, dare hope? She practically ran up the steps, breathless with excitement. No matter how foolish it seemed, she had to reach him, thank him for his kindness. No wonder he was cross. He realized she had thought the gift was from Adam. But what he didn't know was she thought it was for Esther. Oh, things could get so tangled. But how wonderful she felt.

At last, she found him at the bow of the deck. The crew had just finished with the blackfish, taking it to the cookhouse for her preparation. "Josiah, might I speak with you a moment?"

He threw her a stern look. "I'm rather busy right now, Adelaide." He rinsed his hands in a bucket of water and wiped them with a cloth.

"I know about the dress and bonnet."

His hands stopped midair as he looked at her.

Her voice softened. "I know you bought them for me, and I want to thank you. It is by far the finest garment and bonnet I have ever owned."

"It was foolishness," he said, though his eyes searched her face for more encouragement.

"Foolishness or no, it is beautiful, and I am deeply grateful for your kindness." She touched his arm in a tender gesture then turned and walked away. Her heart felt giddy with the idea of leaving the mighty sea captain speechless. Besides, she had a new dress and bonnet to try on. Perhaps she would wear it if they went gamming on another ship. She could hardly wait for that to happen. Visiting with other ships brought relief to the lonely days at sea.

⟳

Dumbfounded, Josiah stared after Adelaide as she walked across the deck. What had happened, he wasn't sure, but he liked the idea she wanted to keep his gifts. Before he could get too puffed up in his thinking, though, he reminded himself of the look on her face when he had entered their cabin. She was just as happy with the gifts when she thought Adam had purchased them for her. It was the dress and bonnet she wanted, not Josiah.

His clenched jaw relaxed. This was a start, after all. She liked his presents. With any luck, her feelings would eventually grow for him.

⟳

The next morning after breakfast, Josiah poked his head in the cabin. "Looks like a whaler close by, Adelaide. The *Majestic*. We shall perhaps have company by evening."

"Wonderful!" Adelaide clapped her hands together. She hoped the captain's wife was on board. She so missed the company of women.

"Good, then. We'll plan on that." With that, he closed the door.

Adelaide could hardly wait. Josiah kept a large tub and a pounding barrel in the house on deck where Adelaide did her laundry for most of the day. Once the starching and ironing was done, she made her way back to the cookhouse for dinner preparations. After dinner, she would clean up for gamming. The excitement of it all carried her through the tiring day.

"I've sent word to the *Majestic,* and they are expecting us within the hour," Josiah said to Adelaide in their room after dinner. "Can you be ready?"

Barely able to contain her joy, she smiled.

"Fine," Josiah said, rising from his chair. "I'll be back to get you in, say, half an hour?"

"Thank you, Josiah."

Adelaide cleared the dishes from the top of her trunk while Josiah went back on deck. Her heart thumped hard against her ribs. She wasn't sure precisely what one would wear for such an occasion, but she certainly wanted to look her best and knew just the dress and bonnet she would wear. She opened her trunk and pulled out the gifts she had so carefully placed there. She scurried about to get ready. By the time she was finished, she had a few minutes to spare, so she decided to go on deck and meet Josiah.

She could feel the heat rise to her cheeks as she stepped across the deck and felt the admiring gazes of the crew upon her. But when her eyes met Josiah's, her heart took wings.

"Adelaide—" He stopped abruptly.

She looked at him, waiting for him to continue.

He kept staring at her, and she felt a bit awkward with the moment, noticing the crew was watching the two of them. Josiah cleared his throat. "Well, shall we lift you into the gamming chair and lower you to the whaleboat?"

She smiled and nodded. Something told her Josiah was pleased with her appearance, and that thought thrilled her. The crew helped to get Adelaide lowered and settled into the whaleboat, where Josiah joined her. A few of the crewmen accompanied them, while members of the *Majestic*'s crew came from their boat to visit the *Courage.*

Though Adelaide was disappointed there were no women aboard the *Majestic,* she enjoyed the visit with Captain Winifred and Josiah. Captain Winifred presented daguerreotypes of his wife and children for them to look at, which Adelaide greatly enjoyed.

As they departed, Captain Winifred gave them two dozen nice oranges. Also, Adelaide left him with some letters to send home as he was going to port before them. She hoped the letters would reach her family soon.

∽

The weather had been uncomfortably warm, the seas calm, which made for bad whaling. Earlier in the day, they saw whales from the masthead, but before the crew could reach them, the whales had disappeared.

After lunch, Adelaide freshened up in her room, cooling her face with water from the pitcher. She heard another call of a whale sighting. Quickly, she dabbed once more at her face and made her way up the steps to the deck.

Very soon, she saw the sea creature blow and turn flukes, as they called it, or dive toward the ocean bottom. She thought him a formidable creature.

The two mates went off in their boats. Then Josiah went with his boat's crew. The ship received word one of the boats had fastened. The whale continued to spout.

The crews returned in low spirits. Several boats were stoven, and they had to cut from the whale. Adelaide thought they should at least find that whale and make it pay for their boats.

Adelaide watched as the men boarded the ship from the whaleboats. Ebenezer brushed past her mumbling some obscenity, caring nothing about using such language in the presence of a woman. The man infuriated and frightened her. She thought him capable of almost anything. Presently, he walked toward a corner where a few other men were gathered.

What he was up to, she didn't know, but it bothered her. She'd talk to Josiah about it, though she knew Josiah had his own suspicions about Ebenezer Fallon.

Adelaide felt sure they would soon find out more than she wanted to know. She wanted to pray for Ebenezer, but she couldn't push away the feeling of distaste she had for the man. The farther she could stay away from him, the better. He was up to no good. No other way to say it.

Ebenezer Fallon meant trouble.

Chapter 11

Though blackfish and porpoise provided some oil along the way, Josiah wondered at the lack of whales thus far.

Standing at the stern, he looked out to sea. A slight breeze barely lifted the mast. The *Courage* inched its way toward the shores of Rio de la Plata, traveling at three or four knots an hour. Known as good whaling ground, the area raised Josiah's hopes that they would be able to get a few barrels of whale oil.

Breathing in deep of the sea air, Josiah thought about a life on land. How could he ever stop sailing? He shook his head. What would make him ask such a question? A vision of Adelaide popped into his mind. Her delicate features, her gentleness looked so foreign on the likes of a whaling ship. Yet she had her stubborn side—how well he knew. He couldn't help but smile. Deep down, he supposed that's one thing that drew him to her. He liked a woman with a little spirit.

All at once, the breeze kicked up, causing the snap of sails as the wind caught the rigging. The noise temporarily muffled the cry of the crew. Finally, a whaleman approached Josiah. "Captain Buchanan, sir. . ." Panic, coupled with running to the stern, caused his words to squeeze between chokes and great gulps of air. "Your wife—"

Josiah felt his blood run cold. "What is it, man? Out with it!"

The whaleman tried to straighten himself. "Overboard" was all he could manage.

Before the word had left the man's tongue, alarm bolted Josiah half-way across the rolling deck. Men shouted and pointed starboard side. Josiah rushed to a crowd just as a sailor lifted Adelaide onto the ship.

Dripping from their clothes, seawater pooled onto the deck. The man carefully laid her down. He saw Josiah and stepped aside.

Rushing to Adelaide, Josiah's heart felt like a block of ice. "Adelaide." He turned her, trying to push the water from her lungs. She laid there for what seemed an eternity, then finally coughed out the water and began to breathe. It was then he realized he had been holding his own breath. He took great swigs of air.

Adelaide appeared dazed. Josiah looked up. "Everyone back to your post. She'll be fine." He looked over to the man who had rescued Adelaide.

Josiah lifted his face to him. "I would like to thank you for—" His words froze in his throat. Only then did he realize it was Adam Bowman. The look on Adam's face made Josiah's heart stop. Concern etched the young man's visage, but it was more than that. Perhaps fear of losing the woman they loved gripped them both. A sinking feeling balled in the pit of Josiah's stomach. Before he could say a word to Adam, Adelaide spoke up.

"Who. . . ?"

Josiah swallowed hard and stepped away, pointing toward Adam. "Looks like the first mate came to your rescue."

She reached her hand out to Adam. "Thank you," she managed to say with a weak smile. The look between them said more than Josiah could bear.

In all his days at sea, Josiah had never felt more alone than at that very moment.

෨෬

Josiah took Adelaide back to their room. She put on dry clothes and went to bed. He told her the crew would handle the meals for the rest of the day. She needed to rest. He couldn't make sense out of how she had fallen overboard. Seemed she wasn't quite sure herself; it had all happened so fast.

"You'll be all right, then?"

"I'll be fine."

He turned to go.

"Josiah?"

"Yes?"

"Thank you."

"No need to thank me. I did nothing. I was nowhere around when you needed me. If left to me, you would have drowned." He knew his words sounded harsh, but so be it. Something flickered across her eyes. Most likely sympathy. She felt sorry for him. Sorry that he had failed. They both knew it. The mighty captain couldn't save his own wife. Ah, but the first mate—well, he always stood a stone's throw away, ready to help the lady in distress.

"You're here now."

Her words were barely audible, but they shook him from his self-pity. He grunted. Before he could comment, her eyes closed.

Josiah turned and slipped quietly from their room and latched the door behind him.

Ebenezer met Josiah as he walked up the stairs toward the deck. "Is Mrs. Buchanan all right, Captain?"

Something in Ebenezer's eyes made Josiah want to tell him to mind his own business, but instead he replied, "She's going to be fine."

"Glad to hear it." Ebenezer scratched the whiskers on his chin. "Sure was a good thing Mate Bowman was nearby to save her. Who knows what might have happened." His gaze probed Josiah's eyes, as if he wanted Josiah to read more into his comment. "But then again, guess he's always nearby, isn't he?"

Josiah stared at him.

Ebenezer shrugged. "One can't do without a first mate, that's for sure. Right-hand man, that's what he is. Takes care of business, right down to saving the captain's wife, if need be."

Just then Josiah noticed a few other crewmen nearby listening in. Was this some staged event thought up by this evil man? Did Ebenezer want Josiah to take a swipe at him and give the men an excuse to fight? No, Josiah wouldn't fall for that. He was a captain. He would conduct himself in such a manner.

"Yes, that's right, Ebenezer. A captain can't do without his first mate. I'm thankful to have such a great man for the job." Josiah made himself say the words, though his teeth rebelled at letting them through.

Surprise registered across the crusty sailor's face, and Josiah headed up the stairs, his shoulders relaxing a bit. Once Josiah looked toward the other men, they scattered.

He knew he'd warded off another possible confrontation. He also knew one day soon things would not be so easily smoothed over.

One thought plagued him. Did Ebenezer have something to do with Adelaide's fall? She wasn't sure what had happened. Josiah pounded his right fist into his left palm. If he found out that man had tried to hurt Adelaide. . .

∞

When Adelaide woke up, a black sea sloshed against the hull. A dark sky shadowed the porthole. She couldn't imagine the time. How long had she been in bed? Lifting her head, she raised herself to a sitting position, trying to acclimate herself to what was going on. Her right arm automatically reached down the back of her leg as she remembered hitting it on something just before she had fallen into the water.

She thought back. As she had picked up her washing from a line on deck, a gust of wind had carried a garment from her, and she'd gone to retrieve it. The cloth landed on the railing. She didn't think it that risky to climb up and get it, so she did. The ship suddenly pitched. In her horror, she had tried to balance herself and screamed for help from the nearby sailor. He'd stood motionless and watched her drama unfold. The last thing she saw before being engulfed into the cold, dark sea was the look of pleasure that lit the face of Ebenezer Fallon.

The next thing she knew, she shivered in layers of wet clothes, lying on the hard surface of the ship's deck.

Why hadn't Ebenezer helped her? Could any man be that evil? That inhuman?

Who had helped her? A flash of remembrance came to her. Adam. He stood before her, hair drenched tight to his head, anguish written on his face. Where was Josiah? Oh, yes, he had been there, too. But the look on his face was one of—what? Disgust? Frustration? She couldn't decide.

Then it hit her. She, no doubt, had embarrassed him. After all, she was the captain's wife. What kind of example did she set by falling off the ship? Humiliation washed over her. She had failed poor Josiah. Again.

How could she make it right? How he must regret bringing her with him. Right at this very moment, he probably dreamed of being able to take back those words he had uttered on the shore during the church social.

Her heart ached. How she wanted to make him proud of her. She wanted him to hold her and love her. Be her true husband.

She laid back in her bed, willing herself to forget her responsibilities, her endless chores, her aching heart, everything. Perhaps her dreams would take her to a different life, a life where love prevailed.

∽

Several weeks of snow and hail squalls plagued the *Courage* as it rounded Cape Horn. When the calms came, Adelaide used the time to catch up on her washing, mending, and ironing. She tried to stay out of Josiah's way.

With those chores finished, she wondered what to do with herself. She decided to have one of the men kill a hog from their livestock so she could make sausage meat. Once the killing was done, Adelaide prepared the meat and filled eight good-sized bags.

Her back ached and her body felt sore from her recent chores. She made her way to their cabin. Josiah caught her on deck.

"There's a ship close by, Adelaide. Maybe we can visit with them tonight."

Though she felt tired, she could hardly wait to enjoy the company of the captain and hopefully his wife. "I'd like that."

"Good. You rest for a while, and I'll let you know when we're close enough."

She nodded and decided to do that very thing.

The next couple of nights, Adelaide and Josiah enjoyed gamming with the *Victory's* captain and wife, sharing meals together and talking of life on the seas.

A few days later, they parted company, each heading in different directions with little hope of reconnecting in the near future.

Adelaide hated to see them leave. The distance between Josiah and her had greatly lengthened since her dip in the ocean. She knew without a doubt she had failed him. On the one hand, shame filled her for her stupidity in falling off the ship, but anger also filled her because he had so harshly judged her. People made mistakes. She didn't know perfection was a qualifying factor to be Mrs. Josiah Buchanan.

No doubt Catherine Buchanan had been perfect in every way. Not a clumsy fool. Adelaide sat on her chair in their room and pulled a needle through the material a little too fast. She poked her finger. "Oh!" She pulled her hand free and instinctively sucked on her finger. The pinprick did little to encourage her spirits.

She threw the material down and paced the tiny room. "Why should I feel bad? It's not as though I planned to fall." She took three steps, turned, and headed in the opposite direction. "It's not as though he never made a mistake," she said, shaking her hands in the air—though it made her mad to know she couldn't think offhand of any mistakes he had made.

The more she thought about it, the angrier she became. Who did he think he was, bringing her on this dirty ship to feed a crew of burly seamen? And to have the nerve to pretend he was doing her a favor at that! Oh, sure she had wanted to sail the seas, but like this? He had played on her emotions, that's what. She paced some more, each new footstep hitting the plank harder than the last.

Her chin pointed heavenward. Well, she needn't feel embarrassed. So she had fallen. Wouldn't be the first time someone had fallen into the ocean and most certainly wouldn't be the last. She would not let him make her feel stupid or small. From what she knew of other captain's wives, she felt herself just as qualified.

Oh, the more she thought about the whole affair, the angrier she got. She could hardly wait for Josiah to come to their cabin. She'd let him know in no uncertain terms she was just as good a captain's wife as any of the other wives. Including his precious Catherine. And furthermore, if he didn't like how she conducted herself, why, he could let her off at the next port and she'd get herself home somehow. She was tired of feeling used and unappreciated.

Self-pity engulfed her, and she didn't care. She was tired and spent. Did the men appreciate all her hard work? Clearly, Josiah did not. She could have been a crewman for all he cared. He noticed nothing about her except her cooking. Though she knew that wasn't entirely true in recent days, she refused to go soft.

A voice went off inside her head. *Isn't that what the agreement was? You would cook and get to sail the seas.* Adelaide kicked her boot across the floor. "I hate the agreement. I never wanted that agreement. I wanted. . .Josiah."

Before the tears could flood her eyes, their door swung open. A flushed Josiah stood at the entrance. "Adelaide." He stopped, licked his lips, and looked at her again. "I don't feel so—"

His words were cut short as his body hit the floor in a crumpled heap.

Chapter 12

"We have to stop at Pequeno Island, Adam." Adelaide wrenched her hands together. "Josiah is sick. Very sick. I think he contracted something from the last ship with which we made contact."

Adam looked at her thoughtfully. "Have you been able to discuss this with Josiah?" Adam's eyes held worry.

Adelaide shook her head. "He's feverish, doesn't have a clear thought. We will get to help."

"How long will we need to be at Pequeno?"

"However long it takes Josiah to get well," she said with a voice that let him know he dare not challenge her.

"The men won't like it."

"Doesn't matter. It's what we're going to do." She surprised herself at the authority in her voice.

"All right, Adelaide. We'll stop. Should get there tomorrow by nightfall."

Adelaide took a deep breath. "Thank you." She walked away and immediately made a mental note of the things she would do once they reached port.

The next night after the ship anchored, Adelaide and Adam made their way into town in search of someone to help them. Once they located a doctor, he quickly followed them and came on board the ship.

Adelaide took him to their room and sat in the corner while the stranger went to work. He pulled open his bag, lifting various instruments with which to poke, prod, and stick her husband.

Round spectacles circled his beady eyes, giving him a doctorly appearance. He said very little as he worked with his patient. Josiah lay very still. The fever had subsided, but his skin looked pale as muslin. Fear held Adelaide's breath in place. She was afraid to move until the doctor spoke, letting her know Josiah's condition.

Before long, the doctor began to stuff his things back into the bag; then he stood to look at her.

"Can't say what it is for sure, but most likely the tropical fever that's been going around. I've seen more than one ship come in of late with men groaning of the fever. He'll be all right, but it will take several days to work it out of his system. Makes a fellow weak, though. Most important thing is that he has to rest. If he doesn't rest, it can go into something far worse, so you have to keep him still no matter what. Hopefully, no one else will get it."

Her mind raced for answers. How could she keep a busy sea captain down? Especially one with a restless crew?

"How long?"

"Week, two weeks. Depends." The man shrugged. "I don't know your husband's condition before the fever. That makes a difference on the recuperation period." He walked toward the door. "Keep him sponged off with cool water. I've left you some medicine packets," he added, pointing toward the table. "Just to make sure it is the fever, you'd better not leave for a couple of days. I'll be back and check on him then."

Before she could say another word, he was out the door. Adelaide sighed. She stood in place, trying to decide which way to turn next. First, she would inform the crew. But how could she leave Josiah, even if only for a short time? What if he needed her? What if he woke up delirious? She bit her lip. Seemed she could always think better that way.

Fortunately, she didn't have to think too long. Another knock sounded at the door.

"Yes?"

"Adelaide—I mean, Mrs. Buchanan?"

Adelaide recognized Adam's voice and opened the door. "Come in, Adam."

He stepped in and took off his hat. "How's he doing?"

Adelaide explained what the doctor had told her. Adam looked worried. "What is it?"

He shook his head as he heard her explanation. "The crew is mighty restless. I shouldn't say it, but I don't trust Ebenezer Fallon."

She blew out a sigh of understanding. "It's all right. We feel the same way." She turned a worried look to Josiah. "Let's give him a couple of days and see how he does. Maybe by then, Josiah can tell me how he wants to proceed." She turned back to Adam. "We must stay near help for a couple of days to get through the worst of it. I will not risk his life, not even for the entire ship."

Adam nodded. "I'll try to keep them calm. We'll get through this. I'll be praying."

"Thank you, Adam."

He closed the door behind him, and Adelaide stood staring. She hadn't had a chance to think about praying until now. Quietly, she eased onto her knees beside her trunk.

She didn't know how long she had prayed, but sometime later, with aching legs, she rose to her feet, her face wet with tears, but her heart feeling much lighter. She knew God had heard her prayer and would help them through. Just how, she didn't know, but she knew they were not alone.

The next morning, Adelaide awoke as Josiah was groaning and speaking unintelligible words. She got up and went to him. His face burned with fever. A rush of alarm spread through her. The doctor said he should be getting better with rest. What had happened? Maybe it was more than what the doctor had suspected.

She quickly ran to the pitcher of water, grabbed a rag, and went to Josiah. She bathed his face over and over until the cloth itself felt warm from his body heat. Bringing a cup to his lips, she tried to get him to drink, but he couldn't. She didn't know where the doctor lived, and it was too early for him to be in his office. A glance at her timepiece told her it was almost four o'clock.

What could she do? She hurried to the pitcher, dipped the cloth, wrung it out, then went back to his bed and continued to bathe him.

"Catherine."

Adelaide's hand froze midair. She held her breath and waited for him to say more.

"Why?" Josiah's head turned back and forth, back and forth. Agonizing groans escaped him.

Adelaide shook his arms to free him from his painful memories. "Josiah, it's Adelaide. Josiah." He never opened his eyes, but his head stopped turning, and his groans grew silent.

When his fever had somewhat subsided, Adelaide walked over, exhausted, to her own bed. The light of day had dawned, and she could hear the sleepy town rising to greet it. She collapsed in her blankets with one agonizing thought. Josiah still loved Catherine.

∞

Five days later, Josiah woke up with a start. What had happened? His eyes adjusted to the morning light that filtered in through the porthole. The ship didn't feel right. Must be in another calm. Why was he in bed? Were they in port? If so, who had given the orders to pull into port? He rubbed his head. It hurt. Questions rushed through his mind, but he couldn't work through the tangled maze. He had to get up. He attempted to lift himself from the bed, but his elbows were too weak. He fell back. Something stirred in Adelaide's bed. She lay sleeping and hadn't drawn the curtain between them.

Obviously, she wanted to watch him. Why? He saw the chair near his bed, the rag, the pitcher of water. The medicine. Had he been sick? The throbbing in his head and the weakness in his limbs answered his question.

He lay still, looking at Adelaide. She was so different from Catherine. His first wife would never have bothered with him in his sickness. She left him. Her thoughts were selfish and cruel. While Adelaide cared so generously for others—even him—when he least deserved it.

Just like God.

Where did that thought come from? The only sounds he heard were the thoughts rushing through his mind. Adelaide did love God, and it showed. A God of whom he knew very little. Did he want to know more? What about the people at church who talked about him and about Catherine's rejection? What about his pain at sea—did God care about that? Why did He let her go? Why did God let Catherine hurt him that way?

He wanted to shake his head and make all the thoughts go away, but his head hurt too much. Was he going to die? What if what they said about God and eternity were true? Was he ready to meet his Maker?

Fear gripped his heart. He knew he wasn't ready. Being ready required forgiveness. And God could not forgive Josiah until Josiah forgave Catherine and the church people who had hurt him. He knew that much about the gospel message.

He didn't want to make a deathbed confession. His integrity would not allow it. Would he merely use God to make it to heaven? No, he had to mean it regardless of whether he lived or died, and Josiah wasn't sure he could forgive Catherine. Ever.

"Josiah!" Adelaide scrambled from her covers and rushed to him. "Oh, Josiah, you're awake." Tears flooded down her cheeks.

Her concern touched him deeply.

She looked as though she would throw herself over him in one swoop, but her steps came to a sudden halt. Josiah managed a half smile, which she matched.

Adelaide settled herself into the chair beside the bed and told him what had transpired in the last five days. He thought on what she said, trying to sort out what to do from here.

Someone knocked on the door.

Adelaide stood. "Yes, who is it?"

"Dr. Walters."

Adelaide looked at Josiah then opened the door.

Dr. Walters walked in, weariness on his face. "Is he any better?" His expression told her he had little hope.

"See for yourself," Adelaide said with a smile, motioning toward the bed.

Dr. Walters let out a laugh. "Well, if you aren't a sight for sore eyes." The doctor expertly went through his routine and checked Josiah out. When the exam was over, he announced the good news that Josiah could sail the next day if he so chose, but he'd still need to take it somewhat easy in the days ahead.

Following Josiah's instructions, Adelaide told Adam they would be setting sail the next morning at dawn. The crew should be ready to go.

Adelaide purchased a few things for dinner and brought them to their room. The pleasant scent of spices, meat, and potatoes made Adelaide's stomach growl. Only then did she realize how little she had been eating.

Though Josiah could eat very little, he tried a few bites. He stirred the potatoes on his plate. "Thank you for taking care of me."

Adelaide looked up and smiled. "You'd have done the same for me."

"Catherine would never have done that."

Adelaide dropped her fork. She wasn't accustomed to him bringing up his first wife's name.

"She hurt me, you know."

"I know." Adelaide felt his pain. "I'm sorry, Josiah."

He shrugged. "I don't know why I let it bother me so much over the last couple of years. I suppose it was pride. I just hadn't expected her to do that."

Adelaide listened, never saying a word lest he stop.

"I've been a fool." He ran his fingers through his hair. He stopped and looked at her. "I want to know God the way you do, Addie."

Warmth rushed clear through her.

"I don't understand why she did what she did, but I don't want it to keep me from God."

"People make choices, Josiah. Those choices affect others. Good or bad. Catherine's choice affected you. The good news is that God's choice to love sinners, shown through the death of His Son on a cross, can change a life that trusts in Him. You don't have to let Catherine's choice cause you to make the wrong choice about God. He is there for you. Always has been. Always will be."

Josiah nodded.

"The church folks you told me about probably just didn't know what to say. Sometimes folks feel it's better to say nothing than to say the wrong thing."

He nodded. "You're right. I've allowed my own imaginings to run away with me. I want to make the right choice now, Addie. Will you pray with me?"

Tears plopped on her dress, and she nodded. She led him in a prayer of confession and repentance to God.

Once they had finished praying, Adelaide wiped her tears and looked at Josiah. She placed her hand on his. "You know, Josiah, the prayer is only the beginning. The joy comes from having a continuing walk with Christ. Spending time with Him through His Word, allowing Him to lead you through life. It's an incredible journey."

He wiped his face, smiled, and nodded. "That's what I want—a changed life."

Adelaide smiled while her spirit soared. Though their situation hadn't changed, she felt certain their future would never be the same.

Chapter 13

Adelaide stepped up on deck to get some fresh air. Josiah was feeling much better, though his strength still waned. The sickness allowed him to get up only a few hours each day; then he headed back to bed. The admission of weakness didn't come easily for the rugged sea captain. Adelaide knew he would never go to bed unless forced to do so.

She took a deep breath. At least no one else got the sickness, and for that they could all be thankful. Still, she knew the extra days in port did little to help the morale of the crew.

Footsteps sounded just behind her. "Mrs. Buchanan?"

Adelaide turned to face Adam. She smiled. "How are you?"

His expression turned sober. "Not good." He looked at his feet. "I'm sorry to bother you with this, but, well, with the captain down, I don't know what else to do."

"What is it, Adam?"

"It's the men. Ebenezer's got 'em stirred up. Convinced them the whales are in the Gulf of Alaska, and the captain is wasting their time if he heads only as far as the Sandwich Islands."

She stared at Adam, biting her lip. "If only we could catch another whale."

"I fear a mutiny, Adelaide," he whispered. "I mean, Mrs. Buchanan."

She waved away his formalities, her mind already trying to figure out how to handle the situation. "I'll see what I can do. Thanks for your help."

He nodded, a worried look still on his face.

"Keep praying," she told him. With that, Adelaide turned and walked toward the cookhouse to prepare lunch.

Working hard on the meal, Adelaide prepared a feast of ham, Irish potatoes, cabbage, string beans, and goat's milk for the crew, hoping to calm them down through their stomachs. Once her work was finished, she left the cookhouse and carried a meal for her and Josiah to their room.

Adelaide felt Josiah's gaze on her when they settled into their chairs.

"You want to tell me about it?"

She flipped out her napkin and looked up in feigned surprise. "What do you mean?"

His hand swept across the table. "This meal tells me something's wrong.

This is not our normal fare for lunch."

Of course he would pick up on that. How silly of her. Adelaide sighed. "The men are restless, Josiah. It's Ebenezer. I believe he's trying to convince them the whales are in the gulf and you're wrong to go only as far as the islands. Adam told me, though we have no real proof, unfortunately."

Josiah rubbed his chin thoughtfully. "I see."

Adelaide said little more, knowing Josiah was working out the issue in his mind. They finished the meal in silence.

Before Adelaide could clear the table, Josiah grabbed her hand. "Join me in prayer, Adelaide. We need direction."

How those words thrilled her heart! The two of them prayed for discernment. Afterward, the exercise of prayer seemed to have tired Josiah. "I'm afraid I'll have to deal with it when my strength returns." He looked at Adelaide apologetically and climbed back in bed.

Adelaide still feared for him. Though the doctor had told her the danger was over, she had never seen him so frail.

She stood and gathered the things she wanted to take back to the cookhouse. She needed to clean up after the crew. First, she would clean the dishes; then she would go.

Once the dishes were cleaned, Adelaide stepped from the cabin to make her way to the cookhouse. She heard a commotion from the forecastle. Though a woman should never go near the men's quarters, she edged her way closer in hopes of hearing what was going on. She stopped short when she saw Josiah's form standing in the shadows. She could hear the men grumbling among themselves, Ebenezer's voice urging them on. Then out of the rumble, she heard Adam's voice.

"Now look here. Captain Buchanan has been good to us. He feeds us far better than any other whaling ship on these waters, and you know it. He sees to it we stop in port when we need a change. He's been entirely fair in his dealings with us. Now all of a sudden you think he's trying to cheat us. Why?"

Adam's voice held more authority than Adelaide had ever heard before. She felt proud of him for standing up for Josiah.

"I say this sickness is turning him yellow," Ebenezer called out. "He's weak and afraid to take on a whale now. Too bad for him. We still have to make money with or without him. I say we go to the gulf!" Ebenezer's voice was raised now, exciting the men to action.

Adelaide gasped as she watched Josiah step through the shadows, bringing the room to instant silence.

Josiah raised his arms. "I understand your concerns. No one wants to waste time. We're all trying to make a living here." He turned his unrelenting gaze on Ebenezer. "I'm not trying to make you suffer because of my illness." Josiah measured his words evenly, as if carefully considering what to say next. "In talking with the other captains along our journey, I've been told the weather will be severe this year in the gulf. It didn't seem prudent to risk being trapped by the ice. We've heard of more than one incident where ships have been trapped and eventually destroyed by the icebergs—"

Ebenezer waved his hand. "Yellow, like I said. We ain't afraid of no ice!" His voice thundered with rebellion. He turned to the men. "You gonna let him scare you into missing an opportunity of a lifetime? I'm telling you, the whales are there!"

Adelaide heard a faint sound on deck. She turned. The masthead. The sound came from the masthead. She slipped up the stairs.

"There she blows!" the seaman cried.

Excitement surged through her. She ran back toward the forecastle as fast as her legs could carry her. "A whale. We have our whale!" she cried. The men scattered as fast as the words left her lips.

Relief washed over Adelaide. Josiah looked at her and smiled. They would catch this whale.

God had heard their prayer.

∞

A squall kicked up, making it difficult for the men to fasten the two whales. The ship reeled to and fro like a drunken man. Adelaide could not bear to watch the whaleboats being tossed about from wave to wave.

Her fear subsided when the crew returned with somewhat small, though in Adelaide's view impressive, whales.

The crew immediately set to cutting in and boiling, working day and night. Adelaide watched the pilot fish, skipjack, and albacore that followed the ship for the refuse of the whale that was thrown overboard. The air seemed black with the hundreds of storm petrels that hovered just over the surface of the water. The stench and sight, though still gruesome and overpowering, did not make Adelaide sick like before. She felt proud she was growing accustomed to the life on a whaling ship.

The next morning, Adelaide prepared albacore for breakfast. The crew finally stowed away sixty barrels of oil from the blubber and commenced to salting down some albacore for trade at the islands.

They caught more pilot fish. Adelaide thought them a pretty fish, about the size of a trout, blue with black stripes, and considered very nice eating. She decided to prepare the pilot fish for dinner.

Just after lunch, Josiah asked Adelaide to summon Adam Bowman into their quarters. She knew Josiah didn't care much for Adam, though she couldn't understand why. Josiah seemed to have taken a dislike to Adam from day one. Not that any of it should concern her. Josiah was the captain. Be that as it may, Adam was her friend, and she hoped the two men could settle their differences.

Once back in their room, Adelaide tidied the area while Josiah relaxed on his bed. A knock sounded at the door, and Adelaide opened it to allow Adam entrance.

He pulled off his cap. "Ma'am." He turned to Josiah. "Captain? You wanted to see me?"

Josiah raised himself from the bed and walked over to the table. "Have a seat, Bowman."

Adam complied.

"Would you like me to leave, Josiah?" Adelaide asked.

"No, I'd like you to stay."

Not knowing what to do with herself, Adelaide sorted through her clothes just to keep her hands busy.

"First off, I want to apologize to you," Josiah began.

Adelaide's fingers stopped moving through the cloth. She couldn't imagine what Josiah would say next.

"I've been utterly unfair to you from the start."

Adelaide dared a glance at Adam and thought his expression priceless. He looked as though he'd swallowed a fish whole. She stifled a chuckle.

"I allowed foolish thinking to get in the way of good sense."

Though Adelaide hadn't a clue what he meant, and she could see confusion on Adam's face as well, she was proud of Josiah for taking this hard step.

Josiah swallowed hard. "I never did properly thank you for rescuing Adelaide from the water that day, and I want to thank you for helping me with the men before a mutiny erupted. You've been a top-rate officer, and I'm beholden to you."

Adam blushed. "Wouldn't Esther be proud?" Adelaide said with a smile.

Josiah turned to look at Adelaide. "Esther?"

"Well, yes. Didn't you know Adam was sweet on my sister?"

Adam fingered the cap in his hands. "I'd say it was more than that, Mrs. Buchanan. I want her to be my wife—if she'll have me."

Adelaide saw the surprise on Josiah's face and laughed. "You mean you didn't know?"

Josiah shook his head. "No idea."

Adelaide watched as a pleasant countenance fell upon Josiah. No doubt about it, things were changing for them.

⌒

Adelaide fried the pilot fish for dinner and served the remainder for breakfast the next morning. Josiah didn't much care for the fish, so he ate some eggs. About ten minutes after their breakfast, Adelaide's face began to burn, and her head ached. A glance in the looking glass made her gasp. Her face was as red as a lobster all over: chin, forehead, ears, and neck.

Adelaide got into her bed and prayed Josiah would come back and check on her. At this rate, she would not be able to prepare lunch.

About midmorning, Josiah stepped into their room, took one look at her, and made a face. "I didn't know what was wrong with the crew until I looked at you. Now I know that you've all been poisoned by eating the fish that we kept overnight."

"Oh dear, Josiah. I'm so sorry."

He shrugged. "You didn't know. Everyone will be fine by tomorrow. But you all will feel pretty nasty for the remainder of the day. I don't think there's much need to worry about lunch and dinner. Most of the crew ate the fish."

She nodded.

A smile tugged at his lips. "You are a sight for sore eyes," he teased.

Adelaide grabbed her head. "Just wait, Captain Buchanan, I'll get you for this." She managed a smile then a groan.

"Rest well, Mrs. Buchanan," he said, slipping out the door.

Chapter 14

Adelaide and the crew felt better by the next day. With the crew's renewed strength came restlessness for more whales. Long days of inactivity did little good for them. The head winds and calms added to a great deal of rough weather didn't help matters. The calms caused the ship to move slowly, and Ebenezer continued to let them know there was little time to lose.

Adelaide prayed they'd catch another whale soon, before Ebenezer could cause more trouble.

One of the whalemen grew sick with pneumonia. Josiah said if the man didn't get better soon, they'd have to leave him at the islands. The forecastle offered few conveniences for sickness. Adelaide worried the illness would overtake some others.

While sitting in her room mending clothes, Adelaide thought of the last months at sea. Her head had been so full of romantic notions. Pa had told her what she wanted to hear. He'd left out the bad parts. She smiled and let out a sigh. So like Pa. How she missed him.

Though she still loved the sea, Adelaide had learned much from her short time aboard the *Courage*. It was a hard life. Sickness, disgruntled men, accidents, loneliness—they all plagued the seafaring man. An ache squeezed her heart as she thought of Ma and Esther. Adelaide wondered about their health. Did Ma have enough help with only Esther there? Adelaide breathed deeply and closed her eyes. What was done was done, and she couldn't go back and change things now. She had to make the best of it. And so she would.

Josiah burst through the door, quite out of breath. "Another whale, Addie." He grabbed something from the room and left.

She lifted her gaze heavenward. "Thank You." As long as the whales appeared, Ebenezer couldn't stir up the crew. She said a prayer for the men then rushed to the deck.

Adelaide held tightly to the ship's rail, watching the wind toss about the whaleboats. Strong waves lifted them to great lengths, then dropped them without mercy. The men continued to row vigorously. In the distance, the whale spouted his presence, almost in a teasing fashion. Adelaide's stomach spasmed from the constant motion. The angry seas pelted hard against the ship, biting into her skin. She fought against worry.

After the boats were a distance out, Adelaide decided to go to the cookhouse and work on dinner. Before she turned, someone yelled, "Stoven boat."

Adelaide jerked around and looked back out to sea. Her heart caught in her throat. She watched as the men in the other whaleboats paddled hard and fast to get to the men tossed from their boat. She pulled a handkerchief from her dress pocket and twisted it in her hands. Her lips uttered another prayer. Where was Josiah?

She strained her neck to get a glimpse, desperately trying to find Josiah in the crowd. The ship tossed about, and water formed a mist across her eyes, making it impossible to recognize the men in the distance. She finally gave up and went downstairs to nurse her queasy stomach.

By the time the men came back, Adelaide had returned to the deck, though still feeling a little out of sorts. As the men climbed aboard, she saw that they had fastened the whale, though their countenance showed no trace of excitement. Something was wrong, but she didn't know what.

Fear sliced through her until Josiah came into view. She breathed a sigh of relief. He walked over to her. "We've lost a man, Adelaide."

She gasped. "Oh Josiah, no." Her eyes searched his face. "Who was it?"

"Ebenezer Fallon."

A pain shot through her. "Not Ebenezer. He wasn't ready to meet the Lord, Josiah." She lifted tears to him.

"I know." Josiah reached up and tenderly brushed the tears from her face. Someone called to him for assistance. "Be right there." He turned back to Adelaide.

"How did it happen?"

"He was drunk. Couldn't handle himself with a stoven boat."

"Once the oil is stowed, are you planning a service for Ebenezer?"

Josiah nodded then turned and walked away.

Adelaide walked near the vicinity of the whale and stood in awe. She could never have imagined such a sight. Her pa had told her a right whale's massive head contained fifteen hundred pounds of bone. Looking at it now, she believed him. The display before her was both gruesome and spectacular.

The crew quickly commenced to cutting and boiling. They worked tirelessly stowing the 155 barrels of oil just before another gale stirred up, obliging them to put out the fires and stop the tryworks. The weather would not permit them to gather on the deck. Josiah decided the service for Ebenezer would be put off till after they went to port.

Following their hard work, a dead calm plagued them. Miserable whaling weather. The *Courage* pulled into the nearest port for trading. The customhouse officer came on board, and shortly after, the ship anchored.

Knowing the stop was strictly for business, Adelaide stayed on board.

Once Josiah returned, he told her they had received $1.50 per pound for the whalebone. An unheard-of price.

"I suppose we have the ladies, with all their hoops and corsets, to thank for such a fine price," Josiah teased.

Adelaide's face grew warm. "May the fashion long continue," she said with a smile.

❧

With the ship back on course, Josiah made arrangements for the crew to meet on deck in the evening for Ebenezer's service.

Josiah spoke of the vastness of the heavenly Father's creative power. With a sweep of his arms, he talked of the majesty and dangers of the seas and the surety of eternity.

Genuinely mourning for Ebenezer's soul, Josiah spoke of forgiveness. Who knew what Ebenezer's life had been like? Josiah explained to the crew someone had once told him life was full of choices. He turned to Adelaide and smiled then continued with his speech. "Our choices tangle together with the choices of other people, each affecting the other." He spoke words of comfort and finally ended the service with a prayer for all who were still living, that they might learn to make the right choices.

The crew dispersed. A whaleman came over to Josiah. He fidgeted with the cap in his hands. "After what he did to you and your wife, I don't know how you could forgive him."

"After all that God has forgiven us, can we do any less?"

The man scratched his head.

"I'm not saying it's easy to forgive people who wrong you, only that there's no peace without it."

"I let him get me stirred up." The man looked down at the deck. "I'm sorry, sir."

"People can be persuasive. Let it be a lesson to you to stand strong next time."

The sailor stopped fidgeting with his cap and looked at Josiah with thankful eyes. "I'm proud to serve with you, sir."

He smiled. "And we're proud to have you. My prayers are with you."

The man's eyes grew wide. "I'm obliged." He turned and walked away.

Josiah knew God was working in the hearts of the crew. He prayed that through this misfortune, the men would come to know the Lord.

❧

Over the next several weeks, the *Courage* made good headway. The catch of another large whale kept the crew busy.

Once the deck was scrubbed back to normal, Adelaide enjoyed walking on board and watching the clouds that hovered overhead. The weather, calm and warm, provided the perfect setting for Adelaide as she pulled her chair out on the deck. With her journal in hand, she made her entry: *March 4.* Making it a point to stay current with the news every chance she got, Adelaide remembered having read in a newspaper that on this very day the newly elected president, James Buchanan, would take his seat in the presidential chair. She wondered if Josiah could be distantly related to the new president.

Life seemed so different on the seas than on land. She thought it a wonder they were fortunate enough to hear who had won the election at all when they were so far from home.

"Enjoying yourself?" Josiah's voice warmed her more than the sun.

"Uh-huh." She closed her journal and looked at him. They were growing closer, but would they ever be man and wife? She dreamed of the day. She hoped it would happen. One day.

"Walk with me to the rail?" He extended his hand to her. Adelaide reached for it and rose from her chair. Together they walked to the railing and looked out to sea.

"We've been on our journey over three months now." His gaze fixed on the waters, he seemed to be speaking to no one in particular. He hesitated as if afraid to say the next words. Turning to her, he asked, "Are you happy, Adelaide?" His eyes searched hers.

She looked him full in the face and said with certainty, "I'm very happy, Josiah."

Lost in the moment, neither one pulled away. Josiah looked for all he was worth as though he wanted to kiss her. Wanting him to desperately, yet not wanting to create a spectacle in front of the crew, Adelaide blinked, bringing both of them to their senses.

Josiah cleared his throat. "Good," he said matter-of-factly. He looked back toward the sea. "We should arrive on Akaroa Island sometime tomorrow afternoon. Hope to stay about a week, do some trading, give the men a chance to relax, buy more supplies."

Adelaide smiled, excited at the thought of being on land awhile. "We're still a ways south of New Zealand, right?"

"Right," he answered with a smile.

She smiled back, knowing he understood her struggle with directions.

"I'll let you get back to your journal," he said. Once more he turned to her and brushed a strand of hair from her cheek. He smiled then walked away, leaving her cheek burning where his finger had been.

⁓

The following morning, Adelaide prepared for fishing. Josiah helped her place a piece of white cloth onto a hook and instructed her to bob it up and down to make it look like a flying fish. By morning's end, she felt a bit puffed up with pride for having caught several large fish. Josiah seemed proud of her and suggested she cook her catch for lunch, which she immediately set out to do.

By early afternoon, the ship had arrived at the shores of Akaroa Island. The wharf bustled with activity when the *Courage* finally anchored. Ships lined the port. Crewmen spilled onto the shores, anxious to explore the island. Some stayed behind and worked busily on ship repairs. Adelaide thought the sights spectacular. As soon as they anchored, the customhouse officer came on board with a boat's crew of natives. Josiah followed them for the purpose of obtaining a boarding place while on shore.

Within a couple hours, Adelaide and Josiah were in the boat on their way to the house of Paul and Ruth Burks. Longing for the company of another woman, Adelaide was disappointed the Burks were traveling abroad and would not be there. Still, she could hardly wait to get settled into a real home.

Upon arrival, the straw cottage surprised her. Exotic trees and flowers surrounded it, making it appear every bit the island home. Its backyard faced the shoreline.

The cook and two women who took care of the house greeted Adelaide and Josiah and showed them around.

The house consisted of four rooms: a sitting room, two bedrooms, and a dining room. The sitting room extended the whole length of the house with a door opening at either end. Crimson and white drapery adorned four windows. Chinese chairs, lounges, and a sofa provided comfortable and decorative seating. Other furnishings included a secretary and library and center and side tables, while bright paintings and engravings hugged the walls, giving the room a homey feel.

"Do you like it?" Josiah whispered when no one was around.

"Very much."

"Good."

A knock sounded at the door. Josiah opened it. An islander stood in the entrance. "Captain Buchanan?"

"Yes?"

"You have an urgent letter, sir," the young man said in polished English as he handed Josiah an envelope.

Fear gripped Adelaide as she worried that it might be bad news from home.

Josiah thanked the man and worked quickly to open the envelope. Adelaide watched as he stared at the paper, all color draining from his face. "What is it, Josiah?"

He turned a glazed look her way. Staring for a moment, he finally said, "It's not about your family. I can't talk about it now." With envelope in hand, Josiah pushed through the doors, leaving a speechless Adelaide behind.

Chapter 15

Josiah walked up one street then another. Though the fever had left him weaker than it had found him, he continued to walk. He lifted the crumpled envelope in his hands time and again. Funny how a letter could change your life forever.

A child. He had a child. He paced with only a cursory glance at the colorful birds that swooped down upon the bright green foliage enhancing the land. His thoughts held him captive. What would he do with a child? He knew nothing of raising one. His hand absently raked through his hair. Suddenly, his footsteps came to an abrupt halt.

Adelaide.

He had asked her to be his cook. But a mother? Just when things were growing between them, would he lose her, too?

Why hadn't Catherine told him she was pregnant? Did she despise him so much she would withhold his own child from him? Had he known her so little?

The Bayview Orphanage had written that Catherine had died in child-birth. Though Catherine's mother raised the child for a short time, poverty and ill health had forced her to take the child to the orphanage. The orphanage had been searching for Josiah over the past two years, hoping to unite him with his daughter.

His daughter.

He kicked a stone in his path. Not that he wasn't thankful for a child, but to gain one in this way? He couldn't help but feel somewhat responsible for Catherine's death. She had made wrong choices, true, but he hadn't exactly been the best husband. What kind of father would he be?

While some people took their children aboard whaling ships, he wasn't sure he could do that. Life was hard on the seas. Did he want his daughter raised around a band of rough crewmen?

A more troubling thought nagged at him. Could he continue whaling? The last few whale catches had tired him beyond belief. He thought once he got over his illness, he would be good as new. Yet his former strength eluded him. He questioned his ability to continue. So many questions, so many decisions to make.

What do I do, Lord? Josiah felt at the end of himself. This was something he couldn't fix. After hours of thinking, he decided he'd head back to the cottage. Most likely, Adelaide was in a state of confusion over his actions. How should he break the news to her?

"Yes, Adelaide, you're about to become a mother." He groaned. How could things get any worse? Raw emotion seared through him, with shame following close behind.

It's not that he didn't love children. Thoughts of having a child softened him. A faceless girl played before his mind. A toddler.

Being methodical by nature, he'd take it one step at a time. What else could he do?

The first step was to tell Adelaide the news. Her reaction would determine the next.

∞

Adelaide couldn't imagine what news Josiah had received. Whatever its content, it couldn't be good. Other than when he was sick, she had never seen him so pale. She wanted to help him, but how could she since she didn't know what the problem was?

Of course he didn't share the problem with her. True, they had grown closer, but they weren't truly husband and wife—yet.

She sat on a chair in the backyard, drinking in the liquid blue of the sky, the smell of the sea, the lush greenery. What would her friends back home say if they could see her now? If only she could take these sights home with her to share. Even then, she couldn't imagine adequately describing the place to them. If only Ma and Esther could be with her now.

If Ma were here, she'd know what to do for Josiah. Visions of long talks with Ma on the porch filled Adelaide's mind. "Oh, God, show me how to help him. Give me the strength to hear his news and help him through it."

∞

Josiah rehearsed the words in his mind all the way back to the cottage. He couldn't worry about it. The words had to be said, and they would deal with the situation accordingly. After all, this little girl was his flesh and blood. He would not neglect her. Who knew what her life had been up to now?

Taking the last step up to their temporary home, Josiah drew in a ragged breath before opening the door. He stepped inside.

"Adelaide?" He went from room to room in search of her. With a quick glance out the window, he saw her sitting in the backyard. His heart stirred. He loved her. No denying it. Adelaide was an understanding woman, full of compassion. She'd stand by him. Why did he worry?

He pushed through the door and stepped out into the backyard. Upon seeing him, Adelaide rose from her chair. Her questioning eyes made him want to wrap her in his arms. The unspoken words kept them apart.

"I need to talk to you."

She nodded.

Josiah cleared his throat. He reached into his pocket and pulled out the crumpled envelope. He stared at it a moment. "This letter holds some disturbing news, I'm afraid." Oh, how could he tell her this? How would she react? He decided to go for the lighthearted approach. "It seems..." He stared at his boots, not daring to look at her. "It seems that I'm a father." He glanced up in time to see her teeter in place. His eyes fixed on her. She said nothing. "Addie? Are you all right?"

She looked as though cold water had been doused in her face. "A father?"

Her eyes looked all liquid and brown. He wanted to hold her, tell her things would work out, plead with her to understand. "Seems Catherine was with child when I set sail." He stared across the waters. "I never knew." The words lifted softly out to sea. He turned back to Adelaide. "She died in childbirth."

Josiah thought Adelaide's face looked flushed. Was she angry? Upset? Of course she was upset. How could he think otherwise?

She eyed him warily. "Where is the child?"

"I'm told she's at an orphanage in Bayview, Massachusetts."

"She."

He nodded.

"Does she have a name?"

Her question startled him. He hadn't even thought of that. "I suppose she does. I just don't know what it is."

"How old is she?"

"Three."

"What do you plan to do?"

He thought for a moment. "I have to get her." He looked at Adelaide for understanding. "She's my flesh and blood."

"You had no idea?"

He was puzzled by her question. "No, of course not. What? You think I would keep something like this from you?"

"I don't know what to think anymore, Josiah." Her voice was thick with defeat. "Besides, you don't owe me an explanation." She glanced at her hands and whispered, "After all, I'm just your cook." She looked up at him.

Her words hurt. He thought they had grown closer. But maybe that was all on his part. "Is that the way you want it?"

"Well, that was the agreement."

"Yes, I suppose it was," he answered, wishing with all his heart he could change things.

"When will you get her?"

He stroked his chin. "I don't know. I'll have to check into it."

"I see."

He paused a moment. "Will you go with me?"

Adelaide swallowed hard. "I'll have to think on that, Josiah. I committed to being your cook, but a mother? Well, I just don't know."

He nodded. "We'll talk later."

∽

Now it was Adelaide's turn to walk. Though it wasn't proper to appear on the streets unescorted, Adelaide didn't care. She needed time to think.

Alone.

The beauty of the sights around her did little to lift her spirits. It's not that she minded mothering a child, especially Josiah's child, but she couldn't help feeling—what was it? She took a deep breath. "Might as well call it what it is, Adelaide Sanborn Buchanan. Jealousy." The thought shamed her, but she knew it was true.

She was jealous of Catherine. No matter how hard she tried to rationalize her feelings, she knew the root of the problem. Catherine owned a piece of Josiah's heart that Adelaide felt certain she could never reach. Perhaps Catherine owned all of his heart. Adelaide wondered if he'd ever offer his love to her.

Each time it seemed they were drawing closer, something would happen to make him pull away. The only thing she could imagine to hold him back was Catherine.

How can I compete with memories? What do I do when the "other woman" is no longer living? Josiah's love is buried with Catherine, and I have to accept it.

Stopping for a moment, Adelaide reached for a seashell that had found its way a distance from the shore. She turned it over in her palm, examining the tiny crevices.

She straightened and held the shell in her hand. She decided to keep it. Most likely, she would never come to the island again.

Choices. How much she had learned about choices. Why hadn't she sought God's heart before saying yes to Josiah? Would He have led her to marry him? Would He have whispered no to her heart? Her footsteps carried her to a large rock. She sat on it. The ocean waves stirred with a slight wind. Sounds of the sea calmed her spirit.

How could she be so cold as to turn down mothering Josiah's daughter just because the little girl belonged to another woman? There was no doubt in Adelaide's mind she could and would love the child. What she feared was if the girl looked like Catherine. Would the resemblance be a constant reminder to Josiah of his love for his late wife? Could Adelaide bear to always live in the shadow of another?

Hot tears stung her eyes. She swiped at the tears with the back of her hand. Why couldn't she be strong? She knew Josiah cared about her, but he had never indicated he loved her. If only Adelaide knew that Josiah loved her, she could bear it all, but as it was, she felt like nothing more than a hired servant.

"Oh Ma, I wish you were here. You'd know right what to do." Her thoughts wrestled with her heart.

"Adelaide!"

She turned on the rock to see Adam running her way. Dabbing once more at her face, she rose and walked toward him. A broad grin stretched across his face.

"Adam, what is it?"

He waved some envelopes. "We've got mail."

Energy pumped through her. She clasped her hands together.

"You got one from Esther, and I got one as well," he said with a hint of boasting.

"Is that a fact?" she asked with a smile, hiding the turmoil in her heart.

"Josiah asked that I bring this to you if I saw you. He's tending to some repairs on the ship."

She nodded. "Thank you so much, Adam."

He handed her the envelope. "Well, I know you're anxious to read the letter, so I'll leave you be and let you enjoy the news from home." He smiled again and left her.

Adelaide headed back to her rock and settled into a comfortable position. She looked at the envelope and wondered why her mother hadn't written. Most likely, they both had written and sent it in one envelope, she decided. Anxiously, she tore it open:

Dearest Adelaide,

I trust this letter finds you well. How we miss you! Our home is much too quiet since you've gone. Ma misses you something fierce. She tries to act brave, but you know how she is. It helps her to know you are happy with Josiah.

Guilt pinched Adelaide's heart. She read on.

I regret, dear sister, to tell you Ma is not well.

Adelaide's breath caught in her throat.

She has a bad cough. Doctor says it's consumption.

Adelaide wiped tears from her eyes once more.

I didn't want to tell you, but we fear she is getting worse, and, well, I didn't know if you could get home to see her. Perhaps it is impossible to do so, but I wanted to try to reach you so you would have the choice.

The rest of the letter was lost to Adelaide. She folded it and allowed the tears to freely flow. Too many choices already. Now she must make another. She had to get to Ma. But how? What would Josiah say? Could they make arrangements?

She lifted a piece of her skirt to her face and dried her eyes. "Enough feeling sorry for yourself." Adelaide looked at the sea once more and stood to her feet. She knew what she had to do.

Chapter 16

Though Adelaide's emotions got the better of her at times, once she made up her mind about something, the matter was settled. Sometimes to her detriment. She pushed the thoughts of Catherine, Josiah, and "their daughter" aside. For now, she had to concentrate on getting home to her ma.

She walked back to the cottage. Upon entering, she found Josiah waiting on the sofa, arms folded across his chest, his mouth drawn in a tight line.

"Where have you been?" His words held a father's discipline.

Anger worked its way up her spine. "I've been thinking." She looked him square in the face. "If you must know."

He stood. She could see his chest rise and fall with each breath. "Adelaide, you know it's not proper for a woman to walk the streets unescorted. Especially in an unknown land."

She gritted her teeth. "I care nothing about propriety today, Josiah. I needed time to think."

He took a few steps toward her.

She stepped back. "I'm going home." She said the words more sharply than she had intended.

He stopped. His eyes widened. His gaze never left her face. She felt a stab of regret. It's not that she wanted to hurt him. She just needed time to think things through. More importantly, she needed to get home to Ma.

"I see." His gaze dropped to the floor, as if searching for what to say next.

"Ma's sick."

He looked back to her. "The letter?"

"Yes."

He cautiously took a couple of steps toward her again; still she backed away. She didn't want his nearness to cloud her thinking. He stopped again, a look of sympathy on his face. The last thing she wanted was his pity. She could tell he hadn't expected the wall between them. Sorrow tugged at her heart.

"You wish to travel alone?"

She nodded.

"I won't let you go on just any ship." His words left no room for argument. "You are my wife—"

"Your cook," she corrected.

"And my wife." The tone of his voice told her not to argue, which, of course, made her want to all the more. But she resisted the urge.

"I'll go to the docks this afternoon and see if I can find an appropriate ship on which you can sail home."

She couldn't make herself look at him.

"Adelaide, I..." He reached his arm out to her.

"I need to get things packed," she said, turning away from him. As much as it pained her to do so, she couldn't deal with any more talk. Not now.

Stepping away, she wondered if there was anything more painful than a breaking heart.

☙

The next morning, Josiah walked the streets toward the wharf. Salty comments and raucous laughter seeped through the air from the town's saloon. Those sounds ultimately gave way to carpenters' tools, scrubbing, and fragmented conversations as men worked on the ships in dock. Strange-looking birds called from a clear blue sky. Josiah barely noticed. His thoughts grew darker with every step.

He hadn't expected Adelaide to be so unfeeling about the news of his child. She was softhearted and kind—or so he thought. Of course, he had been wrong before. But that was another woman, another time.

Was it so terrible for Adelaide to think of watching over his child? Did she despise him that much? A thought struck him. Maybe she didn't like children. Surely that would not be the case. He had seen her with the children at church, and she seemed delighted to spend time with them. No, that couldn't be it.

His boots shuffled against the dirt road, kicking up dust behind him. A cloud of despair seemed to follow him to the dock. He wasn't sure if he felt discouraged or angry. After all, why wouldn't she care for his child? If Adelaide could not love his child, he certainly could not love Adelaide! Trouble was, he already did love her. Would she take his love and cast it aside the way Catherine had?

He shook the thought from his head. Well, he would not let her go traipsing halfway across the globe in just any old ship, whether she liked it or not. She was his wife, and he aimed to see her safely home. He made the decision then and there to go with her as far as Bayview. Her headstrong ways would get her into trouble one day but not as long as he could help it.

Josiah made his way from ship to ship, asking where each one was bound, losing all hope of getting Adelaide home until he came upon the next to the last one. He found the *Wallace* was headed for Panama City. He talked to the captain and, through the course of the conversation, found they had a cabin that would house one guest, and Josiah could bunk out with the crew. Not ideal, but at least they could get as far as Panama City. They would have to book passage on the railroad in hopes to catch a clipper in the port of Colon on the Caribbean side. Josiah discussed the trip with the captain, and they agreed upon an appropriate price. Josiah also agreed to help with any whaling endeavors.

Relieved to have that matter taken care of, Josiah decided his next step would be to talk to his first mate about taking over the *Courage* in his absence. Though at first Josiah had refused to see it, Adam Bowman had proven himself a worthy seaman time and again. Josiah had no doubt the man could handle the ship. Granting Adam the captain's position would increase his pay substantially and possibly give him the savings he needed to go home and ask for Esther's hand in marriage. Josiah felt a twinge of envy. If only Adelaide cared about him the same way.

He stooped to pick up a pebble and threw it across the beach—something he did as a child when he was angry. Funny he would think of that now. Somehow, rubbing the smooth stone and throwing it made him feel better. He wasn't sure why. Maybe he liked having control over something. Even if it was only a pebble. He certainly didn't feel in control of anything else in his life. He'd made a mess of things, and he knew it.

The Lord would help him through, but Josiah knew his choices brought consequences. He would pray for guidance in dealing with them.

He turned his thoughts back toward Adam. If Adam agreed to the change, Josiah would send the necessary message to the owners of the ship and settle up the money later. Josiah would sell what oil he could in port and give Adam the instructions for his trip to the Sandwich Islands.

He breathed a sigh of relief to have their trip scheduled. Most likely, Adelaide would be upset once she learned he would be traveling with her. Even the fiercest of whales were easier to tackle than her stubborn ways.

Seemed like she could be a little more understanding about things. He replayed the events of the past several months in his mind. Her life had changed dramatically since he entered it. He couldn't deny that. But then again, he hadn't forced her to marry him. She did so of her own accord. She wanted to sail. He gave her that chance. Did that make him so bad?

How absurd to try and fool himself. He knew his selfishness had brought on the current dilemma. His mind had told him he needed a cook, and Adelaide seemed the perfect solution. He hadn't stopped to consider it was really his heart dictating the marriage idea.

What did it matter how or where the idea germinated? Josiah knew that he loved Adelaide and readily admitted her help as cook on the ship had proved invaluable.

Now with the problem of his waning strength, the idea of leaving the whaling profession seemed a very real possibility. He knew for sure he would lose Adelaide if he stripped her of the one thing she wanted most—to sail the seas. He had ruined her dreams and his own as well.

No point in rethinking it. Maybe wrong choices had brought him to this place, but with the Lord's help, Josiah could make right choices for their future. He didn't know how he could fix things with Adelaide or if they could have a future together; he knew only that he would do whatever it took to make a life with her.

With nothing settled, yet a lighter heart, he walked toward the cottage. But not before throwing one more pebble.

~

Josiah spent the next day helping his crew make some minor repairs to the ship. They also gave the deck a good scrubbing to prepare for sailing.

Adam was more than willing to take charge of the *Courage*. He all but puffed up like a rooster when Josiah presented the idea. At least that matter was settled. With the post sent informing the owners of the change, Josiah could rest a bit easier.

By early evening, Josiah started back toward the cottage to discuss Adelaide's departure. She was already in bed when he had gotten home the night before. With no opportunity to advise her of his news, he needed to get the information to her so she could pack. Would she look forward to leaving for more reasons than just seeing her ma?

He couldn't think about it. Too many problems cluttered his mind. The matter of his child surfaced. His daughter. Hard to imagine himself as a pa. With his own pa gone on a whaling ship for months at a time, Josiah had little example of what a pa should be. If he continued on the *Courage*, he would be the same kind of pa for his child. A pa who was never around. Was that what he wanted?

What was he thinking? He could hardly change his whole career for this child he didn't know. After all, what else would he do? Whaling had been his life up to now. Much as it frightened him to admit it, he couldn't deny his weakness since the fever. He feared his whaling days were changing, but did he possess skills for any other profession? He couldn't imagine what it would be if he did. His head hurt from thinking.

Before his thoughts could travel further, he arrived at the cottage. He pushed through the doors and found Adelaide sitting on the sofa. She looked up from her sewing.

"Do you have a moment to talk?"

She nodded and laid the cloth in a nearby basket, carefully winding the thread and tucking the needle into the material. Once finished, with her hands folded in her lap, she turned her full attention to him.

"Hear me out before you say anything."

Though her expression revealed her curiosity, she merely nodded.

"I have found a ship on which you can sail to get home."

He noticed the way her eyes lit up when he mentioned going home. Had she hated life on the sea after all? Or was it life with him she despised?

"The thing is. . ." He measured his words carefully. "I'm going with you."

"You can't go with me," she protested.

He held up the palm of his hand. "Before you say anything else, let me tell you I'm going only as far as Bayview to pick up my daughter." Saying those words sounded foreign to his ears, as if someone else were saying them.

"I see."

What flashed across her face: disappointment, sorrow? Why? Because he was going along? "Adam will take over the *Courage.*"

A slight smile played on her lips. "That's nice for Adam."

"I thought it might help out his plans with Esther."

Adelaide almost seemed to soften. Josiah wanted to run to her, pull her into his arms, and tell her he loved her. How could he bear her going on to Yorksville? He couldn't lose her. He just couldn't. Neither could he ignore his own flesh and blood. Would Adelaide make him choose?

"Will you be able to meet up with the *Courage* later?"

Josiah nodded. "I expect so. I'll worry about that after I see what's ahead for me." Their gazes held as if they both considered their futures might lead them in different directions.

"How far will it take us?"

"Panama City. From there we will board the railroad and take it to the port of Colon on the Caribbean side. At that point, we'll catch a clipper and head for home."

She nodded.

"One other thing. I thought you might like to know the captain's wife, Elizabeth, and their five-year-old daughter, Emma, are traveling with him." He knew the idea of female companionship would please her.

"Wonderful!" She clasped her hands together, but then as though she'd thought better of it, she put on a serious face.

He stared at her. When she glanced up at him, he didn't turn away. "Once you leave for Yorksville, I will miss you, Adelaide." He didn't like revealing his heart to her, but the words were spoken before he could stop them. Josiah wanted to ask her not to go, fearing he would never see her again.

She looked as though she were about to say something then thought better of it. "What will Adam do for a cook?"

He shrugged. "One of the crewmen. That's how other ships do it anyway. Just whoever happens along, they pick to be cook. That's why I wanted you. I never liked running a ship that way. Meals are important to the crew.

They work better when they eat well."

She nodded. "When do we sail?"

"Tomorrow. It will still be a long trip home but quicker than the *Courage* could have taken you." Josiah saw the worry on her face. "You'll make it in time, Adelaide. I'll be praying."

"Thank you."

He saw a tear trickle down her cheek. He wanted to go to her but feared her reaction. "I guess I'll leave you to your sewing. Just wanted you to know the arrangements had been made."

Adelaide bent over to pick up the material once again. "I appreciate your efforts, Josiah."

He tipped his head toward her then walked out of the cottage.

With skilled fingers, Adelaide poked the needle through the material, her thoughts clearly not on sewing. She stabbed her finger. "Oh, why do I always do that?" Blood squeezed through the tip of her index finger. Adelaide grabbed a scrap of cloth and held it on the small wound.

So Josiah would be sailing with her. Though she wanted time alone to think, she had to admit she welcomed his presence on a strange ship. Dangers lurked on such vessels, especially for women. The thought of his accompanying her calmed her somewhat.

Life was full of changes. Certainly, she had seen many changes in the past four months. Marriage. Moving from land to sea. Now Ma was sick. The very idea of all of it overwhelmed her.

Adelaide checked her finger. The bleeding had stopped. She folded the soiled cloth and tucked it in the basket to dispose of later. How could she sit still? Sunshine burst through the windows, and she decided she'd sit out in the yard, allowing the sea to calm her frazzled nerves. With all she had to do, though, she thought it best to pack first then go outside.

She didn't have much to gather. She had learned quickly the value of packing light. Living on a ship, space was at a premium.

With the packing completed, Adelaide walked outside with a cup of tea. She settled into her chair and tried to shut out the thoughts racing across her mind.

In spite of her anxiety, she could hardly wait to see Ma and Esther again. A shadow of fear lurked in her thoughts. "God, please let me make it in time."

"Good day, Mrs. Buchanan."

Adelaide turned to see Adam standing there. "Hello, Adam. Please join me." She pointed to a nearby chair.

"Thank you." He grabbed the chair and pulled it over near her.

"I understand you've accepted a new position?"

A broad grin lined his face. "Yes, indeed. I sure appreciate Captain giving me this opportunity."

"He has utmost confidence in you," she assured him.

Adam cracked his knuckles. "I hope I don't let him down."

"You won't. You're good at what you do, and the men respect you. That's half the battle."

He nodded. "Sorry to hear about your ma."

"Thank you. I'm praying she'll get better and that I make it home to see her before. . ." She couldn't finish.

"I'll be praying, too." A catamaran drifted by in the distance. "I hope to see Esther when I get back."

Adelaide eyed him carefully. Something in his manner told her he had more to say.

He let the comment hover in the air. "Do you think she'll wait on me?" It took a full minute before he looked at her, as if her expression might tell him what he didn't want to know.

Adelaide smiled. "Well, I can't speak for Esther, but I know she cares a lot for you, Adam."

He let out a sigh as if he had been holding his breath.

Adelaide laughed. "You worry too much."

He took off his hat and smoothed his hair. "I guess I do." The sea glistened before them; large birds called from thick, leafy trees. "When you go home, maybe you could let her know how I feel?"

"I would be happy to let her know."

He slapped his hands on his trousers. "I appreciate it, Addie—I mean, Mrs. Buchanan." He stood.

Adelaide had to hide a chuckle. Obviously, Adam had come merely to make sure she delivered his message. Esther was quite fortunate to have someone love her that way. How Adelaide longed for the same feelings from Josiah.

"You have a safe journey home. I hope to see you in about six to eight months."

"Be safe, Adam. We'll see you then." Watching him leave, Adelaide wondered what her life would be like when next she saw Adam Bowman.

Chapter 17

Six weeks into her trip, Adelaide grew more impatient to get to her ma with every passing day. They'd caught a couple of whales on the way, keeping Josiah busy with the crew. Since Adelaide roomed in the guest cabin and Josiah bunked with the sailors, she spent most of her time with Elizabeth McCord, the captain's wife.

Adelaide stretched on the chair in her cabin. She liked not having to prepare all the meals, though she did miss the *Courage*'s crew. She prayed for them daily. She also missed Josiah. Yet she knew she couldn't go back to him as a cook and pretend wife. As much as she wanted to be near him, she couldn't go on pretending. She loved him, plain and simple. It hurt too much to pretend otherwise. If Josiah declared his love to her, Adelaide would embrace his child with open arms. But to offer her life to him and his child purely as a hired hand, she couldn't bear it.

Adelaide refocused on the page of the book she held in her hands. How many times she had read the same words, she didn't know. She decided to give up and snapped the book shut. A knock sounded at the door. Smoothing her hair, Adelaide walked over to answer it. Elizabeth stood in the doorway. Five-year-old Emma stood bedside her mother, clutching the tattered doll known as Mrs. Plum firmly in her arms.

"Well, good morning," Adelaide said with a smile. "Do come in."

"I hope we're not disturbing you," Elizabeth said, ushering Emma in ahead of her.

"Not at all. You know I look forward to our visits." Once they stepped through the entrance, Adelaide closed the door behind them.

Elizabeth sat in the extra chair her husband had placed in the cramped quarters so his wife and Adelaide could visit. With Adelaide's permission, Emma sat on the edge of the bed with Mrs. Plum. Elizabeth untied her bonnet and pulled it off. She plucked a handkerchief from her dress pocket and wiped the perspiration from her face. "It is so hot on deck today. Not much better down here."

"But at least we can cool off with water from the basin," Adelaide said, pointing toward the pitcher and bowl on the dresser.

Elizabeth nodded.

Pulling open her trunk, Adelaide lifted out a couple of children's books she had purchased on the island. Knowing the McCords had a child, she decided it would be nice to have the books on hand. Adelaide extended them to Emma and was delighted when the child's face perked up at the sight of them. Emma carefully placed Mrs. Plum beside her on the bed and reached for the books. "Thank you, Mrs. Buchanan." Hearing Josiah's name linked to hers made it hard to swallow.

"You're welcome." Adelaide sat down in her chair across from Elizabeth. "You all right?"

Nothing got past Elizabeth. In their six weeks of traveling together, there wasn't much they hadn't learned about one another. Their friendship had blossomed from the start.

"I'm fine."

"You know you can't fool me, Adelaide Buchanan."

Adelaide tossed her a weak smile.

"You don't see him much on this ship, do you?" Elizabeth said the words in such a comforting way, Adelaide wanted to cry.

Instead, she shook her head and swallowed hard to push away the knot in her throat.

Elizabeth reached out and patted Adelaide's arm. "Why don't you tell him how you feel?"

Adelaide sat staring at her lap. "I can't."

"Tell me why."

Elizabeth had a no-nonsense approach to life. She didn't allow her emotions to get all jumbled up with her good sense. Adelaide wished she could do that, but she couldn't separate the two. "You know why."

"I know that *you* say Josiah's still in love with his first wife, Catherine, but I'm not convinced."

Adelaide wiped her nose on a handkerchief and looked up with surprise.

Elizabeth shrugged. "Well, I'm not. I watched him as you came aboard ship, each going to your own rooms, the sadness in his eyes. I would never have guessed—"

"It's all part of the pretense."

"Adelaide, what I saw wasn't pretense. I could see love in his eyes. And fear."

Adelaide tried to understand what Elizabeth meant by that.

"At the time, I thought he feared being away from you, letting you out of his sight. Now I think he fears losing you forever."

"If only that were true."

"It is true. Why can't you believe me?" Elizabeth pulled a wrapped biscuit from her second dress pocket. "Want some, Emma?"

The child nodded her head, causing her golden curls to dance upon her shoulders. Elizabeth walked over, handed Emma part of the biscuit, then sat back down. "Adelaide?" she asked, extending a portion of the biscuit.

"No thank you."

Elizabeth shrugged and bit into her half. "You know," she said between bites, "I live with a ship full of men, and I think I know a little about the male species."

Adelaide chuckled in spite of herself. Though Elizabeth was ten years older, Adelaide loved the woman dearly. The men respected her, and Elizabeth treated them as if each one were her brother.

"I've heard more love stories than I can count, and I can tell you if a man's in love a mile away." She waved her biscuit for emphasis, dropping a crumb or two in the process. "It's written all over his face." She took another bite and chewed heartily. "That's the look I saw on Josiah."

How the words warmed Adelaide's heart. She wanted desperately to cling to them. They offered her the hope for which her heart longed.

"Write him a letter."

Adelaide bit her lip. "I don't know if I can." She paused a moment. "Besides, he's said nothing of coming to get me. We've made no arrangements to meet." Her voice began to rise in pitch with each word. "Once he gets to Bayview, I have no idea if I'll ever see him again."

Elizabeth grinned. "You'll see him."

Adelaide blew out a sigh. "I hope you're right, Elizabeth. Still, I will go only if he wants me for a true wife. I can no longer bear to serve as merely a helper."

Elizabeth laughed and shook her head. "Anyone ever tell you you're stubborn?"

"Too many to count."

"Well, you can add my name to the list."

Adelaide smiled and sent up a prayer of thanks for her friend, who managed to lighten many a dreary day.

⌒

The days were long, and the nights were longer. Josiah wondered how much more loneliness he could endure. After Catherine had left him, his days had seemed hollow and empty. Yet those days paled in comparison to what he experienced now. Without an appetite, he forced himself to eat enough to get by. His stomach churned, and his heart hurt in a way he couldn't put into words. He stood at the railing and stared out to sea.

He made only enough contact with Adelaide to keep the rest of the crew away from her. They barely talked, neither knowing what to say. He didn't like the idea of a future without Adelaide. He wanted to let her know, but pride stopped him. She didn't love him. The fact that she couldn't bear the thought of raising his child proved that.

Nothing made sense to him anymore. He'd go pick up his daughter in Bayview and decide what to do from there. But first he had to think about obtaining passage on the railroad once they arrived in Panama City. Another two weeks should most likely get them there. A little more time left to decide what he would do. How could he win her heart?

"Hello, Josiah."

He turned around and saw Adelaide standing a few feet from him. His heart beat like a blackfish thumping in his chest. "How are you, Adelaide?"

"I'm fine. And you?"

"Good."

She walked up beside him and leaned on the rail with him. "It never ceases to take my breath away."

He stared at her. "Me neither."

She looked at him. He kept his gaze fixed on her without a single blink. Could she tell he wanted to hold her next to him and never let her go, to feel the warmth of her lips pressed hard against his? She turned away. He sighed and turned back to the sea. "Should get there in a couple of weeks."

Adelaide said nothing. Josiah figured she just wanted to get the whole thing over. What a mess he had made of everything. She probably couldn't get home fast enough, for more reasons than just seeing her ma. "I'll get you there quick as I can, Adelaide."

She placed a hand on his arm. "I know, Josiah, and I'm so very thankful for your help."

The brush of her hand sent currents through him like the touch of an electric eel. Torture. That's what she was putting him through, pure torture. Dare he ask her what was to become of them in the days ahead? The mere thought of approaching the subject turned his gut to the consistency of melting whale blubber. He couldn't ask her. Not yet. He couldn't bear to hear what was sure to come. But soon. He'd ask her soon, for he had to know.

∽

Adelaide would miss Elizabeth and Emma once they docked. She could hardly believe they'd be in Panama City in less than twenty-four hours. She prayed she would reach her ma in time.

"Adelaide." With Emma tagging along behind, Elizabeth walked up to Adelaide on the deck. Mrs. Plum dangled at Emma's side. A chicken clucked across the deck, catching the girl's attention.

"Can I play with Henny, Mama?"

"Stay where I can see you, Emma. And don't get in the way of the workers."

"Yes Mama." Mrs. Plum's cloth body bobbed against Emma's legs as she skipped off toward the strutting chicken.

Elizabeth turned to Adelaide. "Are you all packed?"

"Yes. Wasn't much to do, really."

Elizabeth nodded, her mood pensive.

"You all right?"

Elizabeth smiled weakly. She waited. Sounds of the sea, the hum of men shuffling about the ship, and Emma muttering to Henny filled the air. "I'll miss you terribly," Elizabeth finally managed. Tears filled her eyes.

"Oh!" Adelaide reached over and wrapped her friend in an immense embrace. "I will miss you, too, Elizabeth. You have been such a wonderful friend!" They hugged a moment more then pulled apart.

"Aren't we behaving like silly women?" Elizabeth asked, dabbing at her eyes with a handkerchief.

Adelaide laughed, wiping at her own wet cheeks.

"Whoa there, you two. I'll have none of that on my ship." Peter McCord took broad steps toward them. Josiah walked along beside him. Adelaide's pulse quickened.

Shaggy gray eyebrows lifted as Peter McCord smiled tenderly toward his wife. There was something in that smile that warmed Adelaide's heart. Peter's love for Elizabeth was written all over his face. Was that what Elizabeth was talking about? Is that what she had seen in Josiah?

Adelaide dared a glance at Josiah. His eyes were studying her. She felt herself blush.

Elizabeth must have recognized the awkward moment, for she was the first to speak. "I was just telling Adelaide how much I would miss her."

Adelaide looked up to see Josiah still staring at her. This time he nodded his head in agreement. Would he miss her, too? Oh, she had to quit torturing herself.

Straightening the cuff of her sleeve, she looked at Elizabeth, though she could still feel Josiah's gaze upon her. She felt restless beneath his stare.

"Are you packed?" Josiah's voice held such tenderness, Adelaide couldn't help but look at him.

She nodded. "Are you?"

His gaze fixed on her, he nodded. For a moment, it felt as though they were the only two people on the ship. She could almost imagine Josiah reaching out to her, pulling her to him, ever so gently lifting off her bonnet and kissing her right temple, his soft lips eventually making their way to her mouth, claiming it tenderly yet firmly with his own.

A burning seared through her. She actually touched her cheeks, feeling the warmth in them. Whatever was she thinking? She mentally shook herself. Josiah smiled at her as if he knew exactly where her thoughts had taken her.

Someone had said something, but Adelaide missed it. When her eyes refocused, the entire little group was looking at her. "I'm sorry?" she asked, looking at Elizabeth.

Elizabeth threw her a knowing grin. "Actually, Peter was just saying he thought the weather would hold out for your arrival in Panama City." Elizabeth looked as though she were hiding a giggle behind her hand.

Adelaide couldn't leave the group fast enough. "Well, I really need to finish a few things in my room. If you'll excuse me." Before anyone could respond, she turned and walked across the deck, feeling sure they were still watching her.

∞

In no time at all, Adelaide and Josiah stood in the hot afternoon sun, saying their good-byes to the McCords. Among tears and promises to keep in touch, the women finally separated. The McCords boarded the ship, and Josiah led Adelaide to a carriage that would take them to the train station.

Adelaide settled into her seat and tried not to think about the friend she had left behind. She took a deep breath. The stifling air made it hard to breathe. Grabbing her container of water, she took a drink. The carriage ride proved bumpy and a bit unpleasant as they jostled their way to the station. Adelaide didn't feel much like talking, and Josiah seemed to sense it. They said very little during the ride.

Once they arrived, Adelaide watched the scores of people milling around the station. The place buzzed with activity. Josiah purchased their tickets, and he and Adelaide stepped across the wooden platform to board the train.

"You hungry?"

"I think I'm too tired to eat."

"We'll need to get something soon, though. Why don't you try and get some rest? We can eat later."

Adelaide lifted a tired smile. She appreciated how he took care of her, especially now, yet she couldn't help feeling he was desperate to get her to watch his child. Who else could he turn to for fulfilling that responsibility while he ran a ship? She almost bolted straight up in her chair. Did he expect her to stay behind on land and watch his daughter while he traveled the seas? The very idea made her blood boil.

No doubt about it, he was being nice to her so she would watch his child while he continued to go whaling. She didn't like this at all.

When she looked over at Josiah, his gaze caught hers, and he smiled. Oh, she could see beneath his innocent exterior. She forced herself to turn away and watch the scenery that flew by the window.

She could hardly wait to get home.

Chapter 18

The railroad trip passed in a blur. Though she'd never ridden a train before, Adelaide had enjoyed the sights and the experience.

She could hardly believe she and Josiah were now sailing the Caribbean. They had boarded a clipper in Colon, South America. Their next destination was the waters of the Atlantic and home.

The speed of the clipper amazed Adelaide. The *Courage* could not compare to it. She wondered what man would come up with in the future for travel. Certainly improvements were being made daily.

Though thrown together in a cabin, Josiah and Adelaide spent little time there. She avoided him whenever possible. She didn't need him around to confuse her further. He seemed to know she needed her space and gave it to her. How could she think when he stood close to her or when she looked into the blue eyes that made her knees buckle? Sometimes the very way he spoke her name took her breath away.

No, she needed space. Lots of it. The sooner he got off at Bayview, the better. Still, the very idea punctured her heart with pain.

⌒

The days melted one on top of the other. Josiah could hardly believe they were pulling into the Bayview port. He watched as the ship clumsily made its way to the deep harbor. After all these weeks, he was no closer to changing Adelaide's mind than from the start. Their interaction had been minimal since they left the island. Formal and distant, at best.

Adelaide walked up behind him. "You've got all your things?"

He turned to her and nodded. Neither had said anything about where they would go from here. Every time he had tried to approach the subject, she cut him off, telling him she needed time to think. He wondered if he'd ever see her again.

"I hope you find your daughter," Adelaide said almost in a whisper.

The wind caused a wisp of a curl to dance upon her cheek. Before he caught himself, Josiah reached over and tucked it gently behind her bonnet. Their eyes locked. "Look, Adelaide, I know our situation isn't the best—"

"Please, Josiah. Don't." Tears filled her eyes. "We both need some time."

He asked the question to which he feared the answer. "When will I hear from you?" A sadness such as he had never known gripped his heart like a heavy clamp. So many words left unsaid. They clogged his throat, trying to break free, but he knew it wouldn't make a difference. Not now. He swallowed them.

Adelaide stared at him. "I don't know." A tear rolled down her cheek.

What held her back? Had he been wrong about her love for him, or was she being stubborn? The idea that she would allow her stubbornness to keep them apart made him angry, making it easier to let her go. If her love didn't go any deeper than that, she would never be happy raising his child or living out her days with him. Somehow knowing that gave him the strength to release her.

"I hope you find what you want, Adelaide." Without another word, Josiah picked up his trunk, turned, and walked away.

⌒

Scenes of Josiah's departure haunted Adelaide's mind time after time. Today, though, she refused to think about it. For this day would bring her joy or great sorrow. She would either see her ma or learn of her death.

Standing on the deck, Adelaide anxiously awaited the opportunity to step onto Yorksville's shores. Through the light fog, she could just make out Markle's General Store in the distance. July brought summer into full bloom, and despite her aching heart, Adelaide could hardly wait for the ship to dock.

It seemed an eternity, but she finally stepped onto the land, and her heart swelled with thankfulness and a prayer that her ma was still alive. She wanted to pop in and see the Markles but felt she had to get straight home. She didn't want to hear bad news, if there was any, from anyone but family. A kind couple offered her a ride in their carriage, and she was home in no time. At the edge of their property, Adelaide gathered her things then stood and faced the house. She took a deep breath and made her way toward the front door. Before she could get there, a scream sounded behind her.

"Addie!" Esther came running from the henhouse as fast as her long skirts would allow.

Adelaide dropped her trunk and ran to her sister. They embraced and cried tears of joy. When the excitement died down, Adelaide pulled away, looked her sister square in the face, and asked the question that had plagued her for months. She pulled in a ragged breath. "Ma?"

Esther turned toward the house. Adelaide's eyes followed until they stopped at a form standing just outside the front door. Adelaide's blurry eyes focused. "Ma!" she cried, running to her. When she reached Ma, Adelaide pulled her into a firm hug, never wanting to let go. She was alarmed at the frailty of her ma's body beneath her arms, but Adelaide would not let that steal her joy for now. She'd made it home to her family, and that's what mattered.

She looked at her ma's tired eyes and quickly escorted her toward the door. "We have much to catch up on, Ma. Let's get you inside for a long visit."

Ma wiped the tears from her face and nodded. A smiling Esther walked beside them.

Once inside the house, Esther set to making tea while Adelaide and Ma settled into chairs in the living room. Ma told of her near-death experience and how God had brought her through. Though she struggled with weakness, she felt her strength returning day by day, and they all rejoiced in her healing.

Adelaide shared of her life on the seas. Esther sat across from them, starry-eyed as always, while Ma listened with interest. Adelaide felt uncomfortable under Ma's gaze. Ma knew her all too well, and Adelaide had no doubts Ma could read much into what wasn't being said.

To quickly change the subject, Adelaide told Esther of Adam's feelings for her. "Oh, I almost forgot!" Adelaide shot up from her chair and ran over to her trunk. She searched through her things and pulled out a dainty package. Quickly, she closed the lid of the trunk and made her way to Esther. "He asked me to give this to you."

With wide eyes, Esther looked at Adelaide, then the package, then at Adelaide once again.

Adelaide shoved it toward her. "Well, are you going to take it, or do I have to stand here all day?"

Esther smiled and reached for it, quickly opening the package. Inside she found a dainty gold necklace with a small turquoise stone dangling from it. Esther gasped and, with shaking fingers, pulled the necklace from its case. Adelaide helped her put it on.

"Well, that pretty much settles the matter," Ma said in her practical way. "She's had plenty of men calling, but Esther's been waiting for Adam." Ma cradled a cup of tea in her hands and shook her head.

"Well, I'd say he has plans for the two of you if you'll have him," Adelaide assured her.

"I suppose I'm losing another daughter to the sea," Ma said but quickly gave her blessing with a smile.

"There's never been anyone else for me from the day I first set eyes on him."

Another jab of pain struck Adelaide's heart. Oh, to have that kind of love for another and to be loved in return.

"And what of Josiah, Adelaide?" Though she knew Ma would ask the question sooner or later, Adelaide had hoped they could discuss it later.

"It's much too long a story, Ma. Can we talk about it later, after I've had some rest?" Adelaide didn't miss the eye contact between Ma and Esther.

"Certainly, dear. Why don't you go take a nap, and we'll have dinner prepared by the time you wake up."

"Oh, I couldn't have you do that—"

"You can and you will. Ma has spoken," Esther said with a laugh. She lifted one end of Adelaide's trunk and pulled it toward the bedroom.

Adelaide shrugged toward her ma and followed Esther.

Though she couldn't imagine how long she'd been in bed, Adelaide had to admit the nap felt good. She hadn't realized how exhausted she was from the trip. The wooden slats beneath her creaked when she stretched her body and let out a yawn. Reluctantly, she pulled herself from the comfortable bed and straightened herself. A quick glance in the looking glass told her more than she wanted to know. With a tuck here and there in her hairpins, she made herself presentable and went into the kitchen to help with dinner preparations.

"We're almost ready to eat," Ma told her. Adelaide felt ashamed of herself for sleeping while they did all the work. Ma must have read her mind.

"Now, don't you give it a thought, Adelaide. You had a long trip, and we're thrilled to have you home. I'll put you to work soon enough." Ma smiled.

They had a pleasant dinner and a nice visit. Adelaide shared more stories of her adventures, even telling them about Ebenezer Fallon. Ma shook her head and clicked her tongue, adding something about the ways of men.

Esther headed to a friend's house where several of the church ladies were gathering to work on a quilt, leaving Adelaide and Ma behind to do some serious talking.

They finally settled into chairs out in the front yard. The hot air did little to comfort them, but they hoped a slight breeze might stir among the trees.

Not being one to mince words, Ma came right out with it. "You want to tell me what's going on with you and Josiah?" Ma wiped the perspiration from her neck with a handkerchief.

Adelaide sighed before telling the story of her life for the past eight months. Of course, she left out the part of their deceit. She didn't want Ma to know her true reason for marrying Josiah. When she finished, Ma looked at her and said nothing. She could see more than Adelaide intended. Feeling a smidgen uncomfortable, Adelaide looked away and pretended to be interested in a bird that flew by. Ma had a way of knowing when her daughters didn't tell the entire truth, and Adelaide just didn't feel like explaining at present.

"When do you plan to return to him?"

Sometimes Adelaide wished Ma weren't so direct. Most likely, she wouldn't appreciate the answer anyway. "I don't know."

Ma swatted at a bug that flew close to her face. Adelaide wondered if Ma took her present frustration out on the insect. "What's holding you back, Adelaide?"

"It's complicated, Ma."

She raised her eyebrows. "Too complicated for me to understand, is that what you mean?"

No response.

"Does he hurt you?"

Adelaide's head shot up. "Of course not! He's good to me. Well, Josiah's about the best—" She stopped midsentence when she realized Ma had baited her with the question, and Adelaide had fallen for it, rising to Josiah's defense in a heartbeat.

Ma smiled.

Mad at herself for falling prey to Ma's strategy, Adelaide kicked a stone from the ground under her feet. "I'm not ready for a child, Ma."

Ma nodded her head and looked in the distance. "Oh, I see. I didn't realize your wedding vows contained conditions. I must have missed that." She wiped her face again.

Adelaide blew out a frustrated sigh.

Ma turned to Adelaide once more. "Look, Adelaide, I can't tell you what to do. You're a grown woman with a life of your own. You need to search your heart and pray. Pray more than you've ever prayed in your life, because your future is at stake here. How you handle this situation will not only affect your life, but Josiah's and his daughter's as well. But hear me on this, Adelaide. You must return to him sometime. He is your husband."

Without looking up, Adelaide nodded.

"Enough of that," Ma said, brushing her hands together as if wiping the conversation from them. "Let's go pick out a chicken for tomorrow's dinner."

Killing and preparing a chicken for dinner had always been one of Adelaide's least favorite jobs, though after being on the whaling ship, she knew she had developed a stomach of cast iron. Very little made her squeamish these days.

When they entered the barn, chickens clucked and scattered about. From a bowl, Ma threw some feed on the ground, and the chickens greedily pecked their way through the tiny bits of food. Once the bowl was empty, Ma put it on a shelf, brushed her hands on the front of her dress, and pointed toward a fat chicken to her right. "I'm thinking tomorrow night's Mabel's night."

Adelaide groaned. "Ma, how many times do I have to tell you not to name them? I can't eat them if they have names."

Ma laughed until she saw the serious expression on Adelaide's face. "I'm sorry, honey. It's the way of life out here. You know that."

"I know. I just. . .well. . .don't like it."

"Adelaide, they were born to die. They serve their purpose to help us sustain life. That's the life to which they were called."

Adelaide didn't want to think. Seemed like every conversation weighed her down. She loved Ma, but she wanted to go off by herself.

"Why don't you hitch up the team and go into town for some sugar and flour? We're just about out. Besides, the Markles can hardly wait to see you."

The thought made her feel better. A journey to town might be just the thing she needed right now. She definitely wanted to visit with the Markles anyway.

Adelaide hitched the horses to the buckboard and arrived in town fairly quickly. She stepped through the doors of Markle's General Store. The bell jangled overhead, but Adelaide's footsteps carried her into an empty room. Her boots seemed to echo on the wooden floor. Adelaide glanced through the bolts of material and other goods on the shelves. She couldn't help noticing that things were not quite as neat and tidy as before. The Markles must keep too busy.

Upon hearing a stirring behind the counter, Adelaide turned around to see Mrs. Markle jotting something in the logbook.

"Good day, Mrs. Markle."

Mrs. Markle continued writing without lifting her head. "Oh, sorry, I didn't see anyone in here."

Feeling a bit giddy with the surprise, Adelaide quietly edged her way through the room while the storekeeper finished writing.

With the last stroke of the pen, Ida Markle laid it down and looked up. She gasped, jumped from her chair, and, with outstretched arms, made her way to Adelaide. "Oh, dear, dear Adelaide!" She pulled her into a tight hug, almost cutting off Adelaide's air supply. "How we've missed you!"

Adelaide struggled to catch her breath. "I've missed you, too," she finally managed in between coughs.

"Caleb, you've got to come out here and see who's meandering around our store."

Caleb poked his head around the corner. "Why, Adelaide Sanborn!" he crowed with a huge grin.

Ida Markle laughed. "It's Buchanan now, Caleb, did you forget?"

"Oh, I did, at that."

"How could you forget our girl running off and getting herself hitched like that?" The old woman looked around. "Where's the grand sea captain?"

An aching pain rolled through Adelaide. "He couldn't come. I came back to check on Ma."

"Oh, of course," Mrs. Markle said with a wave of her hand. She looked at Caleb. "Can we tell her?"

He nodded.

"It's an act of God that you are here, child. We've been talking about this place. We're not able to keep it up anymore. Now, we know you love the sea, and most likely, that's where you'll stay, but you walking in like a miracle—well, we just have to tell you. If you and Josiah should decide to settle on land, we'd like you to take over running the store. Caleb and me, well, we'd just live upstairs like we do now, but you could live in the downstairs apartment and the majority of ownership in the store would belong to you. We'd maintain only enough ownership to get us by. We'd always planned to give the store to you anyway. You've been like a daughter to us."

Adelaide stared at them, speechless.

"Now, we don't want you feeling obligated. Like we said, we know you love the sea, so it probably won't work out for you. But seeing you walk in today and us just making the decision only yesterday to have someone take over, well, seemed like an answer to prayer."

They looked at her through eager eyes. Adelaide had no idea what to say. "I—I don't know." Her mind raced in all directions. If she didn't go with Josiah, at least she'd have an income, and a mighty fine business at that. She loved working at the store facing the sea. But she knew that life would be without Josiah. The sea owned him.

"I'll have to give it much thought and talk it over with Josiah. I'll let you know. That's the best I can do."

They both smiled. "That's all we ask, dear, that you at least consider it and pray about it."

They chatted a little longer. Other townsfolk made their way into the store and visited with Adelaide. As she finally made her way home, she mulled over their generous offer. In many ways, it seemed the perfect solution. If she knew Josiah loved her, Adelaide could stay on land and raise his child there. Too bad Josiah couldn't give up whaling; the general store would provide a wonderful income and family life for them.

But, of course, that was silly. Everyone knew Josiah would sail the seas as long as he lived.

Chapter 19

Adelaide could hardly believe a week had passed since her arrival at Yorksville. It felt good to be home and see familiar faces. The townsfolk didn't seem to think it unusual she had come back without Josiah. After all, her ma was sick, and Josiah had a ship to run.

After finishing the dinner dishes, Adelaide took a walk around the property. All week, turmoil had churned bitterly in her stomach. Stopping in front of the henhouse, Adelaide thought about her mother's comment, *"They were born to die."* The phrase kept rolling over in her mind time and again.

She paced. Wasn't that true of herself as well? She was born to die to self. As a Christian, her life belonged to Jesus Christ. As she learned from the Lord and grew stronger in her Christian journey, His desires became her own.

So what of her current situation with Josiah? She walked amid clucking and strutting hens. They quickly pattered away as Adelaide moved closer.

"They live to die." No matter how she turned that phrase over in her mind, the truth of it burned in her soul. Josiah was a good man. He treated her well and had accepted Christ as his Savior. Whether he still loved Catherine or not shouldn't matter. Adelaide had agreed to be his wife, knowing full well he had been married before.

Adelaide threw some chicken feed on the ground and watched the chickens cluster toward it. She didn't know how long she stayed there, praying over the matter, thinking, and finally deciding.

With the issue settled in her heart, Adelaide knew what she had to do. She turned and walked out of the henhouse with renewed determination and excitement. Tonight she would talk with Ma and Esther, and tomorrow she would make arrangements to go to Bayview in search of Josiah and his child. She only hoped she could make it before it was too late.

∽

By the time Josiah made it to the orphanage, he had little strength left. He knew he should have gotten a room first, but he couldn't wait a moment longer to see his child. Once inside, he sat on the nearest chair and rested a moment.

"May I help you?" A thin woman with a beak of a nose, small eyes, and a permanent wrinkle between her brows said the words with impatience.

Josiah thought she looked like a bird. Feeling as though he were back in school, he stood and pulled off his cap. "I'm here to pick up my daughter." He took the envelope from his pocket and handed it to her.

She glared at him then pulled out the letter, reading over it briefly. Stuffing it back into the envelope, she looked back at him and eyed him suspiciously. "And just how do I know you're Josiah Buchanan?" Her lips were pulled into a severe line.

Though Josiah understood the reason for her question and appreciated her caution, Bird Woman was getting on his nerves. "I've got the letter, don't I?"

She harrumphed, clearly offended by his comment. The woman lifted her chin, turned, and walked away. Josiah decided he should follow. They entered a small room with a desk and two chairs. Without a window, the room appeared stark and depressing. Over the next hour, Bird Woman grilled him with questions and handed him endless papers to fill out. Finally seeming convinced of his identity, she stood and announced, "I'll take you to her."

"Before we go, I need to let you know that I'll have to make arrangements for a room at a boardinghouse, and I have some other matters to tend to, so I will return tomorrow evening for her. I trust she will be ready?"

The woman reluctantly nodded.

"Um, what's her name?"

She turned a condemning look at him, as though he should be ashamed for not knowing. How could he have known? He hadn't even known he had a child.

"Grace."

The name surprised him. He hadn't thought Catherine capable of choosing such a name. Josiah and the woman made their way to a room full of children preparing to eat dinner. Bird Woman went to the front of the room.

She clapped her hands together in the most annoying way, and the room grew quiet. "I wish to see Grace Buchanan, please."

Josiah's heart pounded hard against his chest. He searched the room for his daughter. Finally, the tiniest of forms with blond braided hair that fell to her waist walked away from the others and made her way toward Bird Woman. Josiah felt his legs go soft. As Grace walked toward him, he couldn't believe what he saw. A shrunken imitation of himself, though her features were softened by femininity. Not a shred of Catherine in her. For some reason, relief washed over him.

With her head lowered, Grace lifted cautious eyes to him as if peering over spectacles. She chewed on her thumbnail while standing a bit behind

Bird Woman's skirt. The woman raised her chin and pulled Grace away from her. "Grace, this is your father, Captain Josiah Buchanan."

The little girl said nothing. Josiah decided he would stay in Bayview for a short while, in an environment with which she was familiar, to give them time to get acquainted. He knew it would take some doing, but somehow he would win Grace's heart, and he would treasure raising her.

With or without Adelaide.

❦

Though tired and spent from her trip to Bayview, Adelaide still had time to make it to the orphanage before nightfall. When she arrived, a lady there told her Josiah had picked up his child, and most likely they had set sail by now.

Exhaustion made her want to cry. But instead, Adelaide merely thanked the woman and made her way out the door. What would she do? Ma had given her some money so she could at least spend the night if she could find a room. Tomorrow she would have to make her way back to Yorksville. Alone.

With heavy steps, she found her way to a boardinghouse where the owner took pity on her and agreed to allow her to spend one night. A heavy heart dictated her dreams that night. Dreams where she found herself very much alone.

The next morning, sunlight peered through the window, making Adelaide feel a little better than the night before. She had given the matter to the Lord, and that's where it would stay. Quickly she got up and dressed. In order to find a stagecoach to return home, she'd have to hurry and make the arrangements. She'd grab a bite to eat first.

Once downstairs, she looked over to see a room full of men dining at the table. As hungry as she was, she didn't feel it proper to sit and eat with them, so she lifted her bag and walked through the door into the sunlight.

Walking only a few steps from the boardinghouse, she heard someone call her name. It almost sounded like Josiah's voice. She turned and looked in all directions. Nothing. Of course, she had imagined it. He seemed to follow her everywhere, even into her dreams.

Adelaide took a few more steps. The sound was clearer now, spoken directly behind her. She turned to see Josiah holding the hand of a beautiful little girl, the image of her father. Adelaide's heart melted.

When Adelaide glanced at Josiah, his questioning eyes held hers. For a moment, both seemed lost in words they couldn't speak. The look in Josiah's eyes warmed her clear through. She loved him. Oh, how she loved him.

Finally, Josiah's tender voice eased through the silence. "Grace, this is my wife, Adelaide. Adelaide, Grace."

"Hello, Grace," Adelaide said, scrunching down in front of the little girl. Grace lifted shy eyes to Adelaide. The little girl offered the faintest of smiles. Adelaide decided that was a good start.

"No question she belongs to you, Josiah." Adelaide chuckled.

He nodded with a grin. His expression grew serious. "We need to talk, Adelaide. Have you eaten breakfast?"

She shook her head.

"We saw you in the boardinghouse. We haven't eaten yet, either."

"You were there? You should eat there."

"No, I'd rather we have a little more privacy."

Together the three of them made their way to the restaurant. Adelaide wondered what the next hour would bring.

∽

Adelaide and Josiah spent most of their meal getting to know Grace. Little by little, the child talked, revealing snippets of her past to them. Already Adelaide could see herself mothering this child, with or without Josiah's love. They could be a family; she knew they could. If Josiah wanted them on the ship—though life would be hard on the sea—they'd somehow survive. Watching Elizabeth and Peter McCord with their daughter, Emma, had shown Adelaide that much.

"Will you be my mama?" Grace asked after she clumsily took a drink of water and wiped her mouth on her arm.

Adelaide stared into Josiah's eyes. Of course, he wanted her to say yes. He needed someone to look after Grace. Instead of the usual resentment, Adelaide had a sense of peace. "Yes, Grace, I will be your mama."

Grace took another bite of her egg, her pudgy legs swinging beneath her.

When Adelaide looked back at Josiah, what she saw on his face surprised her. She thought he would be happy to hear her say yes. Instead, he looked—how—sad? She couldn't put her finger on it, but something was definitely wrong.

Fears assailed her. Did he not even want her around anymore? The rejection caused her more pain than she cared to admit. Just when she thought she had things figured out, when it seemed all the answers were neatly in place, she found herself in a state of confusion once more.

"The beach is only a couple of blocks away. Can we talk there?" Josiah asked.

Adelaide nodded, fearing the worst.

∽

On the beach, Josiah found a couple of chairs for them. Grace immediately set to work building a sand castle while Josiah and Adelaide settled into their chairs. Josiah took off his cap and ran his fingers through his hair. Where would he begin? How could he tell Adelaide he was giving up the *Courage*? That his body would no longer allow him to do the rigorous work he once did. Would she think him an invalid? Why, he didn't even have a job.

Not only would she have to give up her dream of living on the sea, but she would be stuck with a man she didn't love. Further, she'd have a child to raise.

Nausea swelled in his stomach. No matter how he tried to word it in his mind, the truth still spelled misery to his future with Adelaide.

Grace busied herself a few feet away from them. Amazing how well children adapted to new situations. At least that was something for which he was thankful. Adelaide sat motionless in the chair beside him—no doubt waiting for him to spill what was on his mind.

He fingered the cap back and forth in his hands. "I guess you're wondering what I want to say?"

"Yes."

"I don't quite know how to tell you this, Adelaide." He could feel her looking at him. He looked down at his cap, searching for the words. Finally, he turned to her. She looked so vulnerable. So beautiful. Oh, how he did not want to lose her! He cleared his throat and glanced back at his cap. "I know you love the sea, Adelaide. I would never take that away from you willingly."

He lifted his gaze in time to see confusion on her face. "If there was any other way, if I could do anything to make it work—"

Adelaide stretched out her hand and placed it on his arm. "Josiah, what is it?"

He fidgeted in his seat until he mustered the nerve to say the words. "I have to give up whaling." There. He'd said it. Fear would not let him look at her.

"But why? I could help you with Grace on the ship. We can do this."

He shook his head. "That's not it, Adelaide. I should have told you before, but I just couldn't bring myself to do it. Now I have no choice. Remember when I struggled with the tropical fever?"

She nodded.

"I'm afraid the fever has taken its toll on me. I've not been the same since. When it left, it took my strength with it. Truth is, I'm too weak to do what it takes to captain a whaling ship." He swallowed back the pride, hating to admit he wasn't man enough to handle the workload. "I know you must hate me for what I've put you through, and now to take away your dream—"

"Josiah, I don't care about that."

"Well, it's just unthinkable that I would do that to you and—what?" He turned to her.

She smiled. "I said, I don't care about that."

"What do you mean?"

"I mean, I don't care if we can't sail."

Josiah looked at her with shocked disbelief. "But I thought—"

She laughed. "Well, I did, too. But the truth of the matter is that Pa painted a much different picture than the life I found on the whaling ship. While I wouldn't trade the experience for anything and would be happy to continue whaling at your side, I'm equally happy, and more so, to live on land."

He couldn't believe his ears. She wanted to stay with him. More importantly, she actually sounded happy to stay with him. Before he could pull her into his arms, Grace came up to them.

"Look at my whaling ship," she said, pointing toward her rather awkward creation.

"Oh Grace, it's absolutely beautiful." Adelaide reached over and, seeing the child did not back away, gave her a slight hug, to which Grace responded in kind.

"That's a mighty fine ship, Grace," Josiah agreed.

The child beamed at their praise.

"Grace, come here for a moment," Josiah said. She walked over to him. "Would you be terribly disappointed if we don't sail on a ship?"

Grace looked at him, puzzled.

"Adelaide and I, well, we want to find a real home on land with you right beside us. How would you like that?"

Grace smiled broadly, the first time they'd actually seen her pretty white teeth in a full, honest-to-goodness grin. "Can I play a little longer first?"

Josiah and Adelaide laughed. "Yes, indeed, you can," Josiah answered.

Grace skipped over to her creation.

"She's so much like you, Josiah."

He rubbed his chin. "She is, at that. Poor child."

Adelaide laughed. "Actually, I'm rather glad."

Josiah thought Adelaide looked as though she could kick herself for saying that. "I'm glad, too."

"You are?"

"Yes. If she had looked like Catherine, I would have had a daily reminder of my foolishness."

Adelaide looked at him. Josiah turned to her. "I never loved her, Adelaide. I see that now. Whatever I felt for Catherine pales in comparison to what I feel for you." Josiah tenderly covered her hands with his own. "I love you, and I want you to be my wife, in the truest sense of the word." Without a blink, his gaze held her breathless.

"Adelaide Sanborn Buchanan, will you marry me—again?"

Chapter 20

Adelaide wondered if her heart would ever come back to her. It seemed to have taken wings and flown into paradise. "Oh, Josiah." She couldn't utter another word as the tears tumbled from her eyes. "Is that a yes?" he asked with a laugh.

She continued to wipe away her tears and nodded vigorously. Before she could blink, Josiah jumped from his chair and scooped her into his arms.

He held her close, his face burrowed into her neck. His warm breath caused her skin to tingle. Lifting his head, he tenderly kissed her eyes, her nose, and finally her lips. Placing her on her feet, he pulled away slightly and looked at her. His fingers twirled a strand of hair that had escaped her bonnet. "You know, I'd still like to see your hair down sometime. I'll bet it's beautiful."

Adelaide's face burned as though someone held a candle only inches from her.

He smiled and kissed her once more, the emotion of recent days working its way through their kiss.

"I was going to stay in Bayview awhile for Grace to get acclimated to her new life, but she seems to be handling things just fine. I'll make arrangements for us to take the first stage back to Yorksville. I think there's one scheduled tomorrow. Then I'll look around for work."

Adelaide stepped back. "Oh, I almost forgot," she said suddenly, as if waking abruptly from a dream. "The Markles asked if we would consider taking over the general store. Their health is failing. They would retain part ownership, though most of it would go to us. They want to continue living in the upstairs apartment but said we could live downstairs and run the store."

Josiah stared at her wide-eyed. He shook his head. "I can't believe this."

"I hadn't given it much thought till now. I thought we would head back to the ship," she said.

"All my worrying, and God had everything taken care of from the start." He leaned his head back and stared at the sky. With a twist of his wrist, he threw his cap in the air and let out a long whoop. He grabbed Adelaide and twirled her around.

Grace giggled and ran toward them to join in the celebration. Josiah lowered Adelaide and the three of them joined hands and skipped in circles, laughing and praising the Lord together.

∽

Night breezes hovered over the sea, filling the air with a pleasant mist. Josiah finalized the arrangements, and together the little family headed back to the boardinghouse.

Grace skipped alongside Adelaide, holding her hand. "Can I call you Mama?" Grace seemed to have plucked the question from nowhere.

Adelaide turned to her with a start. She looked up to see Josiah staring at her. He threw her a wink. Adelaide turned back to Grace. "You certainly may call me Mama if you would like, dear."

Grace's pudgy hand squeezed Adelaide's. The little girl said nothing, but her walk turned into a happy trot. A nurturing instinct coursed through Adelaide. How she loved this child already!

Once they reached the boardinghouse, they climbed the stairs and stopped in front of Adelaide's room. She assumed they would get her things and move her into Josiah's room. Josiah turned to her. "I have made arrangements for you to stay in your room one more night, Adelaide."

A wave of disappointment swept over her. Did he notice?

"I want to marry you again. Really marry you. When we get back to Yorksville, we will have a proper wedding. This time, you will truly become my wife."

Adelaide's cheeks burned. "Oh, Josiah, you don't need to do that."

He put his fingers to her lips. "I want to do this for you. For us." He lowered his head and placed a tender kiss upon her lips. Raising his opened hand to her, she put her key in his palm. With a tip of his head, he nodded toward her and opened the door, allowing her entrance. She turned and looked at him. Lifting the key, he pressed it into her palm. "I don't trust myself with it," he whispered with a wiggle of his eyebrows.

She laughed. Grace tugged at Adelaide's dress and snuggled next to her side. "Can I stay with you, Mama?"

Adelaide decided she liked the idea of being a mama. She looked at Josiah. If he was disappointed, he didn't show it. Most likely, he was a trifle nervous about dealing with a child, anyway. He nodded to her.

"Yes, of course, Grace, you may stay with me."

Her small face brightened.

Josiah winked. "Well, little family, I guess I'll see you in the morning."

"Good night, Josiah."

"Good night, Papa," Grace said as naturally as if she had known him all her life.

Josiah scrunched down and kissed Grace on the forehead. "Good night."

He stood. "Night, Addie."

Adelaide smiled then closed the door, her heart beating wildly against her chest. She could hardly wait to go to bed and dream of the man she would soon marry—this time in every sense of the word.

⌒

The trip to Yorksville passed by without a hitch. Once Adelaide introduced Grace to her family and they finished dinner, they settled in for a comfortable chat.

"So tell me about you two," Ma said while Esther skirted Grace out the door to check on the chickens.

Adelaide opened her mouth to speak, but Josiah raised his hand. "No, let me, Addie."

She stopped and nodded.

Ma looked at them curiously. For the next fifteen or so minutes, Josiah explained about the pretense of their wedding, the struggles along the way, the note about Grace, and finally where everything had brought them.

When he finished, Ma sat back in her chair and looked at them. "I knew something wasn't right. I just didn't know what." She looked at Adelaide. "I also knew that behind it all was something to do with your love for the sea."

Adelaide nodded, her eyes carefully avoiding Ma's.

Ma sat back up and brushed her hands together. "Well, that's that."

They both looked at her with a start. Adelaide felt sure they had a long talk coming to them.

Ma laughed. "What's to say?" She shrugged. "Everything's all right now, and that's what matters."

Relief rolled over Adelaide. "Thanks, Ma."

"I just want the two of you to be happy."

Adelaide reached for Josiah's hand and looked at him. "We are, Ma. We are." Josiah squeezed her hand.

Just then, Esther and Grace walked through the front door holding hands. "Auntie Esther showed me the chickens." Grace ran over to Josiah. "She let me throw some feed on the floor, and they ran over to eat it. They make a funny sound. One almost bit me."

The words tumbled out of her faster than chicken feed from a bag. They all chuckled. Josiah looked at Adelaide. "She certainly seems to have overcome her shyness."

Adelaide agreed, muting a giggle behind her hand.

"Hey, I've got an idea," Josiah piped up. "How about after church tomorrow, we have a picnic at the beach?"

Grace clapped her hands together and jumped up and down, causing her loose bonnet to tilt in an awkward fashion on her head.

Once again they laughed. Everyone agreed the picnic would be a good idea. "We've also got a wedding to plan," Josiah said, his gaze never leaving Adelaide's.

∽

After church, old friends welcomed Adelaide and Josiah home with open arms. They'd had a good service, and now Adelaide looked forward to a picnic on the beach.

Ma fixed enough chicken to feed the church. They settled into place and ate a nice meal while Grace played in the sand.

"Esther, have you heard anything recently from Adam?" Josiah asked.

She shook her head, a pout on her lips.

Josiah laughed. "You'll hear soon, I'm sure. He's smitten with you, no doubt about that."

Her pout turned to a smile. "It's so hard not to have word." She fingered the gold chain around her neck.

"That's the tricky part of loving a seaman." He turned to Adelaide and grabbed her hand. "I'm glad we didn't have to go through that."

"Papa, come look," Grace shouted.

Josiah winked at Adelaide, and together they ran to Grace's side. They marveled at her sand creation and sang her praises. Josiah scooped her into his arms. Grace giggled and squealed as he twirled her round and round. When he finally placed her on the ground, she took crooked steps before finally falling into a heap. Grace turned to Josiah. "Again, Papa?"

Josiah groaned. "Oh no, Grace. Papa's too dizzy."

"I'll race you back to the blanket, Grace," Adelaide called.

Josiah counted, "One, two, three." They took off trudging through the sinking sand, leaving Grace behind with her pudgy legs to carry her. It suddenly became a real race for Josiah and Adelaide, though her skirts got in the way. By the time they reached the blanket, they fell together, laughing and gasping for breath. Adelaide looked at his blue eyes as he smiled only inches from her, wanting desperately to kiss him but not with her family around. She quickly straightened herself.

"Good to hear you so happy, Adelaide," Ma said.

"I am happy, Ma."

"I talked to the pastor this morning. The wedding is set for tomorrow," Josiah said.

"So soon?" Ma asked.

"Why wait? We're not inviting lots of people, just family, the Markles, a couple of witnesses, and, well. . .um. . .why wait?"

They all let out a laugh. Adelaide's emotions rose to her face. She wished she weren't so transparent.

A pleasant evening breeze caused a strand of hair to tickle Adelaide's cheek as she made her way to the church. She felt glad they had decided on a church wedding. They wanted a different start this time.

Adelaide lifted her dress—the dress Josiah had bought her on the island—so that she could more easily climb the church steps. She adjusted the wreath of flowers that circled her head.

Having the matter of the store settled with the Markles made her feel a lot better. She and Josiah had already taken their things to the store and would move in after the wedding. The Markles left some furniture for them since Josiah and Adelaide hadn't had time to set up housekeeping as of yet. Grace seemed all too happy to stay with Ma and Esther for a couple of days.

Adelaide wondered if she had stepped into a fairy tale. She couldn't believe how their story had changed for the better. With a thankful heart, she entered the church. Josiah stood with his back to her, talking with Pastor Daugherty. Pastor looked up, and Josiah turned. The pleasure on his face made Adelaide's heart skip. She made her way toward him. He stepped forward and grabbed her hand. "You look beautiful." His breath tickled her ear as he whispered the words meant for her alone.

The pastor began the wedding service, and Adelaide's heart soared. Surrounded by family and friends, standing by the man she loved with all her heart, and with a precious little girl whom they would raise together, Adelaide whispered a prayer of thanks deep in her soul.

When the ceremony ended, Josiah reached over and kissed his wife. Though he didn't make a spectacle, this kiss was different from all the others. A kiss that said they belonged to one another, and nothing would ever change that.

The little group went to Ma's house, ate a wonderful meal together, laughed, and shared stories. Finally, one by one, they trickled away, each going to their own homes.

"Mrs. Buchanan, are you ready to go home?"

Adelaide looked up to see Josiah's blue eyes sparkling down at her, his extended hand ready to help her to her feet.

She smiled, the thrill of truly being his wife running through her. They said their good-byes and headed for the Markles' General Store. Their new home.

The *clip-clop* of horses' hooves echoed through the night sky. The sea murmured softly in the distance. Adelaide leaned into Josiah. He held her tightly with one arm and guided the horses with the other. She thought the night perfect.

"Do you miss the sea, Josiah?"

"I will always miss it some. It's been a part of my life for as long as I can remember. But I have everything I want with you and Grace." He turned to her. "I couldn't be happier." He kissed her long and hard. The team almost ran off the path. They laughed while Josiah snapped the reins to speed the horses along.

Josiah put the carriage away, and Adelaide noticed the lights were out upstairs, so the Markles had already gone to bed. She climbed the steps to the porch and waited as Josiah had requested. He soon joined her and stopped in front of her. "I've never done this before," he said as he lifted her into his arms. Adelaide giggled. Josiah nuzzled his nose into her neck. "But then I've never been in love like this before."

Adelaide shivered slightly. Josiah carried her through the doorway then pushed open the door to the bedroom, Adelaide still in his arms. He lowered her to the floor. "I would like to offer our marriage to the Lord."

Adelaide nodded.

Together they knelt beside their bed.

"Father, we thank Thee for bringing us to this place. Thank Thee for providing us with an income through the Markles' generosity. Adelaide's right. Life is all about choices. Our choices affect not only ourselves but others around us. I thank Thee for helping me make the right choices this time. Thank Thee for bringing Adelaide into my life. And while I hadn't planned on Grace, Thou didst know all about her, and I thank Thee for bringing her into our lives. May our family bring Thee the honor Thou dost deserve. May we be an extension of Thy love, grace, and mercy. And one day may we gather as a circle unbroken before Thy throne where we will hear Thee say, 'Well done, thou good and faithful servant. . . .'

"Now, Father, I pray Thy blessings on our family as we begin our lives together. In Jesus' name, amen."

Adelaide whispered, "Amen."

They rose and stepped away from the bed. Josiah went and closed the bedroom door. He walked back toward Adelaide and looked her square in the face. "I will spend my life proving my love for you."

"And I, you, Josiah. I love you." She brushed the tears that pooled in her eyes and stretched her arms around his neck. He pulled her close to him and kissed her in the way of which she had always dreamed.

When they parted, Josiah looked at her. "You know, whaling has been good to me. Provided a substantial living, true, but most of all it brought me you." Josiah grew silent and serious as his fingers reached for her hair. Slowly, tenderly, his hands pulled away tiny pins, one by one. Adelaide barely breathed. Josiah's fingers caressed the honey brown curls that fell in heaps across her shoulders. He leaned into her, his voice brushing light against her ear as his hands continued to explore her hair. "I told you I'd like it down," he said in a heavy whisper.

Everything around Adelaide seemed surreal. Was it really happening? If she breathed, would the magic end? She wanted to stay in the moment forever.

Holding onto her hand, Josiah took three steps, stopped at the stand beside their bed, and in one puff of air, blew out their candle.

Into the darkness he whispered, "I choose you, Adelaide Buchanan. I choose you."

BASKET OF SECRETS

Chapter 1

Abigail O'Connor watched as the dark carriage rattled toward the train station, taking away the only man she'd ever loved. Her chance for happiness had rushed in like the waters of Lake Michigan to the Chicago shoreline then seemed to flee like an ebbing tide.

"Abigail, come down and eat something," her mother encouraged from the stairwell.

Wiping away the last tear, the twenty-six-year-old dropped the lace curtain from her window, muting the afternoon sun to dull shadows in her bedroom. She walked to the washstand. The cool splash of water against her face erased the tears but still left behind the stain on her heart. A towel lay nearby. She picked up the soft cloth and dried her skin with it, all the while struggling to find relief from the pain that plagued her.

With reluctance, she stepped in front of the looking glass. One glance and she pulled in a sharp breath. Crying did little good for her appearance. Her fingers probed gently around the puffy area of her eyes.

"How could you do this to me, Jonathan?" Her words, a mixture of anger and sorrow, echoed within the confines of her room. Once more, she dabbed the towel on her face with more force than necessary, stinging her delicate skin. Frustrated, she turned and threw the towel on her bed. She thought a moment, then lifted her chin. "Well, if that's what you want, Jonathan Clark, go back east. Build a new life for yourself. I'll get along fine without you." She gulped back a fresh wave of tears.

The dress hanging on a peg on the wall caught her attention. A dress designed by her best friend, Sophia Hill.

Sophia and Clayton Hill. If only Abigail could find happiness with someone as they had found in one another. She couldn't imagine Clayton and Sophia would soon celebrate their first anniversary. Almost a year since the fire.

Almost a year since Jonathan had walked into her life and stolen her heart.

She remembered the day well. She had gone to the Thread Bearer to discuss the Christmas ball with Sophia. Jonathan had arrived shortly after to help Sophia with her ledger books. Catching the fancy of the handsome bookkeeper, Abigail had left with a promise of an escort to the ball. They had been a couple since that time. Until a week ago. When he told her he took another position. Back east. He couldn't pass it up, he had said.

Obviously, he didn't love her. She'd have to move on with her life. But how?

Abigail sighed and fell onto the bed. She sank into the thick blankets and plump pillows. Their comfort did little to ease her misery. Why did Jonathan feel the need for a bigger, better job back east? Despite her anger, she felt a twinge of understanding. He no doubt wanted to go home. She couldn't blame him for that. She wanted to stay near family, too. But would she have given up family for him? Her back stiffened. Without a doubt, she would have given up everything for him. She felt almost sure she would have.

Almost.

Rising to her feet, she brushed down the front and sides of her skirt with her hands, smoothing out wrinkles. She would not wallow in self-pity one moment longer. Quickly, she returned to the looking glass, took a brush through her red curls, and with a sigh watched them spring back into place. Considering it useless to fight her stubborn hair, she placed her brush on the dresser and grabbed her bag. She walked across the hall and stepped down the brown wooden staircase and past the family portraits and colorful tapestries from her parents' travels in Europe.

"Oh Abigail, I'm so glad to see you. Are you feeling better?"

"I'm fine, Mother. I would like to go see Sophia, if you don't mind."

"Well, of course, dear. I'm afraid you'll have to drive yourself in the carriage. Your father is having a guest for dinner, and I have things to do. Can you manage?"

Abigail nodded. "Who's the guest?"

Her mother shook her head. "I don't know. Your father said he was going to town to employ a chauffeur and would invite him to dinner tonight."

Abigail smiled. "He will probably do it, too."

Her mother laughed then said, "Oh, I do hope we find a chauffeur soon. I suppose we should have known Mr. Wickers would leave a great hole when he left."

"I miss him."

"I know you do, dear."

"Well, I'd better go hitch up the horses. I'll see you in a while." Abigail reached over and dropped a kiss on her mother's cheek.

Mother stretched her arms around her daughter. "I know you're in pain now," she whispered, "but it will fade with time. I promise." With a light pat on Abigail's back, her mother pulled away.

Abigail nodded, not wanting to think about it for fear she would cry again.

"Are you sure you don't want to eat first? You hardly touched your breakfast, Abigail." Mother's brows pushed together, scrunching a worry line between them.

Abigail touched her mother's arm. "I'm fine, really. I just wanted to talk a little with Sophia."

Though a worrisome frown still etched her face, her mother gave up with a sigh. "All right, you go and have a nice time. Give Sophia and her family our love. Oh, one more thing, Abigail."

Abigail turned back.

"If you happen by the mercantile, could you stop and pick up some coffee?"

Abigail smiled, nodded, and slipped through the door. With some effort, she hitched the horses to the carriage. Both horses.

Funny how things worked better in twos.

She did miss Mr. Wickers, but not only because he took them where they needed to go. He had been with the family for ten years and was practically like a grandpa to Abigail. Family had called him out west. Abigail wondered why people didn't stay in one place.

With a click of her tongue, she set the horses in motion. The Thread Bearer was situated a ways north of her home, so Abigail settled in and tried to relax for the ride.

Summer's sun had yet to give way to the call of autumn, though the intensity of its warmth had subsided somewhat. Green leaves waved from assorted trees located in a small city park. Abigail felt the need to turn in and meander through the winding lane. With a slight tug, she steered the horses through a path bordered with thick foliage and the season's last burst of blooms sprouting from plentiful plants.

The heady scent of roses followed her. She took a deep breath of the fresh, sweet air and allowed the peaceful surroundings to envelop her. Mothers sat along the few wooden benches, watching their children run and play in the expansive grasses. Abigail's eyes blurred. Would she ever know motherhood? She shook her head. Spurned by love once could happen to anyone. Only a fool would let it happen twice.

Her back straightened. She'd learned her lesson well. No need to go through it again. From this day forward, she would be on her guard. No other man would come close to her heart again. She'd see to that.

As she made her way through the edge of town, Abigail still marveled that last year's fire had left such devastation. People had rallied from all over the United States to lend a helping hand to Chicago. The railroad spilled immigrants into the city on a daily basis: people needing work, knowing Chicago was rebuilding. "The land of opportunity." *Too bad Jonathan didn't feel that way.*

Though it would take time to rebuild, being the hub of importing and exporting goods, Chicago would survive. Already new structures stood taller and boasted brick faces, evidence of stricter building codes. Property values soared. The city throbbed with the excitement of new adventure.

Abigail figured if Chicago could move on after such devastation, so could she. Maybe she would put her teaching certificate to use and go to work somewhere. One thing she knew: She needed to leave her problems with her Savior. Only He had the answers anyway.

Lord, please, grant me direction. Show me what Thy will is for me.

The horses snorted and neighed. Their harnesses jangled slightly as they plodded along the streets of Chicago. Though she loved the thrill of big city life, Abigail couldn't deny her longing for the quiet nights on the front porch of their family home, where crickets called from manicured bushes and fireflies flickered about on distant grassy meadows.

Seeing Manford's Mercantile, Abigail decided to stop and pick up coffee for her mother. Tying the horses to a hitching post, she made her way into the mercantile. Coffee and leather scents reached her the moment she entered. As she meandered through the aisles, the aroma of apples lifted from a nearby bin. Her footsteps left the scent behind and soon carried her to the sharp smell of pickles hovering around a barrel. She spotted the coffee and picked up a bag.

A slight temptation to dig into the jar of penny candy on the counter tickled her fancy, but with reluctance, she turned from it.

The thought of candy so engrossed her, she neglected to see the person in front of her until it was too late. She plowed into the man like a runaway horse cart slamming into a tree. He stopped cold.

A gasp caught in her chest. She looked up and peered into dark brown eyes with golden flecks that seemed to fan from the center like sunlight bursting upon a brand-new day. The pleasure she saw in them warmed her down to her toes. "I–I'm so sorry. I don't know what must have gotten into me." She pulled out her handkerchief to cover her embarrassment then stopped the dainty cloth at her throat as she attempted, but failed, to swallow.

A twinkle lit the man's dark eyes, making her almost light-headed. It was all she could do to hold herself up in her boots. Whatever had gotten into her, she didn't know, but one thing was for sure: she had to get over it.

"Ma'am, the fault was mine." In a polite gesture, he pulled off his hat, and a thatch of heavy blond hair spilled across his forehead. Her cheeks grew warm, and she knew her face must match her red hair. She had to get out of there before her heart jumped clean out of her chest. "If you'll excuse me," she said, pushing past him before he had a chance to say anything else. She started to leave the store when Mr. Manford called to her.

"Abigail?"

She turned and swallowed hard. "Yes?"

"You gonna pay for that coffee?"

She looked down at the package of coffee clutched to her chest. Her jaw dropped in astonishment. "Oh my!" she said, looking at Mr. Manford. Then without thought, she glanced toward the young man with the dark eyes. A full smile spread across his angular face. Could she possibly suffer any more humiliation? "I'm so sorry, Mr. Manford," she said in a whisper. He tried to hide his smile, but she saw it just the same. With shaky fingers, she pulled out her coin purse, plunked money on the counter, and scurried out the door.

⤫

Titus Matthews's gaze met that of the storekeeper. Titus shook his head and smiled then glanced back as the woman stepped out the door. Never before had he seen hair a blended color of autumn leaves. He picked up a sack of flour, but a vision of the woman's crimson face peered from the sack, her bright blue eyes coaxing him to find out her identity.

Maybe he could get her last name from the storekeeper. He'd have to be careful, though. Folks were suspicious of strangers. He shrugged. He might have to do his ma's shopping at Manford's Mercantile from now on in hopes of finding the woman again.

⤫

Once she arrived at the Thread Bearer, Abigail had settled down from her near bout with apoplexy at the mercantile. She climbed from the rig and tethered her horses. Lifting her heavy skirts, she stepped across muddy spots on the pathway and entered the shop. The bell jangled on the door behind her as she closed it.

"Be right with you," Sophia's voice called from the back room.

Abigail smiled and waited, knowing Sophia would be excited to see her. They hadn't visited in quite some time. Sophia had been too sick for church the last couple of weeks. Abigail needed to see how her friend was getting along.

Sophia stepped through the curtain that separated the rooms. "Abigail!"

The two women rushed through the room and embraced. "Oh, how I've missed you," Sophia said, quite out of breath. She pulled back and looked at her friend and gasped. "You've been crying. What's wrong?"

Abigail let out a chuckle and shook her head. "I could never get anything past you."

"Let me make some tea. Come to the back, won't you?"

"Am I keeping you from any deadlines?"

"No," Sophia called over her shoulder. "In fact, this is a very good day for a visit. I have only a few items to mend and one dress to start with no set date by which to deliver it."

Abigail pushed aside the curtain and sat at the scrubbed pine table while Sophia busied herself in the kitchen, putting water on the stove. Once the cups and saucers were placed on the table, Sophia sat down to wait for the heated water. "So, tell me what's going on." Her worried eyes met Abigail's.

Abigail sighed, not knowing exactly where to begin. "Well," she said, looking at her hands and fidgeting with her fingers, "Jonathan has moved back east."

"What?" Sophia's mouth gaped, her gaze fixed on Abigail. "Is someone in his family ill?"

Abigail shook her head. "It seems," she measured her words evenly, "he has a new position."

Sophia covered Abigail's hand with her own. "Oh, Abby, I'm so sorry."

Despite Abigail's great efforts, a tear trickled down her cheek and plopped onto the table. She quickly brushed it off with her hand.

"Oh my dear, dear friend." Sophia stood, came around to the back of her chair, and gave her a hug.

Abigail rather wished Sophia hadn't been so compassionate. It made her want to crumple into a mass of tears.

The water on the stove boiled. Sophia stepped over and lifted the pan holding the hot liquid, pouring it into a teapot to steep their tea. "I can't believe you haven't told me this before now, Abigail."

"Well, you've been away from church, and to tell you the truth, I had no idea of his intentions until a week ago. I felt sure he would change his mind. I couldn't imagine he was serious. But I was wrong. He came by this morning, wished me well, and walked out of my life."

Sophia seemed to sense Abigail's need to stay composed. They waited a little while in silence. Sophia finally got up and walked over to the teapot. Pouring the steaming tea into their cups, Sophia placed Abigail's in front of her.

"Thank you."

Once seated, Sophia took a sip of her own drink.

Abigail gingerly swallowed the hot brew, willing it to calm her queasiness.

Placing her cup back in the saucer, Sophia looked Abigail square in the face. "Well, that's that," she said matter-of-factly. "God has something better in store for you."

Abigail raised her hand to stop the conversation. "No no no!"

Sophia looked at her, puzzled. "What do you mean?"

"He might have something better in store for me, but I can tell you it doesn't include a man. Those days are over for me."

Sophia gasped. "Abigail, you can't mean that. You're too young. You have your whole life ahead of you."

"I assure you, Sophia, I do mean that."

Sophia seemed to stop herself from saying any more. "Well, I won't attempt to haggle with your Irish temper, but I will pray for you," she said with an ornery grin.

Abigail returned a weak smile.

Sophia leaned over and touched Abigail's arm. "Just promise me this. You'll be open to whatever the Lord has for you?"

Abigail nodded. "As long as my heart is not at risk." Even as she said the words, the image of the young man at the mercantile popped into her mind.

She wondered why.

Chapter 2

Titus Matthews ran his hand through his hair, waited a moment, then pulled the watch from his pocket. Four o'clock. He had been walking the streets of Chicago since eight thirty in the morning and still no sign of a job. He looked around for a bench to rest his aching feet. Not seeing any, he moved on.

There had been plenty of ads listed in the *Chicago Tribune*, but it seemed someone always beat him to it. He thought they always needed railroad men, but with the great number of new workers coming into town, the competition grew fierce. His boot shoved a pebble out of the way. Why had his pa agreed to that investment? Why had he placed so much of the family earnings in one pot?

Titus's brown boots thumped hard against the dirt path, anger kicking up dust behind him. "Thomas O'Connor, you will pay for what you did to my pa and to our family," he groused, making his way across the road.

He decided to make one more stop at the mercantile. Though he had checked it out earlier, this time he decided he'd go back and pick up some things he remembered his ma needed. He doubted he'd run into the woman again, but then anything was possible. Not that it mattered. What woman wanted a man without a job? He couldn't provide for his ma and sister, let alone court a lady friend.

He entered Manford's Mercantile. He'd heard his ma say she had a craving for an apple pie. Ma loved to bake. Yet since Pa died, she had had few supplies with which to work. No more familiar smells of boiled chicken and beef or home-baked pies. His teeth clenched, jaw tightened. Resentment churned in his stomach.

Today he aimed to change that.

She needed three apples and some sugar. Though funds were low, Titus decided he would get those for her. She had endured enough in the last six months, losing her husband and caring for a ten-year-old daughter who couldn't walk and hadn't said a word since Pa died in March. Though Titus's ma helped with some sewing, she brought in little income. The responsibility weighed heavily upon his shoulders.

"Good afternoon, Mr. Matthews," a strong voice called behind him.

Titus turned to look into the face of his enemy. Thomas O'Connor.

"Mr. O'Connor," he quipped and started to turn away.

"Wait," Thomas O'Connor said, placing a hand on Titus's arm.

Titus turned around.

"I don't know if you have a position just now, Titus, but I'm in desperate need of a chauffeur and wondered if—well, I wanted to know if you might help our family. I will pay you well," he quickly added.

Help their family, Titus sneered inside. Why, he'd rather spit at this man as to help his family. He took one step to walk away, when a thought struck him. Maybe he could help their family. More importantly, he could help his own family. This was his chance to get even with the man who took Pa's life, destroyed Titus's dreams of becoming a doctor, and took away the Matthewses' fine family home, leaving them to live in poverty in a hovel. Sure, he would help him—and make some money at the same time.

"Titus?"

Titus shook himself from his web of thoughts. "I would be much obliged, sir," he managed.

"Great!" Thomas O'Connor said, slapping Titus on the back. "Here's my address." He handed Titus a piece of paper. "Come by this evening for dinner, say, around seven o'clock, and we'll discuss your duties."

"I'll be there," Titus said, stuffing the address into his pocket. The two men parted, and Titus felt good about getting the sugar and apples. Still, he couldn't deny a gnawing feeling in his gut, something that told him he'd better beware, that he might be stepping on shaky ground. He pushed the thought aside, allowing the bitterness to prevail. Besides, he had a right to feel the way he did.

Didn't he?

∽

Abigail looked up from the newspaper when her father came in the front door. "Hello, Father." She glanced at his parcel. "Oh dear, did you bring mother some coffee, too?"

He looked at his bag then back at Abigail. "Don't tell me you stopped at the mercantile today?"

She laughed and nodded.

He chuckled. "Well, looks like we won't be running out of coffee for some time."

With a long apron draped over her ample middle, Abigail's mother came into the drawing room, stepping lightly on the plush rug at her feet. "What's this? Both of you stopped for coffee?" She placed her hands firmly on her hips and looked at them, a smudge of flour on the tip of her nose.

At the sight of her mother, Abigail smiled. She knew her father had tried time and again to talk Mother into hiring a cook, but she wouldn't hear of it. Her one joy in life, she always said, was to feed her family well.

"Yes dear," Father said, dabbing at the flour on her nose then bending to kiss her.

Mother laughed and took the sack from him. "Well, I suppose it will keep."

"So, what are we having for dinner?" Father followed her into the kitchen. Abigail wanted to hear about the surprise guest, so she trailed behind.

"We're having fried chicken, mashed potatoes, sliced carrots, and applesauce. Apple pie for dessert with coffee." Abigail couldn't help noticing Mother's pleasure.

"I'm sorry I wasn't home to help you cook today, Mother."

"Nonsense." She waved her hand. "I had a delightful day in the kitchen."

Abigail smiled, knowing how her mother loved to cook. She turned to her father. "Who's coming for dinner?" Abigail didn't miss the shadow that flickered across his face.

"Titus Matthews."

Mother turned to him. "Abram's boy?"

Father nodded. "Only he's not a boy, Lavina. He's a man. I'd say about Abby's age."

Abigail had no idea what any of it meant. "Who is Abram?"

Father pulled in a deep breath and pushed it out with effort. "He was a friend whom I tried to help. His business dealings were failing. I talked him into starting an insurance company. I partnered with him, and we insured many of the businesses that thrived before the fire."

Understanding hit Abigail. "You mean—"

Father nodded. "We lost it all. Couldn't pay the claims. Too many. It didn't really affect our family. I have our money divested in many different areas. Abram kept buying up more stock. I didn't want to pry into his affairs. I figured he had gotten back on his feet with his other investments. He wanted full ownership. I sold all my shares over to him a week before the fire. I only started the business to help him in the first place. What I didn't know until recently was that he had put everything in that business. When he died in March, he left his family with nothing but debt."

"Oh, how awful," Abigail said.

Mother went over and touched his arm. "You can't blame yourself, Thomas. Abram chose to do those things."

Father ran a hand through his thinning hair. "I know. I still can't get it out of my mind though."

"So why are you having Titus over?" Mother asked, poking a fork into the potatoes on the stove.

He smiled. "I've asked him to be our new chauffeur."

She dropped the fork on the stove and turned to look at him with wide eyes. "And he agreed?"

Sadness touched Father's face once again. "He lost his job last week. Needs work." He rubbed his chin a moment. "Course I'll pay him more than the job is worth."

"Thomas, it's fine to do that if you want to help him, but don't do it because you feel guilty."

"I can't help but think I'd want someone to help you and Abby if I were gone."

Mother reached up and kissed him on the cheek.

"Abigail, you might want to help us out in the conversation. I'm a little on the slow side of things with young folks."

Abigail nodded out of respect. The last thing she wanted to do was spend her evening entertaining a gentleman.

"Is he married, have a family, Thomas?" Mother wanted to know.

"No. The way I understand it, he lives with his ma and sister. His sister, Jenny, fell from a horse a few years back, leaving her crippled. Titus was going to medical school, studying to be a doctor, until Abram died and the boy had to drop out."

Mother looked at Abigail. A cold knot formed in the pit of Abigail's stomach. She hoped her mother's cooking plans were for dinner only, not romance.

"When will he be here?" Mother asked.

Father had grabbed the paper and was already on the finance page. "Hmm?"

"Thomas, when will Mr. Matthews be here?" she asked again with a nip of impatience.

He glanced up. "Oh, sorry, dear. Should be here. . ." He glanced at his pocket watch. "Any minute now." He looked up and smiled.

"Oh you," she said, flicking the towel at him before she commenced to flutter about the kitchen in a flurry, handing out orders to Abigail. "Abby, get the dishes so we can set the table. Oh dear, where are our good bowls?" Mother asked no one in particular as she fished through the cupboards.

Her ramblings were cut short when a knock sounded at the front door.

"That would be our guest," Father said with a smile. He folded the newspaper back in place and headed to the door.

"Oh, just a minute," Abigail said, racing past him to run up the stairs to her room. Once she reached the top of the stairway, she turned to look at her father, who watched her with his hand on the doorknob. "All right, now you can let him in."

He laughed and shook his head. Abigail saw him twist the door handle. She darted out of sight and into her room. Not that she cared one way or another what some man thought about her. Still, she didn't want to look like an old hag.

Quickly, she slipped from her soiled clothing and put on a fresh combination of a sensible white top and black skirt. As usual, her curls bounced in unruly ringlets. She pulled the abundance of hair into a shapely knot at the back of her neck. A few ringlets slipped from the pins and sprung loosely at the sides of her face. She sighed. "It's hopeless," she said to her reflection. Taking a deep breath, she left her room and headed down the stairs.

She could hear her parents talking to Titus. His voice was deep, confident. Reminded her of someone else. Jonathan. No, she wouldn't think about that tonight. She would make the chauffeur feel welcome, make polite conversation, and go to bed. She was having a miserable day, and the sooner it was over, the better.

He most likely would consider her an old maid. A spinster. How embarrassing—although not as embarrassing as her earlier escapade at the mercantile. At the time, she had been mortified, though right now, as the whole scene played out in her mind, she thought it quite funny. She felt a smile light her face just as she walked into the kitchen.

"Ah, Abigail, dear. I'd like you to meet our new chauffeur, Titus Matthews."

The young man turned from Father and looked at her. Abigail nearly swallowed her tongue. The same dark eyes that had earlier made her almost trip on her boots looked back at her.

At first, surprise etched his features, then something else. What it was, Abigail couldn't be sure. "Well, hello again," he said.

"Um, he–hello."

"You two have met?" Father asked with a puzzled grin.

Titus turned to him. "Yes, in fact, only this afternoon. In the mercantile."

Father glanced from Titus to Abigail. "Ah yes, the coffee." He threw a wink at his daughter. She wanted to throw a towel at him.

Oh, why did she have to stay and make conversation? She wanted to go to her room. This man made her uncomfortable, though she wasn't sure why. After all, it wasn't his fault his presence lifted her to a hazy vision of a crackling hearth on a winter's day. Goodness, how could those thoughts pop in her mind when she had said good-bye to the love of her life only that morning?

"Abigail?" Mother was saying.

"I'm sorry?"

Everyone looked at her.

"Would you help me carry the serving dishes to the table, please?"

"Oh yes." Abigail quickly ran to help.

Once the table was laden with an abundance of food, the group settled themselves quite comfortably in the dining chairs, and Father led them in prayer. Titus cleared his throat and shifted in his seat. Abigail wondered of his thoughts toward God. Was he bitter because of his pa's death and the circumstances in which he now found himself? She'd have to remember to pray for him.

Amid the clinking of silverware against dinner plates, Abigail felt the conversation moved along at a reasonable pace. Before long, she felt herself actually relax and steal a glance or two at the gentleman seated across from her. So different in appearance from Jonathan, and yet something about him...

She snapped her cloth napkin back in place at her lap. No matter how nice or friendly he seemed, she would keep her distance. Although she did not want to be unchristian, she would not allow herself another heartache. The more she could avoid their new chauffeur, the better.

She took a bite of potatoes and glanced up in time to see Titus looking at her. He smiled. She turned away and struggled to swallow.

Yes, she would avoid him.

⌒

"Titus, did you have a nice dinner?" his ma asked as he settled into the chair and pulled off his boots.

"Yeah, it was fine, Ma." He attempted to keep the agitation from his voice.

He looked up in time to see a frown on Ma's face. He let out a long breath. "Sorry, Ma. I'm just a little tired."

She gave a short nod. "Would you like some tea or coffee?" she asked in a whisper. His sister, Jenny, slept on a mat in the corner of the room.

"No thanks. I'm going to bed, too." He rose to his feet, clutching his boots with his right hand.

"Titus."

He winced within. Nothing got past his ma. He looked to her.

"They're good people. Things happen beyond our control."

He shrugged as if he had no idea to what she was referring.

Her eyes sparked with understanding. "Bitterness never helped anybody."

"I don't know what you're talking about, Ma."

"Sit back down."

Reluctantly, he complied.

"I see the blame in your eyes, Titus. Your heart has grown cold. I know your dreams have been put on hold for now—"

"On hold? Is that what you think, Ma?" His hands slid down his stubbled jaw. "They're not on hold. They're gone," he said with finality.

"I don't believe that," she insisted. "The Lord gave you a love for people and the intelligence to help them. He'll see that you use your gifts. Trust Him."

His jaw clenched. It wasn't Ma's fault things turned out this way. He wouldn't take it out on her.

"Don't allow bitterness to separate you from your Lord and your gifts. You'll have a much different future, son, if you give in to this temptation."

"Meaning no disrespect, but I'm going to bed, Ma."

She lifted her chin. "Mind you, my prayers will not let you go. I can be as stubborn as you are." Her expression emphasized her words.

He lifted a slight smile, walked over to Ma, and kissed her on the forehead. As he started to walk away, she grabbed his arm. "I will bombard heaven till you set things right in your heart, Titus Matthews."

"You're right. You are stubborn." He winked at her and walked away.

Once ready to go to sleep, he settled onto his makeshift bed on the floor. The wooden boards that held their tiny home together creaked and groaned with the night winds, reminding him of the depths to which they had fallen. He pulled the thin blanket up around him to shut out the draft seeping through the boards. How could he not be bitter?

Thoughts of Abigail played upon his mind, adding to his bitterness. Why couldn't they have met under other circumstances, another time? He couldn't deny his attraction to her, but he wouldn't entertain that thought. She was an O'Connor. Plain and simple. And O'Connor was a name he planned to bring down. He didn't know how or when, but he figured every family had a weak spot, a place of secrets that the outside world didn't see. His job was to find their weakness and expose them to all of Chicago.

A cold chill whipped through him. He buried himself deeper into his blanket. Yes, he would bring the proud O'Connor family down.

Just as they had done to the Matthews family.

Chapter 3

Abigail walked onto the porch and glanced up at the moisture-laden clouds. She went back inside and grabbed an umbrella from a tall basket then stepped back outside. A carriage creaked and rattled as it rolled past her house. Neighbors Jack and Nan Forrest waved at Abigail. She returned the greeting. Just then her attention turned to the wheels of another carriage that bit into the hard ground and ultimately came to a halt in front of the porch.

Titus jumped from his seat and walked over to her. He took off his hat. "Miss O'Connor."

"Good afternoon," she said with a smile. "And please, call me Abigail."

His eyes twinkled with pleasure. "Abigail then." He stood a moment, as if forgetting the task at hand. "Where would you like to go?"

She smiled. "Have you heard of the work that goes on at Barnabas House, located in the Irish neighborhood?" She didn't miss the surprise on his face.

He nodded.

"I want to go there." She thought she noticed a look of disapproval flicker upon his face.

He hesitated. "That's no place for a lady, Abigail. Are you certain?"

Why, by giving her such advice, he had quickly taken on an air of familiarity that she wasn't at all sure she liked. In fact, she felt quite sure she didn't like it. Her back bristled. Her parents approved of the work at Barnabas House, and she certainly did not need the approval of the family chauffeur. "It is a respected program put on by one of the churches in town. I am certain," she said with finality.

His right eyebrow rose, his gaze never leaving her eyes. He looked almost as if he dared challenge her request. Why, of all the nerve. What was his problem? She lifted her gloved hand, letting him know the discussion had ended and he could now help her onto the seat of the open carriage.

Which he did.

Once on the seat, she settled in for the ride, straightening her skirt, adjusting her hat, fingering her loose strands of hair back into place. Though it did little good. With the open carriage, her hat barely held her hair in place. She didn't know what to think of Titus's response. What was

145

it to him where she went? He wasn't her husband, after all. She wasn't about to let the family chauffeur tell her what to do.

Her shoulders heaved as she sighed. Her Irish temper would get the better of her if she wasn't careful. It was the one temptation to which she succumbed almost daily. Abigail bit her lip. *Why can't I work past that, Lord? Sophia has the sweetest demeanor, calm, peaceful. I flit around my little world, barking at anything that stands in my way.*

She kept peering to the right of her, being careful not to look at Titus on her left. She gazed absently at the passing scenery. *My temper is my thorn in the flesh, I suppose,* she thought. With another sigh, she attempted to calm herself before arriving to work at Barnabas House.

The carriage continued, jostling about as it traveled over potholes and ridges in the dirty streets. The scenery had turned from sprawling houses with plush green lawns, pruned bushes, and rambling honeysuckle vines to tattered yards splotched with mud holes, random sprouts of grass, tangled weeds, and overgrown bushes.

Trash littered the streets, and dirty children played in front of the tenements. Rats searched through discarded debris in hidden alleyways. Hundreds of houses were unconnected with the street sewer. Abigail's heart bled for her people. The Irish were her people, weren't they? She shrugged off the doubt. With her red hair and temper, she figured she had to be related.

God had been merciful to her, placing her at the O'Connors' front door when she was a mere three days old. Countless times Mother had told her shortly after they found out they couldn't have children, Abigail had shown up in a basket on their porch. Nothing short of a miracle. Abigail smiled at God's kindness. . .to all of them.

She would live her life in thankfulness to Him by helping the Irish immigrants. Even if they weren't her blood relatives, the O'Connors were related, and well, she was an O'Connor.

That was enough for her.

⚭

Titus pulled the carriage to a stop, and Abigail waited for him to help her down. Once they walked a few feet, the stench from the stables wafted over her, taking her breath away. She wanted to grab a handkerchief but didn't want to offend the people. She told herself she could do this.

Helping her over some mud holes, Titus saw her to the edge of the property.

"Thank you, Mr. Matthews."

"Please, it's Titus."

"Titus," she repeated. "I'll most likely be here an hour or so. You might check back around five o'clock?"

"I have nothing else to do. I'll wait here."

She had a sneaking suspicion he was playing the guardian again, but distracted by the poverty, she left his comment alone. "As you wish." She stepped past him and made her way through the door.

Dark with shadows, the room smelled of sweat and dirt. The outside stench seeped sparingly through the open cracks. Despair met her through the eyes of the people. Abigail mentally rolled up her sleeves. First thing on her agenda was to make the place look happy. The former drawing room needed paint. Lots of it.

"Abigail O'Connor?" a masculine voice called beside her. She turned to him.

The man had raven black hair and a charming smile, and hidden only slightly behind wired spectacles were blue eyes that sparkled like Lake Michigan on a sunny day. She liked him instantly.

"Hello. I'm Christopher Doyle, director of Barnabas House."

"Hello, Mr. Doyle."

"Please, call me Christopher." Before she could comment, he continued. "Might I call you Abigail?"

She nodded.

"I'm afraid there's not much need for formalities here." His gaze swept around the room, causing Abigail to do the same. He turned back to her. "I understand you have a teaching certificate?"

"Yes."

"Good. Once the children return from school, we need someone to help them with their studies."

She nodded with understanding.

"Let's go over to the table where we can talk." He led the way. "Would you like some coffee?" he called over his shoulder.

"No thank you."

They arrived at a wooden table marred and nicked with use. Christopher pulled out a seat for her. "We have five bedrooms upstairs where the cook, the cleaning lady and her child, and a couple of other workers stay. I have a room in the basement since I'm the only man." He smiled. "Neighbors come in for various supplies. Before handing out health items, we teach them about taking care of their bodies. With the distribution of free food, we discuss nutrition and proper eating. We cover the importance of being good neighbors and reaching out to those around us in need. They come to us to learn what job opportunities are available in the city, and we try to find the best jobs for them."

Abigail couldn't imagine such poverty with people struggling to afford the dilapidated dwellings she had witnessed in the neighborhood.

"I wish we could do more," Christopher said, looking absently ahead. He blew out a frustrated sigh and turned a weak smile her way. "The main thing is to get them off the streets, working, and into homes."

Abigail nodded.

"Well," he said, smacking the table with his hands, "that's where you come in." His broad smile was back. He then led Abigail to a group of five children, thin, wide-eyed, fair-skinned, with assorted freckles sprinkled across their noses. Her heart melted at the sight of them. Christopher introduced Abigail. They eagerly pulled out their school slates. The more talkative ones began chattering about their school assignments. Christopher smiled then let her commence to work. She hardly noticed when he walked away. The children had already captured her attention. And her heart.

⟳

Titus grabbed a cup of coffee from a nearby store while he waited for Abigail. He passed some time talking with the neighborhood men, who groused about no work and poor living conditions. Titus barely tolerated the strong coffee but managed to get it down just the same. He had to agree the Irish neighborhood conditions were worse than what he and his family had to endure.

Of course, with people like Abigail O'Connor to help them. . .

He ignored the dip of his heart with the thought of her. His thoughts turned smug. *Abigail O'Connor and her charity work. Just like her father trying to salve his conscience by hiring me, most likely she, too, has something to hide.*

He would find out their weakness. It might take some time, but if he remained patient, they would crumble. He'd see to that.

After a while, he went back to the carriage and waited in his seat. The front doors finally creaked open, and his head jerked up.

"Thank you, again, Abigail, for your fine help today. I can see the children have immediately taken to you," the man beside her was saying. Abigail smiled at him and waved good-bye. The sight of the man standing beside her brought an uncomfortable twist to Titus's gut. He jumped from his carriage seat and went over to escort her.

"Have you been waiting all this time?" Abigail asked.

"I went down the road and had some coffee, talked with a few of the neighbors."

Abigail looked at him for a moment. A pleasant smile came to her lips. "What?"

"Oh, nothing," she said as he helped her into the carriage. "We do have one more stop. I need to check on my gramma. She has been ill lately."

"All right. How do I get there?"

Abigail gave him directions, and soon they were on their way. Titus could see his days were going to be filled with carting Abigail around town. The horses *clip-clopped* their way through the dusty streets, and his mind wandered to the man at Barnabas House. He seemed a mite too friendly, to Titus's way of thinking. But then what was that to him? It's not like he cared one way or another how friendly the man was to Abigail. Two reformers. They deserved each other.

☙

Maeve O'Connor lifted hooded eyes to her granddaughter. "Good day to ye, Abigail darling," she said with a voice frail and thin as she settled into her deep chair.

Abigail slipped off her hat and crossed the floor to her gramma. Thin arms wound about Abigail's neck, and kisses pressed into the top of her burnished curls. The smell of medicines and sickness surrounded Abigail in the embrace. Once they parted, Abigail scooted a chair closer to the old woman.

"How are you feeling?"

"Ah," Gramma said with a wave of her hand, " 'tis better I'm getting. The doctor says this pneumonia won't kill me." She shrugged. " 'Tis me old, worn-out body takes a long time to mend, it does." A smile lit her lips and reflected in her eyes.

"I miss you, Gramma."

"And I be missing ye, too, Abigail darling." Then, as if to dismiss sentimentality, Gramma picked up a lighthearted voice. "So, tell me now about ye chauffeur. I saw him when the carriage pulled up." She wiggled her eyebrows.

"Gramma, you've been spying!" Abigail said with a giggle.

Gramma shrugged with mischief. " 'Tis true," she admitted shamelessly. "And what else is it that an old woman is to do when she be bored?"

Abigail laughed again. "He is Titus Matthews."

"Quite the laddie," Gramma encouraged, all the while studying Abigail's face.

"Not a possibility," Abigail said, shaking her head. "I'm through with men." She used a carefree tone so as not to worry Gramma. She figured there was no need for anyone to know the depth of truth to her statement.

Gramma studied her a moment. "God has a plan, Abigail darling. Ye must trust Him." She pointed a bony finger toward her. A fit of coughing followed, causing Abigail to run for a glass of water. Once the coughing stopped, Abigail pushed the water to Gramma.

Abigail stayed close to her, dabbing at her face with a cool cloth. "Are you sure you're all right?"

Gramma raised a smile. "Ah, I be fine."

Abigail spent a pleasurable hour talking with Gramma and telling her about the work at Barnabas House.

As evening fell upon the city, Abigail kissed her gramma good-bye and walked toward the door.

"Abigail?" Gramma called.

She turned. "Yes?"

"I'll be asking ye the same question ye asked me, wee one. Are ye sure ye be all right?"

"I'm fine, Gramma. I'm fine." With that, Abigail turned and walked through the door. Her eyes locked with Titus's, and she prayed it was so.

Chapter 4

By the time the carriage rolled to a stop, Abigail felt thankful to be home. She yawned just before climbing down, the lantern on the carriage lighting the way. A soft yellow light spilled from the house onto the outside lawn, giving Abigail some ability to see where she stepped. A small wail sounded behind the bushes.

"What's that?" Abigail stopped in her tracks, her finger pressed against her lips. Titus listened. Another cry. Together they edged forward, careful not to get too close to the bush. "I think something is back there and it's hurt," she whispered. With caution, she pulled apart a cluster of the bush and peered in. There sat a mutt covered in long, white hair with patches of brown thrown in seemingly as an afterthought. A blob of disheveled fur lopped over one eye, while his tongue drooped rather disgracefully from his mouth. Abigail glanced at his front paw. The bone poked in an odd angle.

"Oh Titus, he's hurt."

"Watch it, Abigail. A dog in pain could bite."

She pulled back. "Will you get Father? We need to take him to the veterinarian."

Titus nodded and went to the house while Abigail cooed softly to the animal, trying to ease his pain.

In no time, the lucky hound went from rags to riches as the O'Connors swept him into the veterinarian's office, had his broken leg set, then whisked him happily off to his new home.

"Abigail, I have no idea what we're going to do with a dog," Mother said, staring with disapproval at the animal in the house. The dog seemed to sense her dislike. He hobbled over behind Abigail's legs.

Abigail chuckled. "Oh, you poor thing." She patted his head then looked up at Mother. "I told you. I'll take care of him. You won't have to do a thing. I'm not a little girl anymore. I can handle it." Abigail scrunched down and scratched him behind his ears. "Besides, I think he will be a great encouragement to the children at Barnabas House."

With arms crossed, Mother looked him over once more and finally sighed. "Well, just see that you do care for him. I'll not have a dog tearing up our things around the house."

Feeling much like a child again, Abigail jumped up and gave Mother

151

a squeeze. "Thank you."

Mother returned the embrace then looked back at the dog. A sudden softness came to her voice. "The poor thing has been through enough for one day." She paused a moment before adding an admonishment. "But mind you, tomorrow he will have a bath. You'll just have to be careful of his leg."

Abigail nodded, then picked the dog up and carried him to her room while Mother just shook her head and watched.

With her feet, Abigail maneuvered a small rug beside her bed. Carefully, she bent down and laid the dog on the rug. He looked up at her with dark, melting eyes. Abigail stroked his fur and talked in whispers, lulling the animal to sleep. She'd have to think of a name for him.

Quietly, she pulled off her clothes and changed into her nightgown. Sinking into her soft bed covers, she reached for her Bible and read a passage. Afterward, she placed it back on her stand then glanced once more at the sleeping hound. "Barnabas. I think I'll call you Barnabas," she whispered. Satisfied, she blew a puff of air into the lamplight, snuffing the room into darkness.

Abigail rolled over to her side, pulling the covers just under her chin. It had been a long day but a rewarding one. Not until that very moment did she realize she hadn't thought about Jonathan the entire day.

Still, she wondered if he slept peacefully tonight in the comfort of his bedroom so very far away.

∞

The smell of breakfast alerted his nose, and Titus opened his eyes. Sausage? Eggs? He couldn't remember such a breakfast in some time. He sat up and stretched on his bed. He turned to the sounds of clanging pots and sizzling bacon.

"Well, good morning, sleepyhead," his ma said with a smile. She finished setting the table. Thrusting himself from his bed, he stretched his tired muscles and walked over to the table. Jenny sat smiling from her chair. Ma had pulled Jenny's blond hair back from her face into a long braid. Hollow eyes looked up at him. Titus's heart flipped with the sight of his little sister. So weak. So vulnerable. He grinned back at her. "Boy, I love Sundays! The one day I can be home. Right, Jenny girl?" He reached over and ruffled the hair on top of her head then turned to Ma. "How long till breakfast is ready?"

"Almost ready," Ma said, turning the eggs in the pan.

"If you don't mind, I'll step outside for a breath of air so it can wake me up. I'll be right back."

She nodded as she placed steaming biscuits on the table.

Walking into the backyard, Titus felt the morning chill prick his skin as he surveyed the area. Weather-beaten homes with sagging porches stumbled over one another along the street, leaving no gaps between neighbors. Broken glass, tattered furniture, and fragments of yesterday's trinkets littered neglected lawns. Being one for privacy, Titus hated the intrusion of other people so close to his home. He could hear their conversations, their thumps across wooden floors, their heated arguments. He shook his head. It wasn't like him to dwell in resentment, but he was there for now and wasn't ready to give it up. Not until somebody paid.

By the time he stepped into the kitchen, Ma was seated beside Jenny, and they both looked up at him. "Oh, sorry, didn't mean to take so long." He quickly seated himself and reached for a biscuit. Ma's words stopped him.

"Dear Lord, we thank Thee for the wonderful meal this morning. We ask that Thou wouldst bless the kind people who so graciously shared of their abundance with us. In Jesus' name, amen."

Titus knew their family tradition of prayer before meals, but he found himself forgetting such things more and more each day. He reached for a biscuit and pulled it open. Careful to save some for Ma and Jenny, he spread a tiny dollop of butter inside. "So, which *kind* person shared with us today?" Titus bit into his biscuit and looked at Ma.

She didn't even blink at his snide remark. "The Barnabas House brought some food over for us yesterday," she said matter-of-factly, while spooning some food onto her plate.

The impact of her statement hit him full in the face. He stopped chewing and glared at her. "Abigail O'Connor," he said with distaste.

Ma looked up pleasantly. "I would suspect so. Very kind of her and—"

He hit the table with his fist, stopping her words. His lips snarled, and he shoved his plate away. "How ironic that they would help us!" He barely spat out the words. "We don't need *their* charity! The O'Connor family brought this on us in the first place!"

Ma's face turned red. "Now, you listen here, young man. You'll be going to an early grave talking like that. The O'Connors are good people. Your pa made a choice. It turned out to be bad. Nobody is to blame. Things happen. The good Lord—"

"I don't want to hear about the good Lord," he shouted, rising to his feet.

Ma rose to her feet, too. "You'll not be talking like that in this house, Titus Matthews!" A whimper sounded from the table, causing them to turn to Jenny. Tears streamed steadily down her face.

As angry as he was, Titus couldn't hurt his sister. He swallowed hard and took a deep breath as the anger slinked away. Ma and Titus exchanged a glance. Titus walked over to Jenny and hugged her. "It's all right, Jenny."

He held her tight, kissing the top of her head. "I'm sorry. I was wrong." He felt tears moisten his eyes. How could he do this to Jenny when she had so much to deal with already? "Ma. . .is right," he heard himself saying, though he refused to believe it.

Jenny hiccupped a time or two then wiped her tears. Ma settled back in her place, and Titus did the same. They finished their meal in silence.

After breakfast, Ma cleared the table and grabbed her Bible. With Jenny's inability to walk, they found it too difficult to get to church, so Ma saw to it that they got religious training through her daily reading of the scriptures.

Out of respect, Titus stayed in his seat, but it took everything in him to keep himself there. After years of hearing the scriptures, he could recite verses without thinking. But they rang hollow in his dark heart. He knew he was traveling a path better left alone, but he couldn't seem to stop himself. Bitterness fed on his soul like termites on wood.

Hadn't King David of the scriptures avenged himself on his enemies? Titus tried to convince himself of that, but he knew his thoughts were a distortion of the truth. David had left Saul alone, though countless times Saul had tried to kill David. David left his enemies in God's hands.

Enough! Ma had filled his mind over the years with Bible teachings, making him weak. He needed to think like a man, not a weakling who depended on God as a crutch. No, this was one battle he could handle himself.

⚭

Abigail walked across the lawn to the stables in search of Titus, the morning dew soaking the hem of her dress. She peered into the barn. "Titus?"

At her side, merely a breath away, he answered. "Yes?"

She turned to face him. His breath was close enough to cause her face to tingle. "Oh," she said with a gasp. She took an awkward step back, tripping over her skirts. He reached out his hand and grabbed her to keep her from falling backward. For a moment, he hovered over her slightly bent form and looked down into her eyes. Neither said a word. A horse neighed, seeming to bring Titus to his senses. He looked as though he'd been splashed with cold water. Pulling Abigail to a standing position, he cleared his throat. "Are you all right?"

Abigail's hand pressed hard against her chest. "I'm fine. I don't know what got into me." She looked around a moment, not knowing how to handle the situation. Finally, she lifted her head and looked back at him. "I wanted to let you know I won't be going anywhere until this afternoon when it's time to go to Barnabas House. So if you want to groom the horses, you'll have the time." She pulled at her handkerchief and gave a delicate cough.

"Thank you. I'll do that."

She nodded then turned to go.

"Did you have Barnabas House bring our family food on Saturday?"

She stopped in place. Did she hear resentment in his voice? Maybe she had stepped out of line. Father had said the Matthews family was proud. She turned to him. "Well, I might have mentioned your ma could be in need of a few items."

Looking a bit uncomfortable, he hesitated a moment. He rolled his hat around in his hands a few seconds before looking back at her. "Thanks."

Relief washed over her. "You're welcome." She felt herself smile.

In fact, she smiled all the way back to the house.

☙

Titus brushed the horses with more vigor than necessary. Had he really thanked her for her charity? What had gotten into him? He knew the answer all too well.

Those blue eyes. The way her curls spilled across her shoulders and reflected the brilliance of the morning sun. Her kindness and gentle ways.

He yanked off his hat and slapped it against his pant leg. "It's not supposed to be like this!" he grumbled to the horses. "I have my plan all set, and I don't need Abigail O'Connor to mess things up." He plunked his hat back on and brushed the horse's coat once again. If his plans were to succeed, he'd have to stay away from Abigail, keep his relationship with her strictly business. He could do this.

He had to.

☙

"Abigail, are you all right?" Mother asked when Abigail stepped into the house quite out of breath.

She looked up with a start. "Oh yes, I'm fine."

"Look at the hem of your skirt," Mother said, pointing. "Where have you been?"

"Oh, I went out to tell Titus I wouldn't be going anywhere until this afternoon if he wanted to groom the horses."

Her mother studied her a moment.

"What?" Abigail asked, feeling uncomfortable under her mother's scrutiny.

"Oh, nothing," Mother said with a smile. "Nothing at all."

Abigail wasn't sure what that meant, but she knew one thing. She didn't like the sounds of it. Not one bit.

Making her way up the stairs, Abigail went to her bedroom. She needed to take Barnabas outside. When she pushed through the door, she saw the dog standing, admittedly a little crooked, waiting on her. Abigail laughed and walked over to him.

His tail wagged furiously as she edged closer; thankful eyes looked to her. Abigail bent down to the animal, speaking words of comfort to him. She wanted to nuzzle him but decided since she hadn't given him a bath yet, she'd better wait. Instead, she scratched the top of his head and worked her fingers down his back. He leaned in toward her as if begging for more. Father had found an old leash and collar in the barn and brought them in the night before. Abigail fastened the collar around Barnabas's neck then clamped on the leash. She carried him down the stairs, but once they reached the bottom, she lowered him to the floor, allowing him to adjust to his new way of walking.

"I'm taking Barnabas outside, Mother," she called before opening the door. Once outside, Abigail took Barnabas to a secluded spot in the backyard. She lifted her face to the morning sun, allowing its warm rays to wash over her. The warmth gave her a good feeling. Like when she and Jonathan shared happy times together. Jonathan. Her good feeling plunged. She lowered her head. "Where are you, Jonathan? Do you miss me at all?"

Just then, Barnabas stood erect. His body tensed, muscles flexed. A low, menacing growl simmered in his throat, and his lips rolled back, revealing pointed teeth.

Abigail turned. "Titus. You startled me."

"Oh, I'm sorry," he said. "Looks like you've got a good watchdog though."

Abigail laughed. "I guess I do," she said, rewarding Barnabas with a scratch on the head.

"I saw you out here and thought I'd find out what time you were thinking of leaving this afternoon. I wanted to clean out the stalls."

"Oh, probably around three o'clock. Will that work for you?"

"That's fine." He stood there for a moment. "Well, that's all I needed."

She nodded and smiled. Abigail watched as he walked away. Funny he should come out here to ask her that. She thought he had known they would leave at three. Could it be he was looking for an excuse to talk to her? She couldn't help feeling a little giddy at the thought. But then, what woman didn't appreciate a little attention from a handsome gentleman once in a while?

You're through with men, remember? The thought rang in her ears. *Of course, I remember.* "Come on, Barnabas, time to go in." The dog instantly hobbled to her side. She could hardly wait until three o'clock. The children would enjoy meeting Barnabas.

Or was she looking forward to three o'clock for another reason?

Chapter 5

The autumn winds swept the rest of September and all of October right into history. Abigail pulled her dark, woolen cloak tight against her as she stepped into the wintry November chill. Titus tipped his hat. "Abigail." She smiled and offered Barnabas to him as she stepped up to her carriage seat. Once she situated herself, Titus gave the hound a friendly scratch and lifted Barnabas to her. The two laughed as they watched the dog curl up in her lap.

Titus climbed onto the carriage and flicked the horses into a steady trot. "Barnabas seems to be getting around a lot better since his leg has healed."

She nodded.

"His fur looks better, too, since he's moved in with your family. You're taking mighty fine care of him." Titus reached over and stroked the dog down his back, causing Barnabas's left hind leg to stretch with delight.

Titus and Abigail laughed. "Looks like you've won him over at last," she said with a smile.

"I don't know who's won who over," Titus admitted. "But one thing's for sure: those kids at the house love him."

Abigail warmed to his words. "Yes, they do." She gave Barnabas an affectionate hug. Then remembering something, she turned to Titus. "Oh, don't let me forget. Ma said we need to stop at the post office and check the mail."

He nodded.

The afternoon went by quickly as Abigail worked with the children. Their studies seemed to be going well, and she enjoyed each of them. Abigail gathered her things to prepare to leave. She turned to see Katie O'Grady hugging Barnabas tight against her. In characteristic charm, a thatch of white hair drooped over the dog's right eye. His gentle face seemed to hold a smile, suggesting he was quite fond of the children's hugs. He snuggled his face into the crook of Katie's arm, as if totally enjoying the warmth of her embrace.

Abigail softened at the sight. Her heart went out to Katie. Only six years old, the child had suffered much already. Her pa left their family shortly after they arrived in America, just a few years back. Struggling to make ends meet, Katie's ma cleaned Barnabas House in return for room and board for herself and her daughter.

Abigail wondered how Mary O'Grady got through each day knowing the man she had given her life to had walked out on her and their child. Sadly, he could never come back. Shortly after leaving his family, he had stepped off a curb in the dark of night and been hit by a carriage. He died the next day. Such a tragedy. That's what Abigail couldn't risk. A man promising to love her forever then leaving. Like Jonathan.

"I love Barnabas," Katie said when she saw Abigail watching them.

"I know you do." Abigail cringed, thinking that a man could abandon his family in this way. But then isn't that what happened to her? Her parents had left her on the doorstep of the O'Connor family. Did her real parents know the O'Connors? Somehow, Abigail felt her parents did know them and knew that they would take good care of her. And the O'Connors had been wonderful parents. Still, sometimes she craved to know where she belonged. Where were her roots? Were her parents still living?

Abigail felt a tug on her leg and looked down. "Yes, Katie?"

The little girl clung to Abigail's dress and through messy hair looked up. "I love you, Miss Abigail." She squeezed Abigail's skirts once more.

Without warning, tears sprang to Abigail's eyes. She related to this child in many ways. After all, she, too, had been abandoned. By her parents. By Jonathan. Abigail hunkered down to the child. "And I love you, Katie O'Grady," she said, hugging the child with abandon.

"You won't ever leave me, will you, Miss Abigail?"

Abigail's breath caught in her throat. Only God knew the future. How could she make a promise she wasn't sure she could keep?

"I will be here, Katie, for as long as I'm able."

The child seemed satisfied with the answer and squeezed her once more before trotting off to play with the rag doll Abigail had given her weeks ago.

"Come, Barnabas," Abigail called. Once the hound was on a leash, she waved good-bye to the children and made her way out to the carriage. The strain of the child's sincere question had tired Abigail. She kept her tears at bay, refusing to think further on parents who abandoned children and gentlemen who left broken hearts behind.

❧

Titus pulled the carriage to a stop in front of the post office. Abigail waited as he opened the door for her. "I'll only be a moment," she said, making her way to the door.

Once inside, she exchanged pleasantries with the woman who ran the post office. The woman then pulled Abigail's mail from the proper box and handed it to her. Abigail sorted through it and looked curiously upon one parcel in particular. A letter from Uncle Edward out in Colorado Territory. Why would he be writing to their family? She fingered the envelope, turning it over in her hands. Uncle Edward had cheated her father out of a job at least fifteen years ago. Pa forgave him, even tried to keep in touch, but Uncle Edward avoided his brother. Father had said Edward needed the Lord and they should pray for him, Aunt Elizabeth, and their daughter, Eliza. Her father had prayed faithfully over the years. The letter could bring good news. The mere fact he was writing would encourage Father, she felt sure.

Abigail thought of her cousin. Eliza and her pa were just alike in looks. . .and behavior. Spoiled, mean, and selfish.

Remembering her mother's scolding on the subject over the years, Abigail chided herself for such thoughts. After all, those were childish pranks Eliza had pulled, tattling and lying to the adults. They were grown up now. Abigail wondered what had happened to Eliza.

She could hardly wait to get home and get the mail to her parents.

"Good news?" Titus asked, helping her back into the carriage.

"Possibly," she said, holding up the letter.

"I'm glad," Titus answered. A look of affection flittered across his face. Abigail was pleased she had noticed.

⊝⊃

Abigail and Mother sat on the sofa in the drawing room while Father opened the letter. The solemn look on his face made Abigail a little uneasy. Concern shadowed Mother's face as well.

"Thomas, what is it?" Mother asked.

He rubbed his chin and thought for a moment, as if searching for the right words. "Well, it seems Edward has been down on his luck. The gold rush didn't work out. He's in Colorado Territory now and without work."

Ma lifted her chin.

He held out his palm. "Now, hold on, Lavina. Before you get yourself out of sorts, let me finish." He dropped his hand and glanced at the letter again. "It seems they barely have food on the table. Eliza is down to skin and bones, and he fears for her. He says here that since we're good Christian folks—" Father glanced up. "He's sending Eliza to live with us."

Ma gasped. "What?"

Abigail felt her stomach turn to lead. All the childhood memories once again burned across her mind like a fire out of control. How silly, she thought, pushing the immature matter aside. She looked at Mother, who seemed to bite her tongue. "What is it?" Abigail asked.

No one answered. Mother sucked in a long, deep breath and wiped her hands on the front of her skirt. She kept her gaze on her skirt. "When will she be here, Thomas?"

"It looks as though she'll arrive by train within a week."

"Nice of Edward to give you an option," Mother said through clenched teeth.

"Now, Lavina."

This time she held up her hand. "I know, I know. Just let me have a moment of self-pity to get used to the idea."

Father walked over to her and pulled her to her feet. He placed his arms around her waist. "Lavina, if ever there is a woman who forgives, it's you. It's your gift. Besides, it's not Eliza's fault her pa is the way he is."

Mother seemed to melt in Father's arms. "You're right. We'll make her welcome, Thomas, because she's family and because God loves us even when we don't deserve it."

Father smiled. "I love you, Lavina O'Connor."

Abigail quietly stepped out of the room, giving her parents a moment of privacy. The love between them had always made her feel secure. Eliza had probably never known that kind of security with a pa like Uncle Edward. Despite their differences in their childhood days, Abigail decided she would do what she could to make Eliza feel welcome.

A knock sounded at the door. Abigail looked up from her novel. Barnabas barked and ran toward the sound. She put a marker in her book and walked over to answer the door. Pulling on the knob, she was surprised to see her best friend standing at the entrance.

"Sophia!" she exclaimed, reaching over to hug her. "Come in."

The two walked into the drawing room, Barnabas prancing at their feet. "So, you're the wonder dog I've been hearing so much about," Sophia said with a laugh as she settled into her seat. She pulled off her gloves and let Barnabas sniff her hands. When he finished, she tousled his hair. He seemed to lose interest in the visit, ambled over to Abigail, circled three times, then plopped in a heap at her feet. They both laughed.

"How is the little mother doing?" Abigail asked, looking at Sophia's growing midsection.

"I'm doing fine. The sickness has subsided, so things are looking up."

"Oh Sophia, how are you?" Mother entered the room and gave Sophia a hug.

"I'm fine, thank you."

"How would you ladies like some tea?"

"That would be nice," Sophia answered.

"Thanks," Abigail agreed.

In the blink of an eye, Mother was out of the room, with the sound of clanging dishes coming from the kitchen.

"I hope you don't mind I stopped by. Since I haven't been able to make

160

it to church as much lately, I had to see for myself how you were getting along." Sophia flashed a look of concern toward Abigail.

"You mean without Jonathan?"

Sophia nodded.

"I'm fine, really. I mean, I miss him, but I'm getting along all right." Abigail shrugged. "Just wasn't meant to be."

"What about your chauffeur?" Sophia asked with raised eyebrows. "He seems like a good catch."

"You and Gramma!" Abigail said with a laugh. She shook her head. "I'm not sure I want another relationship. I'm happy with my work at Barnabas House, and—"

"You don't want another relationship? Of course you do! My child has to have a playmate!"

They both laughed. Mother brought in the tea and handed a cup and saucer to each one.

"Tell her, Mrs. O'Connor," Sophia encouraged. "Tell her she has to find someone and get married soon so my child will have a playmate."

The older woman smiled and shook her head. "I learned long ago that once Abigail's mind is made up, I'm hard-pressed to change it." She threw a wink at Abigail and started to leave the room. Turning, she looked at Sophia. "But you're more than welcome to try." She laughed and went back to the kitchen.

"What about this Christopher you told me about at Barnabas House? Any chance of something with him?"

Abigail smiled. "Christopher is a wonderful friend, but it's not like that."

Sophia sipped her tea. "Well, the way I view it, you have two handsome men in your life, and you just can't throw away good prospects. I can see I'm going to have to pray harder."

Abigail groaned before taking a sip of tea. "How's your ma and Mrs. Baird?"

Sophia chuckled. "Mrs. Baird is ornery as always."

Abigail laughed and nodded.

"It's all Mama can do to keep up with her."

Abigail could hear the affection in Sophia's voice for the women. And rightfully so. They were both easy to love. "She has a lot of energy; I'll give her that." They paused a moment. "Still keeping busy sewing?"

Sophia nodded, put her cup in the saucer, and placed them on a nearby stand. "Do you remember Marie Zimmerman?"

"Uh-huh."

"She still helps me. I don't know what I'd do without her."

"How is her husband—wasn't it Seth?"

Sophia nodded. "He found a job with the railroad. They've managed to move out of the shanty and into a fine little cottage and are doing well. Their girls love school."

Abigail smiled, thinking of the little girls. "They are so cute." She took another drink of her tea.

Sophia looked into the distance. "I love those two." She absently rubbed her stomach.

Abigail looked at her and laughed. She put her teacup on the table then turned to Sophia. "I can't believe you're married and expecting your first child! Where does the time go?"

Sophia shrugged and smiled. "I don't know."

"So, tell me about you and Clayton."

Sophia nodded with a sparkle in her eye. "I never knew I could be so happy, Abigail."

Abigail smiled. "I know. I can see it in you. You practically glow!" A comfortable silence followed. "His business is going well then?"

"Yes. And his father and mother are doing well."

"You've been very blessed." Abigail looked away for a moment.

"It will happen for you one day, Abby. If not with Jonathan, then with someone else God has in mind for you."

Abigail shrugged. "It doesn't matter."

"Don't give up. There are eligible men out there besides Jonathan Clark."

"I suppose."

They each drank some more of the tea while Mother answered another knock at the door.

"You know," Sophia said, "it's all so exciting. Why, the man of your dreams could walk through that door at any moment!"

No sooner had the words left Sophia's mouth than Titus appeared in the doorway. "Abigail?"

Her head jerked up with a start. With teacup still in hand, her sudden movement caused it to rattle on the saucer, sloshing the hot liquid about.

"Oh, I'm sorry," he said, hat in hand.

Sophia and Abigail exchanged a glance.

"What can I do for you, Titus?"

"I wanted to see when you would be heading for Barnabas House so I could have the carriage ready."

Sophia chimed in, a smile on her face. "I really need to be going anyway. We'll visit again soon," she was saying, already on her feet.

Titus looked to Abigail.

"I'll be ready in ten minutes."

He gave a quick nod and left. Sophia looked back at Abigail, and they both burst into laughter.

Chapter 6

The weekend passed much too swiftly for Abigail. The children had most of their homework caught up, leaving her little to do at Barnabas House. Deciding to leave early, she asked Titus to take her to visit Gramma. She needed to see how Gramma was faring.

Once they arrived at Gramma's, Titus helped Abigail and Barnabas from the carriage. With his leash trailing behind him, Barnabas ran to the front door, barked a couple of times, then scurried over to a tree for a good sniffing.

Though Abigail was put out by Barnabas's moment of freedom, she laughed with Titus at her dog's antics. Upon hearing the creak of the front door, they turned to see Gramma standing at the entrance in a sensible gray dress. Titus stayed near the carriage and lifted his hand in greeting.

"Good day to ye," Gramma said, embracing Abigail at the door and nodding to Titus. "Come in, come in." Abigail stepped through the door. Barnabas rushed in behind her just before Gramma closed the door. Abigail made her way toward the sofa and settled in. Paws and leash clinking lightly against the wooden floor, Barnabas strolled up beside her and snuggled at her feet. Abigail gave a token scolding to the independent hound then patted him for reassurance. Gramma opened the door again and called, "Ye come join us, laddie."

A scuffle sounded at the step, and Abigail turned in surprise to see Titus in the doorway. He fingered his hat as he talked. "I don't mean to intrude, ma'am."

" 'Tis no intrusion. No intrusion at all," Gramma said with a brush of her hand. "Please, come in." She turned back to Abigail and winked.

Abigail sighed and shook her head. Gramma was up to her frolics again. Abigail looked at Titus, and he smiled, throwing her a what-could-I-do look. They settled down to tea.

After Gramma gleaned every bit of information out of Titus that she could possibly gather, she proceeded to list Abigail's attributes. By the time Gramma had finished her little speech, Abigail thought herself a saint by Gramma's standards.

"Enough of this, Gramma. You're making me blush."

Gramma shrugged. "So ye add a little color to ye face, aye?"

Titus walked over to her piano. "May I?" he asked.

A pleasurable smile lit Gramma's face as she nodded her approval.

Titus scooted onto the piano bench and began to play some classical themes that Abigail had heard before but whose titles she didn't know. She closed her eyes and listened, letting the music lift her from her fatigue and stress of the day and carry her to a place of comfort. Once the last note faded, she lingered a moment longer then opened her eyes.

Gramma's eyes, alight with sparkle as if she had stumbled upon a well-kept secret, stared at her. The expression on Gramma's face brought Abigail to her senses. She turned to Titus, who was also looking her way. "It's beautiful, Titus. Where did you learn to play like that?"

He shrugged. "Ma taught me. She used to be quite the pianist and occasionally helped out at Hooley's Opera House."

Abigail found the information intriguing. She didn't know that about Titus. But then, she didn't know much about him at all.

He turned in his seat and started another tune. "Amazing Grace." This one she knew; she hummed the melody then started singing the words. Before they knew it, beautiful music filled the air. They passed the hour playing and singing such tunes as "Buffalo Gals," "Oh! Susanna," "Jim Crack Corn," "Jeanie with the Light Brown Hair," song after song until they were finally spent.

They laughed and visited awhile longer then decided they had to leave.

"This afternoon ye have brought great joy to this tired heart, that ye have," Gramma said, cupping Abigail's face in her hands. Gramma kissed Abigail's cheek then turned to Titus. "And ye, laddie. I'll be thanking ye for the fine music."

Titus's face lit up. The smile that stretched across his face made Abigail's heart flip, startling her. They turned and walked out the door, Barnabas following close behind. Once they reached the carriage, Titus stopped and looked at Abigail for a fleeting moment. Her pulse drummed hard against her ears. Neither said a word. Yet their silence spoke volumes.

☙

Titus led the horses through the streets as dusk crept into the sky. He took off his hat and shoved his fingers through his hair. What had gotten into him? He couldn't let this woman get under his skin. He had a job to do. Abigail and the O'Connors were muddling everything. Why did they treat him like family? He wanted to think it was their guilt, but deep down, he knew such a burden didn't drive them. Their faith made them care about others. Not just him. They weren't doing good for appearance's sake. They lived a "life of thankfulness," as Mr. O'Connor had put it, for what God had done for them. That knowledge pricked him. Why couldn't God do things for him, too? Why did God take his pa? Why did God strip Titus of his dream to one day be a doctor?

By the time the horses arrived at Abigail's home, he had worked himself up good. He wanted no part of that woman. Keep his distance—that's what he'd do. No more letting her rattle him with her gentle smile, the sparkle in her eyes, and her kind ways. No, he had to stand firm, find what he needed to bring them down, and get on with his life.

He jumped off his carriage seat and helped Abigail down, his jaw taut, teeth clenched. She smiled, then upon seeing his face, quickly lowered her eyes. "Thank you," she whispered before heading for the door.

He felt like a heel, a scoundrel. She didn't deserve his treatment, but he couldn't stop now. He'd come too far. The O'Connor family had to pay. He'd suffered too much.

Unhitching the team from the carriage, his thoughts rambled on when he was struck with an idea. He would go to their church and see what he could find out, see what made them tick, so he'd know better how to bring them down. Putting the horses back in their stalls, he decided that's what he'd do.

Come Sunday, he would go to church.

⌒

Abigail went straight to her room. She had had a wonderful afternoon, but what just happened out in the stable? One minute Titus seemed wonderful, and the next, well, she didn't know what to think.

She laid across the bed, but Barnabas whined from the floor. "Oh you!" she said, pulling herself up to console him. "I'm the one who needs a kind pat or two, not you."

Barnabas seemed to ignore her completely. Abigail continued to comfort her dog while thinking of Titus. Where had his thoughts taken him during the carriage ride? Was he afraid she would read more into their afternoon than was there? Perhaps he had another young lady in his life. She gasped, causing Barnabas to look up. Until that very moment, she hadn't thought of that possibility.

Abigail heaved a big sigh and plopped back on her bed again. As long as she lived, she would never understand men. One minute you felt quite sure they were smitten; the next minute their attention was focused fully on newspapers, horses, or who knew what.

Maybe when her cousin arrived, she and Abigail could share secrets. Some cousins were close like that. Abigail hoped they could be. Of course, Sophia was her best friend. Still, it would be nice to have a cousin with a shared spirit. Kind of like having a sister.

Her mind replayed the afternoon's events. Titus playing on the piano, the look in Gramma's eyes. The look of affection filled Titus's eyes when he watched her from the piano. She hadn't missed it. It warmed her clear through.

Thoughts of Jonathan had grown fewer with every passing day. Perhaps she had moved on without him. Much sooner than she had expected. Quite possibly she didn't love him after all. That revelation surprised her.

Then another thought came to her, surprising her even more. Perhaps she could give love one more chance.

∽

"Where are you going?" Ma asked.

"I'm going to church," Titus said matter-of-factly.

Ma looked like she would faint dead away. "Where are you going to church?"

"I'm going to the O'Connors' church."

Her eyes narrowed. "Why the sudden interest?"

He shrugged.

Ma's eyes turned big as coins. A smile broke out on her face. "It's Abigail, isn't it?"

"No, it's not Abigail. I just want to go."

"Oh son, you don't have to hide your feelings. I think she's a lovely young lady."

"Ma, it's not Abigail," he barked. One look at her face made him feel bad for his tone. "I'm sorry, Ma. I'm just going to church. That's all."

Her expression grew serious. "Titus, you watch yourself."

"Don't worry, Ma."

She walked over to him and kissed his cheek. "Don't let hate rule you, son. I love you. I don't want to lose you, too." Before he could answer, she turned and busied herself with breakfast preparations.

Jenny smiled at him. "What are you smiling about?" he teased, tousling her hair. For a moment, his heart pricked. He was doing this for Jenny, too. After all, she was affected by what the O'Connors did to them. He justified his actions, cleaning his heart of any trace of guilt. After breakfast, he gave Jenny a kiss on the head then did the same to Ma. "I'll see you later."

He walked through the door, barely hearing Ma's words that she was still praying for him.

∽

Titus walked into church with the O'Connor family. His boots scuffed the wooden floors. It had been awhile since he'd darkened the doors of such a place. The building was small, not at all like what he had imagined. Every eye seemed to turn and look at him, making him uncomfortable. The boards groaned when they finally settled onto the rough-hewn benches. Titus took great care as he scooted across the worn and splintered bench.

The reverend, somewhat familiar in his approach to the people, surprised Titus. He liked it though. Oh, there he went again. Getting his mind off of his reason for being there. This wasn't a real church visit. He was there for one reason: to find out how to bring down the O'Connor family.

The reverend's sermon spoke of forgiveness. Of course. What else? Ma was praying. She did this to him. Though he loved her, sometimes she made him want to spit. He often wondered if she had a direct line to God. Seemed God answered all of her prayers.

Well, maybe not all. Had Ma prayed about their current situation? Surely Ma had prayed about Jenny. Where was God in all that?

Titus shifted in his seat and refocused on the reverend's words. He talked of David's forgiveness toward his enemy Saul. Of all the things to talk about. Hadn't Titus already rehashed those stories in his mind? The reverend reminded them that though Saul had made several attempts on David's life, David stayed true to God. He would not touch the Lord's anointed.

Well, Titus could rest easy. The O'Connors were not the Lord's anointed. Were they? What did that mean, anyway? Someone chosen of God? To do what, preach? Saul wasn't a preacher, but a king. The O'Connors wouldn't fit. God understood Titus's feelings. God would approve.

He had to.

⁂

Church was over faster than the flutter of a hummingbird's wings, and Titus had little time to mingle with the people to find out anything on the O'Connors. It would take time, no doubt. He'd have to be patient. Still, he didn't want to risk too much time. He didn't like the way his heart turned over at the sight of Abigail. The sooner he could leave their home, the better.

"You will join us for lunch, Titus?" Mrs. O'Connor asked.

He looked at Abigail. "Oh yes, and you have to play me in checkers," she encouraged. "But I'll warn you, I'm good."

His eyebrows lifted. "Oh, a challenge? Well, I don't see how I can refuse." He turned to Mrs. O'Connor. "I'll be there." He mentally kicked himself. What was he thinking? He wasn't. The words were out of his mouth before he had time to think.

After a meal of beef, potatoes, corn, and biscuits, Titus and Abigail settled into a game of checkers in front of the hearth. Barnabas lay coiled at her feet. Over the next hour, they played a couple of games, stopping to chat between moves, each winning one game. Titus insisted on a third to break the tie. Abigail took up the challenge, and much to his pleasure, Titus won. Abigail gave in agreeably; then Mr. O'Connor invited Titus to a game of chess.

Titus couldn't remember when he'd passed such an enjoyable afternoon. He only wished it hadn't been with the O'Connors. Oh, he was learning more about them, all right, but he was learning things he didn't want to know. Like the fact that they seemed genuine. He hadn't expected that. He had thought they would be like most people who claimed religion. Fake. Yet this family was different. They actually believed what they said they believed. Made him almost sorry he didn't share in their faith.

Before leaving, Titus edged his way out to the barn to check on the horses. Although it was his day off, he had grown to care about the animals and wanted to see to them.

"They kind of grow on you, don't they?" Mr. O'Connor's voice came from behind Titus.

Titus turned to him and smiled. "Yeah, I guess they do at that."

"Look, Titus, you've done a good job for us, and I want to thank you." Mr. O'Connor waited a moment. "There's something else." Titus looked up at him. "I've never told you how sorry I was about your pa. He was a good friend. I never meant for him to. . .well, I. . ." Tears welled up in the older man's face, confusing Titus. This was all wrong. He didn't want to see genuine concern on his enemy's face. This man was his enemy. Titus did not want to care about him or his family. Titus turned away.

"I didn't know he had put everything into that business, or I would have tried to stop him."

Titus turned back to him. Mr. O'Connor placed a hand on Titus's shoulder. "I want to help you, Titus, because I know your pa would have done the same for my family had the tables been turned."

Titus was speechless. What could he say? His thoughts warred. He wanted to. . .

Get even.

Before his heart could thaw, Titus fought back, allowing the chill to return, cold and hard like icicles. He said nothing.

Mr. O'Connor looked into Titus's eyes and paused. Without a word, he patted Titus on the shoulder then turned and walked away.

Chapter 7

Shaking the snow from her boots, Abigail stepped into Barnabas House and pulled off her cloak. She thought it best to keep Barnabas at home today since it was so cold. A pleasurable smell of stew meandered from the kitchen through the front room to greet her. As she hung her cloak on a nearby peg, she glanced at the freshly painted white walls. It hardly seemed to Abigail the same place as when she first started working there.

She walked over to the fireplace to warm herself a moment. Her cheeks were still stinging from the biting cold, but she felt refreshed, invigorated, and ready to work. Winter did that to her. Rubbing her hands in front of the open fire, she spoke greetings to a few of the workers. A movement in the window caught her attention. Outside, delicate snowflakes fluttered to the ground, reminding Abigail of a scene from Currier and Ives. With a happy sigh, she pulled herself away and headed toward her table to work with the children.

"Abigail, how are you?"

She turned with a start to see Christopher standing there. "Oh, hello! I'm so glad you're better."

A huge smile spread across his face. "That makes two of us." He looked around the room. "I've missed this place. And I'm so thankful you and the others were able to keep it going while I was gone. Thanks, too, for organizing the painting. The place looks nice."

"Well, Mary O'Grady did most of the organizing. She worked hard to keep things going while you were gone."

Christopher's eyes sparkled. "That woman is a wonder."

Abigail thought she heard something in his voice. Admiration? No, it was more than that. Definitely more. Her face must have revealed her thoughts.

Christopher cleared his throat. "Well, it's hard to believe here it is December 10th already. Christmas will soon be upon us."

Abigail smiled then turned giddy with the thought of Christmas. She loved Christmas with all the trimmings and festivities the holiday brought.

"I see you like this time of year."

"Yes, I love it."

"Miss Abigail, I have something for you." Katie O'Grady tugged at

Abigail's dress. She held something behind her back.

Abigail looked down at her and smiled. The sight of the child brought out her maternal instincts. "Is that a fact?" she asked, looking at Katie.

Katie beamed and nodded with vigor.

"Well, I'll leave you two for now," Christopher said with a wink.

"Thank you, Christopher," Abigail returned then scrunched down in front of Katie. One thing about it: Mary O'Grady might be poor, but her daughter's face was as shiny as a scrubbed apple. Hems had been dropped on her two dresses and tears mended. "Now, what is it you wanted to show me?"

"Could we go over there?" Katie pointed to a vacant corner out of the way of others.

Abigail smiled. "Certainly." Together they scuffled through the busy room, across the wooden floor, and hunkered in the corner as if sharing a wonderful secret.

"This is my favorite necklace. I wore it every day until Bobby broke it." Katie's eyes filled with tears as she stretched out her hand. "I want to give it to you." There in her delicate palm lay a golden locket with a broken chain.

Abigail gasped. "Why, Katie, I could not take such a wonderful gift from you. Where did you get it?"

"Ma gave it to me. It don't have her picture, though. She didn't have one." Katie opened the locket and showed an empty shell where a picture should have been.

"You cannot give away such a precious gift, Katie. Your ma meant that for you."

She lifted worried eyes to Abigail. A look that said she wanted to give her best gift yet didn't want to part with such a treasure. "Ma said when you love someone, you give them your best gift, just like God did when He gave His Son, Jesus." All wiggles and energy, she couldn't seem to stand still but moved about and scratched as new itches seemed to surface. "I know it's broke, but it's still my favorite thing." Suddenly, she pulled herself straight, squaring her shoulders as if she were about to recite a memory verse word for word. "Ma said broken things could be fixed. But only God can fix a broken heart." She snapped her head and grinned at her own delivery of the speech.

Abigail felt a squeeze on her heart. No doubt Mary O'Grady still ached over her husband's abandonment and death. Abigail's pain over losing Jonathan was nothing compared to what this woman had suffered.

Katie swayed in half circles as she talked to Abigail. Her hands waved with her words. "Ma says I have to forgive Bobby for breaking my necklace just like she has to forgive Pa for leaving us," she said matter-of-factly. She stopped and licked her lips very slowly, like she was tasting honey from a biscuit. Raising her right arm, she swiped her wet mouth with the back of her hand. "I'm still mad at him, though." As if someone pushed a button, her eyebrows crinkled at the same time her lower lip jutted out. "Ma says she'll pray for me." She frowned and stared at the necklace in her hand and lifted teary eyes to Abigail. "Don't you like my gift, Miss Abigail?"

"Oh!" Abigail pulled the child into an enormous hug. When they finally separated, Abigail looked into Katie's green eyes. "Katie, I love your present."

With only a slight hesitation, Katie dropped the precious locket and broken chain into Abigail's waiting hand. Abigail knew Katie had sacrificed her most treasured gift. "Thank you."

The little girl's face brightened, and her tears dried. Without another word, Katie skipped over to the table where she worked on her homework, and no doubt the entire scene was quickly forgotten. But Abigail knew she would never forget the sacrificial gift given to her by a pink-cheeked, little Irish girl on a chilly winter's afternoon.

☙❧

Sunday morning, Titus walked behind Abigail as they made their way out of the church. He found himself spending more time with the O'Connors than necessary but couldn't seem to turn them down when they invited him. As much as he hated to admit it, he enjoyed their company. His plan gnawed at him, but he pushed it aside for now. It didn't hurt to enjoy life a little, did it? He'd get back to his plan, but for now, he wanted to spend a little more time with Abigail.

"Abigail!"

Titus was just helping Abigail into the carriage when they heard her name. They both turned to see Sophia and Clayton coming toward them.

"Oh, I was hoping to catch you before you left," Sophia said, somewhat out of breath.

"Titus," Clayton said with a grin, extending his hand.

"Good to see you again, Clayton."

"Well, I wanted to know if you and Titus could join us for lunch." Sophia looked hopeful. Abigail hesitated a moment then looked at Titus as if she feared what he might say or think.

"It's fine with me," he said.

Abigail visibly relaxed. A smile lifted her lips. "We'd like that. Let me tell Mother."

"Good," Sophia said with a snap of her head. "We'll see you there."

Titus turned to Abigail. "You'd have to ride with me in my buckboard since your parents will need the carriage."

She smiled, putting all his fear to rest. "That will be fine."

Somehow he knew she meant it, too.

Her parents gave their blessing. Titus and Abigail waved good-bye and headed toward Sophia and Clayton's home. He felt a little self-conscious being a mere chauffeur with Clayton an attorney and all. He reminded himself these people didn't seem to care in the least. So why should he?

Titus pulled the buffalo skin up from the wagon, brushed it off, and gave it to Abigail. "Here, you'll need this."

"Thanks," she said, adjusting it around her to ward off the biting chill.

Soft white flakes filled the air as they traveled the roads to Sophia and Clayton's country home. Meadows once filled with wildflowers lay in frigid heaps, waiting for spring's thaw.

"I'm sorry it's cold. But at least it's pretty to look at, don't you think?"

Abigail smiled with pure pleasure. "I'm glad to find someone else besides me who loves the season. I was beginning to think the world was full of grouses."

Titus laughed. His eyebrows quirked and lowered. "I guess I'm not a grouse, at least when it comes to winter."

Abigail studied him for a minute, making him feel a little uncomfortable. "So tell me about your ma."

His spirit dropped. He didn't want to talk about his family. That was too personal. They were stepping into intimate territory. Yet it was a perfectly sound question. After all, he'd spent lots of time with her family. He decided to answer.

"Ma's amazing. Her spirits are always up, despite the circumstances."

"I'm sorry about everything, Titus. I know things haven't been easy for you."

The sincerity of her words tugged at him in ways he didn't want to explore. "The main thing is to get Jenny walking—and talking again."

"Oh, I knew she didn't walk, but I didn't realize she couldn't talk."

"Just since Pa died. She talked before then."

"Oh, how awful. I'm so sorry."

"We'll get by," he said, scratching his jaw. He just didn't want to tell her he had to take her family down to bring his family peace. His heart constricted. The truth was he was getting soft. Second-guessing himself. Abigail seemed to sense his inner struggle. She kept silent the rest of the journey.

꩜

"Abigail, you must see what I've made for the baby," Sophia said, placing the soup ladle on the stove. Grabbing Abigail's hand, Sophia took her friend to the bedroom. She bent down in front of her trunk.

"Oh Sophia, your mother gave you the trunk?"

Sophia looked up, beaming. "You remember?"

"How could I forget? That's the one Clayton found in the fire, right?"

"Right." Sophia ran her fingers along the top of the trunk. "Papa's gift to Mama, Clayton's gift to me." She lifted the lid almost as if there were something sacred inside. Carefully, she picked up a knitted yellow blanket woven in an intricate pattern.

Abigail gasped. "Oh my, Sophia, you knitted this?"

Sophia smiled with pride. "Do you like it?"

Abigail held it tenderly, pressing it softly against her face. "It is beautiful." She handed the blanket back to Sophia. "Your baby is very blessed to have you and Clayton for parents."

"We are the ones most blessed," she corrected, slipping the blanket gingerly back into the trunk. She closed the lid and looked to Abigail. "Do you still miss him?"

"Who?"

Sophia laughed. "Well, I guess that answers my question."

"Oh, you mean Jonathan?"

Sophia nodded, her eyes probing.

"Only a little. It's not so bad now."

"You never hear from him?"

Abigail shook her head. "It's all right. I've moved on."

"I can see that," Sophia said, nodding her head toward the door with a laugh.

"No, no. I don't mean that."

"Titus is handsome, don't you think?"

"There you go again."

"Well?"

"All right, he's handsome, but I'm not ready for another relationship, Sophia. Really."

Sophia studied her a moment. "You will be one day. I hope Titus is still around." She pulled herself up from her knees and walked through the door, but her words lingered in the room with Abigail.

⟳

When the women walked into the room, Abigail overheard Titus talking to Clayton about his dream of becoming a doctor. Her heart ached as she heard the longing in his voice. Dreams obliterated. She wished there was something she could do to help him get back to medical school. His mother had her hands full taking care of Jenny. He was their sole provider. How could he possibly come up with money or time for medical school?

Titus turned to see her looking at him. He stopped talking. Clayton seemed to notice the awkward moment. "How's the soup coming, Sophia?

This man is hungry," he said with a laugh.

"It's almost ready."

Abigail placed the dishes on the table, and soon they gathered around for prayer and eating. Sophia scooped ample portions of steaming stew into hefty bowls. The sight of the stew, thick with vegetables, made Abigail's stomach growl. She could hardly wait to eat. Sophia's mother had taught her daughter well in the art of cooking.

By the time lunch was over and the afternoon spent, the snow had subsided. Abigail and Titus said their good-byes to Sophia and Clayton and headed home just before dusk.

"Thank you, Titus, for coming along. I hope it didn't make you uncomfortable to be paired with me today." Feeling her words were too forward, Abigail almost wished she hadn't spoken them.

He looked at her and smiled. "I didn't mind it at all. I had a wonderful time." His eyes locked with hers long enough to make her heart skip. She pulled her gaze away, not daring to dwell on what was happening between them.

They traveled the way home in comfortable silence. Abigail found herself wishing Titus didn't have to leave. When he drew the buckboard in front of her home, he turned to her. He looked like he wanted to say something. He leaned in, and she lost her breath, feeling quite sure he was about to kiss her, but before she could react, he pulled away and jumped out of the buckboard. He came over to her side and helped her out, walking her to the door. "Good night, Abigail," he said without looking.

Befuddled, she watched as he quickly boarded his wagon and headed home.

She watched him leave. "What was that all about?" The wind lifted her words into the night air, but the question remained on her heart.

Chapter 8

Wednesday morning, Titus stood in the drawing room of the O'Connor home, circling his hat between his fingers. "Sorry to keep you waiting, Titus," Abigail said, lifting her bag. An abundance of volunteers at Barnabas House had left her with fewer hours to work. She hadn't talked to Titus since their afternoon at Clayton and Sophia's on Sunday. She felt a little nervous talking to him since their last meeting, wondering what was going on inside of him. Without saying a word, he shoved his hat on his head, and they turned to leave.

Before they left the drawing room, a knock sounded. Barnabas barked and ran through the hallway, skidding to a halt at the front door.

Mother's footsteps sounded in the hallway. "I'll get it."

While they waited a moment, Abigail felt anxious to fill the silence. "How have you been this week, Titus?"

He lifted his gaze to her. "I've been fine. How about you?"

"Good." An awkward moment stretched between them. Titus looked like he wanted to say more. If only she could read him. He filled the gap with talk of the horses. Ignoring Barnabas's warning barks of a stranger in the house, they slid into a comfortable discussion. So lost were they in conversation that when Mother entered the room, it took them completely by surprise.

Abigail looked up to see an attractive, blond-haired woman, dressed in the latest fashions and colors, standing beside Mother. The woman tilted her chin and seemed to look Abigail over as if she were a bolt of cloth. It unnerved her a little.

"Abigail, it's been awhile since you've seen her, but this is your cousin Eliza."

Abigail felt her stomach plunge. Most likely a response brought on from years gone by. *Let it go, Abigail*, she told herself. Eliza walked over to Abigail, extending her hand. "Hello. You haven't changed a bit," she said with a sugary whine. "Same freckles and—" Eliza's gaze ran over Abigail. "Well, everything."

Somehow Abigail felt the comment was meant to dig under her skin.

It did.

Eliza O'Connor. With the same personality as Abigail had remembered.

"And I see you haven't changed," Abigail said, all the while noticing Eliza didn't appear the sickly cousin that Uncle Edward had described in his letter. They shook hands rather awkwardly.

Eliza turned to Titus and gave him a look that made Abigail blush. Before Mother could introduce them, Eliza stepped up to him. "And you are. . . ?" she asked with obvious interest.

Titus took a step back. "Um, Titus Matthews, ma'am," he said, tipping his hat.

A sly smile curved the corners of her mouth. "I like that name," she said with unreserved boldness.

Mother coughed, seemingly taken aback by Eliza's behavior. "Titus is our friend and our chauffeur."

Eliza's eyebrows rose as she seemed to consider this information; then she smiled again. "I'll look forward to a pleasant carriage ride then," she said, eyes twinkling.

Abigail's jaw dropped in astonishment, never before having seen such a lavish display of feminine daring.

"Will you be staying at Barnabas House all day, Abigail?" Mother wanted to know.

Abigail clamped her mouth shut, swallowed, then looked at her mother. "No, I won't be working with the children today, so I'm going over long enough to help Christopher with a few things, and I'll be back around eleven o'clock."

"Good," Mother said. "I'll plan on lunch around then." She turned to Titus. "You'll join us today, Titus, or do you have other plans?"

He cleared his throat. "Um, I'm beholden to you, Mrs. O'Connor."

"Good. Lunch at eleven o'clock," she said with a snap of her head. She turned to Eliza. "That will give you time to get settled in your room and freshen up, if you so desire."

Eliza turned to Titus. Her eyes never leaving his face, she responded, "I do so desire to freshen up. A lady must always look her best." She threw a delicate smile his way then turned to Abigail. "Isn't that right, Cousin?"

Abigail's cheeks flamed, no doubt giving Eliza the answer she sought. Eliza laughed and followed Mother to the stairway, leaving Abigail speechless.

⌒

Arriving home from Barnabas House, Abigail pulled her wraps tighter around her neck, making her way from the barn to the house. The winter winds had picked up, biting into her face. She looked at the heavy clouds overhead, noting snow would most likely cover the ground by evening.

Once inside, she pushed hard on the front door to shut out the cold.

Barnabas yapped at her feet until she finally reached down and paid attention to him. "I'm sorry you didn't get to go today. Maybe next time," she said to the lovable hound as he scooted around so she could scratch every possible itch. Once she felt sure he was satisfied with the reassuring rubs and words of greeting, Abigail tugged at her scarf and headed toward her room. Before she could reach the stairs, her mother came through the drawing room and stepped into the hallway.

"Abigail, glad you're home, dear. I hate to do this, but before you take off your wraps, would you let Titus know that lunch is ready?"

Abigail smiled. "Certainly." Mother turned to go, and Abigail pushed her scarf back in place, bracing herself for the cold winds.

Once at the barn, Abigail poked her head around the stall. "Titus?"

He stepped from the shadows toward her. "Yeah?"

"Oh," Abigail said with a laugh, "you startled me. Mother wanted me to tell you lunch is ready."

"Thanks. I'll be there in a second."

She nodded and walked away. Knowing Eliza would join them for lunch, Abigail couldn't help wondering how Titus felt about her cousin.

∞

Titus put the hay in a corner and brushed the fragments from his hands. He wondered why the O'Connors allowed him to eat with them. After all, he was merely their servant. The idea burned him. Yet he couldn't deny they had been very kind to him. Too kind. He didn't like it. Constantly, he had to remind himself their goodness stemmed from a guilty conscience. Why else would they treat him like he was one of the family?

With deliberate steps, he made his way toward the house. In a weak moment, he had to admit their kindness made his job all the more difficult. How could he burn with hate toward people who reached out to him? He mentally shook himself. All of a sudden, he found himself getting soft, and he didn't like it. Weak. Next thing he knew, he'd be using God as a crutch. . . .

Once inside the house, they gathered around the table, said the blessing, then passed the bowls. Titus tried to eat and get away from the table as soon as possible. Eliza stared at him most of the way through the meal, making him uncomfortable. He wasn't used to pushy womenfolk. It troubled him. She wasn't bad to look at, but something about her didn't ring right with him. He glanced at Abigail. She pushed the food around on her plate, not talking much, not eating much. He wondered why.

"Titus?" Mrs. O'Connor caught his attention.

"Yes ma'am."

"We would like very much for you and your family to join us for Christmas."

He looked at her with a start. "I...uh, I..."

She shook her head. "Now, we won't take no for an answer. You have them here at about noon for Christmas dinner." Mrs. O'Connor winked at him and continued with her meal. He looked at Abigail, who blushed beneath his stare. Then he glanced at Eliza, who seemed put out about something. Yet once she realized she had his attention, she smiled sweetly.

Mrs. O'Connor started talking about how nice it was to have Eliza in their home. He looked at Eliza again. She rolled her eyes, as if totally bored with her aunt's and Abigail's company. Somehow he knew that didn't include him. She made sure to throw plenty of other signals his way. The sooner he could get back to the stables, the better.

Horses were much easier to contend with than women.

⌒

After lunch, Abigail plopped on her bed. Barnabas jumped up and nudged her hand with his nose. She stroked him as she allowed her thoughts to wander. What had gotten into her? She saw the way Eliza looked at Titus. Surely he had noticed, too. What Abigail couldn't understand was why that bothered her. So what if Eliza and Titus were attracted to one another? Why should Abigail care?

Barnabas padded over the plump covers and finally curled into a ball at the foot of the bed. Abigail threw herself back on the bed and stared at the ceiling. True, she and Titus had become friends. After all, they were together every day, going on some errand or another. Perhaps she was being protective of him, knowing Eliza's true character.

She scolded herself. Maybe she didn't know Eliza's true character. Abigail didn't want to jump to conclusions because of her cousin's comments upon first meeting. It was quite possible Eliza was sincere in her remarks. Abigail couldn't deny, though, the obvious sneer in Eliza's voice. She was like a dog marking territory.

A knock sounded on her bedroom door. Eliza's voice called, "Abigail?"

Abigail jumped up from the bed, stopped a moment at the looking glass and fussed with her hair, then walked over to the door and opened it.

"Are we going to visit Gramma O'Connor this afternoon?"

"Yes. I'll just get my things." Abigail turned to gather her bag. Eliza stepped into the room and looked around. "How quaint. My quilt print was much the same as yours before I got a more fashionable one. I always liked that *old* quilt, though," she said, as if looking into years long gone.

Abigail seethed. Of all the nerve! It wasn't as if her bedroom furnishings were all that old. Besides, it didn't matter. She liked them. Her chin lifted. She would not let Eliza's meanness get to her.

Eliza raised her gaze to meet Abigail's. A knowing smirk played on her lips. Eliza would like nothing more than to get under Abigail's skin. Not wanting to give Eliza the satisfaction, Abigail offered a smile before walking through the doorway. "We'd best be going."

Hearing Eliza's dress swish along the floor in an effort to keep up made Abigail feel better. Her feet padded along at a stress-driven pace.

"Titus will be taking us, right?" Eliza wanted to know.

"Of course. He's our chauffeur."

"And a mighty handsome one at that." Eliza had caught up with her now and peered at Abigail.

Abigail looked at her a moment and turned away.

"Come on, surely you've noticed?" Eliza insisted.

"Eliza, Titus Matthews's physical appearance is of no concern to me."

"Oh? Then he's fair game?" Her voice held a thin veil of challenge.

"Well. . ." Abigail didn't know what to say. Finally, she lifted her chin. "Yes. Yes, of course."

Eliza flashed a victory smile. "Good."

They stepped through the front doorway into the flutter of falling snow, though Abigail couldn't help but feel they were heading into something much more ominous.

⌒

Abigail and Eliza sipped on hot tea in Gramma's front room. Gramma shared wonderful stories of their fathers' childhood days, which kept Abigail on the edge of her seat. Eliza, on the other hand, drank her tea and worked on some needlework she had brought with her.

"That's a fine piece of needlework ye have there, Eliza."

For a moment, Abigail thought Eliza looked genuinely pleased. "I've worked with stitches for years," she finally announced, as if she wondered how they could think her work would be less than exquisite.

"So ye have finished your Christmas shopping, have ye?" Gramma asked, changing the subject from Eliza.

"I have everything done, but I was wondering if I should get something for Titus," Abigail said, searching Gramma's face.

Eliza's head jerked toward Abigail. "You're buying your chauffeur a present?" she asked, her eyes glaring.

"Well, I. . ." Abigail thought it had seemed a friendly gesture. After all, Titus was practically like one of the family.

Gramma came to the rescue. "Ah, 'tis a lovely idea, Abigail darling. The laddie is like ye family."

Eliza frowned at both of them. Her nose pointed upward. "It seems odd to me that a young lady should buy a present for her chauffeur, that's all," she said, lowering her gaze only long enough to stab her needle into the cloth she held and, with obvious irritation, yank the thread through to the other side.

Abigail thought it amusing that suddenly Eliza would concern herself with propriety.

Gramma ignored her comment and went on with another story about her sons, Thomas and Edward.

Midway through Gramma's story, Eliza turned to her cousin. "Abigail, shouldn't we be going? No doubt Titus is waiting on us by now."

Abigail was appalled at the unchristian thoughts about this woman that assailed her mind. She threw an apologetic look to Gramma and looked back to Eliza. "I'm sure we can stay long enough for Gramma to finish her story." Her words held chastisement, and without blinking, Abigail kept her gaze locked with Eliza's.

Eliza tilted her head to one side and frowned at Gramma. "I thought you were finished." She began to put her needlework materials in a bag.

Sorrow shadowed Gramma's face. Abigail wanted to hug her. She wanted to do something else to Eliza but refused to allow herself the luxury of lingering on that thought.

Gramma finished her story, although Abigail suspected Gramma had shortened it to please Eliza. " 'Tis time ye be going. I'll see ye on Christmas Day, then?"

Abigail stood and dropped a kiss on Gramma's cheek. "Yes, we'll look forward to it."

Without looking back, Eliza pranced across the floor and called, "Bye, Gramma," over her shoulder before disappearing through the door. Gramma and Abigail exchanged a glance, and Gramma gave her an extra squeeze. Abigail wondered how she would get through these days with her difficult cousin.

Stepping into the sunlight, Abigail's thoughts drifted to Christmas once again. If she'd had any doubts about getting Titus a present before, they were now gone. Feeling a trifle rebellious over her cousin's display of distaste toward the idea, Abigail suddenly thought a present for Titus seemed the perfect idea.

∽◯∾

The children could hardly concentrate on their studies as talk of Christmas filled the air. The workers had covered Barnabas House with Christmas greenery and holly. The smell of cider permeated the building, along with aromas of roasted chicken, potatoes, glazed carrots, applesauce, and cookies. Many kind folks had contributed to the Christmas lunch.

Abigail passed around candy to the children as her gift to them. Barnabas sported a handsome red bow around his neck, which made the children giggle at first sight. They decided he looked like a Christmas present, and everyone wanted to take him home. Abigail had to remind them he stayed with her but truly belonged to all of them. Barnabas strutted around the frolicking group, seeming quite pleased with all the attention.

Having alerted Mary O'Grady to what she was about to do, Abigail called Katie over to a quiet corner. "Katie, I have a special present for you." Mary watched from nearby.

The little girl's eyes grew wide, the light in them sparkling with excitement.

"Remember the very precious gift you gave to me?"

Katie nodded her head with all the energy of a six-year-old. "Well," Abigail continued, "here is what I have for you." An open locket holding Mary O'Grady's picture dangled from a new golden chain and dropped into Katie's chubby palm. It had taken some doing for Mary to find a picture for Abigail to place in the locket, but they finally came up with one. Abigail waited, holding her breath. She didn't want to offend Katie by giving back her gift, yet she knew how much the child had not wanted to part with it.

Katie gasped. Large tears toppled from her eyes and streaked down her plump cheeks. "That's Ma! And you fixed my broken chain!" Before Abigail could respond, Katie threw her arms around her and squeezed her tight. When Katie released her, she bit her lip for a moment. "But now you don't have a present."

"Ah, but I do, Katie. My gift is the pleasure of seeing your eyes when you looked upon your ma's picture and your special locket. I'll feel happy every time I see you wear it."

Katie hugged her once again. "Ma says the gift that brings the most pleasure is the one that is hardest to give." She wiped the tears from her face. "I didn't want to give you my special locket. But since it was the hardest to give, I knew you would like it most."

"Oh!" Abigail's words caught in her throat. She closed her eyes to the tears that sprang forth. Once she opened her eyes, she saw Mary O'Grady smiling and wiping tears from her own face.

If she never took another breath, Abigail knew Christmas had already come to her. For in that moment, she learned the most precious gift she had to give was her heart. And she understood that she must risk giving it away in a manner she had never done before.

One day. . .

Chapter 9

Abigail rubbed her eyes and opened them to the morning light that streamed through her windowpane. Outside, lacy snowflakes fell from a frosty sky to the ground below. A childish excitement swept through her like a December blizzard. Quickly she pulled on her slippers and robe then ran to the window.

She turned to look at Barnabas who, with droopy eyes, watched her, all the while staying curled at the foot of her bed.

Abigail laughed and looked back out the window. With childish abandon, she thought herself in the most magical of places. She drank in the scene of frosted trees topped by an icing of snow and imagined the frost on the fence post was a smattering of fairy dust.

It was Christmas! The one day in all the year when she refused to be sad about anything.

Quickly dressing for the day, Abigail made her way into the kitchen, where she ate her breakfast.

Morning gave way to afternoon as Abigail worked alongside her mother with the meal preparations. Just when dinner was ready to serve, someone knocked at the front door.

"Oh, would you get that, Abigail?" Mother called from the kitchen.

Abigail went to the door and opened it. There stood Titus, holding his sister in his arms, his ma standing beside him, and Gramma beside her. "Oh, come in," Abigail said, hastily moving out of the way.

The little family went into the drawing room. Abigail pointed to a sofa, where Titus carefully laid his sister. After quick introductions, Titus took Jenny's cloak from her, as well as his own, and handed them to Abigail. Mrs. Matthews and Gramma did the same.

Abigail put the winter wraps away then rejoined them. After a short visit, Mother announced the meal was ready, and in no time at all, they were sitting around the dinner table. Father offered the prayer. Finally, the sounds of clanging silverware, bowls thumping against the wooden table, and soft chatter filled the room.

"Jenny, would you like some of this?" Abigail asked, pointing to the potatoes. The little girl nodded slightly and lifted a shy smile. One by one, Abigail found Jenny's preferences and placed food on her plate. Abigail glanced up to see Titus watching her, a look of appreciation in his eyes.

Eliza cleared her throat. They both looked at her then went back to their business. "So, Titus," Eliza said, lifting her fork in the air, "tell me more about yourself." The chattering at the table stopped. With a curious glance, Mrs. Matthews looked at Eliza. Titus squirmed in his chair, seemingly uncomfortable with the attention.

"Eliza, we've talked about me many times before. This is Christmas. There is much more to discuss."

"All right, then," she said, not to be deterred, "I can tell you about me."

Heat flamed Abigail's cheeks at Eliza's selfishness.

"You may not know this, but I've actually won awards for my needlepoint. I have quite a lot of things at home decorated with needlepoint—pillows, pillowcases, and the like. But of course, I brought only the bare essentials to work with when I had to come here." Instead of reflecting gratitude for a roof over her head, Eliza's voice was tainted with disgust.

Feeling her Irish blood shift from simmer to a rolling boil, Abigail opened her mouth to say something but caught her mother's discreet shake of the head. Abigail clamped her mouth shut. All the angry words bunched in her throat, and she swallowed them.

It took two hard swallows.

"You do a beautiful job with your needlepoint, Eliza. I noticed the pillow you are currently working on is very nice, indeed," Mother said.

Eliza straightened her shoulders and lifted her nose, ever so slightly, but said nothing.

Mother changed the subject. "You know, I was reading in the newspaper—"

"Did you hear about the woman who tried to befriend a prison inmate?" Eliza interrupted. "It seems while attending to the female prisoner, the kind woman had taken quite ill. The prisoner gave her a drink of water, sprinkled with morphine, which promptly put the volunteer to sleep. When she awoke, she was void of her teeth." Eliza laughed heartily.

"Oh dear," Mother said with a gasp. "That's positively scandalous."

"I'd be in a fix without me teeth, I can tell ye that," Gramma admitted.

Eliza nodded her head. "The prisoner took out the woman's teeth for the gold in them. The police found them later stuffed in her things."

Mother tsked and shook her head. "What is the world coming to?"

"I think it's funny," Eliza continued.

" 'Twouldn't be so funny if ye didn't have ye teeth," Gramma chided before chewing heartily on a piece of turkey. Then she shrugged. "I'm afraid they wouldn't get much from me, though, they wouldn't. Not a piece of gold in there. Me teeth be worth their weight in gold to me, though." Gramma laughed at her own joke.

"I still think it's funny," Eliza said, lifting an eyebrow and lifting her nose in a snoot.

Mother pinned Eliza with a look that said *enough*. "I think it's quite unfortunate, Eliza."

"It's Christmas. We should talk about happy things," Abigail put in.

Eliza scowled at her.

"If everyone is quite finished, I say it's time we share our presents," Father said pleasantly, as if trying to lighten the tension in the room.

Abigail's heart squeezed. Her mother had wanted the day to be perfect, and Eliza seemed bent on ruining it. Why did she have to come, anyway? The sooner she could leave, the better. She was just like her father.

Dusk had settled over the town as the group shared their presents and got to know one another. By the time Titus, his family, and Gramma left the gathering, a wintry moon hung suspended above a cluster of oak trees. Making their way out the door, Abigail called out to him. "Oh, Titus, I almost forgot." He turned to her. She ran into the kitchen and back to the door.

Since her family had given Titus a new hat for Christmas, Abigail had decided to bake some cookies for him and his family as her gift. Though it wasn't as nice as the scarf Eliza had given him, she decided she preferred something a little less personal. She lifted a plate of assorted cookies to him. "I know it's just cookies, but I baked them for you and your family." A twinge of embarrassment heated her cheeks.

He stood looking at her without saying a word, but he didn't have to. His eyes spoke of his pleasure.

"What a lovely gesture, Abigail. A gift of time is one of the finest treasures of all," Mrs. Matthews said.

Abigail heard Eliza "humph" behind her then clomp up the stairs.

Gramma winked at Abigail.

"Well, Merry Christmas," Abigail said. A flurry of holiday greetings filled the room as the Matthews family and Gramma went through the door, allowing the wisp of a wintry breeze to slip inside before they stepped into the cold night.

∞

By the time Titus had dropped off Gramma O'Connor and reached their home, he was pretty worn-out from the day. Lifting his sleeping sister from the carriage, he hurried through their front door with Ma close behind. After laying Jenny on her bed, he braced himself for the cold, went back outside, took care of their horse and wagon, then went back in the house. Ma had hot coffee waiting.

Long legs stretched out before him as he settled into his seat. "This is nice, Ma. Thanks," he said, wrapping his cold fingers around the warm cup.

She sat across from him at the table, took a sip of coffee, and looked at him. "We had a wonderful Christmas, didn't we?"

"That we did," he agreed.

"Jenny seemed taken with Abigail."

"I noticed that," he said with pleasure.

"Abigail is a fine young lady."

Titus looked at Ma, throwing her a look that said he knew exactly what she was up to. "There's no denying that."

"She'll make some man a fine wife one day."

"I suppose so," he said matter-of-factly, hiding a smile behind his cup.

"Tell me what you think of Eliza," Ma said, studying his face.

Titus shook his head and blew out a sigh. "Now there's a woman who could make a man choose the company of his horse."

Ma seemed to struggle with holding back a chuckle. "I must agree she is, well, a tad bold." Ma took another drink. "It's obvious she's taken by you."

He whistled. "I know you're a praying woman, Ma, and the man Eliza O'Connor snags will need much prayer, but I don't plan on getting snagged."

"By her?"

"By her."

She looked at him, her eyes twinkling. He suddenly realized he had been trapped. "All right, I see what you're doing here."

Ma feigned innocence.

He rubbed his head. "Aw, Ma, I plan on getting married one day. When I find the right woman."

Her eyebrows lifted.

"What?"

"Anybody I know?"

He smirked at her. "I'll let you know when I meet her. Until then—"

She cut him off. "I'll keep praying."

He smiled, rose from the table, and dropped a kiss on her head. "I love you, Ma," he said before taking his cup to the sink. "Good night."

Titus had made a habit of attending church with the O'Connors but was no closer to finding out anything substantial against the family. It seemed everyone liked them. He could see why.

After lunch, the O'Connors prepared to go visit Gramma, who had felt poorly and stayed home from church. Titus needed to get back home to Ma and Jenny. He started to board his wagon when he realized he'd left his hat on the kitchen table. Remembering the O'Connors left their home unlocked, he decided he'd better retrieve his hat. Barnabas greeted him with a wagging tail when Titus stepped back into the house. Titus stooped and scratched the old hound behind the ears then walked over to the table where he'd left his hat.

As he turned to go, he walked through the hall and noticed the open door to the sitting room. This was Mr. O'Connor's study area. He glanced in as he walked by and noticed a box by Mr. O'Connor's chair. Though the notion of getting even with this family lessened with each passing day, he couldn't deny he hadn't given up on the idea entirely. No one was home. They need never know. He stood in the doorway, biting his lip, hesitating, wondering.

Before he could think any further, his footsteps carried him into the room. He scrunched down by the box, and though guilt plagued him, he reached for the box and opened it. Assorted business papers filled the pine box, most of which meant nothing to him. Then he saw the letter to his pa from Mr. O'Connor, agreeing to sell his remaining shares of the business to Pa. He quickly scanned the letter, taking in the fact Mr. O'Connor did mention diversifying and making sure Pa wanted full ownership. Titus stared into books that lined the wall, though not really seeing them. By the sounds of the letter, Mr. O'Connor didn't want to sell off the business. The warning to diversify was obvious.

Mr. O'Connor had been telling the truth. He felt as if a load of bricks had been lifted from his shoulders. All this time with all his bitterness and resentment, he had been wrong. Maybe Ma was right. Maybe Mr. O'Connor had not tried to break their family. Pa's wrong choices took them there. Titus's hand shook with thoughts of days wasted, energies spent, bitterness eating away at him.

He heard a jostling at the front door. Barnabas ran to the door and started barking. Quickly, Titus placed the letter back in the appropriate place in the box. Grabbing his hat, he hurried through the sitting-room door and walked down the hallway toward the front door. Eliza stepped in.

"Hush up, you no-account dog!" She looked up and saw Titus. "Oh my, you startled me," she said, holding a gloved hand to her throat.

"Sorry. I just came in to get my hat," he explained.

She eyed him with suspicion. Her gaze glanced around the area. His pulse raced in his ears. He hoped he had put everything back in order.

"Yes, well, I need a heavier cloak," she said. "Would you mind helping me out of this one?" Before he could answer, she walked over to him and turned around with her back to him. He slipped off her cloak. She turned around, mere inches from his face. "Thank you," she whispered. He could feel her breath on his cheek.

She raised her arms to his chest and with a gloved hand ran her finger down his jaw. "You know, Titus, I'd really like to get to know you better." Her tone was one of definite boldness. He took a step back.

"Titus, why do you avoid me?" A pout played on her lips. "Aren't you attracted to me?" She walked over to him again. This time her arms went up around his neck. "Don't you desire me even the least little bit?" Pulling his head farther down to her until their lips finally met, she pressed her mouth hard against his own. He wanted to pull away, but he hadn't kissed a woman in such a long time. A warning seemed to sound inside him. He mentally shook himself and broke free, pulling her arms from his neck. He stepped back.

"I've got to go, Eliza."

She lifted her chin. He felt pride rather than modesty stained her cheeks red. The look on her face spelled trouble. He knew that look, because he'd worn it himself until ten minutes ago.

Just then the front door opened. They both turned to see Abigail.

She stopped short, as if she realized she had interrupted an awkward moment. "I'm sorry. I didn't mean to intrude."

"No intrusion at all," Titus said, his heart feeling lighter by the minute. Especially with the sight of Abigail. His reassuring smile seemed to put her at ease, though the scorn on Eliza's face must have told her a different story altogether.

He brushed by Abigail and turned back. Seeing Eliza's back to him, he looked at Abigail. "I'll see you tomorrow," he said in hushed tones, his gaze lingering on her.

Chapter 10

The next morning, Abigail stepped into the blazing yellow sunlight. The town glistened in a whitewash of snow. The January air smelled clean as a new year. An early chill prickled her skin as Abigail stepped toward the carriage. Stopping short of the carriage seat, Abigail turned to Titus, wondering how to approach the matter.

"I was hoping maybe after we visit Barnabas House, if we might perhaps—well, uh, I was wondering. . ."

Titus appeared perplexed by her struggle with the words.

She took a deep breath. "Could we stop by your house? I have something for Jenny."

He looked like he might object then seemed to think better of it. His glance went to the cloth rag doll in her hands.

She held it up. "This is Laura. She used to be mine when I was a little girl."

His eyebrows spiked upward. "You can't give her something so valuable, Abigail." His words were soft.

Lifting her head in confidence, she looked at him. "A wise friend once told me that when you love someone, you give them your best gift, just like God did when He gave His Son, Jesus."

Titus stared into her eyes, never blinking. "Well, I guess I can't argue that." He waited a moment, still looking into her eyes. "Thank you, Abigail." His voice was husky and low. His hand touched her arm. He had never touched her, even slightly, unless it was to help her into the carriage. Somehow she felt something was changing between them.

The thrill of presenting her doll to Jenny kept Abigail excited all morning while working at Barnabas House. Once they arrived at the Matthewses' home, Abigail was taken back by the poverty surrounding them. It made her admire Titus all the more. Rather than wallowing in self-pity, he got out there and made the effort to feed his family. The more she thought about him, the more she liked him.

He helped her from the carriage. "I apologize for the area." His hand swept across the neighborhood.

"Please." Abigail stopped his hand midway and held it. "Don't. I didn't come here to see the neighborhood. I came here to see your ma and Jenny."

"You're a wonder, you know that?"

She laughed. "I'll bet that's what you say to all the ladies." Her steps continued toward the door.

He laughed and jumped forward to keep up with her. He grabbed her hand and turned her to him. "No. Just you."

Abigail swallowed hard. The front door opened. "I thought I heard someone." Mrs. Matthews's face sparkled with pleasure. "Abigail, so good to see you. Come in. Come in."

Once inside, Mrs. Matthews pulled Abigail into a warm embrace. When they parted, she smiled and pointed to Jenny. The little girl lay in a heap on a mattress on the floor. She looked up at Abigail, a huge smile on her face, a twinkle in her eyes.

"Well, hello, little one," Abigail said, walking across the floor and stooping down to her. Holding the rag doll behind her back, she said, "I have something for you, Jenny."

The little girl's eyes lit with excitement. With her strong arms, she pushed herself up.

"Funny how they have the strength when they need it," Mrs. Matthews said with a laugh.

Abigail smiled and brought the rag doll in front of her. "This is for you."

Tears made wet tracks down the little girl's cheeks. "Oh," Abigail said with a gasp. She pulled Jenny into a hug. "You like it then?" she asked, once she released her.

Jenny nodded.

"I'm so glad, Jenny. You see, this is Laura. She used to be my doll when I was a little girl." Jenny smiled and immediately pulled the doll tight against her chest.

Abigail stood.

"How about some coffee?" Mrs. Matthews asked them.

Abigail looked to Titus. "Fine with me, if Abigail doesn't mind."

"I'd like that," she said.

"Good."

The three sat down at the kitchen table. Though the place looked old and revealed little wealth, Abigail noticed the room was clean. An apple pie baked in the oven, spreading a pleasant scent around the room.

"You finally made your apple pie," Titus teased.

"I wanted to save it for a special day. And as it turned out, today is special. Jenny received a wonderful gift from Abigail." Mrs. Matthews looked at Jenny and smiled then turned to Abigail. "Thank you."

"My pleasure. I did have another matter I wanted to talk with you about," Abigail ventured.

Titus looked at her with surprise.

"I wanted to know if I might come over and work with Jenny on her words." Seeing the surprise on their faces, she hurried on. "I'm a certified teacher, you know, and I can get some books. If you'll allow me, maybe I can help her."

"You would do this for our Jenny?" Mrs. Matthews asked with disbelief.

"Of course."

More charity. Titus knew Abigail's heart was right, but he didn't like charity. Even from her. "I don't think so, Abigail," he said.

Abigail and Mrs. Matthews looked to him with a start.

"But why, Titus?" Mrs. Matthews wanted to know.

"We don't need charity. When I save enough money, we'll get the help we need."

"You'll allow your stubborn pride to keep your sister from getting help?" There went her Irish temper again. She took a deep breath.

His jaw set, his cold, hard gaze held hers.

"What do you say, Mrs. Matthews?"

Mrs. Matthews looked from Abigail to her daughter, and then to Titus. "I say, I love my son." She caught his attention then continued. "But this time he is wrong." She turned to Abigail. "I would appreciate anything you can do."

Titus took a deep breath. He drank his coffee more quickly than anyone should drink something hot, and then he went outside.

Abigail stood to leave.

"Don't worry. He'll come around. He's got his pa's stubborn pride."

Abigail smiled at the kind woman. "I'll be by three times a week."

"May God bless you for your kindness."

◌◌

Two weeks later found Titus walking around the O'Connor property, trying to sort things through in his mind. He supposed Abigail's charity caused old doubts to resurface. Though he had found the letter in Mr. O'Connor's box revealing some of the man's intentions, Titus still had suspicions. It didn't strike him right that his pa would bear the entire brunt of things. Why would he put everything into that business? Things didn't add up. Titus and his pa didn't talk much about business things, but Titus thought his pa was a wise businessman. Had Titus been wrong?

With gusto, he kicked a pebble in his path. He was tired of thinking. Abigail had been to their home several times now. Jenny's face lit up every time Abigail walked into the room. He couldn't deny her presence seemed to help Jenny. The way Abigail pored over those books with Jenny, the painstaking lessons for a girl who showed little response, he had to admit were admirable. Still, he didn't like feeling in debt to the O'Connor family just to appease their consciences.

He shouldn't have taken his family to the O'Connors' for Christmas. That's what started the whole mess. And he couldn't understand Eliza. Why was she staying there if she so obviously hated it? Did they have guilt over something done to her, as well? Maybe he should find out just why she was there.

Ma said pray about it. How could he pray when he hadn't talked to God in more than a year? Titus once served Him, but that was before everything went wrong. *You don't serve God because He does things for you, Titus. You serve Him because of who He is.* His ma's words haunted him. Aw, why did she have to pray all the time? He kicked the ground once more with his boot.

A movement in the front of his house caught his attention. Abigail was waving. Upon seeing her, his heart flipped. Why did he do that? He didn't want to turn weak-kneed at the sight of her. But he did.

Every time he saw her.

With a heavy sigh, he walked straight toward the woman who had turned his world upside down.

⌒

On Thursday afternoon, Eliza stayed outside talking to Titus while Abigail visited with Gramma.

"Does it bother you?" Gramma asked.

"What?"

"That your cousin visits with the handsome chauffeur?"

"Why should it?"

"Never be trustin' an answer that asks a question, said me pa." Gramma laughed, causing Abigail to smile.

"All right, maybe a little."

Gramma gave her a knowing look. "Ye care about him. I can see it in ye eyes, wee one." Gramma pointed her crooked finger at Abigail. "He cares about ye, too."

Abigail shook her head.

"You didn't know?"

"No Gramma, he doesn't. He cares about Eliza."

"Surely ye don't think so? If he does, he's not the man I be thinkin'."

"He spends time with her."

"She spends time with him," Gramma corrected. "There's a difference. Ye must trust ye heart again, Abigail. Ye be afraid to trust. Ye fear getting hurt?"

Abigail nodded. Tears spilled down her cheeks, and she couldn't imagine what had gotten into her.

Gramma stretched her arms wide and walked over to Abigail, pulling her into a hug. " 'Tis no' wrong to fear, Abigail, darling. 'Tis only wrong to let it hold ye prisoner." Gramma lifted Abigail's chin and looked her full in the face. "Life, 'tis full of hurts. Things are not always what they seem, and expectations are set too high. People fail. Remember, we make mistakes, too." Gramma smiled and kissed Abigail's temple. "Never forget, everyone is imperfect. 'Tis why we need a Savior."

Abigail nodded and blew her nose into a handkerchief. "Thank you, Gramma. Pray that I can trust again. I really want to. I just don't know how."

"I will pray."

Just then the door flew open, letting all the winter's chill in and the stove's warmth out. Eliza stood in the doorway. "Are you ready to go yet, Abigail?" she whined, one hand on her hip. "I'm tired."

Abigail looked at Gramma and lifted a weak smile. She stood to her feet and kissed Gramma good-bye. "I'm coming," she called to Eliza, who was already down the stairs, leaving the door wide open. Abigail ran to the door and pulled it almost closed. "Thanks for everything, Gramma. I love you."

"I love ye, Abigail darling."

Abigail turned to go, wondering about the glimpse of pain that flickered across Gramma's face.

∽

Later that evening, sunken between soft sheets and plump blankets and pillows, Abigail felt she was lying on a cloud. She did some of her best thinking in the comfort of her bed. Barnabas whined until she stroked his fur. Then with a look of satisfaction, the mutt trotted clumsily to the foot of the bed.

Watching him, Abigail laughed. She leaned back once more and stared at the ceiling. Since her visit with Gramma, she had felt uneasy. She wasn't sure why. Maybe it was the realization of knowing that her feelings for Titus were growing, or maybe it was the shadow on Gramma's face when Abigail left. What was that about? Did she think Abigail wouldn't trust another man? Did she fear Abigail's heart would break again? If so, why?

She wanted to pray yet struggled. Her thoughts toward Eliza hadn't been exactly Christian. How could God hear Abigail when her heart had shadows where Eliza was concerned? She didn't like herself when she acted that way. It just seemed Eliza brought out the worst in her. She shook her head. No, she couldn't blame someone else for her own actions. It was time to change things. This seemed as good a time as any.

Abigail slipped from her covers and knelt beside her bed, asking the Lord for forgiveness for her treatment of Eliza. After all, the Lord loved

Abigail enough to die for her, and she didn't deserve it. In her own strength, Abigail had to admit she didn't have it in her to love Eliza. It would take God's strength to work through her and make it happen. Amid a flurry of tears, Abigail laid her heart's cry at the foot of God's throne, knowing when she had risen, that the Savior had heard and answered her prayer.

She blew out the light in her lantern then slipped beneath her covers once again. Tomorrow would be a good day. No matter the circumstances.

Abigail slept the night through like a baby. By the time the morning's light had flooded into her room, she felt refreshed and fully alive. She could hardly wait to start her day. God had worked in her heart; now came the time to roll up her sleeves and get to work.

Quickly, she dressed and pulled her hair back with a ribbon, allowing the curls to flow down her back. She took one glance at the looking glass and decided her appearance would do for breakfast.

Practically running down the stairs, with Barnabas right on her heels, she had a definite hop to her walk by the time she made it into the kitchen.

"Well, someone is feeling mighty chipper this morning," Mother said with a smile.

"I feel wonderful today," Abigail replied.

"Well, I'm glad someone does," Eliza said as she entered. "Is the coffee ready?" She lifted sleepy eyes toward the stove.

Mother laughed. "It's ready. You ladies go sit at the table, and I'll bring you your breakfast."

"Can I help?" Abigail asked.

"No dear, I can manage."

As she walked to the table, carrying the coffeepot, Mother explained that Father had to meet his boss at the railroad station early that morning. "What's on your schedule today, Abigail?" she asked, pouring coffee into the empty cups.

"Barnabas House has taken on more workers, so I'm not needed as often. I miss the kids, but Jenny helps fill the void. I thought I'd go over and work with her today."

Mother smiled, placing the coffeepot back on the stove. She sat down once more. "How about you, Eliza? What are your plans?"

Eliza let out a long sigh and glared at Mother. "Same thing day after day. Work on my needlepoint; take a walk; wait, wait, wait on word from my pa."

Tempted to snap a retort to the young woman for her ingratitude, Abigail felt a prick of conscience and threw up a silent prayer for help. This whole business was going to be harder than she thought.

"You can go with me today, Eliza, if you'd like."

She looked at Abigail. "Well, I wouldn't like. I don't want to sit around while you're teaching a girl who won't even talk. I don't know why you waste your time."

A spurt of anger shot through Abigail in an instant. Her body trembled, but she said nothing. Yes, this assignment was much harder than she had anticipated.

Mother winked at Abigail.

Just then, a knock sounded at the door. Barnabas bounded to the door ahead of Mother. Abigail could hear Titus's voice from the hallway. In a moment, boots scuffled against the floor, and Titus entered the kitchen. "I'll get your coffee, Titus."

He looked up rather sheepishly at Abigail. "Morning, Abigail." Almost as an afterthought, he turned to Eliza. "Eliza," he said with a tip of his head. She suddenly sprang to life. Her back was straighter, fingers absently brushed stray hairs into place, and a smile found its way to her face.

Mother poured some coffee and handed the cup to Titus, who stood at the entrance. "Come in and join us."

He stretched out at the table near Abigail. Eliza frowned. Mother attempted to sit then seemed to think better of it. "Oh!" she said with a start. "I almost forgot. I stopped and picked up the mail in town yesterday, Abigail. You have a letter."

Abigail was surprised. She couldn't imagine who would have written to her.

Mother walked over to the counter then walked back to Abigail with a reserved smile, holding an envelope. She paused then handed it to her daughter.

Abigail took it, wondering why the hesitation. She glanced down at the envelope and saw the return address.

It simply read, "Jonathan Clark."

Chapter 11

Abigail glanced up to see Titus staring at her with a question in his eyes. Eliza seemed to sense something going on and perked up considerably.

"So, who is Jonathan?" she asked Abigail, though her gaze stayed firmly fixed on Titus.

Mother piped up, "He's an old friend of Abigail's."

Abigail shot her a grateful look then stared into her breakfast plate. She didn't want to talk about anything just now. Suddenly, she didn't want breakfast.

"Dear, if you'd like to go read your letter, that's fine."

Abigail nodded and made her way from the room. "Well, he must have been a special friend," she heard Eliza say with a laugh. The scooting of a chair sounded from the kitchen. Abigail slipped into the sitting room and heard heavy footsteps in the hallway and finally the opening of the front door. She glanced out the window to see Titus walking across the lawn, a scowl on his face. She wondered if Eliza had said something more to upset him.

Turning her attention back to the letter, Abigail settled into a chair and began to open the white envelope. She read through the words that told her his job was going well and he was glad to be back east. But the next few lines took her breath. "I miss you. I thought I could get along, but it's hard being here without you. I see you everywhere I turn."

The letter continued with more superficial news, and her eyes kept going back to the part about him missing her. She read it over and over. Finally, she leaned back in the chair. What did this mean? Would he come back to Chicago? Did she want him to? She wasn't sure anymore.

Her thoughts flitted to Titus. Every day her feelings grew a little stronger toward him. She wondered if he sensed it at all. He seemed to enjoy her company, though she didn't know if he wanted only friendship or something more between them.

Eliza knocked at the door. Abigail motioned her in.

"Good news?" Eliza asked, looking hopeful.

"It was a nice letter."

Eliza plopped at the desk chair. "Tell me about him."

Abigail didn't want to share intimate details with Eliza. They did not have that kind of friendship. In fact, Abigail felt a twinge of resentment toward Eliza for asking. After all, it was quite obvious she wanted to glean information for her own selfish purposes. To win Titus.

Maybe that's what troubled Abigail about Eliza. Abigail was jealous. The thought irritated her even more. Why should she be jealous? It wasn't as though Abigail and Titus had a relationship of any kind. He could certainly see whom he wished. She would not fight with Eliza over him as if they were silly schoolgirls.

Abigail rose to her feet. "There's not much to tell, really. He's a good friend." With that, she left the room, leaving Eliza alone with her schemes.

"Mother, I think I'll go visit Sophia. Would you like me to pick up anything for you while I'm out?"

Her mother appeared at the drawing room door. "No dear, I don't need anything." She glanced curiously at Abigail. "Everything all right?"

"It's fine," Abigail said with a smile.

Mother nodded, wiping her hands on a towel.

"I'll just let Titus know." Abigail grabbed her cloak and went outside with Barnabas trotting at her heels, his head up, ears pricked with the thrill of an adventure, and a long wagging tail that spiraled into a gentle curl at the very tip. Abigail looked at him and laughed.

She glanced around at the spots of persistent grass that poked through the melting snow. The sun breathed down warm rays, causing the remaining snow to sparkle and glitter on the lawn.

Abigail took in a huge helping of new morning air. "Isn't this wonderful, Barnabas?" She looked at her faithful companion, who looked up at her in a satisfied fashion, as though he couldn't agree more. Bending over, she scratched his head. "You're always so agreeable, not like some people," she said with a glance across her shoulder toward the house.

"And who might that be?" Titus's strong voice startled her. She jerked back to look at him.

"Oh, I—"

Something in his expression made her heart go soft. When did he start affecting her in this way? He smiled. "Were you looking for me?"

She threw a thankful grin. "Yes. I wanted to know if you could take me to Sophia's in, say, half an hour?"

"Be happy to." He hunkered down and scratched Barnabas. "How you doing, ole boy?"

Abigail watched the scene and smiled. Barnabas had grown very fond of Titus. The dog happily nuzzled into Titus, leaning into the scratches as if he were having the most pleasurable of experiences.

"I do believe if he were a cat, he'd purr," Titus said with a laugh.

Abigail laughed, too.

Titus finally stood and looked at Abigail again. He lingered a moment. "You doing all right?"

His question warmed her. The fact that he cared meant a lot to her. She nodded.

"Don't let anyone hurt you."

The comment caught her off guard. Before she could respond, he continued. "He did hurt you once, didn't he?"

"How did you know?"

"Your expression tells a lot."

She looked at the ground.

"Do you still care about him?"

His bold question surprised her. Eliza must have been rubbing off on him. She nodded. "But not in the way I did before."

He shoved his right hand into his pocket. "That's good news."

Her head jerked up with a start. "It is?"

"Yes, Abigail. It is." His face broke into a happy grin. Their gazes locked, and they stood, lost in the wonder of the moment, neither saying a word.

"I'll get the carriage," he finally said.

Abigail smiled and practically floated back to the house, carried on the whisper of the wind.

∞

"Look at you," Abigail said when she entered the Thread Bearer and saw Sophia stand and come toward her. "You are a beautiful mother-to-be." They embraced, a glow emanating from Sophia's face.

"Thank you." She grabbed Abigail's hand and led her into the kitchen. Promptly she pointed to a chair at the table where Abigail could sit while Sophia started the kettle for tea. "So, tell me what brings you here today." Sophia settled onto her seat and smiled at her friend.

Abigail proceeded to tell her about the letter from Jonathan and finally her exchange with Titus before she left to come to Sophia's shop.

"What do you think of it all, Abigail?"

"I don't know what to think."

"Well, there's no question of Titus's interests. He's made that quite clear," she said with a smile. The water boiled, and Sophia got up and prepared their tea and poured it into thick mugs. She placed them on the table.

"How do you feel about Jonathan?"

Abigail toyed with a curl at the side of her face. "That's just it. I don't know anymore."

"It's different now, though, isn't it?"

Abigail nodded. "Do you think I ever really loved him?"

Sophia shrugged. "It's hard for me to say. Only you can really answer that, but I'm thinking no. Another person could not take his place so soon."

"You mean Titus?"

Sophia nodded. "He has, you know."

Abigail stared into her cup. "Yes, I know."

"Is that a bad thing?"

Abigail looked up. "I don't know. I mean, I know he cares about me, but it seems like something is holding him back. I just don't know what it is."

"Maybe he's afraid you won't feel the same way. Does he know about Jonathan?"

"A little." Abigail looked toward the distant wall. "I suppose he could be afraid of my feelings for Jonathan. Although, I think I may have cleared that matter up for him in our conversation before we arrived here."

Sophia grinned. "Perhaps now things will get interesting." She shot a teasing glance at Abigail, and they both laughed.

"Are you going to write Jonathan back?"

Abigail thought a moment. "I suppose I will. After all, he will always be my friend."

Sophia nodded. "How are things going with Eliza?"

Inhaling a big breath and blowing it out, Abigail said, "Where do I begin?" She related Eliza's antics and how the Lord was helping Abigail to work through the situation and try to be a friend to her cousin. After some discussion, the two women prayed together; then it was time for Abigail to go.

"I'll see you soon, Sophia. You know, I can't wait to spoil your baby," Abigail said with a laugh.

"That makes three of us!" Sophia replied before shifting into her seat at the sewing machine. The hum of the machine started once again as Abigail slipped through the door.

∽

Not much later, Titus took Abigail to Barnabas House. She walked over to her station to check on the children's progress with their studies. Julie Barnes, the woman who in recent days had volunteered to share responsibilities with Abigail, stood smiling.

"Miss Abigail!" Katie O'Grady shot out of her chair and squeezed her arms tight around Abigail's skirts.

"Hello, Katie!" Abigail bent down and hugged the little girl. Soon the other children followed suit and gathered around Abigail.

"We've missed you," said a brown-haired boy with freckles sprinkled across his nose. The others nodded in agreement.

"And I've missed you." She took time to hug each one. She glanced up at Julie. "I'm sorry to disrupt, Julie."

Julie smiled. "No problem at all. They've been asking for you. I'm glad you came in."

Soon the children were back in their seats, busily at work. Abigail checked on their progress with Julie and found they were doing just fine. Truth be known, Abigail missed serving as she once had at Barnabas House, but Julie's help freed Abigail to work more with Jenny Matthews.

Once satisfied the children were in good hands, Abigail walked through the room to leave. Mary O'Grady stopped her.

"Mary, how are you doing? It's so good to see you!"

Mary pulled her aside. The largest of smiles spread across her face. She took a deep breath.

Puzzled, Abigail looked at her. "Mary, what is it?"

"Christopher asked me to marry him."

"What?" Abigail said with a squeal. "That's wonderful, Mary!" She pulled her into an enormous hug. "I'm so happy for you both. When is the big day?"

"We're getting married Saturday, February 1, here at Barnabas House." Mary's eyes sparkled with excitement. "We're inviting the workers and the people who come in here most often. Just a little neighborhood gathering."

"Oh Mary, how wonderful for you and Katie!" Another hug. "Let me know if I can help in any way."

"Please tell your chauffeur, too. He and Christopher have become good friends."

"Really? I didn't know that."

Mary nodded. "He slips out for coffee with him while you're here."

Abigail laughed. "All right, I'll see that he knows."

When she stepped out of Barnabas House, her heart was light with the good news and the thought that love could strike anyone at any moment. Life was good.

"Hello, you ready to go?" Titus reached a hand to her as her foot landed on the last step.

Her heart flipped as she nodded to him. Yes, life was good.

∽

Titus took Abigail for her visit with Jenny. When Abigail stepped into the house, she saw Jenny on the floor, clutching Laura, her rag doll, next to her. Jenny glanced up and smiled. She lifted Laura for Abigail to see.

"Oh, I see you're keeping Laura great company," Abigail said upon entering. She turned to Mrs. Matthews. "Hello."

Mrs. Matthews walked over and gave Abigail a hug. "How are you?"

"Fine, thank you. I want to see how my little friend is doing." She walked on over to Jenny.

"I'll get you some hot tea," Mrs. Matthews called.

"Thank you." Abigail hunched down to Jenny, who had pulled herself to an upright position, still holding Laura. She grinned and held Laura out again. Just then Abigail noticed one of Laura's shoes was missing. "Uh-oh, I think her shoe must be in your bed," Abigail said, glancing around.

Jenny stopped smiling and looked down like something was wrong.

"I'm afraid it's not there. We've looked everywhere for her shoe." Mrs. Matthews stood beside her, wringing her hands together.

Abigail frowned. "Hmm, maybe I dropped it at home and just didn't notice. If not, I've seen some shoes for rag dolls at the mercantile. I can take Laura into the store and find one that matches her clothes," Abigail said brightly.

Mrs. Matthews smiled and shook her head. "You're too good to us, Abigail."

⌘

Titus watched the whole exchange between Abigail, his mother, and sister. As if truth had finally settled over him, he knew that Abigail didn't befriend them out of guilt. She did so out of love. She loved them, and they all loved her. Including Titus. He stepped outside a moment to leave Abigail to teach Jenny. When he had fallen in love with her, he didn't know. He only knew that it had happened. Whether he wanted it to happen or not, the fact remained. He loved Abigail O'Connor. Now what could he do? He couldn't bring this family down after all the kindness they had shown his family, not to mention his love for Abigail.

He took off his hat and scratched his head. Yet he couldn't deny that a tiny part of him still felt uneasy, like a hungry wolf in search of food. He knew, too, if he didn't let it go, the ultimate result would lead to sorrow. He wanted to release it so he could be free to love Abigail. Yet, could he? The wall of bitterness he had built against the O'Connor family was bigger than anything he could break down on his own.

It would take an act of God.

He stepped back into the house and spotted Abigail rising to her feet after she dropped a kiss on Jenny's head.

"I need to take Laura with me and buy her shoes. I'll bring her back." Abigail lifted Laura from Jenny's strong hold. "It's all right, Jenny. I'll bring her back."

Abigail walked over to the door beside Titus and said good-bye to Mrs. Matthews. Titus opened the door, and they prepared to leave when Jenny's voice cracked through the room, stopping them cold.

"Laura!" she wailed.

Chapter 12

Abigail, Titus, and Mrs. Matthews turned to Jenny with a start. Jenny's arms were stretched out toward her doll, tears streaming down her face. Mrs. Matthews ran to her. She fell at her daughter's feet. "Jenny, you talked!" Tears flooding her own cheeks, Mrs. Matthews grabbed Jenny hard against her and rocked back and forth.

Abigail and Titus exchanged a glance of disbelief. She walked over to return the doll but stood aside a respectable distance to give Mrs. Matthews a moment with her daughter. When they finally parted, Abigail returned Laura. "I'll find shoes for her without taking her," Abigail said as she gently placed Laura back into the sobbing child's arms.

Jenny's tears slowed to a trickle as she held her doll close, patting her back, rocking back and forth. An occasional hiccup escaped her. Abigail leaned down. "I'm sorry, Jenny. I didn't mean to hurt you. I won't take Laura from you."

Jenny looked at Abigail. Her wide eyes pooled with tears, and her chin quivered slightly. "Laura," she said simply.

Abigail ran her hand along Jenny's soft, blond hair and nodded. "Laura."

Titus waited close by. Standing to her feet, Abigail stepped out of the way so Titus could get near his sister. He immediately crouched down beside Jenny and began to smooth her hair away from her face. The tenderness in his eyes, the gentle touches made Abigail's heart squeeze. The love he displayed for his family moved her more than anything. He would make a wonderful father someday. That thought made her blush. Seeing such affection coming from him for his sister made Abigail uncomfortable to be a witness. She felt the sight almost too sacred for her presence.

Her footsteps whispered across the wooden planks to the front door. She turned once more and looked at the family then snuggled into her winter wraps and stepped into the open air.

Huddled against a corner of the porch, she waited for Titus to come out. In a few minutes, he joined her. "You didn't need to come out here."

"I wanted to give your family time together. It was a special moment."

Titus walked over to her, pulled her gloved hands into his, and looked into her face. "You are special, Abigail. And I thank you for what you're doing for Jenny."

She felt herself blush under his gaze. He didn't blink as he continued to stare into her eyes. Almost in slow motion, his head bent forward, and he pressed her waiting lips with his own. The tender kiss, moist and sweet as the morning dew, lasted a heartbeat, but Abigail knew she would remember it for days to come.

By the time Abigail and Titus returned home that evening, her heart felt light as a feather. He helped her out of the carriage, his hand holding on to hers longer than necessary. "I had a wonderful day, Abigail."

She swallowed hard. "Me, too, Titus."

"I'll see you in the morning," he said, his voice low and soft. He released her hand, tipped his hat, and turned to put the carriage away.

Abigail watched him a moment, wondering how she could feel this way toward him when she thought she had been in love with Jonathan. The thought frightened her a little. What if she wasn't really in love? She had been fooled once. Yet something told her this was definitely different. An icy breeze whipped through her cloak, breaking her free from her musings. She pulled the wool closer to her neck and headed for her house. It had been a wonderful day.

When she stepped into the house, a flurry of barks assailed her as did Barnabas's paws as he jumped and pushed against her. He wouldn't quiet down until she took the time to say hello. With affection, she rubbed him a moment; then she stood and shook the snow from her outer wraps and pulled off her boots. Placing her cloak on a nearby peg, she walked into the drawing room to find Eliza sitting in front of a blazing fire in the stone fireplace, studying the stitches on the cloth in her hand. The room smelled of pine logs and spiced cider. Abigail took a deep breath, thinking the scent heavenly.

Eliza looked up with a scowl. "Where have you been?"

The anger in Eliza's voice took Abigail by surprise. "I went to see Sophia, Barnabas House, and then over to see Jenny Matthews."

Eliza's eyes tightened to slits. "Well, how convenient."

"What do you mean?"

"Little Miss Charity Worker out spreading cheer to all around her. Of course, if her kindness happens to spill upon the sister of one handsome chauffeur, all the better," Eliza said, her voice thick with jealousy.

Abigail did not want to play into her hand. She prayed a quick prayer to get through the anger Eliza's words had evoked. Taking a deep breath, Abigail walked over to her cousin. "Look, Eliza, I don't want to fight with you. You're my cousin, and I want—"

"You want," Eliza spat. "What about what I want? No one cares one whit what I want!"

Abigail suddenly knew this was about more than mere jealousy. This was about Uncle Edward dropping his daughter off in their care. It was about Eliza feeling sorry for herself.

Filled with compassion for her cousin, Abigail measured her words carefully. "I know things haven't been easy for you coming here."

"Easy? I'll say it's not been easy! How would you like to be ripped from your home and stay with people whom you hardly know? And then Titus comes along, giving me hope of rescue from my eternal boredom, but he takes no interest in me whatsoever. Of course you've seen to that!" Eliza glared at Abigail as though she could chew her up and spit her out.

Abigail stared at her, not knowing what to say.

"You are in love with him, aren't you?" Eliza said in a sneering voice.

When Abigail said nothing, Eliza stabbed the needle into her cloth piece. "Oh, how nice for the both of you. Abigail, who always gets what she wants, has won once again." Eliza folded her cloth and stood now, inches from Abigail's face. "Just don't turn your back, Abigail. You never know what a woman scorned might do."

Abigail drew in a sharp breath at the comment and stood trembling as she watched her cousin stomp across the room with resentment and anger guiding every step.

⬭

A full moon sailed high above him as Titus made his way to the barn. It had been a long week, and he was glad it was Saturday. He was tired and ready to go home. Hearing the snap of a twig behind him, he turned around to see Eliza standing just inside the barn.

"Eliza, what are you doing here?"

Absently running her gloved hand along the door frame, she pouted, "Can't I come and say hello?"

"I just spent dinner with you," he said, scratching his head.

"Yeah, me and the whole O'Connor family," she said, watching him closely.

What was she up to? Eliza always had something up her sleeve. After she kissed him that night, he'd stayed clear of her. Not one to beat around the bush, he stepped over to her. "What's going on, really, Eliza? Why did you come out here tonight?"

She looked up at him with an innocent look. "Don't you know?"

He shook his head.

"I can't seem to get you to myself for a moment." She lifted her arms around his neck.

"Not this time, Eliza," he said, pulling her arms away from him.

An icy glaze filled her eyes. "Why, because of Abigail?" she spat.

"Listen, I don't know what your game is, but I don't want any part of it," he said, turning toward his wagon.

"Look who's talking. As if you don't have a game!"

He stopped in his tracks and turned to her.

She gave a hollow laugh and lifted her chin. "That's right. I know you're up to something. After catching you lingering outside the study that night, I decided to investigate and see if anything was amiss. So after the family went to bed, I came down and looked around."

His heart thundered against his chest.

"I noticed a tiny edge of paper hanging outside of Uncle Thomas's box by his chair. I opened the box and there was a letter to your father from Uncle. I figured there must have been a reason you wanted to see that." She watched him closely, as if looking for any clues he might give her.

"Now, I may not have all the pieces together in the puzzle yet, but don't play innocent with me. I know I'm not the only one around here with a plan."

"It's not like that, Eliza. At least, not anymore."

She stepped closer. "The way I see it, you need me, and I need you. We can work together and both get what we want." Her eyes flickered with excitement.

"I don't want to bring them down, Eliza." He couldn't believe he was saying that.

She ran a finger along his jawline. "Well, if you change your mind, I'm here," she said in a seductive voice that made him sick. A laugh escaped her before she walked out the door. Fear gripped his heart. Eliza was the type of woman who would do anything to get her way.

Just when he felt things were turning around in his heart, the freedom that had lifted him from bitterness seemed to drain from his soul like life ebbing from a dying man.

Once again he felt trapped, but this time by the bitterness of another.

∞

Sunday morning Titus once again sat on the church bench with the O'Connor family. Sandwiched between Abigail and Eliza, he felt a bit awkward. Eliza had been following him around like a hovering shadow. He didn't like it at all.

The pastor spoke of Solomon and how he had served the Lord faithfully then ultimately allowed other gods to infiltrate his heart. Titus wondered how someone could be that strong in their walk then so blatantly turn from the truth. Then he thought of his own life. Isn't that exactly what he had done? He had once believed. But that was before his father's business was destroyed and the family funds had dwindled, taking Titus's dreams with them.

Even so, he wasn't sure he was ready to change that. A root of bitterness lingered, but God was dealing with him. Of that, he was sure.

By the sermon's end, Titus felt at war with himself. He wanted to get things straightened out with God. The O'Connors seemed to have proven themselves genuine, but he couldn't shake the notion that someone needed to pay for his suffering.

Someone did pay. Jesus.

He pushed the thought aside, not wanting to think about it. Despite his efforts to ignore the matter, though, he could feel his mood diving south. He needed to get home. Think things through.

After the final prayer, the people shuffled across the wooden floor toward the exit. As people crowded in around them, he reached over and touched Abigail's elbow. Seeming to sense it was he, she turned up and smiled. They had just stepped into the sunshine when a voice called from the side. "Abigail!"

Titus and Abigail both turned their heads to see a tall man with spectacles and a wide smile coming their way, hand extended.

"Jonathan," Abigail said with a smile. Though she hesitated just a moment, she offered her hand in greeting. She turned to Titus and introduced him to Jonathan. Did her face light up with the presence of her old friend, or was Titus imagining it? He felt like a jealous schoolboy. He glanced at Eliza. She tossed him a smirk. Perhaps she could see it, too.

Abigail's preoccupation with her visitor coupled with his own jealousy made Titus sick of heart. Deciding to go home, Titus slipped from the gathering and headed for his wagon.

"Titus," Eliza called out.

He turned to her.

She stepped up to him and raised her hand to his arm. "Just remember what I told you. I'm here for you if you change your mind."

Titus glared at her then turned back to his wagon. Her laughter taunted him the entire ride home.

Chapter 13

Abigail took a moment to collect herself from all the excitement Jonathan's visit brought. She and her family stood talking with him in front of the church. Buggies were pulling out and most likely heading home.

While her father talked to Jonathan of business things, Abigail glanced around. She saw Eliza standing with Titus, her hand on his arm. He didn't pull away. Eliza still pursued him; that much was obvious. How did he feel about her? Was she winning him over? Did the kiss Abigail and Titus had shared mean anything to him? She glanced at Jonathan then back to Titus. Her heart felt a tangle of confusion.

Titus turned and climbed into his wagon without saying good-bye to any of them. Eliza walked over and stood under an apple tree in the distance. She pulled open a book.

Abigail sighed, wondering where her heart would take her, what her future would hold. From a low branch of a nearby tree, a sparrow fluffed his feathers and seemed to snuggle into them. Abigail was reminded of God's love even for the sparrow. If He could take care of the sparrow, He could take care of her. Just then a brown squirrel with a plume of a tail scurried up the tree, startling the sparrow and causing him to fly away, taking Abigail's gaze upward. A spattering of heavy clouds hung low in the wintry sky with occasional patches of soft blue blinking in and out between them.

Abigail thought the day would bring snow. Jonathan loved to ice-skate. Perhaps they could go ice-skating while he was in town. She wondered what had caused Jonathan to return to Chicago and how long he would stay.

"Jonathan, you must join us for lunch," Mother was saying.

Jonathan glanced at Abigail. She smiled at him.

His face broke into the familiar grin that had flipped her heart so many times before. She couldn't deny it felt good to see Jonathan again. Yet things were different somehow. This time, her heart didn't flip. Perhaps she had built a wall to protect herself from further hurt. Not that it mattered; he probably popped in to see her like any good friend would while in town for a visit.

She felt tired and confused. Titus had been acting strange lately, and now with Jonathan showing up, Abigail didn't know what to think about anything.

By the time they got home and ate lunch, midafternoon was upon them. Father glanced out the window then turned to Abigail and Jonathan. "I know it's cold out there, but with the snowflakes falling, it looks like a good afternoon for a sleigh ride. You're welcome to use our sleigh, Jonathan." A wide grin stretched across his face.

Jonathan turned and smiled at Abigail, his eyes lit with adventure. "What do you say?"

Abigail giggled. "I think it would be fun." Then almost as an afterthought, she looked at Eliza. "Would you like to come along?"

"No, thank you, I'd prefer the company of my needlepoint," she said with a tone that made no apologies for her comment.

Abigail ignored the comment and turned to Jonathan. "I'll grab my things from upstairs. I'll only be a minute."

He nodded.

Before long, they were settled comfortably in the sleigh, the horses hitched and ready to go. She snuggled into the warm skins and breathed deeply of winter's scent. He looked over at her and smiled. "I've missed you."

His comment surprised her. "I've missed you, too," she said. And she meant it.

The horses' *clip-clop* echoed through the afternoon air. Jonathan told her of his new job and new life. Finally, when they had traveled just outside of town, he pulled over near a rotted-out tree. The horses stood pawing the ground, puffs of warm air blowing from their nostrils.

"I've been wrong," Jonathan said, clutching Abigail's hands. "I thought I could go on with my life, that this job was the best thing, and we both should start over, but I was wrong. The vision of you follows me every moment of every day and haunts my dreams at night."

Abigail stared at him, not knowing what to say.

"I love you, Abigail O'Connor." He touched the edge of her hat, pushing it slightly from her face, and he leaned in, his mouth brushing against hers in the familiar way of the past. She kissed him back, surrendering to his touch, relaxing in his arms, until she realized the man she kissed was not Jonathan.

It was Titus.

She pulled away. Her mind and heart became a flurry of confusion and contradictions. First Jonathan loved her, and then he didn't. Then Titus cared; now he hovered in secret corners with Eliza. Why did they toy with her heart? She wanted to get away from both of them. Her heart weighed heavy with distrust of everyone. She was tired of being tossed about. Didn't anyone care how she felt? Oh, now she was acting like Eliza. Tears sprang to her eyes.

"Are you all right?"

"I want to go home, Jonathan."

Surprise touched to his face. "Look, Abigail, I'm here for two weeks, and that's it. I have a lot to say to you—"

Abigail turned to him. "I need some time, Jonathan. I don't know what to think about anything right now."

"Does this have anything to do with your chauffeur?"

Abigail wasn't sure how to answer that, because she didn't know the answer. She shook her head. "It has to do with me. I don't want to get hurt anymore." Her words choked to a mere whisper.

He grabbed her by the shoulders until she looked at him again. "I don't want to hurt you. You've got to believe me. I thought I was doing the right thing by both of us when I left. Now I see I was wrong." When she looked at him, he winced. "But by the look in your eyes, I'm afraid I'm too late."

Jonathan turned around and tugged the horses back into a steady trot. "Give me the week. That's all I ask."

Abigail nodded and leaned into her blankets, wondering what the week would hold.

⌒

"Titus, sit down and talk to me. What is troubling you, son?" Ma asked him as he paced the small room.

His fingers raked through his hair, and he sat in the kitchen chair at the battered wooden table. Ma placed some coffee in front of him. His gaze lingered in his cup. "I don't know."

Ma wisely kept silent and waited.

He looked up. "I think I'm in love with Abigail."

"And that's not a good thing?" she asked with motherly gentleness.

He looked away and fell silent a moment.

Ma seemed to catch on. "She has someone else in her life?" She took a drink of coffee.

His eyes darted back to Ma. "That's just it. I don't know." He blew out a frustrated sigh. "This man Jonathan Clark moved out east, though she had loved him. Now he's back."

Ma put down her cup. "Ah, I see." She paused. "Titus, if she loves you, love will win out."

"And if she doesn't?"

"If she doesn't, then God has other plans."

"God," he spewed. "It's always you and God." He stood to his feet and began pacing again. "What about *my* plans and what *I* want?"

"Your plans, Titus Matthews, will get you into trouble. You must trust the Lord."

"Trust. That's another thing. Abigail would never love me if she knew—" He stopped himself short.

Ma's eyes seared through him. "Titus, what have you done?"

He dropped back into the chair. "I haven't actually done anything, but, well. . ." He looked at Ma. "Well, I wanted to get even with the O'Connors."

"Oh Titus, no. Tell me you haven't hurt this precious family." Ma's eyes pleaded with him.

"I haven't done anything. It's just that Eliza knows I happened upon a paper—"

"Happened upon? Don't color the truth for me, Titus Matthews. Tell me exactly what happened."

He explained the situation with the letter to Pa and how that letter changed his heart. Then about Eliza catching on and knowing he had been searching for something. "So you see, if Eliza puts her spin on things to Abigail, how will I get Abigail to believe that I wasn't using her to get to the truth—or that though it may have started out that way, things changed for me?"

Ma took a drink of coffee and frowned. "Eliza O'Connor needs a good prayer session."

Titus smiled in spite of himself. Those were about the meanest words he could imagine his ma ever saying.

"I see your dilemma, Titus. You'd better pray yourself and ask the Lord to help you through this mess you have made—after you ask Him to clean up your heart."

Titus looked at her a moment. "You pray, Ma. I'm not sure I'm ready."

∽∾

Monday morning Abigail and Eliza settled into conversation with Gramma at her home once again. Though she added occasional laughter and a comment here and there, Abigail could tell Eliza was not truly concentrating. She kept looking around the room as if searching for something. Abigail couldn't imagine what.

"Have you heard from your father yet, Eliza?"

Eliza shook her head. "Guess they've forgotten about me." She said the words then stood to her feet and began to meander about the room. Abigail wondered if Eliza was afraid her emotions might show.

"Do you have any books, Gramma?"

Gramma nodded. "There be some in me bedroom. Feel free to look, Eliza. I believe I have a copy of *Little Women*, if ye have never read that one."

Eliza's expression showed surprise. "You've read that, Gramma? I didn't picture you as one to read."

"Ah, I love to read. Just can't see as well as I used to. 'Tis a good book, that one."

Eliza nodded. "I'd like to read it."

Gramma smiled and nodded, pointing toward her room.

Eliza slipped out of the room and into Gramma's room. Abigail and Gramma continued in conversation. Abigail explained her dilemma with Jonathan and Titus.

"I see. If ye thought ye could trust them both fully, Abigail darling, and they both truly loved ye, who would ye choose?"

Abigail bit her lip and twirled a ringlet between her fingers at the side of her face. "I—I don't know for sure. I mean, a few months ago, I was convinced I was in love with Jonathan. Then a few weeks ago, my heart moved to Titus. Now? Well, I just don't know." She looked at Gramma in desperation. "What shall I do?"

"Pray, wee one," Gramma said, reaching over with her old, bent hand and patting Abigail's shoulder.

Abigail nodded. "Sometimes I wish the Lord's answers would come more quickly."

Gramma laughed. "His ways would not be our ways. 'Tis on a different time schedule, He is."

Abigail had to laugh at the thought. She knew Gramma was right. People tried to shape God into their own understanding of Him. He was so much more. Though she still did not have any answers, Abigail felt better just talking about things. She also was certain God would guide her.

"I guess Eliza decided to read in your room," Abigail whispered, leaning into Gramma.

"She tires of me company." Gramma covered a chuckle. "Ye be coming back later this week and letting me know about ye gentlemen friends?" She winked.

Abigail took in a breath. "Gramma, please! You make me sound like a frivolous woman!" They both laughed. "Of course I will be back. I wouldn't miss my visits with you," Abigail said, giving Gramma's hand a squeeze.

"How things be at Barnabas House?"

"Going well. The director is getting married on Saturday. I'm looking forward to going to the wedding. I told you about Mary O'Grady and her daughter, Katie?"

"She'd be the one whose husband left her and later was killed?"

Abigail nodded. "That's who Christopher is marrying. They will make a lovely family. I'm so happy for them all."

"See how God, He works through life's difficulties? No doubt she had many dark hours after her husband left."

"You're right, Gramma."

"God will get us through the questions of life, He will. We need only trust and wait."

Abigail thought a moment and smiled. "How did you get so smart?"

Gramma laughed. "Ah! I'm old. I've seen many things, I have, and listened well."

"Guess I'll have to work on that listening part," Abigail said with a chuckle before rising to her feet. "Well, I really need to go. I'd better get Eliza." She walked to Gramma's bedroom. Peering into the room, Abigail saw Eliza sitting on a rocking chair, looking through what appeared to be a journal of some type. "Ah, you've found something, I see."

Abigail's voice startled Eliza. She dropped the journal to the floor and quickly poked it back into a basket under the stand by the bed. She grabbed the copy of *Little Women* and looked up as if nothing had happened at all. "Yes, in fact I did. This looks like a great novel," she said, standing and brushing off her dress. "I can hardly wait to get started on it."

Watching her closely, Abigail wondered what Eliza had been reading. No doubt snooping into Gramma's things. Abigail shrugged. Eliza was always up to something. As long as no one got hurt, Abigail supposed she shouldn't worry about it.

Keeping Eliza occupied and her sharp tongue silent was the important thing. Then she couldn't hurt anyone.

Chapter 14

Abigail peered out her bedroom window at the frosty air. The wind had swept the sky clean, and it looked like beautiful weather for a wedding. She felt almost giddy as she dressed for Christopher and Mary's big day. No doubt Katie was all giggles and curls this morning. The thought brought a smile to Abigail. The family had suffered much, and God had turned things around for them.

If only she could learn to trust in the hard times. She chided herself. After all, she hadn't really experienced hard times like some people. If she was so shallow on the little things, how would she make it through the really difficult events that were sure to come? Life wasn't always easy, but in her few years, she had seen God take care of a good many people who trusted in Him.

"Abiding joy," Gramma called it. And Gramma had it. When her husband of fifty-eight years died, God brought her joy in the sorrow. Oh, she had grieved, but through her tears, she kept saying over and over, "I'll see him again one day."

Walking to the washbasin, Abigail splashed water on her face. As she patted her skin dry with a towel, she thought further. She served the Lord, but truth be known, she wasn't wholeheartedly committed. She really didn't know what held her back. Life, she supposed. She was busy with life. There wasn't always time to ponder the Creator or read His Word. She didn't actually rebel against Him, she just, well, ignored Him.

Her hands held the towel midair. Is that what she did? Ignored Him? She hadn't thought about that until now. She certainly hadn't meant to ignore Him. The truth of the matter was she put other things first. Gramma's talk had made Abigail see some things in her own life. She wanted the deep-rooted faith of which Gramma talked, the kind that dug deep into the soil of God's love and stood strong in the thrashing winds of life.

She plopped onto the bed. Roots stretch deep in search of water. There are twists and turns, but still they probe, ever onward, doing whatever it takes to survive. That's it. Her heart needed living water. She needed to dig deep into God's Word, always stretching, bending, yielding to His plan to drink from the living water. As she walked with Christ on this level, she would never thirst, because her roots would grow deep. She would not topple in life's struggles.

The very idea seemed somewhat overwhelming to Abigail. She supposed it took years of service and maturity to get to that place. Like Gramma.

She shook her head and stood up, pulling out her dress for the wedding. What had made her think such deep thoughts this morning, she couldn't imagine. After all, her only problem was to choose between two handsome suitors. Thankfully, it wasn't as though she had any overwhelming concerns in her life. When she grew old like Gramma, then she'd be strong.

Until then...

∞

The wedding was beautiful, and Abigail couldn't have been happier for Christopher and Mary. Mary's face glowed with joy, and Katie looked cute enough to squeeze. Christopher stood strong and confident beside his new bride, and Abigail knew they would have a bright future together.

Titus was unusually quiet as they made their way back to the O'Connor homestead. She wondered if Jonathan's return to town bothered him. But of course it didn't. It wasn't as though she and Titus had any type of arrangement between them. They were friends. Maybe a little more than friends. After all, he had kissed her.

She rubbed her temples, feeling a headache coming on. Titus looked at her.

"You feeling all right?"

She nodded.

"Christopher and Mary look very happy."

"Yes, they do," she agreed, knowing he was struggling to make small talk. She decided to help. "How is Jenny getting along?"

Talk of Jenny always made him smile. "She's doing well. Saying more words every day. I haven't seen Ma this happy in a long time." He turned to her, a look of gratitude on his face.

"I'm happy for Jenny...and thankful for you."

Abigail felt his gaze on her. He seemed to study her a moment. She shifted in her seat.

"When is Jonathan leaving?" he asked.

She turned to him. "He's leaving next Saturday."

Titus nodded.

"Why do you ask?"

"No reason."

They lapsed into silence once again. Since Jonathan's arrival, things had definitely grown strained between them. Abigail didn't know how to fix things just yet. How could she, when she couldn't untangle her own emotions? She didn't know how she felt about anyone these days and grew tired of thinking about it.

Titus pulled the wagon into their yard.

"We have time to eat lunch before going to Gramma's. You hungry?" Abigail asked.

He shook his head. "Don't have much of an appetite today."

With the way he looked at her, Abigail felt somehow responsible. "I won't be long."

After lunch, Eliza had decided to join Abigail on her trip to Gramma's, which surprised Abigail. Eliza always seemed bored, so Abigail assumed she'd stay home and work on her needlepoint. But today she was different. Almost perky. Abigail couldn't help but wonder what she was up to this time.

Gramma waited with open arms when they arrived. Abigail knew Gramma looked forward to these visits as much as she did. When she and Eliza stepped through the door, Abigail could smell the tea, the aroma lifting from the teapot on the table.

In no time they had settled into their chairs and talked of the wedding and the Doyle family's future together. Once Eliza finished her tea, she excused herself to Gramma's room to read *Little Women*. It seemed she liked sitting in there on the rocking chair, away from the noise of discussion. Gramma consented.

"I don't know how to reach her," Abigail finally whispered to Gramma after Eliza left the room.

"She is hurting, she is. I'm afraid me son has put his child through a lot." Gramma shook her head. "His rebellion against the Lord has brought grief to his family."

"I want to care about her, Gramma, but sometimes she isn't easy to love," Abigail confessed.

Gramma shrugged. "The Lord, He must feel that way about us at times," she said thoughtfully.

Abigail felt chastised. Once again, Gramma was right.

"Any decision yet on ye handsome suitors?"

Abigail shook her head. "Jonathan is still pressuring me. Titus has withdrawn, so I'm not sure of his feelings at all anymore. Maybe he's not interested."

Gramma took a swallow of tea and shook her head. "I'm not thinking so. He probably feels a trifle displaced with Jonathan here and all." She stirred more sugar into her tea. " 'Tis hard to see the competition at work." Gramma winked.

"Please keep praying. I want to do the right thing. I just don't know what that is."

"I think ye mind is made up already."

"You do?" Gramma's wisdom tickled Abigail. "And just what have I decided?"

"Ye will choose Titus."

Abigail laughed. "How do you know?"

Gramma lifted a gnarled finger. "I've been around a good many days." She tapped the side of her temple with her finger. "'Tis ye heart that tells me."

Abigail stared at her, considering her words. "I wish it would tell me," she said with a halfhearted laugh.

"Would ye be listening?"

Abigail sat in silence. After a little while, she could finally see the truth. "You're right, Gramma. Why couldn't I see it before?"

"Perhaps ye are afraid of Titus's feelings now, since he has pulled away. Perhaps ye think if ye let Jonathan go, ye will be alone."

Abigail looked down, nodding her head. "Yes, I hadn't realized that until this very moment."

Gramma got up from her place and hobbled over to sit by Abigail. She clutched Abigail's hands with her own. "Then ye know what ye must do, Abigail."

Tears spilled onto her dress. She nodded once more.

"Me prayers will cover ye, wee one." Gramma placed a kiss on Abigail's temple. "He will give ye strength."

Huddled together, Gramma led in a prayer for direction and strength. Once she finished, Abigail's heart felt lighter. Though she didn't know how she would tell Jonathan her decision, she knew it's what she had to do.

With the matter settled, Abigail stood. "Thank you, Gramma, once again, for showing me things I don't know myself."

Gramma smiled.

Abigail headed to Gramma's room and found Eliza reading a newspaper. She jumped. Abigail wondered why Eliza appeared nervous lately. "You ready to go?"

Eliza nodded. Abigail noticed Eliza slipped two books into her bag. She wondered why Eliza needed two books. They would be back before long; she could pick the second one up then. She shrugged it off. Maybe Eliza wasn't coming the next time. Oh well, Abigail felt weary from the day's discussions. "Let's go."

⚭

Friday morning after breakfast, Abigail took one more look out her window. A thin mist of frost covered rooftops. The air was white with falling snow. It seemed a perfect day for ice-skating. She wished Jonathan hadn't invited Eliza and Titus to go along. With her mind made up to say good-bye to Jonathan, seeing Titus and Eliza together would be all the harder. Pulling on her winter woolens, she glanced once more around her bedroom to make sure she had everything she needed. She did. With that, she turned and walked out of the room, setting out for the stairway.

Eliza left her room at the same time, both arriving at the stairway together. "Good morning, Eliza."

"Abigail."

They walked the wooden stairs together, the wood creaking beneath their feet. Eliza adjusted the gloves on her hands. "So you must be unhappy with Jonathan's soon departure."

Abigail knew Eliza well enough to know she was digging for information. "I will miss him, but he has to return to work."

Eliza nodded. "And you will not return with him?"

Abigail looked at her in surprise. "Of course not. What made you think so?"

"Oh, I just assumed."

"It's not like that between us."

"Oh?" She stopped a moment. "Pity," Eliza finally said, skipping down the last two stairs and moving toward the door as if to avoid further conversation now that she'd found out what she wanted to know.

The very idea annoyed Abigail to no end. She knew Eliza's plan. To win Titus's affections. Period. The thought threw Abigail into a huff. It's not as though he were a toy to be tossed about between the two of them.

"Good-bye," Abigail called toward her mother, who sat reading the newspaper at her chair in front of the fireplace. Folding the paper, she walked over to Abigail and kissed her cheek.

"You children have a wonderful time."

Eliza smiled, and Abigail hugged her mother good-bye. Eliza and Abigail then slipped through the door into a winter wonderland.

Jonathan and Titus both greeted them. Abigail detected a hint of tension, though she wondered if she imagined it. "You ready to go?" Jonathan's face sparkled. He reached toward Abigail almost possessively to assist her into the carriage he had borrowed from a friend. She felt a little embarrassed by his behavior. The morning was perfect, though, and she didn't want to spoil it. She kept her thoughts light.

Titus helped Eliza in the backseat. Everyone settled in for a pleasant ride.

"How is Jenny doing, Titus?" Abigail turned back to him in time to see Eliza snuggle close beside him. Eliza tossed a victory smile.

"Doing better every day. She misses you, though. Wants to know if you're coming over today." He shifted an inch away from Eliza. She scooted closer. "I wasn't sure since we were going ice-skating."

Jonathan shot Abigail a look of disapproval.

"Well, I guess we'll have to wait and see how tired we all are after this morning," she said with a forced chuckle. She turned back around. With a slight attitude, she smoothed her skirts. After all, she did not appreciate Jonathan's pushiness. Perhaps he had forgotten, but he had walked out on her, not the other way around.

She would not be pushed.

Once they arrived, they all climbed out of the carriage and headed toward a bench to put on their skates. The pond was full of people once again. It was the most popular place to skate when the water iced over. It seemed to freeze faster than the other spots in town. Much safer.

Though frustrated with the men in her life, Abigail had to admit she was excited about ice-skating. She hadn't gone in quite some time and looked forward to it. While she waited for Eliza to finish strapping her ice-skates over her shoes, Abigail glanced up to watch the other skaters. A light snow drifted all around, adding the perfect touch to the scene. Bundled in heavy wraps, the crowd gracefully moved along, the sounds of their blades cutting into the ice, leaving iced shavings behind. Childish squeals and laughter filled the air as one or more spilled upon the frozen ground, causing others to pile one on the other.

Abigail laughed.

"You ready to give it a try?" Titus asked, surprising her. He reached out a hand. She dared not look at Jonathan but rather grabbed Titus's waiting hand. Before Eliza or Jonathan could protest, Titus helped her onto the pond, and they were soon drifting around the sidelines with the greatest of ease.

"They'll never forgive you, you know," Abigail said, daring to give him a sideways glance.

He looked her full in the face and laughed. "I know."

She bit her lip and couldn't help the excitement bubbling up inside her. For now, she wouldn't care about what they thought. She would enjoy the pure pleasure of the moment. "I didn't know you were such a good skater," she said.

He shrugged. "I came here a lot as a kid." He looked at her. "I wanted to say the same thing about you."

"I came here, too. You were probably the boy who always bumped into me when I was little, forcing me to get up and try again."

Titus chuckled. "I knew you weren't a quitter. Even then."

They laughed together. He put his arm around her back and escorted her around the pond at a fast pace. She wondered if Titus did that so Jonathan couldn't catch them. The sides of her bonnet flipped back with the breeze. The cold air pricked her skin, filling her with delight. Their laughter joined the others' and mingled into the air. For the moment, Abigail forgot all problems and responsibilities. She was a little girl again, caught in the rapture of the moment.

After a while, Titus slowed his pace and pulled her aside to rest. He looked into her face, his eyes twinkling. "You all right?"

Quite out of breath, she stopped laughing a moment and tried to calm herself. Her teeth smarting from the cold, she closed her mouth and breathed through her nose. "It was wonderful!" she said finally. Truth was, she hadn't felt so alive in a very long time.

"Good," he said, staring into her eyes.

Just then, Eliza and Jonathan skated up to them, neither looking quite happy.

"Well, I trust you had a nice lap or two around the pond, Abigail," Jonathan said, his glare evident to all. Titus cleared his throat and glanced at Abigail. For some reason, she wanted to giggle. Suddenly, Jonathan seemed the harsh taskmaster, and she and Titus had been like two schoolkids sneaking away for a moment of mischief.

She caught Titus's gaze. He winked at her then turned to Eliza. "So, Eliza, do you care to go around?"

Eliza lifted her chin and threw a triumphant look to Abigail. "Certainly, Titus," she said to him then glanced once more at Abigail before disappearing into the crowd.

Abigail watched them a moment, still smiling in spite of herself.

"Well, I don't see what is so funny, Abigail." Jonathan looked as mad as a March hare.

"What, Jonathan?"

"After all, you came here with me."

"I came here with everyone, Jonathan," she said, giving his tirade little notice.

"I see. Are you giving me your answer this way, Abigail?"

She looked at him with a start. His eyes had softened, sadness replacing his angry stare. As much as she hated to do so, she decided this was as good a time as any.

"I'm sorry, Jonathan."

"I thought as much." He stared at the pond's floor. "I brought it on myself. I should never have left."

Her hand touched his arm. "No, Jonathan, it was right that you left. It's better we know now how things really are between us so we can move on with our lives."

His proud jaw lifted. "I see you certainly have." His words were biting, but she understood. She had felt the very same when he went back east. "I hope you and Titus have a happy life together."

His words jolted her. Would they have a life together?

She could only hope.

Chapter 15

After talking with Jonathan, Abigail felt the ice-skating was pretty much ruined. She loved Jonathan in a special way and didn't want to hurt him for the world, yet she couldn't deny her feelings. What they had shared was a wonderful friendship, not love. She could see that now. Though she didn't know what the future held for her and Titus, she knew her future was not with Jonathan. Still, she didn't want to hurt him.

After a quiet drive home, Titus and Eliza got out of the carriage, and Jonathan stayed with Abigail. "I'm sorry it didn't work out, Abigail."

Tears sprang to her eyes. "Me, too, Jonathan."

"You're sure?" He lifted her chin, causing their eyes to meet.

She swallowed hard, tears trailing down her cheeks. "I'm sure," she said.

"If I thought I could change your mind, I'd stick around, you know. Give up my job, everything."

She looked at him. "Please, Jonathan, don't do that."

He shook his head. "No, I won't. We both know there's no future." He looked toward the barn. "I wonder if Titus Matthews knows what a lucky man he is."

Her breath stuck in her throat.

"I will never forget you, Abigail O'Connor." His finger wiped the tears from her cheeks. Like the quick brush of the wind, his lips lit softly upon where the tears had been; then he got down and helped her from the carriage. Once they arrived at the door, Abigail turned to him.

"Thank you, Jonathan, for being a wonderful friend. For understanding."

"Good-bye, Abigail."

"Good-bye." Abigail turned and pushed through the front door. Her parents and Eliza stood just inside, as if waiting for her. She lifted tear-stained cheeks and knew she didn't have to offer an explanation just yet. "Good night, Mother, Father." She turned to her cousin. "Eliza."

Before they could answer, her legs carried her hastily up the stairway and into her room. Barnabas followed closely behind. Abigail dropped onto her bed and buried her face in her hands. Barnabas seemed to sense her sorrow. He whined as his cold nose nudged her arm, as if wanting to comfort her. When she didn't respond, he gave up and curled up at her feet.

After a little while, she fell back against her pillow. "Good-bye,

Jonathan Clark. I'm sorry," she whispered into the air before falling asleep with her tears.

∞

Titus finished feeding the horses and heard a sound at the barn door. He turned around to see Eliza standing there holding a book. Inwardly, he cringed. Hadn't he had enough of her for one day? Right now all he wanted was time to think. Alone.

She lifted an eyebrow as she waved the book in front of him. "I've found what I've been looking for."

He didn't like the look on her face. It spelled trouble. Something he didn't need right now. He had enough confusion going on in his life.

"Look, Eliza, I'm tired and—"

She would not be put off. "You don't understand. I've discovered a family secret. A secret no one knew but Gramma and Thomas O'Connor."

Titus knew he shouldn't listen further, yet curiosity got the better of him. "All right, what is it?"

She smacked her lips like one with the juiciest bit of gossip. "Let's go over there." She pointed toward a secluded corner in the barn. Once they settled in, she pulled open the pages of Gramma's journal and began to read:

"Thomas left me house a moment ago. Me heart is heavier than 'tis ever been. What shall we do? With Lavina unable to have children, the baby on their doorstep had seemed such a miracle. Never would I have guessed such deception in me son. I knew the past year had brought ill health to him, but I hadn't realized it stemmed from guilt.

" 'Tis a business trip had led him to a night of indiscretion. A night that would bring blessing and pain. Unable to live with the guilt, Thomas surrendered his heart to Christ tonight. He came to me to help him pray. 'Tis why he revealed this hidden sin to me. Still, the blessing of it 'tis the gift of baby Abigail.

"I wondered how the child's mother could leave her baby. She didn't want the responsibility, says Thomas. He gave her money for her trouble, and she went on her way. Me heart breaks at the thought of the future. Thomas has decided it best to keep the truth from Lavina.

"After the doctor told Lavina she would never have children, despair overtook her. One day a knock sounded at their door, and she opened it to see a tiny child wrapped in warm blankets, sleeping peacefully in a basket. Lavina was convinced God had seen her distress and come to her aid. Thomas could not bring himself to hurt her once more.

"He means well, but I wonder at his wisdom in this matter. Can it ever be good to conceal a truth? I'm afraid only time will tell."

220

Eliza closed the book with a triumphant *snap*. Titus felt sick. He had dreamed of this day, and now that it was here, it loomed over him like a dark shadow. How could he hurt this wonderful family who had brought him into their home, treated him as a son? He couldn't deny pain still lurked and rekindled his pride, but he refused to surrender to it.

"So, when shall we bring this to light?" Eliza was asking, pulling Titus from his thoughts.

He sighed and ran fingers through his hair. "Eliza, I don't know. I need to think on this."

She looked at him a moment. "All right, we should have a plan to get the most from this. You give it some thought, and I will, too. Then we'll meet back here in the barn tomorrow night. Will that work for you?"

He stared at her.

She placed her hands on her hips. "Well, will it?"

He knew she had him where she wanted him. She could tell the O'Connors he had been snooping in the study that day. They would piece things together as to why he was there. No matter how it turned out, he would lose. He needed to think things through, stall Eliza in any way he could.

"Yes."

Her face relaxed. "Good. It's all settled then." She turned to go.

"One thing, Eliza."

She looked back at him. "What is it?"

"When the truth is revealed and their family torn apart, where will you go?"

She smiled. "My parents will have to take me back. Where else would I go?"

"So this is about you going home?"

Her face turned hard, rigid. "It's about bringing down this goody-goody family. I'm sick of their religion, their wealth being shoved in my face." Her face contorted with every word. Titus wondered if bitterness made him look like that. "Ever since I was a child, it was always their family with the money, the happy times, while our family struggled. Just ask my father. He will tell you. He's tired of living in the shadow of his big brother. I don't blame him. I detest them all."

Titus cringed at the venom in her voice. This family didn't deserve her harsh words. Still, he couldn't fault Eliza when he had thought the same about them at one time.

But not anymore.

He nodded at her. "Tomorrow then."

"Tomorrow," she said with a gleam in her eye. She turned and walked away. He watched her, amazed at how bitterness had taken this woman's beauty and destroyed it. Something told him his ma had seen that same look on him.

He had much to think about.

∞

The next day, Titus knew he should feel guilty about not going to the O'Connors' house, but it was the only chance he had for stalling Eliza. He stepped from his barn after feeding the horse and walked toward his house. Abigail's horse and empty wagon stood out front. His feet stopped. Had she come? With Eliza?

He took a deep breath and stepped inside. Pulling off his hat, he turned to his ma and Abigail. "Hello. Is everything all right?"

Ma cut in. "She wanted to drop off some chicken noodle soup for Jenny." With her gaze pinned on him, she added, "Since Jenny is feeling so poorly." He didn't miss her look of disapproval. Did Abigail see it? He quickly looked at Abigail, but she didn't seem to notice Ma's chastisement.

Fortunately, Jenny was taking her morning nap, so Abigail could believe his sister might be sick.

"I do hope she is feeling better soon," Abigail said, glancing at Jenny's form on her bed. "Father told me you stopped in last night and let them know you wouldn't be there today because Jenny was feeling ill, so I thought I'd bring her something."

He glanced at Ma. She still glared at him. "Thank you, Abigail. That's very kind of you."

She smiled.

"Well, it's almost lunchtime. Would you care to join us?" Ma said.

"Oh no, I couldn't do that."

"Oh yes, you could," Ma persisted.

Titus knew Ma was inviting Abigail to make him uncomfortable. One thing about it, Ma could sure be stubborn. He supposed that's why her prayers got through. No doubt the Lord got tired of her nagging.

"Well, if you put it that way," Abigail said with a laugh.

"Good. Titus, help set the table, please."

Titus threw her a wait-till-I-get-you-alone look and commenced to set the table.

Once the meal was over and the good-byes were said, Titus walked Abigail out to the wagon. "I'm glad Jenny seems to be doing better today. Maybe lunch helped."

Titus swallowed hard. "Do you think your parents would want me to come today?"

She shook her head. "Though it's hard to get along without you, I'm sure we could manage for one day." She laughed.

"Is Jonathan leaving today?"

She looked down and nodded.

"I take it you've decided to part ways?"

With her head still bent, she answered, "Yes."

He lifted her chin in his hand. "I'm glad."

His heart turned over with the sight of her. He loved this woman and could see in her eyes that she loved him, too. He wanted her to be his wife, but their future rested in the hands of another.

Eliza O'Connor.

☙

"You want to tell me what that was all about?" Ma said when Titus went back inside.

He scratched his head and took the load from his feet, falling into a kitchen chair. Bowing his head, he stretched fingers through his hair, staring at the table.

Ma sat down nearby, her hand reaching over to him. "Titus, what is it?"

He explained the whole story to her. His life, his bitterness, his need for God, his love for Abigail, and now Eliza's scheme.

Ma thought a moment. "I see. The only solution I can see to this problem is God."

He looked at her.

"You've been running long enough, Titus. You see where your way has taken you. Our way is never the right way. God's way is always right. Now, mind you, I'm not saying everything will turn out the way you want it, but I'm saying He will help you through it."

Titus hung his head and nodded. His eyes filled with tears. He couldn't remember the last time he had cried. He thought his tears had all dried up. Ma led him in a prayer. Titus recommitted his love for the Lord and offered himself as an empty vessel for God to use as He saw fit. No matter what the consequences. Once the prayer was over, he knew things were different. He felt better, lighter.

He would face Eliza directly come Monday. He wouldn't discuss the matter at church. She'd have to wait.

Eliza did wait, though not happily so. Titus would not ruin Sunday with their talk of destroying the O'Connor family. He hoped the Lord would give him a way yet to get out of the whole ordeal. Most of all, he didn't want to hurt Abigail. Perhaps Eliza would give it up—though he knew that was about as likely as Chicago turning into a ghost town.

He was right. Come Monday morning, bright and early, Eliza stood ready to greet him at the barn when he pulled up, the journal held firmly in her hand. He prayed once again for strength and hopped from his wagon.

Bitterness pushed her forward. Her eyes lit with the thrill of hurting another. "Are you ready?"

He grabbed her hand. "Listen, Eliza, why are you bent on doing this? The O'Connors have been good to both of us, taking us in—"

She jerked her hand away. "Oh, don't tell me you're going soft!"

He blew out a frustrated sigh. "It's just that I don't see the sense in all this."

"I don't believe you. You know Uncle Thomas stood by and watched your pa go under financially. No wonder your pa had a heart attack!" Her words hurt him to the core, but he saw his old reflection in her. The bitterness had twisted and marred her face in a way he hadn't seen before on himself. But God saw it. And He had set Titus free.

"There's a better way, Eliza. God can help us—"

She gasped. "What? You've got religion now?" She looked at him incredulously. Once again she took a proud stance. "Well, if I have to do this myself, so be it." With that, she stomped across the yard toward the house.

His stomach knotted like an old rope as he followed Eliza to the house. Chills pricked up his arm, and he broke out in a cold sweat. He hurled a frantic prayer for wisdom toward the heavens and stepped in just behind Eliza. She turned to him with surprise. The look on her face said she thought he would back her up. *God help us.*

"Oh, good, I was just going to come out for you both. Breakfast is ready," Mrs. O'Connor said. Titus felt it was more like the Last Supper.

The family took their seats at the table. Titus glanced at Abigail. Her eyes questioned him as if she knew something was amiss.

The dishes were passed, and Titus shoved eggs around on his plate, dreading what was sure to come.

"Titus, I hope you're not getting what your sister had. You've hardly touched a bite," Mrs. O'Connor said.

"Yes ma'am."

"Well, I discovered a bit of news the last time I went to Gramma's house," Eliza offered before biting into a piece of toast.

All eyes turned to her. Mr. O'Connor spread some butter across his toast. "What might that be?" he asked in all innocence.

A smile lit her face, and she looked the happiest Titus had ever seen her. She sickened him not only because of her behavior but because she reminded him so much of himself. How God could forgive him, Titus didn't know. He only knew God had forgiven him, and he was thankful.

Just then a knock sounded at the door.

"I'll get it," Mr. O'Connor said, wiping his mouth with the cloth napkin then laying it on the table.

Titus glanced at Eliza, who was frowning.

"You were saying, Eliza?" Mrs. O'Connor continued.

Eliza lifted her head. "Oh, nothing. It can wait. I'd rather share it with everyone here."

"Well, it seems I have to go out of town for railroad business, dear," Mr. O'Connor said upon his return to the dining room.

"Can't you finish your meal, Thomas?" his wife asked.

"No time. I've really got to run."

Mrs. O'Connor stood. "How long will you be gone?"

He shook his head. "I'm not sure. Probably about a week." His steps were already carrying him out of the room.

Titus and Eliza exchanged a glance. She huffed and stood.

"Are you all right?" Abigail wanted to know.

"Nothing a week won't cure," Eliza said with a scowl.

"I'm sorry?" Abigail asked.

"Nothing." With that, Eliza stomped out of the room.

"What's wrong with her?"

Titus shrugged but said nothing. He pushed his plate aside. "I'm going back to work," he announced before leaving Abigail alone at the table.

Chapter 16

"Titus, feel free to grab a cup of coffee, if you want, and come back in about an hour," Abigail said once she stepped from the carriage. It was ten o'clock, but the light fog persisted upon the city. Horses clip-clopped past them, with rattling buggies following close behind. Gas flames flickered from the streetlamps, mingling with the haze, wrapping the street in a mysterious glow.

"You certain you won't be finished before then? I don't want to make you wait."

Abigail smiled at his consideration. "I'm certain. I need to spend some time with Sophia."

Titus turned his hat around in his hands, a familiar gesture to which Abigail had grown accustomed. "Are you all right, Titus?"

He looked at her with eyes that said he had much to say. Still, he kept silent. He finally nodded and shrugged on his hat, and then turned back toward the carriage. She watched him pull away, her heart heavy. Grabbing a fistful of her skirt, she walked toward the Thread Bearer.

The bell jangled overhead as she entered. The smell of coffee drifted from the kitchen. Sophia was at her usual place in the room, head bent over a sewing machine. She looked up with surprise.

"Abigail, I'm so glad you came!" She got up and walked over to her friend.

"You did say Wednesdays around ten o'clock was a good time for you, didn't you? Is this still a convenient time for a visit?" Abigail hoped so, since she had already told Titus to leave.

"This is perfect," Sophia said. She grabbed Abigail's hand. "Let's get some coffee and sit down for a while in the kitchen."

Abigail pulled off her wraps and settled into her chair while Sophia poured the coffee into their cups. Once they both were seated, Sophia looked at Abigail. "So, tell me what's going on in your life these days. Seems we never have time enough to talk at church."

With a nod, Abigail smiled.

"Jonathan has left?"

"Yes." Her hands hugged the coffee cup. "It wasn't the same. When we were together, things had changed. I think for both of us, though he wouldn't admit it just yet."

"I'm sorry, Abby."

She shrugged. "It's all right. I'm glad I had the chance to find it out rather than always wondering what might have been." Glancing up with a smile, she said, "We did go ice-skating."

Sophia's eyes sparkled. "Oh, you did? I haven't gone ice-skating since I went with Jonathan on your behalf ages ago. Remember, when you had to go out of town with your parents and you wanted me to keep Mary Nottinger away from him?"

They both laughed.

"I'd forgotten all about that!" Abigail took a drink of her coffee and thought a moment. "Whatever happened to Mary, anyway? I haven't seen her in a long time."

Sophia shook her head and looked away, lost in thought. "Mary. Bless her heart. Her mother, Alice, tells me Mary is off seeing the sights of Europe with a favorite aunt." Sophia took another drink then put her cup down. "To tell you the truth, I think she was brokenhearted after your cousin Patrick left."

Abigail shook her head. "Mary pursued him like a hound after a fox, and Patrick couldn't leave town fast enough." They laughed again. "Truthfully, Patrick's job at the railroad wasn't what he wanted. He went back home." Abigail paused a moment. "But he married shortly after, so I think he just wanted to get back to the woman he loved. I think Uncle Mark and Aunt Emma were glad he came home."

"How many uncles do you have?"

"Just two. Three boys in the family; that's it."

"Only two cousins, right?"

"Right. Patrick is Uncle Mark's son, and Eliza is Uncle Edward's daughter."

A comfortable silence fell between them as they sipped on their drinks. "Are you doing all right, Abby?"

Abigail looked at Sophia. "Yes. Why do you ask?"

Sophia held her gaze. "Something seems not quite right. I can't put my finger on it."

"We really are like sisters, you know."

Sophia lifted an eyebrow. "Oh?"

"You can't put your finger on what's wrong because I can't put a finger on it. I mean, I did the right thing by Jonathan. I love him dearly but as a friend. I see that now. And I know that I love Titus. It's just that, well, I thought he felt the same way."

"And now?"

"That's what I mean. I don't know. I once worried he had feelings for

Eliza, but then I changed my mind. Yet for the past few days, he's been acting strange. I've caught him whispering in corners with Eliza, which makes me think perhaps I was wrong. Possibly he does have feelings for her, and I've misread everything."

Sophia looked at her a moment. "I can't imagine Titus falling for someone like Eliza. She doesn't seem his type at all." Sophia clasped her hands together at her chin as she listened.

"That's what I thought, but now I don't know what to think."

"I'll be praying for you, Abigail. And for Titus. Most likely, time will tell what's bothering him. How is Jenny getting along?"

Abigail felt herself lighten with the mention of the little girl. "Oh, Sophia, she is doing so well. She's pretty much back to speaking normally again. Though she doesn't talk a lot, she is able to communicate, which is better than before. I'm so proud of her."

"Sounds to me like the Lord has really used you to help that family."

She shook her head. "It has been my privilege. They have been through so much."

Sophia nodded. "Do you think Titus will ever go back to medical school?"

"I don't know. I pray for his future. I know that's his dream. I pray one day the Lord will open doors for him." Abigail picked up her cup and sipped a little more. "Now, tell me about you and Clayton and the baby. What is going on with you?"

Sophia practically glowed. "I'm happy beyond belief. I feel wonderful, and I'm counting the days till the baby comes." A thought seemed to hit her. "Oh, wait, I have to show you something." Sophia got up and left the room for a moment. Abigail waited, smiling at her friend's enthusiasm. She imagined her own parents' excitement when they found her on their doorstep.

Sophia came back into the room, almost out of breath. "I've finished the baby's booties." She held up tiny knitted booties and wiggled them from the ends of her fingers for Abigail to see.

"Oh, these are adorable!" Abigail ran her fingers carefully along the dainty stitches. She looked up at her friend. "I'm so happy for you, Sophia."

Sophia beamed and carefully placed the booties into a box.

Abigail glanced at the timepiece dangling from a golden chain around her neck. "Oh dear, I'd better go. Titus has been waiting ten minutes already for me."

The two friends hugged. "I will be praying for you, Abigail, and for Titus."

"Thank you. And I will be praying for you," she said, adding a pat to Sophia's stomach, "and the little one."

Sophia walked Abigail to the door and waved at Titus. He waved back and stepped over to help Abigail into the carriage.

"To Barnabas House now?" he asked.

"Yes, please." With one more glance toward the Thread Bearer, Abigail waved good-bye to her friend, all the while thanking the Lord for Sophia and praying for their little family.

❧

No one seemed to notice Abigail as she stepped into Barnabas House. The workers were engrossed in their duties, and children sat at their table with slates in hand, carefully working out arithmetic lessons. Julie stood peering over their shoulders, checking their work. Before Abigail could reach them, Mary O'Grady's voice called behind her.

"Abigail, so good to see you!"

She turned to Mary's smiling face. "Mary O'Grady—I mean, Doyle! How are you?"

The woman blushed. "I'm thanking you for asking. We're doing just fine, that we are."

"And Katie?"

"Ah, my little lassie is happy as can be." They both looked over at the little girl. The tip of her tongue poked slightly through the corner of her mouth as she worked diligently on her slate. The women chuckled.

"I don't know how the wee one would work without the help of her tongue. Would you like some coffee?"

"No thank you. I just came in to see when Julie needed my help. She's a hard worker."

"Aye, she is. Do you mind that she has taken over so much of the work?"

Abigail smiled. "Not at all. As you know, I've been working with Jenny Matthews."

"Aye. How is that coming along?"

Abigail explained Jenny's progress. Before they could continue, Katie's voice broke through their discussion.

"Miss Abigail!" She ran over to hug her. Katie looked up and smiled, revealing a missing tooth on the top, just right of the middle.

Abigail gasped. "Oh my, you've lost a tooth! Aren't you the lucky one!"

Katie beamed, swinging from side to side. Her fingers felt around her neckline, and she pulled out her locket for Abigail to see.

Abigail stooped down. "Oh Katie dear, I'm so glad to see you wearing your necklace."

Without a word, Katie dropped the necklace back into place and threw her arms around Abigail. "I miss you."

"I miss you, too."

"Where's Barnabas?" Katie asked, looking around.

"He couldn't come today. I had other errands to attend to."

Katie nodded and changed the subject. "I like my new pa."

Abigail looked up at Mary, and they exchanged a smile. "He is a good pa, Katie."

"I'm working hard today." She crinkled her nose and quirked her lips into a pucker. "I don't like arithmetic much."

Abigail crinkled her nose. "I don't either. But it's one of those things we need to know." Abigail laughed and touched the tip of Katie's nose with her finger. "Now, you'd better get back to work." After one more hug, the little girl skipped back to the table.

The other children, noting her absence, looked up to see Abigail, and they waved. She smiled and returned their greeting.

"They love you, you know," Mary said.

"I know. I love them, too."

"Well, I'll be letting you talk to Julie. I wanted to say hello before you got away."

"Mary, it's good to see you so happy." Abigail could see the sparkle in the woman's eyes. Such a contrast to what she used to see there.

"Aye, God has worked a miracle for us. We'll be forever grateful."

The two women hugged once more, and then Abigail made her way to Julie to see when next she would be needed to help.

⌒⌒

Titus's heart flipped when he saw Abigail step from Barnabas House. Never before had he felt this way about a woman. And their future held together by a sliver of hope. If Eliza had her way, she would shred every chance of happiness from everyone in her path. He had never seen a woman with such a bent toward evil. Before he could allow his harsh judgment of her to run rampant, he remembered she was no different from what he had been before the Lord cleansed him. God could do the same for Eliza. Titus needed to pray for her.

In the meantime, what would become of Abigail? Her family? *Please, God, protect them from Eliza's evil scheme.*

"Thank you for waiting, Titus," Abigail was saying when she stepped up to the carriage.

"My pleasure, Abby." She looked at him with a start. He could have kicked himself. Why had he called her that? It had slipped from his tongue before he could stop it. Though he had called her that a thousand times in his dreams, he had never used so familiar a name when addressing her before. "I'm sorry," he corrected himself.

230

She touched his arm. "Don't be. I like it."

How he wanted to pull her into his arms and kiss her like before. Would they ever know a moment like that again? He started to lift her into the carriage, and she hesitated a moment. Her eyes looked up to him. "Titus, is everything all right?"

He swallowed hard. "Yes. Why?"

"You've just seemed a little, well, distant, in the past few days. Jenny is all right, isn't she?"

Her worried eyes melted his heart. As always, she worried about someone else. So unlike Eliza. "Jenny is fine."

"And you?"

How he wanted to tell her the truth before Eliza could spread her poison, but he didn't know where to start or what to say. Would she forgive him for his original intention of wanting to get back at her family? Would she believe he had changed?

"Titus?" Her questioning eyes bore into him.

He sighed. "I'm fine, Abigail. Really." He didn't want to lie to her, but the setting wasn't right. He could hardly go into the entire story while standing at the side of the road with buggies and people walking about. Still, how could he be anything less than honest? "Maybe sometime soon we can talk." There, he let her know something was amiss; he just didn't go into what it was.

Her questioning eyes met his once again. "I'd like that." She lifted her hand so he might help her into the carriage. The mere touch of her hand made him weak-kneed. No doubt about it, he had to talk to her. He couldn't live with himself until she knew the truth. Better he talk to her before Eliza did. Eliza would hold nothing back. She would spit the truth out, making it as bleak and ugly as possible.

No, he couldn't let that happen. He had to talk to Abigail first chance they got. Hopefully, he could get to her before Eliza.

Chapter 17

It was midmorning on Saturday before Titus could get Abigail alone. He was careful not to let Eliza see them for fear she would get jealous and spill the news in a fit of anger. When Abigail slipped from the house into the barn, he had the wagon hitched and ready to go.

"Now, Titus, tell me what all this secrecy is about," Abigail said with a chuckle. How he hated to reveal the truth and shatter her happiness.

"I'd rather take you somewhere, Abigail, just the two of us, and talk about it."

"All I know is this has something to do with Eliza, and you're not going to give me even a hint as to what else?"

He smiled at her, trying to keep her at ease. "You'll find out soon enough." His finger trailed her cheekbone. "Just remember, things aren't always as they seem." She studied him. He reached over to help her into her seat when he heard the rattling of a carriage. He looked up to see Mr. O'Connor returning home from his trip. Abigail dashed across the yard with the excitement of a child.

Mr. O'Connor's arrival struck Titus with a heavy blow. For in that moment, Titus realized he was too late.

He slipped back into the barn while the family came out to greet Mr. O'Connor. Their happy murmurings drifted into the barn as he tried to sort the matter through in his mind.

"You coming in?" Eliza's words sliced through the air.

His head jerked up to see her standing in front of him; a face hard as a wagon wheel looked at him. "They're fixin' to sit down to some lunch."

"It's not quite time for lunch."

"Probably just coffee and a pastry or two. Something to celebrate Uncle's return." Eliza laughed. "We'll have something to celebrate, all right." She turned to go.

Titus grabbed her arm. "Eliza, I beg you, don't do this."

She sneered at him. "You're crazy as a loon if you think I'm giving this up after all my planning."

"I don't care beans about all your planning. By hurting this family, you accomplish nothing."

"Oh, I accomplish something, all right."

232

"They have done nothing but extend kindness to you. For that you hate them?"

She jerked her arm free. "What would you know? You're merely their chauffeur. You're soft because of Abigail." She snapped the name off her tongue as if it were poison. "You know nothing of our family history. They blame my father for everything. But I know different. I've heard his side of the story."

"That's right, you've heard his side, and you've allowed it to poison your mind, Eliza. Your father is wrong. If this family is so bad and he's such a wonderful father, why would he leave you with them? You might as well face it, Eliza, your father is a snake!"

Before he could blink, she reached her arm back and slapped him across the face. He stared at her in disbelief. She stepped back, as if shocked by her own action. Without another word, she turned and ran to the house.

He had provoked her, and he knew for that he would pay. Most likely, so would the O'Connors.

<hr />

Once the chatter of Mr. O'Connor's trip and the excitement of having him home once again died down, Mrs. O'Connor passed around the pastries and filled the coffee cups.

Titus's stomach gurgled as nausea filled him. Not knowing when Eliza planned to attack made him weak. Finally, in the quiet of the moment as they passed the pastry plate, she struck like a venomous snake.

"Oh, did I tell you the last time I was at Gramma's house that I found her journal?" She took a bite of pastry and looked at them with a smile, seeming to enjoy their shocked expressions. Titus noticed Thomas O'Connor's face turned pale.

"Honestly, Eliza, I don't think you should be snooping into Gramma's personal belongings," Abigail said.

"That's right, dear. A journal is very personal. People don't mean to share their words with others," Mrs. O'Connor added.

Eliza chewed slowly, as if to draw out the matter. Titus wished her father had taken her to the woodshed as a child. Better still, he wished Mr. O'Connor would do it now. She reached under the table and pulled out the journal. With slow motions, she pulled it open. "Hmm, it says here," she moved her tongue around her teeth as if to stall further, then smacked her lips together. "Um, let's see." She ran her finger along the page. "Oh yes, here it is."

Titus braced himself. Slowly, with great deliberation, she read the revealing words, accentuating those words that would bring the most pain. Her tongue sliced its way into their souls, like the cut of a deadly blade.

After all was read, they sat in a cold silence.

Tears rolling down her cheeks, Mrs. O'Connor looked at Eliza. "Why did you tell us this?"

"Oh," she said with a wave of her hand, "Titus and I thought it would be a good idea. After all you've done for the two of us, separating me from my father and, of course, separating Titus from his father."

Abigail looked at him with the greatest sorrow he had ever seen on the face of another. Her eyes filled with tears. His tongue refused to move, knowing no words could salve the pain for any of them. She got up from the table and ran to her room. Mrs. O'Connor quickly followed.

Eliza continued to eat as though nothing had happened.

"Mr. O'Connor, I—" Titus tried to explain, but Thomas O'Connor held up his hand. The older man turned to Eliza. "I will write your father, Eliza. You can take the first train home. I'm certain that's what you had hoped for, anyway." She offered a smile, but one look at Titus erased the smile from her face.

Titus stood to his feet, hat in hand. "I'm sorry, Mr. O'Connor. Truly sorry." He walked out the front door and didn't look back.

∽

The O'Connor family managed to get through Sunday with little conversation. No one spoke of Eliza's news. Rather, they talked of surface things, attended church together, then hurried home to retreat behind closed doors.

On Monday morning, Abigail opened her eyes to the sound of muffled cries and looked into her mother's tearstained face.

"I'm leaving, dear. Just for a little while," she whispered, using her fingers to brush aside Abigail's hair from her face.

Abigail gasped and sat up in the bed. "What will I do, Mother?"

"You'll be fine. Your father has gone to work, but I've left him a note. He'll need you to see after him. You're old enough to understand that I need time to think, sort things through. I love your father desperately, but I'm struggling with his deception. I can hardly bear it."

"Where will you go, Mother?"

"I'm going to visit an old friend. She lives on Nantucket Island and recently lost her husband. I suppose the time near the sea will do me good, though it's cold this time of year. Perhaps I can help her through her grief. Still, I don't know that I'll be of any good."

Abigail started to cry. "How long will you be gone?"

Her mother looked away. "I'm afraid I don't know. Pray for me."

"I feel like this is all my fault." Abigail pulled her hands up to her face.

Mother's attention jerked back to her. "Oh my, no! You have been the dearest thing to me. An answer to my prayers. I never doubted God used you to restore joy to my life."

"Yet now you want to leave."

"It's not you I'm leaving, dear." Mother smoothed Abigail's hair.

"You would leave Father. But hasn't he suffered in silence for all these years? You heard the words of Gramma's journal—he wanted to spare you the pain."

Mother thought a moment. "Yes, I know. Still, knowing he betrayed my love and lived a lie all these years. . ." Her words trailed off.

"But he didn't know the Lord when he committed the sin."

"Yes, but he knew me." Fresh tears began to flow.

Abigail squeezed her mother's arms. "It was so long ago. Can't you forgive him?"

"I want to, Abigail. I truly do."

"But you've talked to me endless times about forgiving others. Even forgiving Jonathan for the pain he caused me."

Mother nodded. She looked her daughter full in the face. "Perhaps I never fully understood your pain because I've never had to forgive such a betrayal of trust. I've never known such pain, Abigail. The strength to forgive must come from God. I cannot find it in me."

The two women embraced. Abigail allowed her tears to flow. "Please, don't go."

"Pray for me. I will pray for you."

After one more hug, Mother turned from Abigail's room and collected her things. Mother waited by the door for Titus to bring the carriage around. Abigail stood nearby but couldn't bring herself to say another word. She knew her mother's mind was made up.

When Titus finally knocked at the front door, Abigail jumped. "Mother?"

Her mother turned to her. "Pray, Abigail. Pray for us all." With that, her mother walked out the door and out of her life. For how long, Abigail didn't know. She prayed that one day her mother would return. And that her father would be waiting.

Titus carried out some luggage then returned for the last piece. Abigail lifted it and handed it to him. Their eyes met for a moment. His face was red and swollen with dirt streaked across his cheek. His eyes begged for understanding.

A lump grew in Abigail's throat, and she could say nothing. She could only stand and watch as he turned and walked away, and the carriage once again prepared to take away someone she loved.

Two someones.

With a flick of the reins, Titus had the team up and trotting. Abigail stood in the doorway and watched them fade into the flurry of snow. She glanced at the heavy gray clouds looming overhead. Fresh snowflakes fell to the ground, covering the crusty, cold earth beneath. A thought intruded and surprised her. God's love did that for her. Made her black heart pure as new-fallen snow.

Though Abigail had no idea how this would all turn out, her heavy heart quickened with the reminder that God was in control. Barnabas rubbed against her legs, pushing his nose into her skirts. She patted him twice on the head; he licked the top of her hand and snuggled some more.

With a sigh, Abigail closed the door then turned toward the shell of what had once been a home. A home ringing with laughter and joy.

Walking toward the kitchen, Abigail decided she'd better make plans for dinner.

Later that evening, Eliza elected to eat her meal in her room. The next morning's train would carry her home.

Father ate a little dinner with Abigail, though neither had much to say. After their meal, Abigail went into the drawing room and settled by the fire, mending some clothes. Father joined her, reading the newspaper. After a little while, he folded the paper and laid it on the floor beside him.

"Abigail, might we talk?"

She looked up and nodded, carefully laying aside her needle and thread.

"I was wrong. I thought I had done the right thing by keeping this from your mother, but I was wrong." He pulled his hands to the sides of his head. "Oh, how I wish I could wipe that painful sin from my life." She watched him agonize with the pain of it. She walked over to him and knelt by his feet. Lifting red, weary eyes, he grabbed her hand. "I'm thankful for you, child, but I loathe myself for the sin I've committed."

"I know, Father. But God has forgiven you."

"God has forgiven me, but what if your mother cannot?"

Abigail didn't have the answer for that.

"I don't know what I'll do if she doesn't return," Father said, tears running down his face. Abigail had never seen her father cry before. She touched his shoulder.

"Mother loves you, and she knows deep down that you love her."

He looked at her through red, watery eyes and merely patted her hand. He struggled to his feet. Bent and weary, he shuffled out of the room, looking much older to Abigail than she had ever seen him.

The next morning, Eliza had her bags packed and ready to go by the time Titus came to the door. Abigail stepped up behind her cousin.

"Eliza?" Abigail said.

She turned around with a start. "Yes?" Her stance showed her bracing herself for anything Abigail might throw her way.

Abigail wanted to show her anger, to hurl pain upon her cousin for all she had done to Abigail's family, but with one look at Eliza, Abigail changed her mind. "I—I wish things could have been different," was all she said. To Abigail's amazement, she meant it. Expecting an unkind retort, Abigail was surprised to instead find a look of sorrow flash across Eliza's face.

Eliza gave a slight nod. So slight, Abigail almost missed it.

Perhaps God had not given up on Eliza.

∞

When Titus showed up for work on Tuesday morning, Abigail heard her father talking to him.

"Titus, I thought we had an understanding. I never knew the depths of the hatred that simmered in your heart. For that I am dreadfully sorry. I cannot fix the past, nor can I undo what happened to your pa. I had hoped to help you, but not from a guilty heart, as I'm sure you supposed. Rather, out of a heart of respect for the friendship I had shared with your pa." He blew out a sigh of regret. "Knowing you feel as you do, I suspect it's best you leave your position with us."

"But I don't feel that way, sir, I—"

The older man held up his hand. "I need time, Titus, to think this through. You understand?"

"Yes sir," was all Titus said. His head drooped, and he walked away. A sharp pain went through Abigail's chest. She struggled to ignore it. How could she feel soft toward this man who had used her affections and worked side by side with Eliza to bring the O'Connor family to ruin?

Abigail had renewed her vows to the Lord, making every effort to give Him first place in her life. She knew now that in order to please her heavenly Father, she must forgive, but like her mother, she didn't have the strength on her own. Only after much prayer would she find the strength. And even then she might be able to forgive, but she now knew there would never be a future together for her and Titus.

That brought to Abigail the worst pain of all.

Chapter 18

By Wednesday afternoon, the silence in the house made Abigail restless. She decided to go to Gramma's house. She wasn't there very long before she crumbled in a heap.

"Gramma, everything is terrible." Abigail wiped her nose for the hundredth time on her handkerchief. "Our family will never be the same."

"There, there, Abigail darling," Gramma said, patting Abigail's hand. "We will get through this, we will." Gramma looked away. " 'Tis Eliza I'm worried about, I am."

Abigail jerked her head toward Gramma with a start. "Why ever would you worry about her? She brought this disaster to our home."

"No," Gramma was saying. " 'Tis your father's sin brought this about. Eliza merely made the hidden sin known." Gramma thought some more. "I shouldn't have written about it in a journal. What was I thinking? Someone would have surely found it after I was gone." She shrugged. "I'd forgotten I'd even written the words. So very long ago."

"It's not your fault, Gramma."

"No. No. Your father committed the sin, and he should have told your mother. Still, he thought he was doing the best thing by her." Gramma looked away again. " 'Tis all so tragic."

"Why do you worry about Eliza?"

Gramma stood and hobbled over to her chair. With great effort she lowered herself to within inches of the seat and finally fell into the soft cushions with a great *plop*. "Oh dear, me body doesn't cooperate like it used to." Once she settled in, she looked at Abigail. "I worry about Eliza because she has to live with herself. She knows she hurt everyone." Gramma brushed her hand in front of her. "I know she acts tough as an old cowhide, but she's not. Inside, she's still a little girl who wants her father's approval, that she does."

Abigail thought a moment. She hadn't considered that side of Eliza. Truth be known, Abigail didn't want to consider it. She wanted to be angry with Eliza for hurting her family. Yet Abigail knew Gramma was right.

"Do you think Uncle Edward and Aunt Elizabeth are able to take her back?" Abigail asked, smoothing a curl with her fingers.

A pained expression shadowed Gramma's face. "I don't know. Edward can be quite harsh at times."

"What about Aunt Elizabeth? Wouldn't she help her own daughter?"

Gramma offered a weak smile. "Elizabeth is a dear woman, but I'm afraid she's as spoiled as Edward. I'm sorry to say they never should have had children. Eliza has been the one to suffer."

Remorse settled over Abigail. She had only considered her own pain, not Eliza's. Abigail didn't want to feel sorry for Eliza. Yet what if the tables had been turned and Abigail was the one who grew up with Uncle Edward and Aunt Elizabeth? Would she have turned out like Eliza? Here she had thought she never wanted to see Eliza again, and now she wondered if she shouldn't contact her once things settled down. If they ever did.

"I've been harsh in my thoughts about Eliza," Abigail admitted. "She hurt me, and she hurt my family."

Gramma nodded. "Aye, that she did. And it's natural ye would feel hurt."

Before Abigail could comment further, someone knocked at the front door. "I'll get it," Abigail said as she rose and walked over to the door. As she opened the door, she looked at the visitor and gasped.

"May I come in?" asked their guest in a weak voice. Abigail stepped aside.

In walked Eliza O'Connor.

Abigail could hardly keep herself from gaping at Eliza as she moved into the room. "Gramma, am I welcome to come in?"

The small voice surprised Abigail. She had never seen Eliza so vulnerable.

"Of course, dear," Gramma said, motioning to a chair in which Eliza could sit.

Eliza pulled off her outer wraps and sat down. She kept her head bowed. "I couldn't do this." She pulled her hands to her face and started sobbing. Her body heaved with the weight of her burden. Abigail stood silently nearby, not knowing what to do. Gramma went over to Eliza.

After a lengthy time of tears, she finally calmed herself. "I had time to think before the train arrived. I was angry with my father and mother for making me leave. They blamed it on finances, but truth be known, they don't want a spinster daughter holding them back. You see, I received word from a friend that my parents went to Europe. They shipped me off to your family to get rid of me."

Eliza's fingers nervously toyed with the handkerchief in her hands. "I resented your family for taking me." She looked at Abigail. "Though it was a kindness, I refused to see it that way." She looked away and hiccupped, attempting to hold back more tears. "But when I thought of leaving, all I could think about was Uncle Thomas and Aunt Lavina and. . ." Once more Eliza looked up at Abigail. "And you." She shook her head and wiped her nose on the handkerchief. Her gaze was fixed on her lap. "I was jealous of you, just like my father has always been jealous of Uncle Thomas. I've allowed my father's words to poison my thoughts. Your family did not deserve what I did." She lifted tear-filled eyes to Abigail. "Will you ever forgive me?"

A flood of compassion swept over Abigail, surprising her. Her heart filled with forgiveness. The Lord had once again intervened. She went to her cousin's side. "Yes Eliza, I forgive you." The two women hugged through their tears. When they parted, Gramma joined them with tears of joy.

"Well, this calls for some tea," Gramma announced, wiping away her tears. In no time at all, the three had prepared the tea and brought it with them into the living room. They settled comfortably into their chairs.

"Since you missed your train yesterday, what did you do last night?" Abigail asked.

After taking a drink of tea, Eliza carefully placed the cup on the saucer on a nearby stand. "I stayed in the hotel nearby to sort through things. I knew I could catch another train. I just couldn't leave things the way they were." She twisted her handkerchief in her hands. "I've behaved abominably; I know that."

"How did ye get the money for ye train trip, Eliza?" Gramma asked, stirring sugar into her tea.

Eliza smiled. "I saved some money while living at home. I took it with me, not knowing what the future would hold for me with my father practically throwing me out of the house."

They sat silent for a moment.

"I don't know what you will think of this idea, Abigail, but I have enough money that I think we could go together to Nantucket and fetch Aunt Lavina."

Abigail's eyebrows rose. "Really?"

Eliza nodded enthusiastically.

"I have a little money of my own I could contribute." Abigail turned to Gramma. "Do you think she would come?"

Gramma thought a moment. "I don't know. I'd hate for ye to get all the way out there and her not come."

"We've got to try, Gramma," Abigail said.

"I think ye would be best to wait at least a week or two. Give her time to think. Take time to pray about the matter. Then the two of ye do what ye think ye must," Gramma said.

They all decided that's just what they would do.

Friday night, Titus shuffled across the porch of their home and stumbled into the house. Exhausted from searching for employment but finding none, he fought hard against the despair threatening to overtake him.

"Titus," Ma said as he entered. The kitchen chair scuffed hard against the wooden floor as she grabbed it and pulled it over to him. "Are you all right?" She lifted his hat from his head, smoothed some hair from his forehead, and looked into his eyes. "You're pushing too hard, Titus. Have you eaten today?" Before he could answer, she continued, "Day after day you don't eat. You must eat, son. You need your strength."

Titus looked up at her. He knew she was right, but he had no appetite. How could he eat when the woman he loved would have nothing to do with him? Worry lines etched Ma's eyes. He grabbed her hand. "I'm all right, Ma."

She would not be dissuaded. "You didn't answer me. Have you eaten today?"

He smiled. "You're too smart for me."

"Oh Titus." She dropped his hand, picked up a plate, and began to pile on the evening's meal for him. Once his plate was full of chicken, potatoes, and a biscuit, she put it in front of him. She poured hot coffee into a cup and set it down, along with a glass of water.

"Thanks, Ma." He bowed his head in prayer.

The chair groaned as she sat down across from him. "You will find work, Titus. The Lord will provide," she said after he finished his prayer.

He nodded then took a bite of potatoes. She looked at him as if she wanted to say something then hesitated. "What is it, Ma?"

"You've heard nothing from the O'Connors?"

He shook his head. "They never want to see me again."

"They just need time, Titus." Her eyes searched his face.

"No Ma, I haven't heard from Abigail. She wants nothing to do with me." He knew Ma couldn't understand the depths of Abigail's pain. Pain he had caused.

"You must see her again."

He didn't look up. "Not likely. She's pretty much finished her work with Jenny. She doesn't need to come around anymore."

"You must."

"And why is that?" He glanced up at her. She sat smiling, holding one of the books she used with Jenny.

"Because you have to return this to her."

Titus looked at his ma and shook his head. A tiny smile slowly lifted the corners of his mouth.

Titus blew out a sigh. He could hardly believe four weeks had passed. Sophia had told him Abigail was out of town but hadn't offered any other information. The construction work he had obtained kept him busy but not too busy to think of Abigail. He didn't know if she had returned, but he had to find out. Reaching his hand out on the seat beside him, he patted Abigail's book.

As Titus neared the O'Connors' home, he looked at the neighboring lawns. Fresh buds poked through forgotten stems stretching toward the warmth of the sun. Still, winter's chill persisted.

A thread of cold ran through him, though he didn't know if it was the cool air or thoughts of Abigail that made him shiver. How could things go so wrong in such a short time? His scheming fell away, and for that he was thankful. But his plans with Abigail, well, they would never be. He had to let them go. The book on the seat beside him was his only hope. If he didn't see her now, he wouldn't have another excuse to drop by her house. Maybe she would refuse to see him, anyway. Her father might order Titus off their property. He hadn't thought of that. The closer he got to their homestead, the more he regretted his decision to come. His mind told him to turn around, to get home as fast as he could. His heart told him to keep going.

His heart won out.

When he reached their home, he took a deep breath, grabbed the book, and jumped out of the wagon. He looked around the place. Everything was quiet. He glanced at the barn and could see Mr. O'Connor was home. Most likely, Abigail would be with him if she was back in town. He glanced at his pocket watch. They would have eaten half an hour ago.

Walking to the steps, he took off his hat, prayed quickly for strength and the right words, then knocked on the door. He was unprepared for what he saw when it opened.

Before him stood Thomas O'Connor, who only a few weeks before had reminded him of a mighty oak tree, tall, sturdy, rugged. Today he looked old, tired, and spent. "Yes Titus, what can I do for you?"

Titus held the book in his hand. He looked at it then back to Mr. O'Connor. "I wanted to return this to Abigail."

Mr. O'Connor reached for the book.

"Is she home, sir?"

Mr. O'Connor shook his head. "I'm afraid not. She and Eliza got it in their heads to go after Lavina on their own. I was on a business trip. When I returned, I found a note telling me where they had gone."

"Eliza?"

Mr. O'Connor scratched his head. "Yeah, that surprised me, too. Don't know what that's about." He looked at Titus for a moment. "Why don't you come in?"

"Well. . ." Titus hesitated.

"Come on. I could use the company."

"All right," Titus found himself saying. He stepped into the house. Barnabas's tail wagged furiously, as if remembering Titus as an old friend. Titus reached down and patted the dog on the head. Mr. O'Connor saw him.

"I'm afraid he misses Abigail," he said.

The hall clock ticked off the minutes. Titus thought it strange he had never noticed that clock before, but then it had never been as quiet in the house. Mr. O'Connor led the way to the drawing room.

"Can I get you something to drink—coffee, tea?"

"No thank you," Titus said as they sat down across from the crackling fire in the hearth. He watched Barnabas circle a couple of times and finally lay at Mr. O'Connor's feet. No doubt the two of them had become fast friends in the lonely house.

A knot swelled in Titus's throat, making it hard for him to swallow. He prayed again for strength. He wanted to get some things out of the way before Mr. O'Connor said anything. "Eliza was right," he said, practically rubbing a hole through his hat. He looked up at Mr. O'Connor, who was staring at him intently.

"Go on."

"I originally came here to get even. I held you responsible for my pa's financial problems and ultimately his death." There. He'd said what had been festering inside him for all these months.

"I know," Mr. O'Connor said in a slight whisper.

Titus was puzzled. "You did? How?"

"It was all over your face when I saw you at the mercantile that day. When I asked you to be our chauffeur, I could almost see you forming a plan."

Titus hung his head.

"That's the reason I asked you to come to work for me. I had prayed the Lord would give me some way to help you and your family."

"Even though you knew I wanted to hurt you?"

"I had hurt you."

"But you didn't do it intentionally."

"No, but you thought I did." Mr. O'Connor shifted in his chair. "I know you had changed your mind before Eliza shared her bit of news. So what changed it?"

Mr. O'Connor listened intently while Titus explained about reading the letter in his box in the sitting room. When Titus finished, Mr. O'Connor heaved a sigh. "To tell you the truth, I'm glad this whole thing happened, though I don't know where it will lead. I've lived with this all these years, and I wanted to tell my wife." He rubbed his jaw and stared into the fireplace. "I thought I was protecting her."

"Like I wanted to protect Ma and Jenny from what I thought you had done to our family."

"Well, something like that," Mr. O'Connor replied. "When I came to the Lord, I should have told Lavina the truth about Abigail. I should have trusted our faith was strong enough to keep us together. Now she'll struggle with trusting me because I kept something from her." He looked at his callused hands as if seeing something there. "It's best to talk things out. Let the people you love know how you feel about them." Mr. O'Connor looked at Titus in such a way, he felt there was a hidden message in the words.

Titus nodded. Just then Barnabas's top lip curled, baring his teeth. A low growl sounded deep in his throat then rolled forth into a full fit of barking. Suddenly the clatter of horses and a carriage sounded outside.

"I can't imagine two callers in one day," Mr. O'Connor said as he strode toward the door. Titus decided he had better leave since company was coming. He pulled on his hat and stepped just behind Mr. O'Connor as the man opened the door. In the doorway stood three women. Lavina O'Connor's face, at the sight of her husband, revealed her surprise at his shrunken appearance.

"Hello, Thomas," Lavina O'Connor said.

He stared at her, speechless.

"Aren't you going to let us in?" she asked.

Titus watched as Lavina, Abigail, and Eliza O'Connor entered the room.

Chapter 19

Once they entered the room, Mrs. O'Connor turned to Titus. "You might as well join us," she said. "We all need to talk things out."

Titus gulped, not at all sure he was ready for this. Still, he obediently followed the others. Once they settled in their chairs in the drawing room, Mrs. O'Connor took a deep breath as if to begin, but Eliza jumped in.

"Before you say anything, I want to apologize to everyone in this room. I brought this whole mess about, and I'm deeply sorry. I've explained everything to Abigail and Aunt Lavina, and I want you to know I'm truly sorry, Uncle Thomas...and Titus." She averted her gaze from Titus.

Mr. O'Connor shook his head. "No, it's not your fault, Eliza. I should have been up-front with my dear Lavina from the beginning." He looked at his wife, and she at him. His eyes seemed to beg understanding. "I never meant to hurt you. I thought I was protecting you from the pain of my sin."

A single tear spilled onto Mrs. O'Connor's right cheek, trailed off her chin, and dropped into her lap. She lowered her eyes and nodded.

Mr. O'Connor stood and walked over to her. He knelt at her feet. "I would never hurt you for anything. I was young and stupid and very. . . drunk." He buried his head against the folds of her dress.

Titus wanted to look away, to leave. The moment between the O'Connors seemed far too intimate for his presence.

"Oh Thomas," Mrs. O'Connor cried, laying her face next to the back of his head.

Both were crying now. Titus was moved by their affection and forgiveness toward one another. Tears streamed down Abigail's face. Eliza wiped her damp cheeks and shifted uncomfortably in her seat. Titus choked back his own emotions.

Mrs. O'Connor lifted her head. She stroked Mr. O'Connor's hair. "We'll talk later, dear." She looked at the others. A smile lit her face. "I just wanted you to know that during the few weeks I've been gone, the Lord has spoken to me through my friend. As you know, she lost her husband about six months ago. She reminded me how foolish it would be to let pride keep me from the man I love."

Mr. O'Connor looked up, and she smiled at him. "Every day is a gift, and we must not waste it." He offered her a weak smile then reached over and kissed her hand. His face was wet with tears.

She dabbed at her face and looked from Eliza to Titus. "Whatever your motives for doing what you did, it doesn't matter. Hopefully, you have learned from it and will come out better people for the experience. I know I have, though it's not been an easy lesson." She patted her husband's hand.

"I want to apologize." Every eye turned to Titus.

"You know my bent on revenge. I was angry with you, my pa, and the Lord." He said the last phrase in almost a whisper. He studied his hands. "I wanted someone to pay for the pain I was feeling—"

"But you didn't want any part of this. You tried to stop me," Eliza cut in.

Titus looked at her. He glanced over at Abigail, whose face held no condemnation, only compassion. At that moment, he realized Eliza must have explained the situation to Abigail.

"I never meant to hurt you," he said, his eyes never leaving Abigail's face. Then he turned to Mr. and Mrs. O'Connor. "Or you." He ran fingers through his hair. "And you're right, Mrs. O'Connor, I've learned a lot. I'm sorry I had to learn it at your expense."

"No Titus, the Lord has helped us all through this. Though I'm not thankful any of it has happened, He does promise to work things together for the good of those who love Him. And I believe He has done just that." Mrs. O'Connor turned to Abigail. "After all, we have our Abigail."

Abigail got up from her chair and knelt at her mother's feet beside her father. She leaned against her mother's skirts.

"Well, I think this is a good time to pray," Mr. O'Connor announced. Sobs poked through his words. "Father, despite my sin, Thou hast restored our family. And I thank Thee." He stopped a moment to blow his nose. "We know the battle is not over. The enemy will try to discourage us in the days ahead, but we bring the matter to Thee. Remind us again and again to leave it there. I thank Thee for my dear Lavina and for her forgiveness. I cannot imagine life without her."

Mrs. O'Connor's soft voice whispered, "Lord, Thou art far more gracious and forgiving to us than we deserve. Thy love and mercy never end. For that we give Thee thanks and our deepest praise."

"Lord," Abigail continued in prayer, "I thank Thee for my mother and father and for allowing me to be a part of this blessed family. Help me to lean on Thee when I don't understand things and when I am hurt by others. Most of all, help me to forgive as Thou hast forgiven me."

The room fell silent. Titus cleared his throat. "I know Thou hast forgiven me, Lord. Please help these good folks to find it in their hearts to do the same."

Eliza's small voice squeaked through the silence. "I don't know much about talking to Thee, Lord. But. . ." She paused a moment. "I'm sorry."

That was all she said.

It was enough.

Mr. O'Connor and Abigail rose to their feet. The others did the same. Titus thought the whole room seemed brighter. Sunlight spilled into the room and sparkled on the carpet. His heart felt clean. Really clean. While the others embraced in the warmth of forgiveness, he decided to slip out quietly.

Stepping into the hallway, he had just reached the door when a hand touched his shoulder. He turned to see Abigail's red face, blotched with tears. "Thank you." A smile lifted the corners of her mouth.

Titus's heart soared. Before he could say anything, Mr. O'Connor walked into the hallway. "Titus, my boy, I do hope you'll show up for work tomorrow. I've had an awful time trying to manage things on my own."

Titus looked at him in surprise.

"I know you've been working construction, but that was temporary, right?"

Titus nodded.

"Well then, what say you come back to work for me?" A wide grin spread across Mr. O'Connor's mouth. He stepped up and clasped Titus's hand in a hearty shake. Behind Mr. O'Connor stood his wife and Eliza. Everyone was smiling.

Titus grinned. "Yes sir," he said, shaking the older man's hand with gusto. "I'll see you in the morning." Titus shrugged on his hat. His gaze locked with Abigail's. Her face turned a deeper crimson, and for the first time since they had parted, he thought perhaps there was hope for him and the lovely Abigail O'Connor.

~

"Eliza, would you come in the sitting room a moment, please?" Abigail's mother called. Abigail looked on, wondering what was happening. "Abigail, you come join us, too."

Once the women sat down, Mother looked at Eliza. "My husband tells me you only came back to clear things up and that now you're planning to leave."

Eliza's gaze lowered.

"I had taken the liberty to show Sophia your needlepoint. She had mentioned she would love to have you help her in her shop, but at the time, I knew you didn't want to stay on here. Perhaps you would now consider that possibility?"

Eliza's head jerked up. Her eyes filled with tears. Abigail felt compassion sweep over her toward her cousin.

"Of course, you know you're welcome to live with us, should you decide to stay."

It took a full minute before Eliza finally spoke. "You'd do that for me?"

"Of course we would."

Tears plopped onto Eliza's skirts. After a moment, she lifted her head, got up, and went to her aunt, embracing her fully. "Thank you, Aunt Lavina. Thank you."

When Eliza stood, Abigail got up. "Sophia's customers will love your work. Oh, and you will love working with Sophia. She's a wonderful friend," Abigail offered.

The two young ladies exited the drawing room, chattering about their future. Abigail felt as if she really did have a sister.

⁂

The next morning after the worship service, Abigail stepped through the church doors and into the spring sunshine. She shielded her eyes from the sun's glare and looked toward Jenny and Mrs. Matthews. She noticed Titus stood in the distance talking with some menfolk. Abigail's heart felt light and carefree like a summer lark. She edged her way through the tiny crowd toward her friends.

"Good morning, Mrs. Matthews. Jenny."

"Hello," they answered in unison.

"Are you keeping up with your studies, Jenny?"

The little girl sat in the wagon. She nodded, setting her blond curls to bouncing.

"Good," Abigail said with a smile.

Mrs. Matthews hadn't climbed into the wagon yet. She grabbed Abigail's hands. "I know it's not my place to say, child, but Titus told me what's happened with your family and all. I want you to know I'm so happy how the Lord has worked through the situation and seen you through." She patted Abigail's hand. Without a thought, Abigail gave Mrs. Matthews a slight peck on the cheek, surprising them both.

The kindness and appreciation on the older woman's face assured Abigail of the woman's genuine love for the O'Connor family. She whispered in Abigail's ear, "I'm praying for you. . . and my son." Then, as if she shouldn't have said anything, she quickly clasped her hands to her mouth.

Abigail smiled. "Thank you, Mrs. Matthews. For everything." Abigail hugged the older woman, said good-bye to Jenny, and headed back to her family's carriage. They still lingered in conversation with friends on the church grounds. As Abigail lifted her skirts to cross the yard, someone tapped her shoulder from behind. She turned to face Titus.

"Hi," he said, as if he didn't know what else to say.

"Hi." She smiled to encourage him.

"Guess you know how sorry I am." His fingers walked around the rim of his hat.

"I know."

"Um, can we start over?"

"Start over as in. . . ?"

"As in. . ." He fumbled for words.

"As in how about you come to our house for dinner tomorrow night? Then after dinner, I can beat you at checkers again."

His face brightened. "I accept." An enormous smile spread across his face, causing Abigail's heart to flutter.

"Tomorrow then."

"Tomorrow."

Feeling like a feather floating on the wind, Abigail turned toward her carriage, when she noticed Sophia catch herself and grab her stomach. Clayton ran to her side. Before Abigail could get to her, a small crowd had gathered.

An older woman turned a worried face to Abigail. "Looks like the little one is coming early."

❧

Though there was little Abigail could do, she felt grateful Clayton had let her come to their home. Mrs. Baird, Mr. and Mrs. Hill, and Sophia's mother prepared food for the little family, and Abigail saw to it that the coffee stayed fresh. Titus came along to keep Clayton from gnawing on his fingernails, and the doctor stayed busy with Sophia.

The hours dragged on, and everyone grew weary. No one dared speak it, but concern lined everyone's brow. Sophia's cries from the bedroom filled the air with tension. Mr. and Mrs. Hill stepped outside for some fresh air. The rocking chair creaked as Angelica Martone, Sophia's mother, rocked back and forth, back and forth. Mrs. Baird worked feverishly on her needlework while Clayton paced. He was as fidgety as a turkey just before Thanksgiving. Abigail wished she could help, but only Baby Hill's entrance into this world would make things better. Titus sat on the edge of the sofa and cracked his knuckles.

Just when the waiting seemed almost unbearable, a baby's wail called from the bedroom, notifying the little gathering that the blessed event had taken place. Clayton stopped in his tracks. It took a full minute for the idea to sink in. Pretty soon, a huge grin spread across his face, and he couldn't get to the bedroom fast enough. Everyone laughed as they watched him stumble across the room to see his wife and baby. After a few moments of suspense, Clayton burst through the bedroom door and made the announcement.

"He's a boy!"

Chapter 20

The evening hour was upon them by the time Eli Clayton Hill entered the world. The room that had been tense with waiting now filled with tears of joy, hugs, and congratulations.

Once Sophia's room cleared out, Abigail slipped into the bedroom to congratulate her friend. She edged closer to the bed and looked upon Sophia holding her baby son in her arms. With disheveled hair and a weak smile, Sophia lifted weary but joyous eyes to her friend. "Isn't he beautiful?" she asked, looking again at her son.

"That he is," Abigail agreed. She stepped a little closer and looked down at the pink, wrinkled skin of baby Eli. With eyes squeezed tightly closed, his arm flailed about until his fist finally came to rest against his tiny mouth, and he began to suck on it.

Sophia and Abigail laughed. "He must be hungry already," said Sophia. She pulled the folds of the soft yellow blanket down around his chin and stroked her finger gently against his face. He turned his head toward her finger.

"Well, I'll leave you two to get acquainted," Abigail said, turning for the door.

"Oh Abigail, would you ask Titus something for me?"

Abigail turned and nodded.

"Though Eliza will be doing needlework for me, I will need another seamstress to help with my business, especially now with the baby here. Would you ask him to ask his mother if she would be interested in sewing for me? She could work from her home, of course."

"Oh, how wonderful, Sophia!" Abigail said excitedly. "I'm sure she will be interested. She's wanted a job for some time but couldn't leave Jenny."

Sophia nodded. "I knew that. I've also heard people at church talk about what a good seamstress she is. It will be a real blessing to me if she accepts."

"I'll ask him tonight and let you know right away."

Sophia nodded and smiled. "Thank you," she said, her attention quickly turning back to her son.

"I love you, dear friend," Abigail whispered as she left the room.

"You ready to go home?" Titus asked Abigail when she stepped into the living room.

She nodded. "Just let me get my cloak." She grabbed her things, and they said their good-byes. Stepping into the cool night air, Abigail pulled her cloak tighter around her. Twinkling stars dotted the velvet sky while the moon hung barely a whisper above a cluster of trees. A shiver went through Abigail, but she knew it wasn't from the cold. It seemed a perfect night. Like her upside-down world had turned upright again. They stopped in front of the wagon, and Titus helped her up. He walked around and stepped up to the seat. She took a contented breath.

Titus turned to her. She could see his smile in the moonlight. "It is a good day, isn't it?"

She smiled back and nodded. Titus prompted the team into a steady trot. For the next few minutes, she explained Sophia's offer to his mother. Seeing God's hand in the matter, they talked excitedly of God's mercy and provision in times of need.

When they settled into a comfortable silence, Abigail thought about the baby. After witnessing the miracle of a newborn baby, she couldn't help but wonder how a mother could leave her child on the doorstep of another. Did she just want to be rid of a burden? What kind of woman could do that? A harsh, uncaring, cold mother.

Her mother.

A chill surged through her, but it was different from before. She pulled her cloak up tighter. The wind had chased the beauty of the night into the dark woods. An occasional blackbird flapped heavy wings against the night sky. A hoot owl cried out in the distance. The air grew cold. A lonely kind of cold. The kind of cold that made you long for the warmth of another. Her mother had died. No one knew the details. Abigail knew only that by the time she had turned three years old, her mother was gone. Her father had told her that much.

"Are you all right?" Titus asked, interrupting her thoughts.

"Oh, um, yes, I'm fine." She could feel him looking at her. She turned to him. "I can't help but wonder how a mother could abandon her child," she said, surprising herself at the intimacy of her statement.

The rhythmic *clip-clop* of horses' hooves echoed around them as the comment hovered in the air. Titus looked at her.

"I mean, didn't she care at all?" She wished she hadn't asked the question the minute it left her. After all, she knew her mother didn't care, or she wouldn't have abandoned Abigail. Still, Abigail wondered who this mystery woman was, what she looked like, what would make her do such a cruel thing.

"It is hard to understand." He grabbed her hand. "But your mother was good to you, Abigail. She gave you to the people she knew would love you most."

Abigail swallowed the tears that threatened. She hadn't thought of that before. Somehow, it made her feel better to think her mother had shown a hint of caring by leaving Abigail with her real father and his wife. And how thankful Abigail was for that! She couldn't wish for a better mother than Lavina O'Connor. "Thank you, Titus."

"For what?"

"For reminding me how blessed I am."

He smiled. "No, I'm the one who is blessed."

She studied him. "And how is that?"

He pulled the horses to the edge of the country road and turned to her. "Because you have forgiven me."

She felt her face grow warm.

Titus grabbed her hands. "I don't know if I dare presume further, but I can't wait another moment."

Abigail heard the seriousness in his voice and looked up at him. "Titus, what is it?"

"Abigail O'Connor, I have loved you from the moment I saw you in the mercantile. I tried to convince myself it wasn't so, but I couldn't deny it. With all that's happened, I don't know if you could ever feel for me—"

Abigail reached up and pressed her gloved hand against his lips. "I feel the same."

He stared at her in disbelief. "You do?"

She pulled her hand away, nodded, and smiled.

Scooting closer to her on the seat, Titus reached one arm around her back and with his other arm pulled her to him. Beneath the twinkling stars, his lips pressed soft and moist against her own, his arms slowly pulling her tighter against him. Dizziness enveloped Abigail. White lights sparked behind her eyelids as she melted into the kiss. A distant train whistle blew softly into the night air while Abigail O'Connor prayed the moment would never end.

⌖

After dropping Abigail off at her home, Titus warred with himself all the way to his house. He wanted to ask Abigail to marry him, but how could he? Being the family chauffeur could hardly appeal to a woman. No, he needed a good job that would provide for a family. But good jobs were hard to come by. He pondered the matter over and over in his mind.

By the time he got the horses unhitched and put in the barn, he was worn out with thinking. His ma and Jenny were asleep when he slipped quietly into the house. His mind continued to work the matter over as he shrugged out of his clothes and pulled on his night clothes. One thing he knew for sure: when he went to the O'Connors' in the morning, he would let them know he needed to get a different job. With that decision made, Titus climbed into bed and went straight to sleep.

❧

The next morning, Titus had barely stepped into the barn when Thomas O'Connor came out to meet him. "Titus, could you come into the house and meet me in my study, please?"

"Sure, Mr. O'Connor," Titus said, tethering his horse to a nearby post.

Fear tugged at Titus as he took steps toward the house. Perhaps Abigail had told her parents what had happened last night and they didn't approve. What then? Would he have to give her up again? No, he couldn't do that. But neither would he want to cause strife between Abigail and her parents. His stomach churned. Abigail let him in. Her smile chased away his fear for the moment, but as soon as he entered the study and saw Mr. O'Connor, the fear returned sevenfold.

"Close the door behind you, Titus, and have a seat," Mr. O'Connor said, pointing to a chair.

The leather chair squeaked beneath Titus as he sat down. He swallowed hard and looked at Mr. O'Connor.

"Now, Titus, I want you to know we've appreciated having you help us out these past months as our driver, and you can continue on if you would like, but. . ."

Titus could feel sweat forming on the back of his neck. *Here it comes. The speech about leaving his daughter alone.*

"What I'd really like to do is get you to work at the railroad."

Titus almost choked. "What?"

"I haven't said anything before now because there just wasn't a position available. But someone has recently moved on, and I'd like to see you get the job. You'd have to be trained, of course. It would be good pay, I can assure you. Enough to set aside a handsome sum for medical school, I would imagine."

Titus's jaw dropped. Mr. O'Connor laughed. "I can see I've caught you by surprise. You don't have to decide right now if you'd rather not, but just let me know—"

"Oh, I can tell you right now. I accept!"

The two men chatted on about the job vacancy and what Titus's duties would entail. Finally, after mustering the courage, Titus asked Mr. O'Connor for permission to marry his daughter. The older man didn't seem at all surprised, and after giving the appropriate fatherly speech, he gave his full blessing.

With those matters behind them, they left the sitting room. Mr. O'Connor took Titus into the drawing room, where Abigail, Eliza, and

Mrs. O'Connor sat in front of the fireplace.

"Well, ladies, I have an announcement to make," Mr. O'Connor proclaimed.

They all looked at him. "Mr. Matthews, here, has agreed to take a position with me at the railroad."

Mrs. O'Connor clasped her hands together in glee. Abigail and Eliza shared a knowing smile. They all jumped up to congratulate him. When the commotion finally died down, Mrs. O'Connor got tea for everyone, and they sat down together.

"You see, Titus, that has been Thomas's plan all along. To get you in the railroad, I mean. He just had to wait for the opening to present itself." She smiled and took a drink of tea.

"You brought me here to work for you with that in mind?" Titus asked, amazed at God's goodness.

Mr. O'Connor smiled and nodded. "I knew the other man was leaving but wasn't sure how soon, so I had to bide my time."

The next hour was spent with excited chatter over the news. When Titus caught Abigail's look, he thought she appeared almost sad. Why wouldn't she be happy for him? He finally said he needed to go outside. He got up and noticed Abigail a little ways behind him. She followed him to the door.

"I left something in the wagon; I need to get it out," she said as she stepped through the door just behind him. They walked out to the barn together. She reached into the wagon and pulled a book from the seat. Starting to turn, Titus grabbed her arm.

"Are you upset?"

Tears sprang to her eyes.

"Abigail, what is it?"

"I'll miss you," she said in a weak voice.

He threw back his head and laughed.

"Well, I don't think it's so funny," she said, her nose pointing heavenward.

He placed his hands on her arms. "No, you don't understand. I thought something else was going on. You had me worried."

She looked at him, puzzled.

"Look, Abigail." He glanced around the barn. "This is hardly the place I wanted to do this, but I don't think I can wait a moment longer. I feel as though I could burst."

"What is it?"

"I want to marry you, Abigail O'Connor. I didn't know how I could ask you on a chauffeur's salary, but your father's offer has made everything possible. Ma has agreed to work for Sophia, so I don't have to worry about her being cared for." He stopped and took a breath. A look of apprehension settled upon him. "That is, if you'll have me." His fingers lifted her chin until their eyes met. "Abigail O'Connor, will you marry me?"

She gasped. "Oh yes! Titus, I will marry you!" Before she could take another breath, he scooped her tiny frame up into his arms and swung her around several times.

They finally stopped to catch a breath. With a gentle touch, Titus's arms encircled her as he pulled her to him. "Abigail, I've never been this happy in my life. I couldn't have dreamed you'd be the one. Yet God knew." He brushed a red curl from her eye. "The tiny baby in the basket was no secret to Him at all."

Abigail smiled up at him.

"I love you, Abigail O'Connor." He leaned toward her, his lips caressing her own with a passion that said she belonged to him.

When she pulled away, she looked into his eyes. "I love you, Titus Matthews."

She snuggled into him, and in the quiet of that moment, their declaration of love mingled with the morning air and lifted on the breeze toward heaven.

Bestselling author Diann Hunt writes romantic comedy and warm-hearted women's fiction. Since 2001, she has published four novellas, nineteen novels and co-authored a devotional for the CBA market.

Her novels have placed in the Holt Medallion Contest, won the prestigious ACFW Carol Award, and served as a Women of Faith pick.

Diann has five granddaughters and two grandsons whom she loves to spoil (hoping one day they will throw her a 50th anniversary bash in Hawaii) and she lives in Indiana with her real-life hero-husband of 37 years.